BY THE RIVERS *of* BROOKLYN

BY THE RIVERS *of* BROOKLYN

a novel

TRUDY J. MORGAN-COLE

BREAKWATER BOOKS LTD.
JESPERSON PUBLISHING · BREAKWATER DISTRIBUTORS
www.breakwaterbooks.com

Library and Archives Canada Cataloguing in Publication

Morgan-Cole, Trudy J.
    By the rivers of Brooklyn / Trudy J. Morgan-Cole.

ISBN 978-1-55081-262-6

    I. Title.

PS8626.O747B9 2009   C813'.6   C2009-900834-3

We acknowledge the financial support of The Canada Council for the Arts
for our publishing activities.

We acknowledge the support of the Department of Tourism, Culture and
Recreation for our publishing activities.

We acknowledge the financial support of the Government of Canada through
the Book Publishing Industry Development Program (BPIDP) for our
publishing activities.

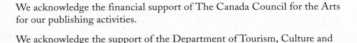

Printed in Canada

Mixed Sources
Product group from well-managed
forests, controlled sources and
recycled wood or fiber
www.fsc.org Cert no. SW-COC-000952
© 1996 Forest Stewardship Council
FSC

THERE'S A LITERARY CONVENTION, which I assume has something to do with laws and liability, in which authors place a disclaimer at the front of a book: "This is a work of fiction. Any resemblance to any persons, living or dead, is purely coincidental." Balancing this is another literary convention which claims that all writers mine their own lives for material.

This novel began with an idea about two sisters whose background and early lives were very similar to those of my grandmother and my great-aunt. I started writing them: they moved out of the shadows of memory and took on their own fictional existence. Joined by a sister-in-law who was not very much like any of my great-uncles' wives, these women went on to make choices and have adventures that carried them far from the paths any of my foremothers had travelled.

This book, finally, is pure fiction, and its story includes things that really happened in my family and in other people's families and a few things that may never have happened in any family. It is a patchwork of memory, lies and dreams, in which a reader who knows me will occasionally be surprised to see a small square of fabric lifted from a dress she once wore, stitched into an unfamiliar pattern.

I'm grateful for these patchwork squares, for the memories of my parents, my grandparents, my aunts and uncles, for the stories of those who went away and those who stayed home. Despite my love for the men in my life – father, husband and son – it is really a story inspired by, and for, the web of women. So this story is dedicated, with particular love:

To the memory of Florence Ellis,
and to
Gertrude Charlotte Ellis,
Joan Gertrude (Ellis) Morgan,
and Emma Charlotte Cole.

By the rivers of Babylon, there we sat down,
yea, we wept, when we remembered Zion.

We hanged our harps upon the willows in the midst thereof.

For there they that carried us away captive required
of us a song; and they that wasted us required of us mirth,
saying, Sing us one of the songs of Zion.

How shall we sing the Lord's song in a strange land?

PSALM 137

PROLOGUE: 1976

ITEMS NOT FOUND IN A TRUNK IN ANNE PARSONS' ATTIC

THE YEAR ANNE WAS eleven, she started looking for a trunk in the attic. Her first glance into the attic made it clear that the trunk could not literally be up there. Every attic she has ever read about has been a cool, gloomy room reached by climbing a ladder at the top of the house, a room filled with old trunks and boxes which, in their turn, are filled with old dress-up clothes, old letters, old diaries. Children in books while away long rainy afternoons opening these trunks and sorting through their contents, losing themselves in past lives, discovering dark or beautiful secrets about their parents and grandparents.

The hatch to the attic is actually in the ceiling of Anne's closet, although no-one ever goes up there except, very rarely, her father, and he never seems happy about it. One day she drags her desk chair into the closet, piles large books on it, and stands atop the teetering pile, pushing and grunting until she heaves the attic hatch open a few inches. Anne pokes her head into a scratchy sea of pink fibreglass insulation, which continues unbroken to the rafters, only inches away. She quickly pulls her head out and closes the hatch, and sneezes for the rest of the afternoon.

But if The Trunk is not in the attic, this does not mean it doesn't exist. Somewhere – in the basement of her parents' house, in Aunt Annie's house, which is much older than theirs, in some forgotten closet or corner, The Trunk must lie. Someone, among all her armies of ancestors, someone must have kept letters, written in a diary, preserved old ball gowns and the ghostly pressed roses that accompanied them.

Her search for The Trunk is similar to the search she conducted when she was eight or nine, for Secret Passages. Every book she read that year involved houses with secret passages linking the fireplace to the basement, or the bedroom to the attic, or, best of all, linking some ordinary room like the kitchen to a secret room high in a tower whose existence you had never suspected. For months Anne went around her house and Aunt Annie's, tugging at bookcases, pressing the stones in the fireplace, lifting rugs – looking for the carefully hidden signs of a secret door. None appeared. When she finally mentioned her quest to her father, he told her that such passages existed, but only in houses much older than theirs or Aunt Annie's – houses over a hundred years old, maybe. When Anne asked if anyone they knew lived in a house that old, her father said no.

Now she realizes that secret passages are firmly in the world of make-believe – for her, anyway. But anyone can keep a diary or save old letters. Anne herself keeps a diary and has since she was nine. And she is never, never going to throw it away, so someday her daughter or her granddaughter can find it. One day she asks her mother if she has ever kept a diary, knowing already what the answer will be.

"No, I'm afraid not," Claire says. "I was never into introspection. That would have been more Valerie's kind of thing."

"Well, did Valerie keep a diary?" Anne persists. Her mother's cousin Valerie moved to Toronto years ago, but perhaps she left the diary behind.

Claire looks both surprised and annoyed. "No, not that I know of. I only meant she would have been the type to."

"Well if she was the type, maybe she did? Maybe it's around Aunt Annie's house somewhere?"

"I doubt it," Claire says. "Anything any of us ever kept would have been thrown out long ago. Your Aunt Annie's not the kind for hanging onto old clutter."

This is certainly true. The spartan neatness of Aunt Annie's house has already discouraged Anne in her search. The anti-clutter gene was passed on in an even more virulent form to Claire who is, as they have this conversation, opening her mail over the garbage can, slicing open envelopes with her neat little letter-opener and dropping flyers, sweepstakes notifications, and Amazing Offers into the trash without a second glance. The small pile of true mail salvaged from this refining process is swept at once into her office to be sorted into the appropriate file folders. Anne can see that a diary would not have survived long, even if her mother had ever been inclined to keep one.

She tries Aunt Annie anyway. "Did you ever write in a diary, when you were younger?"

Annie, folding laundry, laughs. "A diary? Sure, when I was a girl nobody had time for foolishness like that. We were all too busy working."

Anne knows for a fact this is not true. Aunt Annie was born in 1907, around the same time as Emily of New Moon, and Emily kept a diary. So did lots of girls in those old books. Yes, they were busy milking the cows and scrubbing the floors by hand with no vacuum cleaners, but they found time to write in their diaries. Some of them did. Not Aunt Annie, apparently.

Anne pokes through whatever old boxes and cupboards she can find, just in case. Maybe no-one has bothered with a Trunk; perhaps she will open an old family Bible or a musty encyclopedia one day and find old love letters pressed and forgotten between the pages. All she finds are rows of Rubbermaid file boxes in her parents' basement, with their income tax forms going back to 1967, and a few old photo albums in Aunt Annie's closet. Not surprisingly, she chooses the photo albums, hauling them with their heavy burden of dust into the living room, to her great-aunt's dismay.

The pages are black instead of white, the photos black-and-white instead of colour, held in place by little triangles at each corner rather than clingy sheets of cellophane lying on top. Aunt Annie, compelled against her nature, sits down on the chesterfield beside Anne and begins to interpret the lost language of old pictures.

"That's me, with your Aunt Frances, Frances Stokes she was then, that was before she married your Uncle Harold. And that's Jim and Poor Bert, up in the field behind our old house. That was when we lived out in the country. Look, there's Jim and Ethel on their wedding day, that wasn't here, that was in New York. There they are with Little Jimmy and Diane, look at the lovely head of curls on Diane, she was such a pretty baby. There's your Uncle Harold with–"

"Wait, who's that one?"

"What? I can't see."

"There. Isn't that you, and…who's that other girl?"

"I don't know…oh, I think that's Rose, me and Rose. Your grandmother." Quickly, the page is turned.

Anne sits alone with the album later, turns back to that page, to Rose-your-grandmother. Rose and Annie, sisters, somewhere in St. John's, sometime in the 1920s. Teenagers, though maybe they didn't use that word back then. Annie: short and sturdy, plain, wholesome looking, then as now. Rose: taller, with fluffy fair hair, pretty in the alien way people from another era look attractive despite the funny clothes and hairstyles. Something about her is brighter, sharper, more vivid than Annie. Or does Anne only imagine that?

There are not many pictures in the album. Little money was wasted on photographs. But there are enough for Anne to piece together the early lives of

Aunt Ethel and Uncle Jim, Poor Bert, Aunt Frances and Uncle Harold, Aunt Annie and Uncle Bill, and all the various offspring. And in all those pages, only two pictures of Rose – that one snapshot with Annie, and an even earlier sepia-toned family group.

The photo album contents Anne for a while, but she never really stops looking for more clues, more evidence that the past exists. She has ceased to believe in The Trunk; the Evans family, she concludes, are not Trunk-keepers. But she continues to hope for old letters, old diaries, even old schoolbooks with names scribbled in the margins.

By the time she is thirteen, Anne's search has turned up little, but it has not stopped. It has narrowed, too. Once she wanted evidence of anyone's past life, anything that would transport her back to another era. Cousin Valerie's diary, if it existed, would have been almost as good as her mother's. Aunt Annie's or Aunt Frances' old letters would give her some flavour of the past. But now Anne knows she is searching for something, someone, in particular. Through diaries never written, letters never opened or read, a past never sorted and saved, she is searching for Rose.

PART ONE

1924 - 1932

ROSE

～

ST. JOHN'S, SEPTEMBER 1924

"YOU STAY AWAY FROM that one Ida Morris," Rose's mother tells her as she gets ready to go out. "I've heard about her. She goes with the Portuguese and Spaniards."

Tonight Ida has promised Rose and May that they, too, can go with the Portuguese. They meet the boys – young fishermen named Manuel, Luis, Jorge – on Water Street. Rose is paired with Luis, short but handsomer than the other two. He is about her own age, smiling, sweet in his broken English. She lets him put an arm around her. They go to Ida's house, where her invalid mother is forever in bed, in her own twilight world, and knows nothing of who comes in or goes out. Rose lets Luis slip an arm around her waist, closes her eyes when he kisses her.

Rose is nineteen. In the one long mirror in her parents' house, a dusty green oval, she sees an image of herself as faded and discoloured as a flower petal pressed in a Bible. But she knows her hair is blond and curly, that the brown dress with the yellow print is a good fit. In New York, Jim told her when he was home, on Flatbush Avenue in Brooklyn, the girls wear skirts to their knees, bobbed hair, lipstick and high heels. They smoke cigarettes out in the sight of everyone.

Rose's parents, strict Methodists turned stricter Salvationists, would be shocked at the thought of their daughter among the loose women of Flatbush Avenue. But Rose has been sneaking out to dances, kissing boys, even getting drunk, ever since she left school. Bill Winsor, her first boyfriend, has asked her twice to marry him. She strings him along with promises: *later, someday, perhaps.*

Her family cannot understand why she doesn't marry Bill. "He's so sweet, sure, he'd do anything for you," her sister Annie says. "And he's not bad-looking."

"He's a nice young fellow," says her mother, looking Rose up and down as if

14
～

searching for the hidden flaw. "You could do worse. Given time, you probably *will* do worse."

Her older brothers, Jim and Bert, are Bill's friends. Bert, the more serious of the two, tells her when he comes home to visit, "You're cracked if you don't take Bill, Rose. He won't wait forever."

Bill won't wait forever, and neither will Rose. She is waiting, waiting for her life to begin. Perhaps she will not have to wait much longer, she thinks as she dances with Luis to the hissing scratch of Ida's gramophone. A girl she knows, Ethel Moores, is going to New York. Rose has never liked Ethel. Round and pale and bland as a custard, proper and churchgoing, Ethel is Annie's best friend, Bert's long-time sweetheart. Now, with both Bert and Jim away working most of the year in New York, Ethel plans to go too. She has a cousin who will find a job for her. Rose cannot stand the thought that Ethel will walk on Flatbush Avenue before she, Rose, gets there. As Luis whispers to her in Portuguese, she maps out her battle plan. She may have to pretend to be friends with Ethel. Ethel is so slow, she may not notice the difference between a real friend and a false one. When Ethel steps on board the *Nerissa* to go to New York, Rose will be at her side.

Luis, who has had too much to drink, has begun to cry. In his torrent of broken English and weeping Portuguese, Rose hears a name again and again: *Maria, Maria*. His girlfriend back in Oporto, sweet and faithful and unsuspecting Maria, waiting at home as patiently as Ethel waits for Bert on his long trips to New York. For Maria in Oporto, it is the evil women of St. John's, Newfoundland, who threaten her patient Portuguese happiness.

"She is angel...angel to me," sobs Luis, burying his face between Rose's breasts. Rose pulls away. Tonight, lucky Maria will not be cheated on. Rose is skating along the edge of bad-girl, not venturing onto the thin ice. She will not be tricked into having a baby. Bill Winsor's baby or a Portuguese sailor's baby: either would anchor her in St. John's till she died.

Outside, it is dark. Time for Rose to go home.

ETHEL

BROOKLYN, APRIL 1925

"ALL DONE, ETHEL? THAT'S a good girl," said Mrs. Carey. "Put away the vacuum cleaner, now, and go see Mr. Carey, he'll have your pay for you."

Ethel lovingly wrapped the cord around the vacuum and tucked it away in its closet. Half an hour, maximum, to run that marvellous little machine over the Careys' rugs, and not much longer to wipe up and sweep the gleaming parquet floors. At home she would have spent the day scrubbing, waxing, beating the rugs. Washday would have been another whole day, but the Careys had a cylinder washing machine. The machines did all the work and Ethel got the pay, crisp American bills in a white envelope, handed over by smiling Mr. Carey. Then it was take off her apron, hang it on the hook in her own tiny, immaculate bedroom, change her shoes and she was free. Saturday afternoon in Brooklyn, and Ethel Moores waited on the street in front of the Careys' brownstone for Bert Evans to take her walking in Prospect Park.

She walked down the broad front steps of the brownstone, an imposing and solid-looking house in a row of others just as stately. Four storeys, it was shaded by a row of trees that ran along the street. Bert stood under one of those trees, in his shirtsleeves, smiling up at her. It was a sunny, warm day in April, which in itself was a good enough reason to love being in New York. At home, Annie's letters told her, they were still locked into winter, barricaded behind snowbanks and sleet storms. And Ethel was strolling down 7th Avenue with only a cardigan on over her dress.

She took his arm. "You're off early today," Bert said. "I'm sorry. I'd've been here sooner to meet you if I'd known. But I only just got off myself."

"That's all right." Ethel didn't like to talk about Bert's work, suspended between earth and heaven, riveting the high-steel girders on the skyscrapers of Manhattan. But Bert and Jim laughed and joked about it like there was no danger at all. Once, when he'd taken her to Manhattan, Bert had pointed out the buildings he'd worked on, and for many nights after that Ethel had woken from nightmares, heart racing.

But it was good work, everyone agreed on that, and better pay than anything going back home. Both the boys used to work on the boats, but then they hooked up with Robert Doyle, who was married to Ethel's cousin Jean. Robert was from Avondale and a lot of fellows from down that way worked in construction, so Jim and Bert gave that a try and they never looked back. Bert didn't like boats.

Ethel didn't like boats either. She'd been so sick on the *Nerissa*, coming over, that Rose had lost all patience with her. Not that she cared what Rose thought. She'd never liked Bert's hard-faced older sister. If only Annie, rather than Rose, had come to New York with her. But Annie said she no more wanted to leave St. John's than she wanted to parade down Water Street in her underclothes.

"Jim's meeting us in the park," said Bert. "He says he's going to have a girl with him."

Ethel sniffed. "Surprise, surprise. Not Evelyn?"

"No, I think Evelyn gave him the boot. This is a new one, I don't know her name. He met her at a dance last week."

Thinking about Jim, Ethel reflected that the Evans boys were different from most brothers she knew. In most families, the eldest son was serious and responsible, while the younger one was a bit wild and played the fool. She had known the Evans brothers all her life and while they were both good for a laugh, it was Bert, the younger, who was careful and steady, never spending too much or doing anything he might regret the next day. Bert was a smart young fellow, her mother had always said. He'd go far.

They crossed the busy streets at Grand Army Plaza. The huge arch with its metal soldiers and sailors lofted ominously in the sky above them. People flowed down Flatbush Avenue, a living river so thick and fast it made Ethel grip Bert's arm a little tighter. Then Prospect Park opened before them, a lush green space amid the crowded streets of Brooklyn, the ideal spot for lovers to stroll arm in arm. On Didder Hill, where Newfoundlanders gathered, they saw Jim walking towards them, jacket thrown over his shoulder, a very small red-haired girl on his arm.

"Bert, Ethel, this is Dorothy. Dorothy, I'd like you to meet my brother Bert and his girl, Ethel. They're from home, from Newfoundland."

Even before Jim spoke the words, Ethel knew Dorothy was not a Newfoundlander. When she opened her mouth to say, "Pleased to meetcha," Ethel could tell she was a New Yorker, a Brooklyn girl. Ethel wasn't sure how to react, how to talk to her. They were used to the ever-changing parade of Jim's girls, but they were always girls from home – Evelyn from St. John's or Liza from Bonavista or Marina from Grand Bank. Girls who had been in New York six months or a year or three years, more stylish and made-up and loud-voiced the longer they had been here, but always Newfoundlanders, like all their friends, like everyone they danced with and went to movies with and ate Sunday dinner with.

"Me and Dorothy are going to the show tonight," said Jim. "You guys coming?"

Bert looked at Ethel; she paused and then nodded. "We'd love to," said Bert. Ethel had grown up believing that dances and movies and theatres were all sinful, places to be avoided. But here in New York even good churchgoing people seemed to do those things, and nobody talked about sin or going to hell at all. Uneasy at first, Ethel had adjusted. But Bert was so good. He always asked her first, always checked to see if it was all right with her.

Ethel and Bert fell into step behind Dorothy and Jim as they walked along. Dorothy did most of the talking: she worked in a factory making artificial flowers. "It's not bad pay," she said, "the work is awful boring but I don't mind that 'cause I don't have to pay any attention to it. I can carry on and have a few laughs with the other girls, you know?" She seemed so confident, so sure of herself and her place in the world. Her dress was sharper and more stylish than Ethel's, even though she made less money – she had freely broadcast how much she was paid at the flower factory, which amazed Ethel, who thought talking about your pay almost akin to talking about your underwear.

"Oh, I had a letter from Mother," said Bert when there was a break in the monologue. He handed it to Ethel. "She says she's knitting you a sweater. She don't know you'll have little use for a sweater in Brooklyn in summertime."

Ethel laughed as she unfolded Mrs. Evans' letter. Bert had told her how hot it was in July and August but she couldn't imagine it properly. She and Rose had arrived in October and before long a New York winter had been upon them. Jim and Bert had gone home over Christmas when construction work slowed down a little. Ethel had stayed in her little room at the Careys', spent Christmas Day at her cousin Jean's apartment in South Brooklyn, and longed for home.

But now, with spring, she felt no urge to go home. Brooklyn was coming alive around her and she wanted to be there when the streets grew so hot that, Bert joked, you could not only fry an egg on the pavement but a couple of strips of bacon to go with it.

"Mother says thanks for the handbag and shoes, and Annie likes her new hat.

I told her you picked them out," he added. Bert sent frequent gifts along with the money he mailed home out of every week's pay. Ethel did the same with her pay, sending money to her widowed mother and her younger sister Ruby. Beyond that, both Bert and Ethel put a bit aside for the day when they would be able to get married. They had only a little left over for going to the movies and eating out on Saturdays.

When they left the park they ate at a cafeteria on Flatbush. Ethel had never had dinner in a restaurant in her life before she came to New York, and now they ate sandwiches and drank egg creams at restaurants every Saturday. Then they went to see *The Thief of Bagdad* at the Paramount.

"Oh I love Douglas Fairbanks," Dorothy said as they spilled out of the theatre into the street. "Isn't he gorgeous, Ethel? Do they have fellows that good-looking back in NewFOUNDland?"

Ethel giggled, feeling lighter and sillier than usual under the influence of the movie. "You knows what kind of fellas we got in Newfoundland; sure, you can see them all over the streets in Brooklyn. See these two here now, you won't find anything in New York finer than the Evans boys."

"I thought you liked Valentino," Jim said to Dorothy. "I always figured I was more the Valentino type, anyway." He whisked Dorothy into his arms, humming a tune they'd just heard in the theatre. The two of them danced in the streets, singing, whirling, moving into the streetlights' glow like spotlights, while Bert and Ethel laughed at them, told them to be quiet, to stop that foolishness now.

The two couples said goodbye at the corner of Flatbush and Atlantic Avenue, Jim to walk Dorothy back to her boarding house and Bert to walk Ethel back to the Careys'. "I'll come by for you tomorrow at ten," he said as they came within sight of the house.

"I'll be waiting," said Ethel. Bert was good about taking her to church every Sunday. They didn't know any Army people here in Brooklyn so they went to the Congregational church nearest to where Ethel lived. Jim sometimes came and sometimes didn't, depending on which girl he was walking out with. "I don't suppose Jim will be bringing Dorothy to church," she guessed.

Bert laughed. "Not hardly. She's Catholic, I'm pretty sure."

"Your mother would kill him if she knew," Ethel said.

Bert didn't seem interested in talking about Jim's new girl. He took Ethel in his arms, clinching her waist more tightly than usual. "Kiss me, Ethel," he said, and kissed her hard before she had a chance to say anything. "You knows I loves you, Ethel, only you don't know how much." Ethel wondered if watching Douglas Fairbanks had gone to his head.

Spring unfolded into summer that way, weeks of work punctuated by half-days off and dates with Bert and Sundays in church. July and August were every bit as hot as Bert had warned her they would be. Ethel sat in her cousin Jean's kitchen one evening while Jean cooked a feed of roast beef, potatoes, carrots and cabbage on the coal stove in one-hundred-degree heat. Jean interspersed her cooking with complaints: "Ethel, when you goes to have a baby, make sure it's not going to be born in September, because if it is you'll go through the whole of July and August so big as the side of a barn, sizzling to death in the heat. I'm roasted alive, that's what I am."

Jean's baby was due in September. Ethel put a hand self-consciously on her own flat stomach as Jean kept talking. "Never mind, maid, you'll have all that to worry about soon enough, once you gets married. I knows your mother's happy you and Bert finally set a date; she always liked Bert, didn't she? A Christmas wedding would be some nice. If you waited till spring I think that'd be too long."

"Yes," said Ethel, who couldn't have agreed more. "Sometimes I don't know if I can even wait till Christmas," she admitted in an unaccustomed burst of honesty. "It might even be sooner."

Jean frowned at the suggestion of eagerness and abruptly changed her tune. "You don't want to rush into it now; you've got all your life to be married and believe me, maid, 'tis not all a bed of roses. There's no hurry."

There was a knock on the door. Ethel moved across the kitchen to open it and felt suddenly that she was moving through water, slowed down, and everything around her became quite vivid and clear on the oddly long walk across the room: Jean's wooden countertop, the black-and-white tile above it, her own reflection in a glass cupboard door. She didn't realize till afterwards that it was a premonition: at the time she thought she was having another dizzy spell. Her hand closed on the brass knob of the door and she pulled it open. Jean's husband Robert stood there, two hours before he should have been home, with Jim beside him.

Before anyone spoke, Ethel knew everything, the whole story, and then she actually did have a dizzy spell. The kitchen tilted and turned, the linoleum lifted sharply as if she were on the deck of a ship, and Ethel fell into a pile on the floor.

"I knew it, I knew it," she sobbed half an hour later, sitting on the settee in the back room with Jean dabbing cold water on her face. All four of them were crying, the men as much as the women.

Jim repeated over and over, "He was just over from me. Just a few feet away. I could have reached out and caught him. I tried – I'm sure I tried – but when I grabbed for him there was only thin air."

"He was a good ironworker," Robert chanted, dazed. "The best. The best. How could he slip? How could he fall?"

"I knew it, I hated for him to go up there. I knew something would happen," Ethel keened.

Jean went to the store to ring Mrs. Carey and tell her Ethel wouldn't be back that night. Ethel slept on Jean and Robert's daybed – or rather, she didn't sleep. She played the silent movie over and over in her head: Bert standing, turning, losing balance, falling, falling through the blue air to the streets of Manhattan. Over and over, twisting in the sky.

The night crawled on. Ethel felt so many layers of loss she could not grasp it all. Loss of Bert himself, of course: he was no longer in the world, his voice silent, his face gone forever. She would ask his mother to send some more photographs. Or would she go back home, herself? That was the second loss: loss of her own future, of any certainty about what she would do. And the third loss: unspoken and unspeakable. She laid a hand again on her stomach, cradled it.

They got word to Rose in Bensonhurst and she came down the next day. She looked hard, Ethel thought, tough, like a real New York girl. Rose cried, though, for her brother Bert, next in age to her, her childhood playmate. Ethel wondered how much Rose really felt. First thing in the morning they sent a cable to the folks back home with the news, then Jean sat down to write a long letter that would follow the cable.

Jim returned from sending the telegram, red-eyed and quiet. Ethel took his hand in sisterly sympathy and that was when the first germ of a plan, an idea, began to form in her head.

She shook her head as if to clear it away. It was wrong – beyond wrong. It was evil. She had heard that word all her life and never really seen anything so bad it would qualify as evil, but if she did the thing she had just thought of, she, Ethel Moores, would be an evil woman. She could never do such a thing.

Bert's funeral was on Friday. The small chapel was full of Newfoundlanders: Bert's co-workers and their wives and girlfriends, the other men from his boarding house, his landlady, old friends and shirttail relatives from home. Everyone cried and hugged Ethel. "Poor young fellow – he was such a good boy – what a shame. What a waste. What a terrible, terrible thing."

After the funeral, everyone drifted back to Jean and Robert's house. There were cakes and hams that people brought with them, and endless cups of tea, and bottles of beer and rum for all but the strict teetotallers. For all people talked about Prohibition it didn't seem to mean much at times like these. People always knew where to get bootleg liquor – especially Newfoundlanders, who had connections on the boats that came from St. Pierre.

Ethel and Jim and Rose sat at Jean's kitchen table, the centre of the storm of grief, accepting drinks and condolences, talking about Bert. Someone poured a glass of whisky and put it in front of Ethel and she sipped it as well as she could: it was the first drink of her life.

"I remember when he was just a little fellow, couldn't have been more than four or five, he wasn't in school yet," Jim was saying, "and he wanted to build a fort. Well, my son, he was some determined. The two of us hauled wood down from the woods up behind our house, and he got the nails and hammer from Pop's shed, and he kept me at it all day, poor little fella. And finally Pop came home and saw what we were tryin' to do, and he knelt right down there and started in helping. I went off then, and Pop and Bert stayed there till they had some kind of a fort finished."

"I wonder how Pop's taking it?" Rose said. She refilled her glass and lit a cigarette, ignoring Jean's look of disgust. "They'll be broke up at home."

"Pop will be for sure. Bert was always his favourite," said Jim, without apparent bitterness.

People drifted away. Jean and Robert went to bed. Only Ethel and Jim were left alone at the table. Jim was still drinking steadily, crying and telling stories, and Ethel listened, her hand on his arm.

She went to bed that night, still trying to take it all in, to imagine her life without Bert. And again that same idea kept circling, evil though it was. A way out. A chance to escape the consequences of what she and Bert had done.

She stayed a week at Ethel's, and every night Jim came by. Every night they sat together after Jean and Robert and the children were in bed, and talked about Bert. Late one night she leaned across the table towards Jim and said, "He was the sweetest man in the world, Jim, I loved him so much." She felt like an actress even though every word was the truth. "Now I'm all alone in the world, and I don't know what to do. I swear to God I don't know what I'm going to do. I'm all alone in the world...."

Jim moved to put his arm around her; she moved closer; they both cried. Then she turned her face up to his to say, "What are we going to do without him, Jim?" and he kissed her, as she'd known he would. And then he said, "Sorry, sorry girl, I never should have done that," and she said, "No, it's all right, Jim, only I'm so sad, and I feel so all alone...," and he took her in his arms again. And then she said she should go to bed, on the daybed there in the kitchen, and she began to unbutton her blouse, and after that it was all very easy.

When Jim left to go back to his boarding house that night, Ethel lay awake. She wondered if she would ever sleep again. Already Bert himself, the life and the plans they had shared, seemed a long way off. She got up, made a cup of tea and sat at the kitchen table drinking it, thinking that she had just committed the first real big sin of her life.

Going with Bert those few times, in the bushes in the park on those hot July nights – that hadn't been a real sin, not the way they loved each other and with them being engaged and all. And even what happened tonight, she thought, might not have been a real sin – turning for comfort to his brother, overwhelmed with grief, coming together for a brief moment of love in the face of death, sharing their sorrow. If it had really happened that way.

But it hadn't. The sin was this: to do it as she had done it, cold, calculating, serving her own purpose. Planning every step, every move. Her definition of sin was far more elastic in New York than it had been back home, where it was a sin to dance or even to curl her hair too fancy, but by any standard, Ethel Moores had sinned tonight.

She only prayed it would all work out.

ETHEL

BROOKLYN, OCTOBER 1925

Dear Annie,

I hope you and all the folks at home are well. We are all as well as can be expected after the terrible shock we had.

I suppose the news in this letter will be a shock to all of you as well, but I hope you will understand that we did what we thought best and mean no disrespect to poor Bert or his memory.

Me and Jim got married two Saturdays ago in Jean's front room with the Methodist minister. I'm putting in a snap Jean's husband took of us after the ceremony. I hope you will not be too shocked or think it improper so soon after our tragedy, but ever since the funeral me and Jim have been together so much and taken what comfort we could from one anothers company and from our memories. I am sure we will be happy together...

ETHEL TOOK THE CORNER of the paper, ready to tear it, almost a reflex after tearing up the first five copies. Then she paused and reread the letter. "I can't say it any better than that no matter how many times I writes it," she said aloud.

Jim looked up from his chair at the other end of the kitchen table where he was drinking his cup of tea and reading the *Brooklyn Eagle*. "You worries too much, Ethel," he said. "Mom and Pop never had a word to say against you, and Annie's your best friend in the world. No doubt they'll like you a lot better than any of the other girls I might have married." It was no more to him than if a place had opened up on the job and a new fellow stepped into it. Doubtless some new fellow had filled in Bert's place on the worksite, and Jim had moved over to fill Bert's place in Ethel's life, Ethel's apartment, Ethel's bed.

It did seem that way sometimes, even to Ethel. She and Jim lived in an apartment just like the one she and Bert would have rented. She kept house just as she would have done for Bert, missing the lovely convenience of the Careys' vacuum cleaner and washing machine but happy to be sweeping her own floor, beating her own mats, trimming her own curtains with lace she had starched herself in sugar water. The pleasure of making a home was exactly the same as it would have been with Bert; for those purposes, it hardly mattered who the husband was.

Except – except that when Jim came home from work, he wanted to take her out for a hot dog or go out himself for a drink with his friends, not sit at their nice little table in the cheery kitchen and enjoy the good dinner she'd cooked, the way Bert would have done. They didn't have money to go out nearly as much as Jim would have liked, so most of the time they actually did sit down at their own table. Jim would say, "Good dinner, Ethel," when it was all done, but she could tell he didn't take pleasure in it like Bert would have done.

Jim noticed how she looked, if she had a new dress or had her hair done differently; he liked her to look smart and pretty, but he never noticed things like the new trim on the curtains or the rug she'd just bought. He didn't care to hear about how she had gone to Woolworth's and picked out the whole set of china with the pink rose pattern, only she got the girl to knock a dollar off on account of there not being teacups, and how she rode the subway all by herself into Manhattan to another Woolworth's and found the teacups on sale there. She could imagine sharing such things, the little victories and details of her day, with Bert. Sometimes, to her embarrassment, she even pretended Bert was there, talking out loud to him in the empty apartment.

She pounded the stamp up in the corner of the envelope, above where she had written:

Miss Anne Evans
Freshwater Valley
St. John's, Newfoundland

She could picture Annie at her kitchen table, opening the letter on top of her bright red or yellow tablecloth, reading it. But she couldn't quite see the look on Annie's face.

ANNIE

ST. JOHN'S, FEBRUARY 1926

Dearest Annie,

I hope this letter finds you and all the folks at home very well. Has it got real cold there yet? It is cold here in Brooklyn and last week we had a big snowstorm. You should see how fast they shovel it off the streets here. There are so many motorcars that they have to keep the streets cleared.

Jim and I are doing well. Thank you and the folks for the kind gift of money you sent. We used it to buy a new clock for our kitchen wall and some blankets for the bed which are coming in handy now as the nights are so cold.

We have some exciting news and hope you will be very happy for us...

"THERE'S ANOTHER LETTER FROM Ethel, Mom," Annie said as her mother entered the kitchen, tapping her walking-stick ahead of her. As near as Annie could see there wasn't a thing in the world wrong with her mother's legs except maybe varicose veins. But Mrs. Evans had decided some years ago that she was now an old lady, with all the trappings of that position – like the cane – and all the rights and privileges that went along with it.

"Hmmph. I wonder what that one got to say for herself now."

"Don't be hard on her, Mom, at least she writes a letter now and again, not like Rose."

"Rose? Rose!" Louise Evans compressed twenty years of annoyance into the single syllable of her daughter's name. "Don't give me Rose. She's better off not writing letters. There's things I'd sooner not know. Come on now, what do Ethel have to say?" She heaved herself down into a chair, and Annie moved from the stove to the table, sat down, and unfolded Ethel's letter, which she had already read three times. She was just going to read it aloud and let Ethel speak for herself. Annie wasn't about to waste any more time trying to put things in the right words or prepare Mom for anything.

She watched though, over the edge of the letter, and saw her mother's fingers start to twitch as soon as she read, *I am expecting a baby in late spring or early summer.* Counting, counting off the months.

When Annie finished reading her mother said, "Hmm! Well, they didn't waste their time, did they?" Her eyes went to the calendar on the wall and her fingers moved again.

That was all she would say to her eighteen-year-old unmarried daughter. She was obviously bursting with comments and speculations, but she needed another married woman to talk to. Annie knew quite well that babies took nine months to get born and that bad girls sometimes got them started before they got married. She could also count nine months in her head without using her fingers. She knew her mother suspected that Jim had gotten Ethel in the family way before they were even married. She couldn't picture Ethel doing such a thing, but she could well believe it of Jim, who was not always a gentleman, not like poor Bert.

Poor Ethel, Annie thought, how lonely she must have been up there all by herself, without Bert. I hope Jim is good to her.

Annie loved all three of her brothers, of course, but they were so different. She had always admired Jim. He was the oldest, the good-looking one, the hero behind whom they all trailed, amazed at his daring feats, unable to imitate him. Little Harold – not little now, of course, he was almost seventeen, but they were all used to thinking of him that way – was such an afterthought for Mom that Annie had fallen into the habit of looking after him, even though she was only two years older.

But Bert had been the one she was closest to. He always had a kind word for everyone. Better than words, he could walk into a house where everything was topsy-turvy, where something had gone terribly wrong, and Bert could find the one good useful thing to do, like bringing in an armload of wood for the fire or shovelling a path to the door. She had been so happy when he and Ethel had started walking out, because Ethel admired and loved Bert just as she did. Bert would take good care of her best friend, and all three of them could always stay close, not like if her favourite brother had married some stranger.

And now Bert was dead, and Ethel was married to Jim, and they were having a baby. Life was funny. Annie turned back to her pot of stew on the stove and pushed at one of the dumplings, letting it bob back to the surface, thinking of the warm solid weight of a baby in her arms. Ethel would have that, soon. A baby of her own.

"I think it's grand. I hope they'll be very happy," she said.

"Hmm." The stick tapped and the chair creaked as Mrs. Evans got up. "I'm just going over the road to Mrs. Stokes' for an hour. I'll be back before your father gets home. You have supper ready by five, you mind."

In the empty kitchen, Annie sang, "There is power, power, wonderworking power... In the blood...of the Lamb," as she worked on supper. She didn't hear Harold come in behind her until he pulled out a chair and sat down.

"Some cold out today," Harold said. "Jim says down in New York the snow is already thawed by March."

Annie heard his words and what lay underneath them, and felt her heart grow hard like a stone. They would all be gone soon. Harold was the last and he would be gone as soon as he could wheedle his way past Mom and Pop.

"Mom's not going to let you go, you know," she said.

They had never spoken before about Harold going away, but he didn't seem surprised at her reply, only nodded, as if his thoughts had been painted on the kitchen wall and anyone should have been able to read them. "I knows that. But I knows I'm going, too."

"Not yet. It's too soon...after Bert."

"No, not this spring, anyway. Maybe next year. There's nothing in this place for me, Annie."

"I know."

He didn't say, *You should come too.* Nobody ever did. They took it for granted that she didn't want to go, and they were right. The longing for faraway places, for new voices, for a different kind of life, even for more money, drove all her family away, but all those longings were absent in Annie.

"No, girl, I got to give Mom time to get used to the idea. You'll have me hanging around like the millstone around your neck for a good while yet, I'd say." He grinned, his laughter coming quickly as always.

Much as she had loved Bert, Annie now thought Harold was perhaps the best of them all. He had Jim's quick way with words and ready laughter, his wit and light-heartedness, but he was as solid and sensible as poor Bert, as kind and thoughtful, and because he was so quick he could be even kinder, because he could see into what you were thinking or feeling. She felt a sudden rush of affection for her youngest brother. "Here, let me pour you a cup of tea," she said.

"You're a good woman, Annie," her brother said.

ETHEL

❧

BROOKLYN, NOVEMBER 1926

ETHEL PUSHED OPEN THE door of the house with her shoulder, her arms being occupied with Ralphie's carriage and several bags of food. She edged inside the porch to lay down her shopping bags, begrudging even the few seconds she had to leave Ralphie outside in the frigid November air. Then she dragged the huge unwieldy carriage through the door, hoisting it over the doorstep. Once inside, with the shopping bags and the baby carriage, she couldn't maneuver enough room to close the door. November rushed inside, cold air and grey-brown leaves and dirt from the sidewalk all whirled on the wind. Ralphie was crying. Ethel backed up against the landlady's door and shifted the pram a few inches farther into the corner, then squeezed around it to shut the door.

She picked up Ralphie, who was howling, and jostled him around, a tiny squalling mass inside a huge bundle of knitted sweater, cap, booties and blankets. She jiggled and soothed him, partly because she hated to hear him cry but also because Mrs. Delaney, the landlady, had little tolerance for crying infants, as Ethel had good cause to know. When Ralphie was colicky at two and three months, Ethel and Jim would take turns walking the floor with him, trying to quiet him, waiting for the inevitable banging on the door as Mrs. Delaney came up to say that the second-floor tenants were complaining.

Now Ethel looked up at the stairs, towering above her, disappearing into the gloom of the third floor. She thought of Jim, climbing each day up on the naked skeletons of the skyscrapers that towered over New York. Could that be any harder than climbing two flights of steps with a crying baby and five bags of groceries? It couldn't be done, not in one trip. She would have to bring Ralphie up, lay him in the crib, and come back down for the food.

The time it took to settle Ralphie in the crib meant she had left the porch downstairs cluttered with her bags and her carriage. When she came down,

Mrs. Delaney was standing in her doorway, shaking her head.

"Mrs. Evans, I may have told you," she began.

"Yes, yes, I'm sorry, Mrs. Delaney, you did tell me."

"It's not me, it's the fire regulations, you know. What would happen if we had a fire and the doorway was obstructed like this?"

"Yes, Mrs. Delaney. I just took Ralphie up to lay him down. I'll put the baby carriage away in the corner right now," Ethel said, doing it as she said it so Mrs. Delaney would see that she really meant it.

Mrs. Delaney glanced up the steps to the unseen apartment above, from which banshee wails were issuing. "Is your little boy all right, Mrs. Evans? Is he suffering from gas pains?"

"No, Mrs. Delaney, I don't think he's got gas. I believe he's hungry. We were out at the shops for a little longer than I thought. I'm just going up, now, to feed him." Laden with parcels like a pack-horse, Ethel began her long trek up the stairs. Her legs were killing her. The heels of her shoes were slicing into her flesh. She needed new shoes.

"Because if it's gas, you'll want to get the gripe water. As I've told you before, Mrs. Evans, I used it with all six of mine and they never–"

Ethel shut the door of her apartment behind her, very gently and quietly. She wished she could slam it with a huge bang, but she was not that type of woman. Anyway, there was something nice in the idea of Mrs. Delaney in the stairwell, still talking away, not realizing Ethel couldn't hear her.

Ethel wanted to sink down into Jim's chair, the one armchair in their apartment, but Ralphie had managed to pull himself up to a standing position on the bars of his crib and was jumping up and down, his face tomato-red. Last month she had been so proud he could pull himself up. Now she was worried he'd jump so hard he'd shoot right out of the crib and onto the floor. There was no question of leaving him in there while she prepared a bottle. Instead, she scooped him up in one arm – he was so heavy these days – and held his squirming, wriggling body while she used her free hand to open the draft of the coal stove, poke up the fire a bit, put on the kettle to boil, measure out the tinned milk, add hot water once the kettle was boiled, and shake it up to mix it. All this terrified her: she couldn't escape visions of Ralphie twisting violently while she held the kettle, causing her to drop it and splash boiling water all over him, leaving his poor skin scarred for life, so that all the other children would laugh at him. "Hush, baby. Hush, baby," Ethel cooed. "It's all right, your milk will be here soon. Hush, hush-a-bye."

Her hush-a-byes had no effect on Ralphie, who continued to squall. Finally, an eternity later, Ethel was settled in Jim's chair with bottle and baby. "Here you go, here you go," she crooned, but Ralphie pushed the bottle away and screamed twice as loud. Ethel felt panic begin to rise. She was exhausted. She needed to pee. Mrs. Delaney would be hammering on the door soon. And whatever Ralphie wanted, it wasn't this bottle.

She walked with him some more, changed his diaper while he screamed and kicked, tried again with the bottle. Maybe Mrs. Delaney was right and he did have gas. Maybe he had caught something terrible, being dragged out in the cold. Maybe from now on she could buy everything from people who came to the door, or from shops that delivered. But after the long hot months of summer spent almost entirely cooped up inside when Ralphie was too young to take out much, she felt she needed a weekly hour at the shops. But at what cost?

Finally, finally, exhausted, he allowed the nipple into his mouth. He sucked almost accidentally, widened his eyes, looked gratified, and began to drink steadily. Ethel studied his face, so round and serious, the dark red colour beginning to recede now. His blue eyes, calm again, looked so much like Bert's. Or Jim's. Of course all the Evans boys had the same eyes, wide and light-blue and guileless.

He was so much like Bert, Ethel thought as he finally settled down contentedly in the crook of her arm. At moments like this she loved to look at him, to search secretly for hints of Bert. It wasn't easy because Jim and Bert looked a lot alike anyway. And when people pointed out that Ralphie had Jim's chin or Jim's nose, Ethel wanted Jim to believe that. But when she was alone with the baby, she thought, *Bert's chin. Bert's nose.* And, especially – because she missed them so much – *Bert's eyes.*

Jim had been wonderful. He never questioned, never cast a doubt or a suspicion. Yet he must have guessed. How could he not? Ralphie was born eight months to the day from the night of Bert's funeral. Twenty-three hours a day, baby Ralphie was a little bundle to love, an endless round of chores to complete, a screaming nightmare of frustration. All the things a baby was supposed to be. But one hour, at least one hour every day, Ethel had the peace and quiet to sit alone and look at him. Then he was a reminder, a charm hung around her neck, calling back her very best memories and her very worst. He was the living memorial of Bert, and he was also the shape of her own guilt, which she must never forget or forgive. She loved him with every breath in her body.

And so did Jim. Yes, Jim had been wonderful. He gave bottles and had even changed the odd diaper, clumsily. Ethel knew from watching Jean's husband Robert that some men had no real interest in babies or small children, appeared not to notice them except as noise until they were old enough to throw and catch a ball, if boys, or to look pretty, if they were girls. Jim was never like that. Even when Ralphie was the tiniest thing, Jim would talk to him while he walked the floor with him. He would talk the strangest talk – not baby talk, gushing and cooing like a woman would do, but he would carry on these serious one-sided conversations, or sometimes not serious, sometimes telling jokes and stories. Stories from home. He talked about home a lot to Ralphie, talked about taking him to Newfoundland someday, showing him to his Nan and Pop Evans, his Nanny Moores.

At those times Ethel had to turn away, busy herself with dishes or laundry, something noisy. She wanted home so bad it was like a pain in her gut. And she knew they couldn't go, not for years and years anyway.

Ethel moved to the window and looked out at the back of another house just like the one they lived in. They had two rooms – barely. One L-shaped room had Ralphie's crib and a chest of drawers in one arm, the stove, sink, and cupboard tucked in the corner, and the table and chairs, with the one armchair, in the other arm. Their other room, the bedroom, was nestled into the crook of the L and was so small the double bed had to be shoved up against the wall. Only Jim could get out on his side; Ethel had to crawl over the foot of the bed to get out. She remembered herself one year ago, a new bride and a new homemaker, proud of this tiny space and loving it. Now the walls were closing in.

This was Saturday and Jim might have been home early, but lately he had been working all the extra hours he could; all the men were, trying to get more work done before the snow came. Ethel hoped he'd be tired, too, when he got home. Too tired to want anything in bed.

She used to enjoy it in bed with Jim, at the very first, even though she felt guilty and knew she shouldn't. She used to pretend, sometimes, that he was Bert and that she and Bert had had a chance to finish what they'd started, making love in a proper bed with sheets instead of on the damp ground with twigs sticking into her backside. Now, since Ralphie was born, all she could ever think was how tired she was and how she didn't want another baby, not till Ralphie was a little older.

She was lucky; Jim was tired. In the morning, Ethel let him sleep while she went to church. For several months after her marriage she didn't go. The church she had attended in her old neighbourhood was farther away now, and anyway she didn't feel right about going. Then Ralphie came and she couldn't get out. But a month ago Jean had asked her to come to the Methodist church with her, because Jean's oldest, Sadie, was going to be in some Sunday School program. Ethel found it was nice to have an hour to herself, out of the apartment, away from Jim and Ralphie. It was wonderful to have a husband who didn't mind watching the baby for a little while on Sunday morning.

She liked dressing up a little, going with Jean and her children – Robert, who was brought up Catholic, didn't go to church at all – sitting in the small quiet chapel on the hard pews, hearing the organ and the choir. She didn't like the words of some of the hymns anymore, or the sermons. This week, for instance, the minister was preaching about the Prodigal Son. Ethel was the only Christian she knew who didn't like that story. She felt sorry for the older brother, who always got a hard time when preachers told the tale. What was so bad about staying at home and working hard? she wondered. The older brother could be like Annie – the one who stayed behind and kept house when everyone else went off to seek their fortune. Why shouldn't he want a feast, a party for himself once in awhile? Was that so wrong? Why was the old father too mean to slaughter a calf for his faithful older son? Just once, Ethel would have liked to see the older son get some credit.

But the Reverend Darling – what a name! – like every minister she'd ever heard, was all caught up with the younger son, the bad son. He was harping on and on about forgiveness, God's grace, God's mercy. How the worst things we've ever done can be forgiven, no matter what. Ethel looked up at Reverend Darling, his round milk-white face glowing above his black shirt and clerical collar. His hair curled a little around the temples. He looked like a boy. *Little he knows,* Ethel thought.

The small but determined choir stood to sing the closing hymn: "Just as I Am." Back home in the Army, if they sang this hymn at the end of a sermon about the Prodigal Son – sang it with loud and lusty voices, a steady thumping beat, and a clatter of tambourines – people would be streaming down the aisles, tears running down their cheeks, kneeling at the mercy seat. This did not happen in the Methodist church. Methodists sat quietly in their pews, hymnbooks open, singing along.

> *Just as I am, without one plea,*
> *But that Thy blood was shed for me...*

When she was a girl growing up, Ethel had had a friend, Mary Margaret Murphy, who of course was Catholic. Once she went to St. Patrick's with Mary Margaret and waited for her to go to Confession. It was dark and mysterious and popish in the big church, and Ethel wondered what went on in the small closet. Mary Margaret was matter-of-fact about it. "I tells Father my sins and he forgives me and tells me how many Hail Marys to say, is all," she had said. Now Ethel almost wished for a confession booth. Because it couldn't be that easy, could it? As easy as the hymn made it? *Just as I am? Thy love I own has broken every barrier down?* Not so easy. Some barriers were bigger than you might think. The lady that wrote that hymn hadn't done the thing Ethel did. She didn't know.

The hymn was over: the minister was praying. Ethel did not know what foolishness she had been thinking, or what it was she wanted so much she could almost cry. But she prayed along with the minister, prayed silently for the first time in months. *I'm going to try harder, God. I'll be here every Sunday. I'll be a good wife to Jim and a good mother to Ralphie, and I won't complain. I'll be the best you ever saw, I promise. Only please, please…*

She did not know how to end it. Reverend Darling said Amen, the organist played the postlude, and she stood up and walked out with Jean and the youngsters. She felt better and stronger, like her backbone had been reinforced with steel.

ROSE

~~

BROOKLYN, MAY 1927

THE BELL ON THE door clangs again. Rose peers over the edge of the ornate gold cash register, praying it's someone who doesn't matter, hoping she can stay sitting down. Her feet are killing her, even with her shoes kicked off. If it's a young kid or something, she doesn't have to stand up until they actually come up to the counter. Except she might have to watch to see if they're stealing.

It isn't a kid. It's a middle-aged woman, all starched and pressed in a pink cloth coat, the kind who expects to see a shop girl standing behind the counter and will complain to the manager if she doesn't. With a heavy sigh, Rose lays down her cup of tea and stands up, pressing on a smile.

"Help you with anything today, ma'am?" she calls out as the woman begins to paw through tables of five-and-dime merchandise. The woman ignores her.

Rose keeps a mental list of jobs that would be worse than working at Freedman's Five and Dime. Being a maid, of course that was worse. Her first New York job was working for Mrs. Clark, who was more picky than Rose's own mother ever was. Rose quickly got tired of the smell of brass and silver polish, of the horrible brass cabinet knobs and the silver dinner service that had to be shined till Mrs. Clark, the old cow, could see her face in them. Rose hated mopping, dusting, vacuuming, doing other people's nasty laundry and making up their beds and washing their dishes. She didn't last long at Mrs. Clark's.

Then she worked in a laundry, and that was worse: the heat, the steam, the fourteen-hour days, the living-in. But the girls were fun there. Here, Rose is lonely. The shop is small, only three girls working at a time, and the other two "girls" are over fifty and disapprove of her.

At five she'll be off. Mike O'Dea is going to pick her up and take her someplace for dinner. Rose has a good red dress on under her shop coat, for her date with Mike O'Dea the cop. He is a serious young man – serious about police work, serious about Rose. He fully intends to make Rose his wife. In fact he has only one good point, and that is that he likes a few drinks. When Mike gets drunk, he's funny. He laughs and sings and spends money foolishly, mostly on Rose. When Mike is sober, he apologizes for his drinking and swears he'll give it up entirely when they get married. This doesn't help his position any, in Rose's eyes. Rose has no intention of marrying a drunk. She knows where that leads: the poverty, the crying, the hungry children, the dirty tenements. But why would she want to marry the sober Irish cop, Mike O'Dea?

The starched pink woman holds up pairs of cheap cotton drawers and sturdy corsets that remind Rose of the laced steel girders of the bridges and buildings her brother Jim works on. This woman will prod and poke and look for half an hour and buy one item, the cheapest thing on the table. The door clangs again.

A man walks in, young and very handsome. Dark-haired, dark-eyed, Italian or Greek maybe. Rose feels her cheeks flush, and her smile this time grows as naturally as dandelions in the small green gardens in front of city houses. She has not realized until this moment how tired she is of her job, her life, of Mike O'Dea. She has not realized how badly she needs someone new to walk through the door.

He comes straight to the counter instead of looking around, asks if they have belts, men's belts. Yes, they have belts. "Never needed a new belt before this," he says. His English is good but heavily flavoured: he has not been here long, perhaps not as long as she has. "I been working in the Navy Yards ever since I come from Sicily, two years now. One shirt, one shoes, one pants, one belt. No problem. Then last month, I start working for a guy who owns a fruit store, running one of his pushcarts. Suddenly, the old belt breaks. The old man, my boss, he thinks I'm eating too much – eating up his profits." His hands dance, his smile flashes, as he looks through the rack of belts and calls his life story across the shop to Rose.

"You used to work in the Navy Yards? I know lots of guys in the Navy Yards. Did you ever know Paul Starr? David MacKay?" She wonders what kind of girl she sounds like, saying she knows lots of guys, then doesn't care.

Her customer doesn't seem to care either. He tosses names back and forth, casual acquaintances they both share. "But you left the Navy Yards to work on a pushcart selling fruit?" Rose says.

The Italian boy laughs. "It's the family business, back home. That's what I grew up with. I'm gonna get into business for myself someday, own my own store. You know the American Dream, dontcha? That's what I'm here for. I signed up for my little piece of America."

Rose laughs with him. She envies him, too, knowing his dream, having his little piece of America marked out so clearly. She had only one dream, and now she is living it: she lives in Brooklyn, she has a job, she goes out with men, she dances and wears short dresses and smokes and goes to movies. Suddenly her American Dream seems small, and almost worn out.

He comes to the counter, belt in hand. In front of him sails the pink woman with an enormous brassiere dangling before her. Rose takes it gingerly, rings it in. Next in line, the fruit vendor says, "What time you get off work?" The woman frowns and clucks her tongue.

Rose hands the woman back her change, takes the belt. "I get off ten to five," she says.

After that, Tony Martelli waits for Rose outside the shop every afternoon. Mike O'Dea the cop drops from sight. Rose loves the feeling of having a man waiting for her after work; even better she loves having a new man, someone with crisp edges she has not yet worn smooth, someone whose stories, whose jokes, whose hands and lips, can still surprise her.

Tony Martelli has plenty of stories. He fills the space between them with his stories as they stroll arm in arm through the streets of Brooklyn towards the fruit store where he works. He talks about his family back in Sicily, their donkey and the little plot of land where they grow grapes and figs and tomatoes to sell, and how that was never enough, how his father and brothers worked as labourers on bigger farms. How poor everyone was during the war, when he was a little boy.

Rose tries to grasp it all as he talks, tries to form pictures in her mind. Back home she was so good at this, building pictures of New York and the things she would see and do there. Ever since she got to Brooklyn she has been inside that picture, and other people have been telling her stories – about where they're going, sometimes, but mostly about where they came from, because everyone came to Brooklyn from somewhere else. They always want to talk about where they came from. Only Rose never talks about home.

They arrive at Romano's fruit stand and Tony picks a ripe plum and puts it to Rose's lips for her to bite. Romano's daughter, a plump girl of fifteen or so, giggles behind her hand. "Tony, you gotta girlfriend!" she calls. "I thought I was your girlfriend!"

"You gotta grow up first, Gina," Tony says.

From the store they wind their way through the streets, away from Flatbush Avenue, away from the heart of Brooklyn, into Williamsburg, to the street where Tony lives with his sister and brother-in-law, where everyone speaks Italian, where a man peddles fish from a barrow in the street, where barefoot children run between the apartment buildings. Rose wants to protest that Tony is taking her in the wrong direction – away from everything exciting and modern and New York, into some lost Brooklyn world. It is a wrong turn, she is sure, but for now she is under a spell, unable to break the charm, wanting only to stay by his side.

Later, of course, they will return to the real world, after a huge supper eaten at the kitchen table of Tony's sister, a groaning board of mysterious foods and flavours that, Rose has to admit, taste far better than anything she can buy in a restaurant on Flatbush Avenue. Tony's sister, barely thirty, is already huge, ballooned into a caricature of Italian womanhood by three pregnancies and God knows how many thousand rich dinners. Rose eats sparingly, causing Tony's sister to harangue Tony in Italian about Rose's extreme thinness and possible illness.

It's only then that they make their way back to the world Rose knows and loves, the world of movies and dance halls. Tony is a wonderful dancer. The music fills up everything, the outside world ceases to exist, and Rose is perfectly happy. After the dances, Tony always sees her home on the streetcar. But all the time, while they dance, while they sit in the theatre, while they ride the streetcar, even while he kisses her goodnight, she feels the invisible cord that ties him to those dark streets in Williamsburg. She wonders how long the cord is, how far she can pull him.

ETHEL

⁓

BROOKLYN, SEPTEMBER 1927

RALPHIE SAT BETWEEN ETHEL and Jim, squirming and twisting, bouncing up and down. A streetcar ride was still a big treat for him. Ethel tried to talk to him about the apartment. "We'll live on a nice street...there'll be other families with children in our building, you can play with them..." Ralphie only half-listened; he was only two, after all, and probably didn't understand most of what she was saying. Really it was Jim she was talking to, or maybe herself.

She had been delighted, though not entirely surprised, when on Friday evening Jim pushed his chair back after supper, stretched out his long legs, and said, "So this landlord will let us have a look round the place on Sunday, will he?" That was Jim's way. Ethel had been after him for months about getting their own apartment, but she knew Jim worried about money. They never argued about money; they never argued about anything. When they disagreed, Jim would open up the paper and start to read, or look out the window. Ethel would go about doing her usual chores, but more loudly and with heavier sighs. Jim never actually gave in; he simply said a day or so later that they were going to do whatever she'd suggested, as if that had been his plan all along.

The building on Linden Boulevard was only a few years old. It was a warm brown brick with a big paved space in front of it. Old women sat on the steps, most of them heavyset, clad in long black dresses, their hair covered with bandannas, talking in foreign tongues. It wasn't one of the buildings advertised in the *Eagle* with the words "Christian area." Ethel didn't care about that. She didn't mind living around Jews; she really had no opinion of Jews at all, never having met any except in shops. And "Christian area" buildings were more expensive. On the other side of the paved court sat the old men, chewing on pipes or cigars, muttering rather than speaking aloud, casting occasional glances at the women. Jim and Ethel and Ralphie had to step around a clutch of little boys playing potsy right in front of the front steps.

Inside, there were marble floors in the vestibule where you went in and a tall staircase stretching up. But the apartment for rent was on the ground floor, which was the main reason Ethel was so eager for it. She was so tired of stairs, of lugging Ralphie up those long steps when he was asleep or tired. What would it be like when – if – they had a baby as well? If she was going to live out her days in a Brooklyn apartment building, Ethel wanted it to be on the ground floor.

When the landlord – a small man with a low forehead who came scuttling down the stairs as they entered – opened the door for them, they were standing in a short, dim hallway. Directly in front of them, on the long side of the hall, two doors stood ajar, leading into the kitchen and the living room. Closed doors at either end of the hall led to a bedroom and a bathroom. Their own bathroom! Ethel was so tired of sharing a toilet and bath with three other families. Their own bathroom would be reason enough to rent this place, if everything else was all right.

Ralphie barrelled straight through the living room door, and Jim followed him. But Ethel went into the kitchen, and the landlord hovered near her, knowing that the woman of the house would want to see the small, battered gas cooker, the clean white sink with its own running water, a few dark chips out of the porcelain, the space where she could fit her kitchen table and chairs, the place where an icebox could go if they had one. "Lots of cupboard space here," he said helpfully, and he was right: the shelves and cupboards ranged above the white countertop to the ceiling, though she didn't see how she'd ever get at them, short of standing on a stool. She liked the cheerful yellow paint on the walls, which looked almost new.

When she was satisfied she'd seen the kitchen, Ethel went into the front room. Like the kitchen, this room was brightened by a large window that stretched almost floor to ceiling. Sunlight spilled in and made bright patches on the floor, which was covered in a green-and-brown linoleum. Ethel didn't like the wallpaper – a dark pattern that she knew would make the room look gloomy – but that could be changed. She knew just the pattern she'd pick.

Jim walked around the room with a small frown, as if calculating how much each square foot of space would take from his pay packet. He made $150 a month, and the apartment cost $40 a month; they were paying only $20 for their rooms now and it seemed they were counting every penny. Jim always found money for something foolish like going to the pictures or eating in a restaurant, but if Ethel wanted something for the house, something to make their lives a bit better, he muttered under his breath and counted the bills in his wallet. And she could see him counting now, in his head.

Ethel just stood there, trying to picture a couch, a chair, a little daybed for Ralphie in the corner. She imagined painting and papering, sewing curtains for the windows, making this apartment into a proper home.

Ralphie hung out the open window, looking onto the courtyard below. Ethel could hear, as well as see, that the dirty space was full of people – maybe a dozen kids ranging in age from Ralphie's size right on up to tall boys and girls of twelve or thirteen, all playing and laughing and shouting. Several wash lines crisscrossed the courtyard, though no-one had clothes hung out today, being Sunday. She saw women leaning in their doorways or windows, watching the children, talking to each other, and men sitting on steps and benches smoking and talking.

In the middle of the pavement a skipping rope whirled, marking a circle in the air inside which small girls with flying braids hopped on light feet, while the other children chanted:

She is handsome
She is pretty
She is the belle of New York City

Nearer to Ethel's window, a thin dark-haired woman sat on a step darning socks. The woman took up the skipping rhyme with different words and a more tuneful melody, singing as her needle darted in and out:

Let the wind and the rain and the hail blow high
And the snow come tumbling from the sky...

Irish, Ethel thought, because although dark, the woman did not look foreign; she sang in English and the song sounded like Irish songs, a bit like songs from back home. The woman glanced at Ethel and their eyes met. Embarrassed to be caught staring, Ethel looked away.

She thought of home with a pain in her chest that was as real as if she'd taken a bad heart. She saw her mother's dark blue house, square and simple in its design but standing by itself in its own yard on Merrymeeting Road, neighbours always nearby but separated by fences and decency. Her own line of washing stretching across her own yard; her children playing in the quiet streets where no motorcars rumbled and even carts and horses were few. She knew there were people in St. John's who lived crowded into row houses, poor people who lived in little better than shacks and hovels. But for her kind of people there was always a house of your own once you married and had a family: your own land, your own space. She knew from hearing people talk that America had places like that too, little towns where houses grew like flowers in their own neat gardens behind tidy white fences.

Ethel knew now she would never live in such a place. Her life in America was a New York life, a Brooklyn life; it was as bounded and hemmed in as this yard with the brown brick buildings on all sides. The knowledge made her heart fall with a little despair; then she buckled herself into courage as she might into a girdle, and looked out the window again and willed herself to see in the mix of faces, dark and pale, in the babble of voices, a place she could belong.

When she turned from the window toward Jim and the landlord, she gave Jim her brightest smile. Ralphie tugged at her skirt and she scooped him up in her arms and stood with him there, framed against the window with the lively, noisy yard behind them, so that Jim, who was talking money and contracts with the landlord, could not do anything but nod and say, "All right then. We'll take it."

ANNIE

ST. JOHN'S, MARCH 1928

BILL WINSOR TOOK TO walking home with Annie after the Sunday night Salvation Meeting. Annie and Harold used to always walk home together, but now Harold was going out with Frances Stokes. Frances' people were Church of England, but for years she had gone to the Army with the Evans girls. Now that she and Harold were sweet on each other, she went every Sunday, morning and night. Annie made excuses to hang back, to talk to someone after meeting, telling Frances and Harold to go on ahead so they'd have a few minutes alone. Then Bill started waiting for her, saying he didn't want to see her walk alone.

Annie walked home those nights still warm inside from the meeting, warm with the singing and prayers and testimonies, the glory. Sometimes she went down to the penitent form and knelt and prayed, because that week she had been angry and impatient with her mother, and jealous of Harold's and Frances' happiness, and envious when she got Ethel's letter about the new apartment and how Ralphie was talking now. On her knees at the mercy seat all her discontent and petty thoughts and meanness melted away and she felt good and whole again, filled with enough of the glory to make it through another long week.

"You're in a good mood tonight," Bill said the third time he walked home with Annie alone. It was a cold clear night and their breath made white puffs in the air with every word as they climbed the steep slope of Barter's Hill. Slushy snow slopped around their gaiters.

"I'm always in a good mood after meeting."

"Captain had a fine sermon tonight," Bill said. "Some good testimonies, too."

"Yes. I like to died, though, when Mrs. Pitcher got up, didn't you? The look on old Helen Abbey's face, did you see it?"

Annie shot a quick glance of quickened interest at Bill: she knew almost everyone else in meeting had been watching the subtle glances between the two women, but not everyone would have pointed it out. She was dying to talk about it, even if it was the sin of gossip. "I suppose so, when she must have known every word Mrs. Pitcher was going to say. And when she said, 'Praise the Lord for giving me the courage and fortitude to bear up under the affliction of this troublesome neighbour, this false friend–'" Annie imitated the pitch of Mrs. Pitcher's voice perfectly; she was a good mimic, though she seldom had a chance to show off her skills.

"I know! I saw Miss Abbey's lips start to twitch; I thought, She's going to sing her down for sure. I figured next thing we'd hear was 'Throw out the lifeline! Throw out the lifeline!'" Bill's imitation didn't quite catch the timbre of Helen Abbey's reedy voice, but he knew her favourite hymn.

Annie laughed. "Have you ever really heard anyone sung down in meeting? Not just for going on too long, I mean, but because someone didn't like what they had to say?"

"Once, years ago. I was at a meeting around the bay where Uncle David Abbott started to testify about overcoming the sins of the flesh, and there was people there didn't think he should go into as much detail as what he did, so my grandmother, Sadie Bartlett, started in with 'I am under the good old Army flag…'" Bill had a powerful voice once he got going; Annie joined him on the next line. They turned off Prince of Wales Street and walked down Rocky Lane singing.

Bill laughed a nervous little laugh as the hymn finished. "Look at us, making a holy show of ourselves," he said. A wagon rumbled past on the road; the driver lifted his hat and nodded.

"Sure, nobody would mind someone singing a hymn on the way home from meeting," Annie said. "There's no harm in that."

"I s'pose not," Bill said.

She looked up at him sideways, seeing what she had always seen: his fine fair hair, his blue eyes, his strong jaw, but seeing him as if he were a stranger. She felt suddenly distant from him and at the same time quite close, and that strange double vision made her say, "Mom had a letter from Rose this week."

It made her heart fall, to see how quickly the light leapt to his eyes, how quickly their little moment of laughter and music faded compared to a half-dozen words if Rose's name was among them. "Is there any news, then?"

Annie shrugged. "Rose never has much in the way of news. She's still as foolish as the odd sock, writes about going to movies and dancing, just because she knows it will drive Mom to her knees in prayer. She's left off the last job she was at, the laundry, and she's working in a shop."

"And she's…is she…I mean…"

Annie took pity, although she was sorely tempted to let him flounder like a cod on the wharf. "Ah, no, she never talks about her fellows, so I suppose that means there's no-one serious. Although Rose is so close with her news, she could turn up on our doorstep married with four children one day, and never a word said." She glanced at Bill again before going on. "But Ethel now, she writes regular. She says that Rose has been going out with some fellow, some Italian man, for awhile now, but Ethel don't know how serious it is."

They walked along for awhile in silence out Freshwater Road, past the farms and open fields, falling into step together without trying to. "I suppose Rose got to live her own life," Bill said at last, in a voice like you'd hear at a wake.

Annie nodded. "All of us at home figured that out a long time ago, Bill. It's…it's time you did too. You can't go on through your whole life waiting and hoping, you know."

But am I any different? she asked herself later that night, leaning close to the watery green mirror, one foot square, that hung over her dresser. Her face hung in the greenish gloom like a sickly phantom. She thought again of Bill, of his quiet humour and quick eye. *No,* she told herself very firmly. *No, Annie. Don't waste your time waiting and hoping for Bill Winsor, who is in love with your sister and always has been.* She turned away from the mirror, then turned back for one last savage glance.

You don't want Rose's leavings anyway, do you?

ETHEL

BROOKLYN, JULY 1928

"DID YOU PACK ANY more of Mom's cake? We got to give Rose some of that cake!" Jim called from the bedroom, where he was looking for his old bathing suit to loan to Harold. Ever since Jim and Rose had cooked up this scheme to take their brother Harold out to Coney Island to celebrate his arrival in New York, Jim had been giddy, like Ralphie with a new toy, insisting on new bathing suits, new hats, the best of everything.

Ethel cut another big slice off Mom Evans' cake, wrapped it in a napkin and stuck it in the basket. Harold had brought the cake with him on the boat, on top of his trunk, and the first night he arrived he and Ethel and Jim had sat down around the table with a cup of tea and sliced into the cake and it was just like being home.

"Am I supposed to go out in public in this, Jim, my son?" Harold's voice came booming out of the bedroom. He had a big voice for a small fellow. "Sure, I'd be stoned to death if I went down Water Street dressed like that! Things must be some different in Brooklyn!"

"Only at Coney Island, b'y, they're all dressed like that out on the beach there. You takes it out and changes once you gets down there." Ethel squeezed out a smile at that, Jim playing the big New Yorker for his little brother. Jim hadn't been to Coney Island since, oh, maybe 1922, back when he first came. Long before they were married. Ethel had never wanted to go there, maybe because Rose said she went three or four times every summer and loved it. It sounded cheap, crowded and tawdry, not the kind of place Ethel would like to bring Ralphie.

Ralphie was staying home today with Jean and her youngsters. Jean and Robert had promised to take the children to the zoo in Prospect Park. All the same, Ethel and Jim had had a fight about leaving Ralphie behind.

"I just don't see the point, to take a whole day and spend all that money to go to the seaside and not take our own child!" Ethel had said. "We don't have that many outings and it seems mean not to take him."

"And how many outings do we get, just me and you, no kid?" Jim countered.

"There's no need for that! We're adults now, we have a child."

"Yes, but we're going with Rose and her boyfriend, with Harold – young single people. It's not fair to tow a kid along. It'd be no fun for Ralphie and no fun for the rest of us."

She could see his point. You had a different kind of fun going somewhere with a small child, or with another family who had children, as they sometimes did with Jean and Robert. She could see, too, Jim's longing for that other kind of fun, going on dates, going around with other couples, going to the pictures and to amusement parks. Rose's kind of life.

"It just don't seem right," she said again.

"Fine then, we'll take him with us." Jim had shrugged.

"I am *not* taking Ralphie to Coney Island with your sister and her Italian boyfriend!" Ethel had said. "He can stay with Robert and Jean for the day, and that's final!" She raised her voice to cover the feeling that she'd been tricked into backing down.

So here they were, eight o'clock on a Sunday morning, all packed to go and still no sign of Rose and the Italian. Ethel felt a little uneasy about missing Sunday School and church, but Rose and Jim had insisted Coney Island was an all-day trip. Ethel's foot, pinched tight in the pointed toe of her new white summer shoes, drummed a staccato rhythm on the linoleum.

They finally came at nearly eight-thirty, by which time Ethel had Jim and Harold out waiting on the sidewalk with the lunch basket and all their bags. Rose came sashaying up the street in a bright pink dress that showed her knees and a little pink hat so small it was ridiculous. Beside Rose walked a dark-haired young man in a straw hat with his jacket slung over one shoulder, a young man with a wide smile and a swinging, swaggering step. Jim stepped forward and swept Rose into a hug, swirling her away from the Italian, happy to see her as he always was when she crossed their doorstep every two or three months. Jim and Rose were two of a kind, Ethel thought, just like Bert and Annie. She didn't know Harold well enough yet to know which kind of Evans he was.

Harold stepped forward now, letting Jim lead him towards the sister he hadn't seen in five years. Ethel could see him taking in the changes in Rose: the cherry lipstick, the rouge, the hard shiny voice that sounded more Brooklyn than St. John's, which Ethel knew was put on.

"Everybody, this is Tony Martelli," Rose said. "Tony, my big brother Jim, my little brother Harold, and my sister-in-law Ethel." Rose's eyes slid quickly over Ethel's outfit, back up to her face and away.

Tony Martelli shook hands with the boys and took Ethel's fingertips lightly, lifting them, grazing them with his lips. Ethel pulled her hand back and giggled to cover the rudeness, both hers and his. Then she collected herself and said, "Pleased to meet you, I'm sure, Mr. Martelli. Rose has told us so much about you."

The Italian smiled. "Tony, please. Yes, Rose speaks so well of you all." He and Ethel smiled at each other, acknowledging the polite lies.

Jim broke the silence. "Come on, we better get a move on, let's catch the subway."

Ethel never liked travelling on the subway; she preferred trolleys. The dark tunnels and the hot crowded cars bothered her: it was impossible not to think of the cars and horses and people and houses all piled on top of her, ready to collapse. Jim strode onto the car behind Rose and Tony. Harold gave Ethel his arm to help her on. She shot him a look of gratitude. A kindly man, like Bert.

Harold was short, with bright blue eyes and sandy, crinkly hair. "Well, this is something, ain't it?" he said as he squeezed onto the seat next to Jim and Ethel.

"Sit back, kid. You ain't seen nothin' yet," Rose said. She turned to Tony. "I hope you got big bucks today, Tony Martelli, cause we are going to show my baby brother a good time at Coney Island. We're gonna eat a Feltman's hot dog and go for a ride on the Cyclone, right?"

Ethel glanced up at Jim. They had two dollars to entertain themselves and Harold, and fifteen cents was already gone on the subway fare. But Jim didn't look worried.

Finally the car lurched to a stop where the doors opened and people poured out in a living flood. "This is it," Rose said. Ethel scrambled on the floor, feeling for the lunch basket, the bags, her purse. Rose, a tiny handbag slung over one shoulder, stood up empty-handed without glancing down, leaving Tony to carry her bags while she led them out into the glaring sunlight.

Ethel hated Coney Island at first glance. Between the steady flow of people on all sides she caught glimpses of garish signs, heard barkers' voices luring them in to games of chance, smelled food in the air. She felt hot, faint, and queasy. But the others charged ahead, eager to get to the boardwalk. Ethel felt Jim's hand on her elbow and let him propel her along.

Her first glimpse of the beach was a shock too. Already, only ten in the morning, the sand was black with people, swarming like ants down off the boardwalk and onto the seashore. The ocean looked very far away, a narrow line of dark blue at the edge of a seething mass of humanity.

"Look, there's a bathhouse down there. Let's go change," Jim said.

Rose ruffled her brother's hair. "Don't go playing the big-shot New Yorker with me, Jimmy. You might impress Harry and the little woman there, but you don't know from nothin'. See the line-up outside that bathhouse? You wanna wait two hours and throw fifty cents each for a private locker? You follow me."

She led them off the Boardwalk and up onto a sidewalk where they joined a line-up outside a small, dilapidated house. "Ten cents apiece," Rose told them.

Ethel breathed a sigh of relief: thirty cents for her, Jim and Harold instead of a dollar fifty, just for a place to change your clothes. Maybe Rose's street sense had its place. But when she found herself and Rose crowded into a room with twenty other women shiggling out of their clothes and into their bathing costumes, Ethel could have cursed Rose to eternal damnation, never mind the money saved. She had never in all her life stripped full naked in front of another person in broad daylight, not even Jim. Nobody seemed to be looking but she flushed like a boiled lobster as she peeled off her stockings, dress and slip. Nearby, hugely fat women undressed, jiggling breasts and bottoms almost bumping each other. Skinny young girls stripped like snakes shedding their skins, and Rose, caught in the corner of Ethel's eye, undressed like a dancer, swaying her hips as she shimmied into her bathing suit. Ethel looked down at the dirty floor.

By the time they found the boys, walked back down to the Boardwalk, and fought their way to a narrow strip of sand where they could lay out their towels, it was time to unpack the lunches. Tony bought a couple of bottles of Coca-Cola from a beach peddler. Like the ten-cent changing houses, he explained, beach peddlers were illegal, "but how else are poor people gonna enjoy a day at the beach?" He spread his hands and grinned his big grin.

The Coke was warm but not as warm as the lemonade that had made the subway journey with them. Some of it had spilled in the picnic basket, making the sandwiches and cake sticky. Ethel offered some of Mrs. Evans' cake from home to Rose, who shook her head, and to Tony, who smiled and tried it and said it was lovely.

After lunch the boys went down to the water for a dip, weaving through the forest of bodies, quickly lost to view. Ethel was left alone with Rose. Silence descended.

"So, is Harold gonna work on the high steel with Jim?" Rose said at last.

"Yeah, Jim's already got him a job."

"He's not scared?"

"I don't know. I guess he's not. What does Tony do?"

"Works in a store…a fruit store. Says he's gonna own one someday." Rose was not looking at Ethel; she stared straight into the crowd as if gazing at the invisible sea.

That was all they had to say. After awhile Rose pulled a magazine out of her bag, lay down on her stomach and started to flip through it. Ethel wondered how the boys would ever find their way back through the crowd to this exact spot. What if she was stranded here with Rose forever?

The boys, however, came back, swearing they had been for a swim although in the noonday heat their skin and hair and suits were already dry.

By two o'clock they were all broiling, drowsy, dizzy from the sun and ready to pack up and leave the beach. After another horrible interlude in the changing house, they let themselves be propelled with the crowd up to the Bowery, Coney Island's main street.

Every imaginable human experience beckoned to them, but conscious of their few coins they were content mostly to stroll and watch, not feeling the need to go inside and see Bonita and Her Fighting Lions or Laurello, the Man with the Revolving Head. Tony, Jim and Harold each wasted a nickel on two wallops at the high striker, a chance to show off their muscles and impress the girls. Jim wanted to try the shooting galleries, but Ethel patted her purse and shook her head.

Then they drew near the amusement parks, where the roller coasters towered, and Rose said, "This is it. We all gotta ride the Cyclone."

Ethel looked up at the towering, rickety-looking contraption with the cars plunging to earth. It looked like certain death at twenty-five cents apiece. She shook her head again, but all the boys were as eager as Rose was. It wasn't their insistence, their teasing and urging that got her into the line-up and made her hand over the money: it was the dread of being stuck on the ground alone, abandoned in the crowd.

At the crest of the first big climb Ethel saw what a fool she'd been, how much better it would have been to have stayed on the ground, no matter how alone and afraid. She sat wedged between Jim and Harold, with Rose and Tony in the seat ahead, as the car teetered at the top and then plummeted down with a rush of wind, a roar of screaming voices, and the clatter and rattle of the wooden tracks. Fragile as matchsticks, she thought, and as likely to shatter. Screaming, she buried her head on Jim's shoulder and was briefly comforted to feel his arm tighten around her. Then he gave her shoulders a little shake and pried her head up. "Look, isn't it great?"

Oddly, things got better after the ride, as if the worst had been faced. They walked the length of the Bowery again, and everyone wanted hot dogs. Tony showed them the way to Nathan's, where the hot dogs were five cents instead of the usual ten. Ethel felt strange, walking and eating right out on the street, but everyone around her was doing it, so she did.

Then they turned into Paddy Shea's on Surf Avenue, which, Rose said, used to be an Irish bar before Prohibition. Now it was still Irish but it sold only sarsaparillas and lemon sodas. They squeezed around a table and drank their huge sarsaparillas in the slanting late-afternoon light and listened to the tinkle of the player piano. Ethel put her hand in her purse to check: three nickels, exactly enough for the fare back.

A family near them packed up their things and the father shouldered a sleepy, cranky child, just about Ralphie's size. It was a good thing they hadn't brought Ralphie, Ethel thought, looking at the child's flushed unhappy face. She had never spent a whole day apart from Ralphie before. She felt curiously light, as if she might float away, no longer anchored to earth by Ralphie's familiar weight.

The piano began to play "When Irish Eyes are Smiling" and Rose put her head on Tony Martelli's shoulder. Jim reached out and put his hand over Ethel's and she smiled up at him. Her nose and shoulders were burned and she felt tired in a giddy, sunwashed kind of way. She was almost happy, except for the thought of the subway ride back.

But Harold broke the silence to say, "Now ye been treating me all day and it's time for me to treat back. I'm paying the fare for our ride back, and we're going to take that elevated train, not the subway, so you can all show me the sights on the way back. That'll be all right, won't it Ethel?"

ROSE

A RICH MAN, ROSE thinks. *That's what I need next.*

She spins in Tony's arms, the dance floor a blur of light and colour. Music saturates the air. The band is good; she lets herself drown in the mellow sound of horns and in Tony's brown eyes, fixed on her like she imagines sailors might gaze at a lighthouse as their ship runs toward the rocks. He is a beautiful dancer. Her steps match his perfectly, as neatly as if they were really in love, really made for each other.

She is sure now that Tony thinks he loves her. They have been going out nearly a year and a half, a long time for Rose to be with one man. Now autumn is coming again. She heard a song once that said that in spring a young man turns to thoughts of love. But her mother always said that back home, out around the bay where she came from, people got married in fall, when the hard work of summer was over, before long dark winter nights closed in. Maybe it's the same way in Sicily. Soon leaves will drop from the trees in Prospect Park, and Tony Martelli's thoughts are turning to love.

They are dancing at the Plaza Ballroom to "I'll Get By." The words weave in and out of the music, in and out of Rose's thoughts as she dances in Tony's arms.

> *I'll get by as long as I have you...*
> *Though I may be far away, it's true*
> *Say, what care I dear,*
> *I'll get by as long as I have you*

A rich man. Rose steers her thoughts back into line. The song ends; another song starts.

"That's a lovely dress," Tony says.

"Thanks. I bought it at Loehmann's this week," she says. It's the blue velvet and georgette dress she has been saving for and dreaming of, the one that's a cut above anything else she has ever owned. Only from Loehmann's could a factory girl get a dress like this. She remembers the clear bright moment of finding it, squeezed among the others on the rack, pulling it out and deftly stripping down to her underwear there on the floor, pulling the dress over her head, knowing her heart would be broken if it didn't fit.

But it fit. Rose was so happy that she dressed again and went to the counter with only the briefest of glances up the stairs, to the forbidden hallowed chambers, cool and quiet, where the rich women shopped for bargains and tried them on in private dressing rooms. Usually when she came to Loehmann's, she was eaten up with envy, with the desire to go upstairs, to be among the wealthy, to know what it was like on the other side.

"What are you thinking about?" Tony asks as the song ends and they sit down at a table.

"I'm thinking about being rich. How I'd like to be rich."

Tony laughs, a big round laugh. "Yeah, me too! Old man Romano, he says to me, 'You know, Tonio, you ain't gonna get rich pushing my cart down the street, you know.' And I could tell you the same thing, Rose. You ain't gonna get rich working in no boot factory. Specially when it pays less than the five and dime." He frowns: he disapproves of her quitting her job and going to work in the factory. Rose can't explain why she did it. She knows it doesn't fit his image of her, a girl on the go, on the up-and-up, with ambition and plans.

It doesn't really fit Rose's idea of herself either, and she actually liked the shop better, but she got bored with it. She isn't really a girl on the go. She's the girl who's got to go, a girl who gets restless and itchy and bored and does dumb things like giving up a half-decent job and taking a much worse job for no good reason.

Tony leans across the table and takes her hand. "Rose, my beautiful Rose," he says. "I love you, Rose. You know what? I've been doin' a lot of thinking. I want to get married. I want to settle down and have beautiful babies with you. I don't care if I ever get rich. Will you marry me, Rose?"

Rose does not stand up, scream or run. She feels something unaccustomed and soft in her chest, because after all this time she has begun to care about Tony, in a way. So she tries to make it easier, which is always a mistake.

"Tony, you don't know what you're saying," she says. "Your family, your sister…they all want you to marry some nice Italian girl. Not someone like me. We don't have the same…background."

She sees the darkness cover his eyes and knows she has scored a point. It wasn't just a stab in the dark. She knows this to be true. She can read it off Marcella, his sister, like she is the front page of the *Brooklyn Eagle*.

"Let's not talk about it right now, Tony. We're having fun. Let's just leave it at that." The band swings into a livelier number. "Come on, dance with me, Tony." Rose stands up, swaying her hips, holding out her hands. Tony frowns. But she gives him a little smile and he comes toward her, responding to her invitation even as she's pushing him away.

It's America, where every man can be a millionaire. And any girl can be a millionaire if she meets the right man. It happens all the time in the movies, in magazine stories. The poor but pretty young girl wins the rich man's heart, and next thing you know, she's shopping on the top floor of Loehmann's. *I can get there*, Rose figures. All she needs is to meet the guy, and get rid of Tony along the way. It shouldn't be hard.

She keeps Tony dancing till long past midnight, hoping he'll be too tired to propose to her again. He's a lot of fun, and she'd like to keep on dancing and having a good time with Tony till she meets her rich guy. It would be better if she didn't have to come out and say, "Tony, I'm not going to marry you ever, so get lost, okay?"

He doesn't mention it again. When the band finally plays their closing number – "Stardust" – he holds her close and whispers, "I love you," in her ear, but nothing more. He helps her into her light spring coat and gives her his arm as they walk out onto the street.

As the crowd begins to thin and they wind their way in the general direction of Rose's boarding house, looking for a streetcar, Tony does something he's never done before. He starts to sing. Oh, she's heard him sing along with a band before or hum a snatch of tune while he's busy with something else, but Rose has never heard anything like this, from Tony or anyone else.

The words roll out of him, big strange Italian words she can't understand, huge waves of music much bigger than any tune she's ever heard in a dance hall or a club, great oceans of sound flooding from him. She looks to see if he's gone crazy and he's walking along, still with one arm out for her to hold onto, but the other arm is doing these grand wild gestures that match the song, and his eyes are half-closed – he'll smack into a wall if he doesn't watch out – and she has no idea what he's singing or why.

At first she's afraid people will hear and think he's a nutcase. Then she hopes people will hear, sure they couldn't help but clap or cheer. And for a moment in the middle of the music she sees that there is, after all, something bigger than her own dreams, something more important than finding a rich man to marry, something that might make her a better, truer Rose who could really fall in love with Tony and love him for all her life. She feels this thing coming over her, hovering like a cloud, and she has to bite her tongue to stop from saying, *I love you, of course I'll marry you.* She fights that feeling off for all she's worth, and finally, sadly, mercifully, the song ends.

ETHEL

❧

BROOKLYN, DECEMBER 1928

ON CHRISTMAS EVE, ETHEL, Jim, and Harold put up their Christmas tree. It was the first Christmas tree Ethel had had since coming to New York, and she thought she'd cry to see it there in their living room, all done with popcorn strings and sugar cookies. Harold and Jim had come home early from work, dragging the tree and carrying a box with a red and silver tin star in it. Jim stuck his head in the door and told Ethel, who was in a frenzy of scrubbing and cleaning while trying to keep Ralphie out from underfoot, to come outside for a minute.

"I don't want Ralphie to see," he said. "We got it from the guy selling them on the corner. Me and Harold figured we'd put it up tonight after Ralphie goes to bed."

Ethel stood on the front step of the apartment building staring at the small evergreen and at Harold, who was holding it up. The tree was not quite as tall as Harold. She didn't know what to say. Having their own tree had never occurred to her. She pictured Ralphie's eyes glowing when he woke in the morning to see it.

"Where are you going to put it till tonight?" she said. "Somebody'll take it for sure if you leave it out there."

"We'll find some place to stick it," Harold said. "We got this star to put on top, but we'll need some other stuff to decorate it with."

"I'll...we've got popcorn. I can make that, and string it, and maybe some cookies," Ethel said, thinking of all the work she had to do already. They were having Jean and Robert and their youngsters for Christmas dinner, as well as Rose and her young man if they actually showed up. Why hadn't she or Jim thought of a tree? This was Harold, she knew without being told. Only Harold could make such a leap.

Harold brought laughter into the house. He told jokes, ones a lady didn't need to be ashamed to laugh at, and he played with Ralphie by the hour. Jim was good with Ralphie too of course. Both men liked to come home in the evenings and wrestle on the floor with Ralphie, tickle and chase him and play-fight. It sounded so lively and fun with the three of them out there in the living room while Ethel cooked supper, all those male voices, all that energy. And Harold was so kind and thoughtful too. The way Bert used to be. He would carry his own dishes in from the table to the kitchen, and sometimes even pick up a towel to dry for her while she was washing.

And while he dried the odd dish or stood in the kitchen, he talked to her. That was it, really. He talked to her. Jim would come home at the end of the day and give her a kiss on the cheek and say, "How was your day?" but she knew that if she said anything more than, "Fine, dear," he would stop listening. He wanted peace and quiet at the end of a long day; he might play with Ralphie but he didn't want to be badgered with questions or news.

Harold, now, he would come into the kitchen after supper when she was washing up, and say, "You'll never guess what we saw coming home from work on the subway today, Ethel. You'd have laughed if you'd been there. There was a woman, dark-skinned, kind of a foreign-looking woman, and do you know what she had? She had a dog in her purse! In her purse! I said to Jim, didn't I, Jim, 'My, I wish Ralphie was here, he'd get some laugh at seeing that.' Imagine, a dog so small it could fit in her purse. You ever see a dog that small, Ethel?"

And Ethel would say, "No, I never did. I saw a woman walking a dog the other day with a sweater on, though. Can you imagine the like, knitting a sweater for a dog? I wonder where you'd even get the pattern." And Harold would laugh, and they'd share that moment, laughing at New York people and their foolish dogs and their strange ways.

It wasn't much, perhaps, but Harold made a great difference to the house. He'd been sleeping on their couch now for five months, and two or three times he'd made some noise about finding himself a boarding house, but Jim and Ethel both said, nonsense, they wouldn't hear of it. Of course they would have said the same to any relative. It would be a shame to have a member of the family off living in some boarding house when they had room to spare. But even Jim said that Harold was great to have around. It was like he made the apartment warmer, or brighter or something.

As Ethel finished stringing each long strand of popcorn she handed it to the boys, and they twisted it round and round the little tree. Harold had poked holes in the cookies – they were shaped like stars and Christmas trees – and stuck little bits of thread through them, which he was clumsily tying to make hangers. He and Jim got foolish again while they decorated, and started eating the bits of popcorn that fell off and then tossing them into each other's mouths, standing farther and farther back to see how far they could catch it from. And Ethel, who usually didn't have much patience with shenanigans, laughed right along with them.

Suddenly they heard the door to the hall open, and there in his pyjamas stood Ralphie, wide-eyed. Ethel saw the surprise and delight in his eyes and the big grin on Jim's face, seeing him there. All she could think was that this was supposed to have happened in the morning, when the tree was all done and the presents underneath it. Here it was, half-past eleven at night and the tree half-done and the star not even on it. Now he was awake and might have a hard time getting back to sleep, and Christmas morning was all spoiled.

"Look what you done now. I told you you'd wake up Ralphie if you didn't stop carrying on!" she snapped. "Ralphie! You shouldn't be out of your bed this hour of night!"

Ralphie stood still, as if he didn't hear her at all, staring at the tree as if he couldn't imagine how it had grown there so fast. Ethel was just getting ready to raise her voice and order him back to bed when Harold crossed the floor in two steps and scooped up Ralphie – just in time, before she told him he had to go to bed – and carried him across the room and put him in Jim's arms. "Look, b'y, it's our very own Christmas tree," Harold said.

"Saint Nicholas brought it," Jim added, happy again with his little boy snuggled in his arms.

"Christmas now," Ralphie said. He darted a glance at his mother to see if it was safe to smile, and Ethel smiled at him. How could she not have seen that this was right, that he was supposed to come out and find them and the tree all like this at almost midnight? She hadn't seen that, but Harold had, of course. Just like he'd known they needed the tree.

Twenty-four hours later the three of them were in the kitchen, the two men sitting down to the table while Ethel finished up the last of the dishes. Rose and her young man Tony had gone off not long after dinner, but Jean and Robert and their crowd had stayed for supper and so there was a huge pile of dishes. It had been a grand day though; they were all tired out now but Harold seemed to understand Ethel's need to make it all live again, to bring out the bright moments of the day like pieces of the best silver, polished and catching the light.

"Ralphie was some pleased with his stocking, wasn't he? Thought he'd died and gone to heaven when he got those chocolate bars."

"Yes, and when he saw the toy soldiers?" Ethel said. "Sure him and David were playing with them the whole afternoon."

"I had toy soldiers like that when I was a boy," Jim put in. "Remember them, Harold?"

"Yes, b'y, but you and Bert played with them so much, by the time I got them there was only half of them left, and those mostly had legs or arms cracked off. I used to line 'em off and pretend the battle was over and they were all in the field hospital with their limbs blown off."

Jim laughed so hard Ethel thought he'd bust a gut. "All you needed was a little Florence Nightingale," he said, wiping tears from his eyes. "Shoulda fixed one of them up with a little headpiece for you." All three of them laughed, and Jim sighed. "It's hard lines for the youngest, always getting the leftovers of everything," he said. "Ralphie's lucky, just like I was. First one gets all the new clothes and all the new toys."

Harold shook his head. "Not many toys when we were growing up, though. Ralphie'll do better."

"Oh, he'll have the best we can buy for him," Jim agreed. "I was some pleased when I found those soldiers in the shop for him, wasn't I, Ethel?"

"Sure, Ethel's laughing at us, Jim b'y," Harold said. "Pleased as punch we got the little fellow one present for Christmas, and she was a regular Saint Nick, buying every other present for everyone, and all the candy and oranges, and knitting the mitts and the socks and all, and that sweater for me too. It's a lovely sweater, Ethel. I don't know where you finds the time."

"Oh, I do a bit now and then, whenever I gets the chance," Ethel said. She had taken such pleasure in knitting that sweater for Harold, the very blue of his eyes, hiding it from him and knitting whenever he was out of the apartment. For Jim she had bought a new winter coat because she knew he liked bought clothes better than homemade.

"Nice to have Rose here today," Harold went on. "All the family together… all of us that's here, I mean." There was a brief silence, which each of them filled with their own thoughts: the family back home, and Bert of course – the empty spaces where people should have been.

Ethel was too tired for any foolishness when they went to bed that night and she guessed, rightly, that Jim would be too. She was often too tired now but tried to hide it because she wanted it as badly as he did, though for a different reason. It was high time to have another baby: she had always thought they'd have one by the time Ralphie was three, at the very latest, but time was running out for that. Month after month she'd wait and hope, but her period showed up every time, as regular as turning the calendar over.

Ethel was beginning to worry. She never said a word to Jim about it of course, but he'd been so good with Ralphie when he was a baby, she knew he'd like another one. Sometimes he said things like, "When we have another one, Ralphie can go out on the daybed and we'll put the crib in our room," or "By the time our kids are growin' up, we'll have this place fixed up a bit," so she knew he was thinking of having more than just Ralphie. But why hadn't it happened yet?

She'd tried talking to Jean. But Jean only said she was lucky not to get pregnant every time her husband looked at her; she should count her blessings since most women had the opposite problem. "And what's there to worry about anyway?" Jean said. "Sure, it's not like you'd worry you can't have children, you've had one already. So you know everything's working all right. 'Tis only a matter of time till the next one comes along, right?"

Ethel hadn't been able to get any further than that with Jean. Of course when a couple couldn't have a baby everyone talked about the woman being barren or whatever you liked to call it, but Ethel knew quite well there could be a problem with the man too. Not that you'd think it about a man as handsome and strong as her Jim, who was manly in every way. She couldn't say any of this to Jean because as far as Jean and everyone else in the world knew, Ethel and Jim had already had a baby together, so what was there to worry about? But if years and years went by and they never had another one, surely Jim would start to get suspicious.

As far as she knew he had never suspected anything. It was hard to believe he hadn't done some counting up the months and weeks and wondering about her and Bert…but no. He was as proud of Ralphie as any father could be of his son. It was like he knew for a certainty that neither Ethel nor Bert would have been the kind to do anything before getting married. Ethel imagined he must have blamed the whole business between her and him, the week of Bert's funeral, on himself. Jim thought of himself as that type of man, but Ethel couldn't be that type of girl, and so of course, in his mind, Ralphie had to have been his baby. But would he always think that, if Ethel never got pregnant again?

It got so bad that every month, the few days before her period was due, Ethel would be in a tizzy. She knew the day, sometimes even right down to the hour, because she was so regular. She'd get worried and irritable and achy, just like always, and hope that it was because of being pregnant, but then she'd be afraid it was going to come anyway, which would make her even more worried and irritable. What with one thing and another that was the worst week out of every month – the waiting and hoping, and then the letdown when it started after all.

One night when she said her nightly prayers she added, "And please, God, help me and Jim have a baby soon." She added that petition for several months. It didn't seem to make any difference, but then if you were thinking about women in Bible times, like Sarah or Hannah, it might take years for God to take any notice. She began adding, "I'll do whatever you want, God, if you let me and Jim have a baby." Not long after Christmas, when her January period had come and gone and left her more discouraged than ever, she took a more daring step. "Dear Father in Heaven," she prayed, "I know I've asked you to forgive my terrible sin, but I know it will never truly be in the past until Jim and me has a baby of our own. Please show me what I can do to make it up to you so you'll bless me with a child."

She tried to be better, kinder to Jim and more patient with Ralphie. She threw herself into the church, even volunteering to take charge of the spring tea and sale of work, which was nothing but a headache. Maybe, she thought, God would see she was serious. She worked for weeks on that sale, and when it was all over she stayed late that night to clean up, her back aching and her feet sore.

Jim and Harold came by the church to pick her up, and the two of them helped Reverend Darling haul a cartload of tables from the church back to the school they'd borrowed them from. Ethel sent a message to ask Jean to keep Ralphie overnight; she could see there was a night's work ahead of them. One by one the other helpers dropped off as their jobs were done, till finally it was only the three of them, Jim, Harold and Ethel, left working alongside the minister and Mrs. Darling. Ethel dropped into a chair, unable to move another step. "You must be dead on your feet, Ethel girl," Harold said.

"I am," Ethel said. "But it's all in a good cause." They said goodnight to the minister and his wife and stepped out into the street.

Jim looked at his watch. "It's nearly ten o'clock now. I'm starved. Haven't had a bite to eat since lunch at work."

"Lunch? I forgot lunch," Ethel said. She hadn't eaten since breakfast, and she wasn't sure there was anything in the house to make for a late supper when they got home.

"Let's stop somewheres and get a bite to eat, then," Harold said. "I got some money. Let me treat the two of you to a hot dog or something."

"Oh, Harold, we couldn't do that," Ethel began, then ran out of steam, as she really couldn't think of any reason not to, except that there was something shocking about going out and eating in a restaurant at ten o'clock at night.

They did it, though. And the very strangeness of the activity, and their tiredness, gave the adventure a kind of giddy edge, so that all three of them were laughing and carrying on, Ethel as bad as the boys, over their late-night chop suey in a Chinese restaurant that was the first place they passed. Ethel had always refused to try chop suey before and now wondered why: it was so good, and she had missed out on all these years she could have been eating it. She felt light-headed as she tripped down the steps of the restaurant and back out into the street. In fact she was so light-headed that she tripped quite literally, and Jim grabbed one arm while Harold grabbed the other, and neither one let go so that they all walked arm-in-arm down the sidewalk, laughing at Ethel's stories about the church ladies who were so fussy about every little detail of their tea and sale.

It's wonderful…it's as good as having two husbands, Ethel thought. She knew that was a shocking thought and also a silly one, because two husbands would be twice the work, but it would also be more variety, someone else to talk to. Having Harold here was like going back to the time when Bert was alive, when she and Bert and Jim would do things together. Only then, Jim had always had some girl or other. She wouldn't want that now, of course. It would be just terrible if Jim ever – only there she'd be, alone with Harold – no, that would be quite wrong. Worse than what she did with Jim after Bert died. Why was she even thinking such things? She was overtired, and maybe running a fever.

"Well, Ethel, my love, it looks like you'll have your couch free at last," Harold said as they reached the apartment building. "I got my marching orders here in this letter." He pulled an envelope out of his jacket pocket.

"What?"

"Two weeks ago I wrote to Frances and put the question to her. Told her I knew she'd rather I took her out under a tree in Bannerman Park someplace and went down on one knee, but I said I was writing it in Prospect Park, down on one knee, and that would have to be good enough."

"Go on, you never said that foolishness, did you?" Jim said.

"Yes, I did, and what's more, it's the truth. I really did sit in the park to write it. Well, I wasn't down on one knee but I'm sure she knew that part was just a joke. And just today I got her letter and she said yes. I'm going home the end of the month, we're getting married back home and then she's coming back with me on the next boat." His face shone so bright Ethel couldn't help but smile at him. Of course – Frances. Frances Stokes, her own and Annie's best girlfriend back home. Harold talked about her all the time, didn't he? Only Ethel never really paid attention to it, she realized now; she had never given any thought to Harold getting married, moving out of their apartment, setting up housekeeping on his own with Frances. It was wonderful news, of course. But how empty the apartment would be without him.

Ethel was dog-tired but she couldn't sleep at all that night. She lay beside

Jim, listening to his breathing and Ralphie's, thinking of Harold all alone out there on his couch. Of course he'd been missing Frances, lonely for her, wanting a girl and a life of his own all this time. It was just – she couldn't shake that memory of all three of them walking down the street, arms linked. Things couldn't stay that way forever, of course. It would be nice to have Frances around, a friend from home. They would be sisters-in-law. It was the most natural thing in the world, so why was Ethel thinking that she couldn't face getting up in the morning and going on for another day?

She got up in the morning – of course she did. She told Harold again how wonderful it all was and she wrote a letter of congratulations to Frances. She started crocheting a set of doilies for them for a wedding gift, and suggested Jim should ask around about apartments on their street that might be vacant. For the few days Harold was still with them she tried to wring all the pleasure she could out of his company, his talk and laughter, but it was like he was already gone. She hated the distance between them, the way all his thoughts now were on Frances and his future. Perhaps they always had been, and she had never seen it.

The night before he left he hugged her, in that casual brotherly way he often did. "Ethel, you're a saint, that's the God's truth, to put up with me on your couch for nearly a year. You're a saint, and you're a lovely woman, and I hope my brother Jim knows what a lucky fellow he is. You hear that, Jim?" There was a note in his voice at the end that was almost serious and Ethel clung to it, hoping Harold was trying to tell her something but not knowing what. And then he was gone.

He was gone, and they were into June. The day on the calendar when Ethel's period was supposed to come went by, and another day and another, and finally she realized that she'd been feeling tired and logy from more than just the sale and Harold's going. She waited two more weeks before she told Jean, and explained about her symptoms, and Jean said, yes, you couldn't miss that. Finally she told Jim the news, and he was thrilled, like she knew he'd be.

The night she told him, Ethel finally knew it was real and she could stop praying for a baby. She should pray a prayer of thanks instead, that she was going to have another child, her husband's child. Even if it hadn't always been Jim she was thinking of, it was Jim in the bed with her and that was what counted. Everything would be all right now.

ANNIE

～

ST. JOHN'S, MAY 1929

THE LIGHT IN THE Stokes' front room was rosy, filtered through filmy pink curtains and reflected back from a dusty rose carpet. It was a warm afternoon for May and the pink light made the air seem warmer, almost heavy. Frances wore a soft pink dress and carried pink silk roses, so it wasn't sensible to feel, as Annie did, that there was a cloying rose-smell in the air. Annie felt herself sway a little as Major Barrett led Frances and Harold through the vows. She gripped her own bouquet a little more tightly and tried to pay attention.

Frances looked as neat and pretty as she always did. Her dark hair and dark brown eyes were set off sharply against the pale dress. Her small hands, gripping the bouquet, looked like the curled pink-and-white of seashells. She was a tiny little thing, barely five feet and not an ounce over ninety pounds. That was good though, since Harold wasn't a very big man. On the far side of Harold, his friend David Janes stood as best man. Annie was the bridesmaid; Frances had no sisters and she and Annie had been friends ever since they were little girls.

Frances' father, looking quite unlike himself in a suit, sat stern and upright on his chair. He had wanted Frances married in the Church of England, but Frances had put her little foot down and insisted on a Salvation Army officer. Annie remembered herself and Frances and Ethel coming home from Salvation Meeting on Sunday nights when they were all young girls, arms around each other's waists. Nobody ever said a word against Frances going to the Army with them but sometimes people thought differently when it came time to marry out of your faith – though it wasn't as if she were marrying a Catholic.

Mrs. Stokes, mother of the bride, sat on the small settee next to the mother of the groom, the two of them squashed together like two soft old pillows, beaming like angels but no doubt making up catty remarks to say to one another afterwards. They had been best friends for years and were never without an unkind word to say about someone in the neighbourhood.

Annie's own father sat a little stooped, leaning forward in his chair: his back bothered him these days. His eyes were fixed on Harold almost hungrily, and Annie could read his thoughts. One boy dead, another gone for good – and now Harold, too, would be back off to New York almost as soon as the wedding supper was eaten. The Evans name would be carried on among strangers in a strange land.

The rest of the room was filled with aunts and uncles and neighbours and church people, about twenty guests in all, crowded into the little front room, fanning themselves with their hands or with various papers from the table in the front room: *The Evening Telegram, The Ladies' Home Journal, The War Cry*, whatever came to hand. Annie caught Bill Winsor's eye across the room. She and Bill would be the only ones of their old crowd left, now, once Harold and Frances were gone.

The ceremony was done; everyone crowded around to congratulate the bride and groom. Annie folded Frances into her arms, feeling her friend's bird-fragile bones and her brittle strength. "I know you'll be happy, Franny," she said. "Everything was beautiful...the dress came out lovely." Annie had helped sew it.

Frances stepped back and looked down at herself mockingly. "You know what they say," she said. "Married in blue, ever be true. Married in red, better off dead. Married in pink, certain to shrink!"

Annie laughed and turned to Harold, let herself be gathered into his hug. He was so much like Bert: she saw it more every year. So steady and responsible. Here he was, only twenty, with a wife and a good job back in New York, his whole life in front of him. She wouldn't mention to him how much like Bert he was. It wouldn't be fair.

She stepped back and watched her father come up, stiffly, to embrace his son and his new daughter-in-law. Annie smiled at him, radiantly, and took his arm as they went out into the dining room where her mother and Mrs. Stokes had lined off the table with every imaginable variety of tea buns, cookies, squares, sandwiches, and scones, with the wedding cake a magnificent white-topped centrepiece to the whole display. The wedding guests crowded around the table and two dozen neighbours, who had not been asked to the ceremony but had been hanging around the kitchen and the yard, edged in and began offering congratulations to the bride and groom as they moved carefully towards the table. Annie saw her mother catch Mrs. Stokes' eye when she saw old Tim Casey, who was not much better than a tramp, standing with a tea bun in one hand and a glass of ginger-beer in the other. But neither woman said anything: you wouldn't · turn anybody away from a wedding.

Frances and Harold left an hour after the wedding, climbing into the car David Janes had borrowed for the occasion. Everyone else stayed a good two hours longer, reciting over every detail of the wedding and reminiscing about every wedding ever held in the neighbourhood, the family, and the church for the last two decades. Along about seven-thirty, when it started getting duckish, Annie began to circulate, picking up plates and teacups and glasses, moving them to the kitchen, filling the sink to wash them. She found it soothing to be alone in the dim kitchen, lit by only one smoky lamp on the table, plunging her hands into and out of the soapy water. She always liked this part of a party, cleaning up afterwards, clearing away the evidence, returning everything to normal. She hummed "O Promise Me" as she washed, stacking the dishes neatly in the drain board.

She had caught the bouquet, of course. Frances had made sure of that, turning to flick it directly at her just before getting in the car, so that Annie hadn't even had time to duck or dodge. Frances was sure Annie wouldn't have long to wait. "Don't be talking about being an old maid, sure, Annie," she'd say. "You're only twenty-two, you got a long ways to go before you're over the hill yet. It won't be long before Bill comes to his senses and stops waiting around for Rose." Annie said nothing; she paid no mind to that kind of talk, even from Frances.

It was getting dark by the time Annie and her parents walked across the road to home. Mrs. Evans kept up a steady commentary all the way up into their own yard: "My, I don't know what to think of this spending the night in a hotel… there's a bed in our own house good enough for them…must be New York ideas Harold's after picking up…he don't put on airs too much though, apart from that, though I must say he's quick enough to head back there, taking the boat tomorrow morning…I wonder if Frances will be seasick on the trip? Ethel said she was terrible seasick when she crossed…Frances did a good job on that dress, though I don't think pink suits her complexion…lavender would have been nice…never seen anyone married in lavender, have you, Annie?"

No, Annie had never seen anyone married in lavender. Just as well; nothing rhymed with lavender. Pop had gone on ahead of them to lift the latch and go into their own kitchen, which was a bit chilly now. He knelt to stir up the coals in the stove and said, "Needs a bit more coal." He moved to the basement door and started down the stairs as Annie got her mother's spring coat off, settled her in her comfortable chair, hung up her coat and laid her good new hat on the shelf, and filled the kettle for a cup of tea.

Her mother was still talking: "...poor Catherine got herself wore out over this wedding...hasn't slept good in a week...still it's a fine thing to marry off your daughter...doesn't look like I'm going to have the pleasure, does it? You're in no hurry and I don't say we'll hear wedding bells from Rose anytime soon..."

A heavy solid thud sounded in the basement, much louder and more compact than a load of coal being shovelled into the bucket. Then silence. Annie went to the basement door and called, "Pop? Pop? Are you all right, Pop?" Her voice went up a little on each Pop, tighter and shriller each time he didn't reply.

She started down the dark steps, but she was less than halfway before she saw him lying at the bottom, sprawled facedown on the dirt floor, arms thrown above his head. *He's dead*, she thought. *He's taken a heart attack and died.*

Then her father moved: she saw the patch of white as his face turned sideways, his eyes searching for her. "Fell...my leg gave out," he said, but she had to come down three more steps to hear him.

She tried to pull him to a standing position, but he could not sit up on his own, much less stand, and he was far too big for Annie to push and pull around. From the top of the stairs her mother's voice drifted down: "What is it, Annie? What's the matter with your father? Is he all right?"

Annie knelt on the cold damp basement floor beside her father. "Pop, will you be all right here if I go get help? I need to get someone, a man, to help bring you up the stairs."

"My leg...just gave out under me," he said, dazed.

She hurried up the stairs, wishing she was wearing anything but the narrow-skirted bridesmaid's dress and the pointed-toed shoes. "It's all right, Mom," she said, trying to staunch the flow of her mother's worries and questions. "Pop's all right, he's alive. He fell over the stairs."

She was running through a mental list of her neighbours, thinking who would be at home and able-bodied enough to help, when there was a knock at the back door and there stood Bill Winsor. Annie didn't stop to question what Bill had come over for; his arrival was a godsend. He carried her father up over the stairs, settled him on the chesterfield in the kitchen, phoned for the doctor and waited with her till the doctor came and examined Pop.

"His hip is broken, Annie," Dr. Mills said. "We'll have to take him to the Grace, probably put him in a body cast. Even after he comes home, he won't be the same man again."

"Broken hip," she said. This was what she'd been thinking ever since she saw him move, and it was as bad in its own way as if he had had a heart attack and fallen dead at the bottom of the stairs, worse in a way, because he would be confined to bed and need constant care, constant nursing, and he would never be up and walk and work and care for himself again.

"He's young for a broken hip, isn't he?" Bill said. "My grandfather had a broken hip but he was seventy-seven. Mr. Evans is, what, not sixty yet, is he, Annie?"

"No, he is young for it, but it's not unheard of," the doctor said. "It's a terrible blow for a man like him, though, that's what it is. I'm just going to go out now and bring my car around so we can take him to the hospital. Annie, will you come with him?"

"I don't know…Mom…" Annie began, and looked at Bill.

"I'll see Mr. Evans down to the Grace with you, doctor," Bill said, as the doctor went to the door.

Annie thought of Harold and Frances in their hotel room, enjoying their first night together. And tomorrow morning at first light, leaving on the boat. She said nothing aloud, but Bill said, "Do you want me to go down to the hotel and get Harold, tell him what's happened?"

"No. No, don't do that." Harold and Frances had their plans made, their tickets bought, their lives ahead of them. "I'll write a letter after they're gone, tomorrow, and tell Ethel and Jim what's happened. Harold will get the news when he gets to New York. I don't want him feeling he has to stay back here on account of us. Though I'm sure I don't know what we're going to do," she added, staring down at her hands lying on the yellow flowered oilcloth.

One of Bill's hands moved to cover hers. "Don't worry about it, girl. You don't have to solve all your problems today. We'll take one day at a time, that's all. You know I'm here to help you."

ROSE

৵

BROOKLYN, AUGUST 1930

ROSE STANDS IN MARCELLA'S kitchen, the heat from the stove like a slap in the face. Outside it is August, ninety-five degrees, even small children scurrying for shade or water. In five years Rose has still not adapted to the heat of a Brooklyn summer. Marcella's kitchen is the back porch of hell, she thinks.

Marcella, unmoved by heat or, apparently, any other force of nature, stands at the stove stirring her sauce. She moves back and forth between the stove and the kitchen table, quickly and gracefully for such a big woman, sprinkling handfuls of this and that into the pan, speaking to her food in a soft singsong voice. Rose's legs ache. Shooting pains right up the back. She's been standing all day. Time to quit this job, find something where she's not standing all the time. All day in the factory, and now she's here in Marcella's kitchen, watching this thick Italian peasant woman who is only five years older than herself but seems of another generation, this woman who has finally decided to accept Rose into the family as a necessary evil and has, unfortunately, chosen to show her acceptance by teaching Rose to cook.

"Now, a handful of oregano," she says, scooping up what looks like grass clippings and scattering them over the chicken breasts simmering in the big cast-iron pan. Earlier, Rose watched Marcella pound the breasts almost paper-thin and dust them lightly with flour, watched as her plump quick hands sliced through bell peppers and green onions. Marcella is doubtless gratified at Rose's attention; she has not guessed that Rose is watching with what amounts to horrified fascination. Such attention, such passion, such love, even – lavished on something as trivial, as menial, as cooking a dinner.

Did her own mother cherish the act of cooking like this? Rose wonders, dragged unwilling back in memory to the canvas-floored kitchen on Freshwater Road with the Ideal Cookstove that dominated the landscape and set the hours

৵

of the women's days. Did Annie? Annie loved to cook, had taken over most of the cooking from Mom when she was about thirteen. Mostly Rose remembers Annie baking, up to her elbows in flour, dipping her fingers in a bowl of water, sprinkling one drop, two, three…but no more, never too much. Rose, when she tried, would dash half a cup of water into the pie crust, ignoring Annie's shrieks, not caring about the tough chewy crust anyway. Annie flushed with pleasure when the family cooed over her flaky crust. Annie has probably never seen a bell pepper, or oregano either, but perhaps she and Marcella would understand each other.

"This is Tony's favourite dinner, this is what I make for him on a special occasion. You can't afford to do chicken like this on an ordinary Sunday. You know on a Sunday, coming home from church, Tony likes macaroni with meatballs and gravy," Marcella says. She knows Rose doesn't go to church, isn't Catholic. She doesn't know that the first time Rose came for macaroni with meatballs and gravy she was expecting gravy, like at home, a beef gravy or something, and didn't know what to make of the rich red tomato sauce all over the noodles and meatballs. That was a long time ago: Rose has been coming here for meals for nearly three years now. But she knows, and Marcella knows, that she will always be an outsider.

Marcella knows that Rose hates to touch raw meat and loves to eat in restaurants where waiters bring her things on trays. Marcella's words say, *I'll show you how to look after my brother*, but underneath she is saying, *I know you won't look after my brother. I know you're not good enough for him.*

Rose wants to sit down. She knows it will be one more black mark against her but how long, really, can she stay standing up? After three years of keeping company, three years of nothing better coming along, she has almost decided to marry Tony, but worries the price may be too high. Is Tony worth spending hours and days cooped up in the kitchen on the back porch of hell, listening to Marcella? Worse yet, turning into Marcella? Thoughts of getting older, getting fat, making babies, oppress Rose. When she thinks about being locked into a kitchen like this one, what she imagines is lying in a coffin, the lid nailed down on top of her.

She sways a little: heat, exhaustion, the cramps in her legs. She steps back and lets her legs buckle, settles into a chair. Marcella doesn't notice: she is singing to her food now, singing a song in Italian with a high sweet voice that doesn't match Marcella at all. It's like those songs Tony sings sometimes, when he's drunk or happy or sad, the songs that make Rose wish she really did love him. Another memory stirs and Rose is again back in that other kitchen at home, watching Annie knead bread. Annie sang as she kneaded, clear and strong and a little shrill on the high notes, emphasizing the beat more than the melody and punching the bread down on each beat. "*Would* you be *free* from your *bur*-den of sin? There's *power* in the *blood, power* in the *blood!*"

Quickly Rose knows she has to leave; she stands up even before Marcella notices she was sitting down. "I got to go, Marcella, sorry, I'll see you later," she says, grabbing her purse.

"What…where are you going? Tony's coming over, what am I going to tell him?"

"Tell him…tell him I'll see him later. Thanks for the cooking lesson, Marcella." Rose is already out the door, flinging the words back as she runs down the steps, teetering on her heels.

Out in the street, ninety-five degrees seems blessedly cool. Rose walks through the streets, hearing the babble of Italian voices, waiting till the sound ebbs and she hears only English again, out on the broad main streets. She looks hungrily at stores, speakeasies, movie theatres.

A movie. That's what she needs. She wants to get far, far away, and only the movies can take her far enough. She is a thousand miles from home, in Brooklyn, New York, where she has always wanted to be. But now she knows that even Brooklyn is not really far enough; it is full of little pockets, little holes you can fall down and find yourself back home, or someplace too much like it.

She can't go to a movie alone. She walks, aimlessly at first, then with some purpose, down to the candy store at Bushwick and Myrtle, just beyond the edges of Tony's neighbourhood. It's a tiny store spilling over with people. In the lot outside a bunch of little kids play with alleys, and there are two sagging benches laden with old men reading newspapers and muttering to each other through clouds of cigar smoke. Inside, in the dim and crowded interior, Rose can see a row of people jammed elbow-to-elbow at the counter getting sodas or egg creams. But in front of the store, the reason she's here, is a knot of fellows who usually hang out there in the evenings after work. This being Saturday, the ones who get a half-holiday are there early, lounging around the steps, carrying on with each other and checking out the girls. One of them, Danny Ricks, who works at the Navy Yards, whistles as Rose comes down the street.

"You better watch yourself," Rose says, slowing down and smiling at him. "A lady don't take that kind of thing from bums like you."

"My apologies," Danny says, taking off his cap and doing a big fancy bow. He's always flirting with her. She's known him for years, back before she was going out with Tony.

"I can't forgive you that easy, you gotta make it up to me," Rose says.

"How about a soda? Would that make it up?"

"It'd be a start," says Rose. Danny offers his arm and they go up the steps into the store, where they lean on the counter and both order chocolate sodas. After the brilliant sunlight outside, the inside of the candy store seems like a cave. Rose blinks, trying to accustom her eyes to the gloom.

"So, seen any good pictures lately?" says Danny.

"I hear that new one with Gary Cooper is good," she says, flashing her brightest smile.

"*Morocco*?" Danny says. "I hear it's great. It's got Marlene Dietrich in it."

"Morocco? What's that mean?"

"Some place far away in the desert," Danny says with a wink, even though there's really nothing to wink about.

"I like movies about places far away," Rose says. "I wonder if it's as good as *The Virginian*. I loved that movie."

Danny isn't bright but it doesn't take him forever to get the hint. He looks her up and down and smiles again. "Only one way to find out if a picture's any good. Ain't Tony taken you to see it yet?"

"Tony's working tonight," Rose says, "and I want to go to a show. Haven't I got the worst luck?"

"Maybe your luck's about to change," says Danny.

Rose falls into the movie like she's plunging headfirst into water – which is a funny thing to think, because the movie is so dry, the desert sands and all. But that's how it feels: the movie rises up, absorbs her. She is there in Morocco, in a place almost as hot as Marcella's kitchen on an August afternoon.

The very first scene of the movie shows a man struggling with a donkey in the middle of a dusty road, and Rose remembers the first time she heard Tony talking about his home back in Italy. Donkey – they had a donkey. To Rose, the donkey is an exotic creature, something from an alien world. Is this the kind of world Tony comes from: hot, dusty, with voices wailing strange music? Thinking of Tony makes her feel guilty, and she's glad when the Foreign Legion marches onto the road, onto the screen, brushing aside the man with the donkey.

And, oh yes, there's Gary Cooper, with that amazing long face and those eyes, those dark eyes. Rose wonders why she's never met a man in real life like Gary Cooper. That's the trouble, that's why she can't fall in love and settle down and get married like an ordinary girl. She's looking for Gary Cooper.

Then she sees the beautiful fair-haired woman on the boat who looks so sad, so bored and tired, like she'll never fall in love again and nothing will ever make her happy. "That's her, the German girl," Danny says, leaning over. "Marlene Dietrich. Some looker, ain't she?"

Rose tries to shut out Danny's voice, to block out any intrusion from the real world into the movie world. "Yeah, she's pretty," she whispers back. But *pretty* doesn't begin to describe the woman's face, with her high cheekbones, her perfect mouth, and those sad haunted eyes. When she tears up the card with the rich man's name on it and blows the pieces to the wind, Rose knows exactly how she feels. There's a word for it somewhere but Rose is not good with words: she only knows that even though she has never sung and danced on a stage or made love to a man or been to Morocco or had a millionaire fall in love with her, still, she is fundamentally the same as this woman – already Rose can't remember the actress' name but the character is called Amy, Amy Jolly – and she feels that same weariness with everything, like a glass wall cutting her off from the world where people meet and fall in love and are happy.

The knowledge scares Rose. She admires everything about Amy Jolly: she wonders if she can get her hair done just like that – it's almost the same colour – and would she have the nerve to try that trick of lighting her cigarette from a candle, which looks so sophisticated. When Amy Jolly first appears on the stage, dressed up in a man's suit and a top hat, singing in French in a deep rich voice, Danny leans over and says, "She looks a little like you, Rose, dontcha think?"

"Oh, go on," says Rose, pleased with the compliment but knowing in a hundred years she could never be that beautiful, that strong, that alluring. Maybe she needs to be more like Amy Jolly – more cool, more set-apart, so that everyone will know her heart's been broken too many times and she won't let it be broken again.

Rose sits transfixed, thinking about the choice Amy Jolly has to make, between the poor man she loves and the rich man who's so kind to her and who she'll never really love. That's always the way in movies though, there's always some rich man ready to sweep a girl off her feet. And always some handsome devil like Gary Cooper, too. Sometimes the girl gets really lucky and the rich man is also the good-looking one, but there's some other problem to keep them apart till the movie's over.

That's the movie Rose wants to star in – the one where Gary Cooper plays the rich guy from Manhattan who wants to take Rose away from all this, give her a more exciting and wonderful life. She should be waiting for that, holding out for that. Rose watches Amy Jolly at her engagement dinner to the rich man, wearing his string of pearls around her neck, and thinks, *Rose, girl, this is who you've got to be like. You've got to start playing it smart.*

By this time in the movie Rose is confused because she doesn't know whether she wants Amy to follow her heart and go with Gary Cooper, or play it safe and stay with the millionaire. Either way, it seems to Rose, she's got a pretty good deal. She feels Danny's arm slip around her and tighten on her shoulders. His fingers slip under the sleeve of her dress to her skin. He will expect something after all this is over, and why shouldn't he? She's made herself available.

Rose has still never been with a man, not really, though she's gone pretty far. When she was a girl back home there was a book they gave all the young people in church to read: *The Story of a Rose* or something like that. A warning to young men, about how a young girl was like a delicate rose and if you started handling it too rough, the petals would fall off and it would wither and die. The book was about sex, though the word was never said. Her brother Jim read it and used to tease her, because of her name being Rose. They laughed about the book, yet all these years she's been carrying it – virginity – around like it really was a precious rose or something. Now she feels like a woman who's looked down and sees that all she has in her hands is a wadded up piece of paper, a woman who says, "What am I hanging on to this for?" and drops it casually in the street.

Rose is twenty-five. Last year she started lying about her age, which she can get away with. Still, she won't be young and pretty forever. Something needs to happen, she has to make a choice or take a chance. That look is in her eyes, that same bored tired look that's in Amy Jolly's eyes, only this isn't a movie and no-one is coming along to save her. She will have to save herself.

The movie is almost over. Rose can feel Danny's fingers pressing against her hot skin, reaching farther, under the edge of her brassiere to her breast. His other hand is on her thigh. Amy Jolly has just found Gary Cooper and let him slip away again. Then she stands there watching the soldiers march off across the desert, and the poor peasant women with their goats and donkeys and packs on their backs who trail along behind the men, and suddenly, unexpectedly, Amy Jolly kisses the millionaire goodbye, kicks off her lovely shoes, and starts off in her beautiful white suit, barefoot across the desert, disappearing into the sand.

Will she survive the trip? Will her feet get burned so bad she can't go on? Will she catch up to the men and will Gary Cooper really desert and run away with her like he said he would? Rose can't wait for the next scene and is horrified when the words "The End" come up on the screen. She sits frozen in her seat, seeing this beautiful woman walking barefoot across the sand because her perfectly sealed heart has been cracked open like an eggshell. To her horror, Rose realizes she has tears starting down her cheeks, and quickly wipes them away.

"Well, that was a funny ending," Danny says as they stand up to go. "You don't even see what happens. I don't like that, do you? I like a happy ending. Let's go for a soda or something. Or we could go to a speakeasy. I know where there's one not far from here."

"Sure, let's do that," says Rose, who could use a real drink. They pass through the red-and-gold pillared splendour of the lobby and out into the hot crowded night. On the street they look idly into store windows.

Danny stops at a jewellery store window where a sparkling necklace and earring set is on display. "Something like that would look pretty on you, Rose," he says.

"Yeah, I'd like that." The diamonds probably aren't real, but even so, it's more than she could afford. And anyway, a girl doesn't buy a thing like that for herself.

"Maybe you'll get it for a present, if you're a good girl," Danny says, squeezing her waist and grinning. He leads her past the jewellery store to a candy store where, in the back, you can go down a few steps and find yourself in another, dimmer place, and order a gin and tonic.

All the while they're sitting and drinking Danny is talking happily away but Rose doesn't say more than "Uh-huh," and "Is that so?" and "Really?" which is all it takes to keep him going. She is back in the movie, trying to puzzle out Amy Jolly's choices and her own. She watches Danny's mouth move as he talks. He's good-looking, probably about as good-looking as Tony, though neither of them is Gary Cooper, not by a long shot. But the main thing, she thinks, is that he's nothing special; he's not complicated. There's not too much of him there. He's like an empty glass she can fill up. Not like Tony, full of dreams and sorrows and joy and music and a kind of simple goodness that terrifies Rose. Tony loves her and wants to be loved. Danny operates on a more straightforward basis. A fair exchange, she thinks, remembering the necklace and earrings. Like Amy Jolly's millionaire, on a small scale. A first step, she thinks.

Across the room she sees a dark-haired girl who looks like she could be related to Tony, chatting up some guy who's hardly paying attention to her. *There is a Foreign Legion of women, too,* Rose thinks in that low husky voice, thinking of herself, of all the girls here in New York so far from home, hoping to find some dream come true. She tries on Marlene Dietrich's voice again in her head. *There is a Foreign Legion of women, too. But we have no uniforms, no flags – and no medals when we are brave.*

Out into the street again. Danny draws her into an alley and starts kissing her. Rose closes her eyes so it's easy to imagine he's Gary Cooper. This hot Brooklyn street could be Morocco.

Her back rubs against the rough brick of the wall as this man, who could be any man, presses her into it. She feels him hiking her skirt up around her waist, his hands travelling up her thighs. She's gone this far before, and farther. After this there are supposed to be protests and apologies. Not tonight. "I got a safe," he mumbles, and Rose nods without saying anything. *What am I keeping this for?* Toss it away casually. What is she losing, except the silly dream that someday she'll meet someone worth walking barefoot across the desert for?

The man she's with doesn't question his good luck. He pulls her lacy underwear down to her ankles and gets to work. Rose keeps her eyes closed. He can be anyone she wants him to be. Until the sharp moment of pain, when he enters her and her eyes fly open long enough for her to think, *Is this what I want?* She sees the bricks on the other wall of the alley, a few feet away, and a narrow strip of sky above and, worst of all, his face, handsome and bland and common, locked in a horrible grimace. She sees the sparkle of a cheap imitation-diamond necklace. She closes her eyes, wills herself back to Morocco, back to the land of loss and dreams.

ETHEL

BROOKLYN, OCTOBER 1930

ETHEL STOOD IN THE courtyard, her mouth full of clothespins. Jimmy pulled himself up to stand by hauling on her leg. Thrown off balance, she dropped the blouse she was hanging. She bent down to pick it up and saw it had fallen into a puddle and the sleeve was dirty. With a sigh she threw it back in the basket and picked up one of Jim's work shirts.

"Mommy! Mommy!" This was not Jimmy, who as yet could only say "Ma-ma," but Ralphie, who was running around with a small pack of other four-year-olds in frantic imitation of a group of bigger boys playing stickball in the centre of the courtyard. "Mommy, get my ball!"

"Get it yourself!" Ethel yelled back. She shifted her weight as she called out. Jimmy lost his grip on her leg and fell back on his bum, howling with pain and hurt pride. Ethel sighed. Something as simple as hanging out the wash seemed to take forever. It didn't used to be this hard when Ralphie was a baby, did it? Having two was more than twice as hard, although at least there was a decent space between Ralphie and Jimmy, not bang-bang right next to each other like Jean's three. Women who had their babies close together like that must go off their heads, Ethel thought.

"Ah look, he is standing up! What a big boy!" Mrs. Liebowitz was down with her basket of wash too, standing at her line just next to Ethel's, pinning up her clothes and beaming at little Jimmy.

"Yes, he's growing like the weed," Ethel said. "Where's your little one this morning?" She could never remember the name of Mrs. Liebowitz's two-year-old boy, though the four-year-old girl, Rebecca, was one of Ralphie's regular playmates. Rebecca was a pretty easy name to remember, though Mrs. Liebowitz said it with an odd foreign pronunciation.

Jimmy fell and started to cry again; Ethel picked him up and attempted to finish hanging out the wash while cradling him on her hip.

"Oh, my Sarah, she's taken little Levi out, out in the carriage. She walks him up and down the street as soon as she gets home from school. Her and her friends love to take the little ones out. You should let her take your Jimmy, she'd love to, it's a big carriage. She could put him in together with Levi." Levi – that was the baby's name. And Sarah was the eight-year-old. There would be another little Liebowitz within the year, Ethel could see, though Mrs. Liebowitz never said she was expecting and Ethel didn't ask. They were not friends; they were neighbours. Mrs. Liebowitz was friendly, but she and Ethel did not trespass on each other's territory: they talked in the courtyard or on the front step but would not invite one another into their kitchens for a cup of tea. Ethel wasn't sure if foreigners even drank tea.

Ethel was uncomfortable with the other woman's foreignness, her strangeness. She looked dark and severe and older, with the long plain dark dresses and her hair all tucked up under a scarf. Her laundry, caught by the crisp October breeze, danced on the line: more of the long shapeless dresses puffed out like they were alive, the same dresses in miniature for her girls, Mr. Liebowitz's white shirts, even strange underwear. Funny about neighbours, how you saw their underwear and nightdresses and stuff, and yet you might never see inside their kitchens.

Ralphie spun out of the circle of whirling children back to her side, crying and snivelling: the whole happy wheel of children had exploded into separate sobbing bundles, each running to a mother. Ethel looked enviously at the bigger boys who were now heading off to play in the nearby vacant lot. Someday, she thought, Ralphie would be old enough to play like this, old enough to go off with his friends and not need his mother so close by. She bent down awkwardly, Jimmy still in her arms, to hug Ralphie, and was overcome at once by a rush of love and annoyance.

Back in the apartment, Jimmy and Ralphie played quietly for a little while and Ethel worked as quickly as she could to take advantage of the minutes. Her meatloaf was already made up and ready to go in the oven. Like most of the meatloaves she made these days it was more and more breadcrumbs and onion, less and less meat. She had become skilled at finding bargains, making do, dressing up cheap cuts to look and taste better than they were. Two years ago, when they got this apartment, she daydreamed about getting ahead, moving up in the world. Now she stretched meatloaf to try to save a penny here and a penny there, because even when Jim had steady pay coming in she knew the bad times could strike again, any minute.

It was all because of the Crash. When Ethel first heard about the Crash on

Wall Street, last fall, she didn't understand. She thought it was an actual building on Wall Street that had crashed, the Stock Market. She knew Wall Street was an important street in New York. Jim had even taken her there and she'd seen some of the big buildings that he'd worked on. When the men talked about the Crash, she'd pictured one of those big skyscrapers collapsing somehow, bricks and mortar and rubble crashing to the ground like the walls of Jericho.

It was Harold who had taken the time to really explain it to her, carefully and simply, and at the end she felt much better, like he really took an interest. She still couldn't have really said in her own words what the Crash meant, but she knew no buildings had fallen down. Only that rich men who had a lot of money had lost most of it or all of it. Not a thing you'd think would matter to people like them, but Harold explained to her how the rich men were the ones who owned the big companies and built the big buildings. If the rich men were poor now, they wouldn't be able to hire anyone to put up new buildings, which meant a lot less work for steelworkers. Which meant meatloaf made with more breadcrumbs than beef. The Crash was everywhere, even in Ethel's kitchen.

After the Crash, construction stopped on the building Jim was working on and there were five months, cold months of winter, when he had to pick up jobs wherever he could, a few days here, a week there. The pay was far less than he had been making and it took all Ethel's know-how to make those few dollars cover the housekeeping. But she did it. Then, back in March, Jim and Harold got the news they'd been hoping for: that big new skyscraper, supposed to be the tallest in the world, was going ahead on the spot where the old Waldorf-Astoria hotel burned down, going ahead in spite of the Crash and the hard times. Jim and Harold were among the 3000 men who got jobs.

Most of the Newfoundlanders they used to work with wouldn't go to work on the new building because it wasn't a union job. They'd been told if they worked on it, they'd never find jobs with the union again. Some of the men had a lot of loyalty to the union. Jean's husband Robert was one of those: there was tension between Robert and Jim for awhile after Jim chose to betray the union. When anyone got talking about the brotherhood Jim just shrugged. "If the union's gonna put food on our table, good for them. But if not, I'll take whatever work I can get." And Harold, a little less sure about stepping out of line with the union brethren, allowed himself to be convinced.

So the new skyscraper was rising in Manhattan, and here on Linden Boulevard steady pay was coming in again. But Ethel no longer trusted good fortune. She kept on shopping and cooking exactly the way she had when they were almost penniless, and put the money she saved in a biscuit tin for a rainy day.

"Did Harold say anything about what time they're coming over tonight?" she asked Jim over supper. Jim was still eating and Ralphie dawdled over his plate, dipping his bread into the mashed potatoes, making little patterns but not eating much of either bread or potato. "Eat your potatoes, Ralphie," she said, cutting a sliver of meatloaf for herself.

"He said about seven-thirty," Jim said. "Is it just Harold and Frances or have you got a whole crowd invited over?"

Ethel turned her back to him and began slicing bread at the counter. "Same crowd as always, Jim, you know: Harold and Frances, Jean and Robert, Dick and Eileen. Sure, we haves the same people over every Friday night. You'd think you'd be used to it by now."

"Sometimes, at the end of a hard week, a man likes a bit of peace and quiet in his own house, not a crowd of people traipsing in and out," Jim said into his plate.

"Can I get down now, Mommy?" Ralphie said, with just an edge of a whine in his voice. She looked past the broad blue of Jim's shoulders to where Ralphie sat, pale and small and tired. It was on the tip of her tongue to say he hadn't eaten enough supper but she stopped herself. There was no time to fight this battle tonight and the sooner he went to bed the better. "Go on, get down," she said. "You can play for a few minutes and then go to bed."

"I want to play with you, Daddy," Ralphie said. "Come on, Daddy, play with me."

Ethel was always amazed how well Jim took this pestering. He said, "Wait a minute, Ralphie, and I'll come out and we'll set up your toy soldiers, all right?"

Ralphie kept dancing around him pleading, "Now, Daddy? Are you coming now? Come on, Daddy!" Ethel herself couldn't ask Jim two questions in a row when he came home from work without him flying off the handle at her, but he put up with all Ralphie's foolishness.

It was funny how different she and Jim were about having company. Ethel was the one who invited their friends over, who planned and did all the cleaning and getting the sandwiches ready and looked forward all week to this one evening when they'd be able to sit back and relax and have a few games of cards and a little grown-up conversation. Jim mumbled and grumbled and complained. Yet once the crowd was there Jim was the life of the party, telling all the stories, making the other fellows laugh, even flirting in a harmless way with Jean and Frances and Eileen. Ethel usually found herself sitting quietly on the edge, watching and listening, slipping off to the kitchen to put the kettle on, sometimes having a little bit of a headache from all the loud voices and the smoke from Dick's and Jim's cigarettes. Friday night was the one night in the week Jim would have a few smokes. It was as if Ethel liked the idea of company better while Jim liked the actual company.

Part of it was that they always played cards and Ethel was never very good at it. Of course she had been brought up to think card-playing was a sin, so she'd never learned anything but Rook, and even though Jim had explained over and over that hundred-and-twenties was the same game with different cards, that didn't help much. She'd never been any good at Rook either. "I just don't have a head for cards," she'd say, and no-one ever wanted her for a partner because she forgot what trumps meant or what card it was.

Usually Harold took her as his partner just to be kind. She would sit a little dazed as the cards were laid down, trying to follow the game but never really catching on. She felt a little guilty at the sight of the hearts and clubs and diamonds and spades, knowing that they were of the devil and also wondering why nobody else had trouble telling the clubs and the spades apart and why they couldn't just be different colours like the Rook cards. She was glad when the card part was over and they just sat back and talked.

A good bit of the talk was news from home. All four of them were related in one way or another – Eileen Mouland was a cousin of Jean's on her mother's side – so they knew a lot of the same people and shared the bits and pieces of news in letters from home. And they swapped news about friends and family here in Brooklyn. None of them had any friends who weren't Newfoundlanders; they lived in a web of crisscrossing lines of relations and old friends.

Harold asked about Rose. "Has she been around here lately? We haven't seen hide nor hair of her since the summer," he said.

"No, sure, we hardly ever sees Rose unless she takes it into her head to come visit; it's not like you'd run into her anywhere," Jim said, for Rose, unlike the rest of them, had no friends from back home and seemed to live in an entirely different world. "She was over here...what was it, Ethel? A few weeks ago?"

"She came over one Sunday at the end of August," Ethel said, "but she only stayed half an hour, and we never got no news out of her. I don't think she's with that Italian anymore though." She went into the kitchen to see if the tea was steeped.

Frances followed her in to help. Frances was quiet tonight, like she had something on her mind. Maybe it was only worrying about work and money, which all the men were talking about again now. Or maybe – could she be having a baby? She and Harold had been married over a year. It was about time, but it would be better if they waited till things picked up a little. As Frances took down the teacups and laid them in the saucers Ethel wondered if she should ask what was wrong, or let it go till Frances was ready to talk.

But it was Frances who said, "You're quiet tonight, Ethel, anything on your mind?"

"No, girl, just wore out, you know, after all week. Or, if you don't know, you will when you've got a couple of youngsters." That would give her a chance to talk, if it was babies she had on her mind.

But Frances only said, "Yes, I s'pose they must be a handful." As Ethel lifted the teapot off the stove she could see Frances darting little glances at her, like she was trying to work herself up to say something. It couldn't be a baby, after all. That wouldn't be so hard to tell to your sister-in-law and closest friend.

"I don't s'pose Jim is much help, working queer hours and all," Frances said, filling the pink lustre jug with Carnation milk.

"No, he's late getting home these nights. Well, I s'pose you know what it's like yourself, since him and Harold got this job. They're working the men all hours, weekends and holidays and all. Some nights he don't even be home to his supper. Sure, you know one night last week it was eight o'clock before they were home. But it's better than him having no work at all." Ethel lowered her voice. "Like poor Dick and Eileen. I don't know what they're going to do if Dick don't find something soon."

"We're some lucky Jim and Harold got jobs," Frances said. "I worries all the time what will happen when this job is over, don't you? Especially when we got so much of our stuff bought on time: half our furniture, our vacuum cleaner, the icebox. We'll lose it all if we can't make the payments."

Ethel nodded but said nothing, busied herself filling the sugar bowl. She didn't believe in buying on time. Jim would have done it, but Ethel put her foot down. They had saved for their icebox and they did without a vacuum, but everything in the apartment was theirs and she had no worries about losing it. She thought Frances was foolish for buying on credit, but it was no good telling anyone that; they all wanted everything right now and all the best.

Frances set out the teacups on the tray and Ethel carried it out to the living room. It wasn't till later, when they were all gone, that she remembered that Frances had had something on her mind, and she didn't think it was anything to do with the icebox being bought on time.

She had another chance to find out, though. On Sunday Jim left early; it was his turn to work the Sunday shift. Ethel took the children to church and then Frances came round after lunch to ask if Ethel wanted to take them to the park. "Harold's home trying to fix our radio," Frances said. "He likes fooling around with that electrical stuff and there's no money for a new one, so good luck to him. I tells him I misses hearing my stories, so I hope he can get it working again."

"Oh, he's not working with Jim today?" said Ethel, heading out the front door with Jimmy in the carriage and Ralphie running ahead of them. Frances hesitated and gave her a funny look, and Ethel wished she hadn't spoken. Jim might be getting more hours than Harold, which meant more money for her and Jim, less for Harold and Frances. Better not to mention it. "Ralphie! Slow down!" she yelled. "Come back here and hold my hand!"

They walked up Flatbush Avenue to the park and began strolling down the wide tree-lined paths, towards the zoo where Ralphie was dying to go. Above the noise of the children and the park the two women kept up a steady stream of talk, but after awhile Frances fell silent again.

"Is everything all right with…with you and Jim, Ethel?" Frances said suddenly.

"All right? What do you…well, you know, we're struggling to make ends meet just like yourselves, like everybody I s'pose, but we're no worse off than anyone else. We're getting by, I guess. Why?"

Frances frowned and looked away, like she was sorry she'd opened her mouth but determined to go on. "No, I don't mean money, I mean…between yourselves, you know, is everything all right?"

Ethel wondered what Frances was working up to. Maybe she and Harold were fighting, was that it? They weren't newlyweds anymore, for all they were so cuddly and sweet with each other. "I s'pose so, girl. We gets on all right," she said.

"Mommy! Mommy! Can I go on the carousel?" Ralphie was tearing ahead again.

"I don't have no money for no carousel!" Ethel called back.

"You don't need no money, it's free!"

"Go on then!" She turned back to Frances, who was pushing Jimmy in the carriage, looking down at the ground. "Frances, what is it, is something on your mind?"

Frances blew a little sigh out between her lips like a small gust of wind. "I don't know, Ethel, I been struggling with myself over whether to say anything, even praying about it if you wants to know the truth. Harold told me not to say a word but…he told me something last week. Something…something about Jim."

"About Jim?" Ethel echoed. This was a turnabout; she didn't know what Frances was talking about at all.

"Ethel…look, I think you got a right to know. Harold says…Harold says Jim's been…well, Jim's not working late every night he says he is. Like last week, Harold wasn't home eight o'clock no night last week. And he says Jim doesn't have a shift today. He made that up, Harold says."

"What?" Ethel's mind raced, trying to put this together in a way that made sense. It never occurred to her that Harold would not be telling the truth: if Harold said it, it was true. "What is he up to then? Why would he tell me he's working when he's not? He's not…he isn't going out drinking with that Dick Mouland is he? When we hardly got two coppers to rub together?"

Frances shook her head; she looked like she was going to cry. Two horseback riders trotted past, little rich girls in matching riding costumes, erect as princesses. Ethel watched them and their glossy brown horses while Frances fumbled for words. "No Ethel, it's not that, it's…oh, Harold says Jim got a girl. Another woman."

"A woman?" Once, a week or so ago, Ralphie had been running at her full tilt and got her right in the centre of her stomach with his hard little head, right in the gut. She felt like that now, punched in the gut, and then thought, *Ralphie*. She hadn't seen him since he asked to go on the carousel. She scanned the heads of children atop the bobbing horses. "Where's Ralphie? I can't see him, Frances! Is he—"

"He's there, he's right there on the carousel." Frances pointed, and laid a hand on Ethel's arm. Ethel saw Ralphie waving, then looked down to see that Jimmy had fallen asleep in the carriage. Ethel opened her mouth to speak and found to her horror that her throat was tight with tears that would spill over if she said a word.

Frances rushed on. "Harold says…he says he's going to have words with Jim. Try to straighten him out. I didn't know…I wanted to talk to you. Maybe you want to talk to Jim yourself."

"No. No." The tears were here already and Ethel wiped them fiercely on the back of her glove. Ralphie was climbing off the carousel horse and running towards them. She tried to make her voice, her face, normal again as he approached. "Tell Harold he can do what he wants, say what he wants to Jim. I'm not saying nothing to Jim about it. I wouldn't know what to say."

Jim wasn't home for his supper. Ethel put it on a plate and laid it in the oven for him. She put the boys down to bed herself. She stood for a long time by Jimmy's crib, watching him sleep, his face so like Jim's, but round and babyish and innocent. Then she went out to sit on the daybed next to Ralphie, tracing the soft curve of his flushed cheek with a fingertip, wishing he would open his eyes so she could see their startling blue. *Bert's eyes*, she thought again, though Jim's were the same colour. Bert's eyes were so clear and honest; Jim's were always winking and laughing. *This is what comes from marrying the wrong man,* she thought clearly.

Two weeks later – two weeks of sleepless nights, Jim working late, she and Jim mostly silent or snapping at each other, two weeks when the apartment was filled with things that were not said – they were all at Harold and Frances' apartment one Friday night playing cards. Ethel was in the kitchen helping Frances with the tea, wondering how the boys were doing at home with Jean's young niece Carol Ann watching them. When Frances went out, Ethel stayed in the kitchen, tidying things away, and the noise from the living room was so loud she didn't even notice that Harold had come in with an empty teacup which he laid down on the counter.

"Ethel," he said, very quietly.

She looked up at him. Even the way he said her name made her happier than she had been in weeks. It reminded her of that good time before he and Frances were married, when he stayed with her and Jim and there was so much talk and laughter in the house. Harold was standing very close, just a foot or so away. His grey shirt was unbuttoned the top two buttons, and she looked at the hollow of his throat and smelled his nice clean smell of soap and air, like laundry just off the line. He put a hand, brotherly, on her shoulder.

"Frances told me she talked to you about...you know," he said.

"About Jim," Ethel whispered.

"Yeah. About that. I just wanted to say...look, I talked to him the other day. We had it out. I think I made him see sense...I mean, that's all over now. He swears it is and I'm sure that's true. I mean, I don't think he'd do anything so foolish again."

Ethel nodded, the knot in her throat too big for her to speak right away.

"I'm sorry for butting in, but you know, he's my brother and I don't like to see him make a fool of himself. Jim don't know how lucky he is."

Ethel nodded again. She wanted Harold to put his arms around her, to hold her and keep her safe. She wanted Jim and Frances both to melt away like they'd never existed so it would be just her and Harold here in the kitchen, their kitchen.

"Thank you, Harold," she said. "If you're right and it's all over...don't worry, I won't say a word to Jim about it. But it was a nice thing for you to do." She turned away, back to the sink where she rinsed a plate under the tap. "We'll just pretend it never happened."

Harold's hand tightened on her shoulder a minute, he gave her an awkward pat, and then he was gone back to the party.

ROSE

~⟡~

BROOKLYN, MARCH 1931

ROSE SITS ALONE IN her tiny room at Mrs. Borkowski's boarding house. Mrs. Borkowski is famous for not being too picky over her boarders, or too nosy about their private lives. In some boarding houses where Rose has lived, there are rules about young girls coming in by a certain hour of night and not entertaining gentlemen callers in their rooms. Mrs. Borkowski, by contrast, has only one rule: rent is due on first and third Fridays. Beyond that, she cares little about what her boarders do or when they come and go.

Rose has gentlemen callers, on occasion. She finds the narrow lumpy bed a better place to make love – if you can call it that – than back alleys and laneways. Something snapped in her the night Danny Ricks did it to her in the laneway after the movie. Or maybe it was the next day when he gave her the necklace and earrings. It was just like the books and Sunday School teachers said after all, just like *The Story of a Rose*. Once a girl's virtue was tarnished there was nothing left but for her to sink further and further into sin.

So far, Rose doesn't mind being sunk in sin. She gets taken out for dinner and movies, sometimes all the way to Manhattan. Rose knows this is because some of the fellows have girlfriends in their own neighbourhoods and they don't want those girlfriends to see them with Rose. She gets presents, too – more cheap jewellery, dresses, things like that. Fellows know what to expect at the end of the evening and Rose obliges.

It took a few weeks before the talk got round to Tony and he asked her straight out if it was true. Actually what he said was, "This isn't true, Rose. This fellow, I punched his face in for the things he said about you. I didn't mind. I was happy to do this. Only tell me I didn't make a fool of myself, you didn't make a fool of me."

"I can't tell you that, Tony. It's true. I went with all those guys and probably

~⟡~

a couple more you don't know about."

"Rose, this isn't true! Rose, why? Why would you do this to me?" To her surprise he didn't look angry, didn't raise a hand to her. He looked, instead, as if *she* had slapped him. "Why would you do this to yourself?"

"I...I don't know, Tony. I just felt like it, that's all." She couldn't explain the darkness she felt at the centre, the sure and certain belief that there was nothing to save herself for. She couldn't explain why she had to throw away some silly idea of purity and virtue. And she certainly couldn't explain that she preferred a man who saw sex as a straightforward exchange of goods and services. Tony would think she wanted him to start buying her stuff, and that wasn't what she wanted at all.

"You didn't need to do this, Rose. You're a good girl, a beautiful woman. I was gonna marry you, Rose. You know I wanted to marry you, right?"

"But not now, right? You wouldn't want to marry me now, would you, Tony?"

He looked down, still clenching his fist, now grinding it into his palm. But shook his head. "No. Not now. I still love you – I'll always love you – but I couldn't marry you now. Not after you do these things."

Not long after that, she takes the room at Mrs. Borkowski's. She gets a new job, too, at the soda fountain of a candy store. She meets a lot of fellows there, and some of them wait for her after work and come back to Mrs. Borkowski's with her. Gentlemen callers, to use the term loosely.

Rose stops making even the few infrequent visits she used to make to Harold and Jim. There's no point in seeing her family, now. The folks back home thought she was an abandoned woman even before, when she was respectably going around with Tony. Why let them see what her life is like now? She has tried hard to cut all ties to her past, to avoid anyone with a Newfoundland name or a Newfoundland accent. She is cut loose, floating free.

And she is free, and all alone, on this rainy March evening in her room, putting her feet up after standing all day at work, reading *Life* magazine and having a smoke. This is all she has the energy for most days. Apart from working and going out with fellows, she mostly lies on her bed, asleep or only half-awake. In fact she's starting to drift off when a tap comes on her door. She doesn't encourage fellows to come to her place looking for her; she'd rather make a date and meet them somewhere first, but it's only to be expected that someone will take liberties sooner or later. It could be a girlfriend, of course, but Rose has few girlfriends left.

"All right, hold your horses," she calls. She gets up, pulls on a housecoat over the underwear she's lounging in, and opens the door.

Tony Martelli stands there, his shirt soaked almost transparent, his wet hair plastered to his skull. She hasn't laid eyes on him since – when was it? – September. Six months.

"I gotta talk to you, Rose," he says.

She opens the door, stands aside. He sits down on the bed, shivering with cold from the rain outside. "Take your shirt off," she says. He strips off the wet fabric and she sees again what a lovely body he has, the clean lines of his well-muscled chest and arms and shoulders. Not one of the fellows she's been with has been as good-looking as Tony, not really. She hands him a towel and he rubs his head vigorously and then wraps the towel around his shoulders. "It's pouring out there," he says.

"You're still shaking. Here, have a drink." She opens the drawer where she keeps a flask of whiskey and hands it to him. As he drinks she sits down beside him, one leg cocked up on the bed so her housecoat falls open and her bare legs and the frilly edges of her underwear are showing.

Tony looks up, and she sees something in his eyes that echoes the bleak emptiness in her own. She's never seen that before. Tony is full, not empty, full of life and hope and plans. He's still shaking, and she sees that it's more than the rain that's making him shiver.

"What happened?"

"We just got news today. My mama, she's dead."

"Your mama. Over in Italy." It seems so far away. Rose tries to imagine what she'd feel if she heard her mother died back in St. John's. All she can imagine is the echo of an echo of a feeling: sadness, but nothing that would make her shake and go walking blindly in the rain.

"You don't understand, Rose, I never told you about me and my mama. I was always her favourite, always the boy who could do no wrong. The youngest, her baby, her last little boy. I helped her in the house, in the garden, I slept in her bed. She'd say, 'My Tonio, my wonderful boy.'"

Rose nodded. She has not heard it in these words before, but she knows Tony was his mother's favourite. He must have told her, or else it was something Marcella said.

"But you don't know, Rose, what this means to her. To my mama, she has to give one son to God, one son to be a priest. And who better to give than her favourite son, especially when he's so good, such a kind and helpful boy. So from all my childhood days, all she tells me is, 'Tonio, you are given to God. You are my gift to God, you will be my priest.'"

"Really?" Rose can't imagine this, wrapping up one of your children like a package to give to God. Especially when Catholic priests can't even marry, so it's like you're telling him from the day he's born he'll never grow up to love a woman or have a son of his own. She shudders. "That's not fair of her, Tony. You musta known that, since you're not a priest, right, honey?"

"When I was fifteen, sixteen, I knew. I told my mama I was going to America and I wasn't being no priest."

"And what did she say?"

"She cursed me, Rose. No, I don't mean she just said a curse word at me. That wasn't her way. She was a very holy woman. She just said that I was going against God's will, and making her break her vow to God, and God would damn my soul to hell forever, and a curse would follow me to America and ruin everything I did."

"Tony! You don't believe that stuff, do you?"

He looks up at her with a smile that isn't a smile. "Believe it? I don't know. So far, the curse don't hurt me much. I was doing pretty well here, till I lost you. Maybe that's the start of it. But in the next life? She could be right. She made a vow and I broke it. Maybe I am going to hell."

Rose shivers, because she was raised to believe in a hell too, maybe not the Italian Catholic hell but the Newfoundland Salvation Army hell, just a few doors down from it. And from everything she knows, she's going there for sure. She can't quite believe in it, but she can't quite stop believing either. But she says bravely, "Your mama's curse can't hurt you, Tony. That's just old woman's foolishness, something she said to make you feel bad."

"But Rose, those are the last words she said to me. I wrote her letters and she never answered them. She never spoke my name again, like I was dead to her. I loved my mama, and the last thing she ever said to me was a curse."

Rose takes him in her arms and lets him press his face against her chest, where her housecoat falls open and it's just her bra there. He's crying, his shoulders shaking, using her to cry into, but then he's kissing too, kissing and touching in a way none of the other fellows ever did, a way that makes it seem like both of them are in this together, not just him doing it to her. This makes her feel excited, as if she were with someone new for the first time, only better, and that in its turn makes her feel even more like she's going to hell. Her and Tony, going to hell together.

The night seems to go on forever, though morning finds them both asleep. "Rose, sorry, I gotta get to work," Tony says, sitting up in the dawn light, feeling for his clothes. She didn't bother to hang up his shirt last night and it's in a heap on the floor, still damp. "I gotta hurry, get home and change. Listen, tonight…will you meet me for dinner tonight?"

Dinner. Just like before. Tony has changed the rules, and the ground shifts under Rose. But she says, "No, not dinner. You come here, later on in the evening. Just come back here, okay?"

Tony looks disappointed. But he's there that night, and they talk for a few minutes only and then make love again, and sleep together again. Rose is amazed. She is hungry for Tony, for what his hands and body can do for her, and yet she fears him more than ever. Rose feels like a girl in a movie at last – not that girls in movies ever do this. She is the princess in the enchanted castle, living under a spell. It will end, but for now she just wants to be bewitched.

Every night for a week he comes over. She doesn't make any other dates, any other plans, just waits in her small bare room for him to arrive.

One night, the seventh night, he brings something. It's a single pink rose. Not a red one, her favourite kind, but at least it's a rose, and she knows what it means. Rose would like to think of something sweet and romantic but what really pops into her head is that silly poem. She's not a great one for poetry by any means but there was this one poem her friend Nelly read in a magazine years ago, and the two of them used to recite it and laugh to kill themselves, all about the fellow who sends the girl one perfect rose to show his love, and she says,

> *Why is it no one ever sent me yet*
> *One perfect limousine, do you suppose?*
> *Ah no, it's always just my luck to get*
> *One perfect rose.*

Just my luck, she thinks, but manages not to laugh or anything. She looks around for what to do with the rose and finally sticks it in her water glass on the night table because there's no vase or anything to put it in. Then she looks around again and sees her room so shabby and tacky-looking, and thinks that not only is she not going to get one perfect limousine, she's damn lucky to be getting even a rose from a fellow as sweet as Tony.

Tony is neither laughing nor crying; he looks serious. Then he says the last thing she expects. "I love you, Rose. Will you marry me?"

Rose is lying on the bed; she leans up on her elbow and looks at him, to see if he's serious. "You want to marry me *now*? After…this? After all the other guys?"

He puts his finger on her lips. "Shh. No other men. Just you and me. You took away my curse. It's gone. No power. Now I take away yours, and we can be together."

If only it were that simple. Rose closes her eyes. *But you haven't taken away my curse*, she thinks. She's been under a curse all her life and it will take more than Tony to erase it.

"No," she says. "You're very sweet, but it doesn't change anything. I can't see myself getting married. I don't think I'd be a good wife. No, I don't want to marry you."

"You don't want to marry me?" Tony sits up, naked on the bed. "I love you like no other man ever loves you, I forgive you everything, even cheating on me, I give you my deepest secret to keep for me, and you won't marry me?" At first she thinks he is joking, mock-angry, but then she sees the anger is real: finally he's mad at her. He flings a pillow to the floor for emphasis, punches the wall without even stopping to rub his hurt knuckles. His eyes dart around the room looking for something else to break and she prays he won't hit the mirror because that will cost her money. There's only one other thing really and she knows he'll go for it; he grabs the glass with the single perfect pink rose and flings it against the far wall where it shatters and spits shards of glass all around. In the silence after the crash Tony yells, "I love you, Rose! I wanna give you everything, and you're gonna throw it back in my face? Well, all I can say is, to hell with you!"

He stands up, pulling on his trousers as someone bangs on the wall and shouts, "Hey, shaddup in there, willya?" There are no secrets at Mrs. Borkowski's. Rose says nothing, just stands there and watches him storm out. "And I ain't comin' back neither, so don't wait up for me," he adds as he runs down the stairs.

She watches out the window, sees him run down the street, slowing once and turning like he's going to look up at her window but then keeping on going. *To hell with you.* A good line to go out on. Even in a movie, it would be good.

Rose sits at her window. *What's wrong with me?* she asks herself over and over. She doesn't know what more she could want, or why she's sent Tony away, after he's played a scene even Gary Cooper would envy.

Maybe Tony was right. Maybe he did lift her curse, or part of it. Because six days after she sends Tony away, Rose gets her reward. She finally meets the man she's been waiting for.

His name is Andrew Covington and he's from Manhattan. She meets him when he walks into the candy store one day to buy a newspaper for his great-aunt who lives in this neighbourhood, right here in Brooklyn, though the rest of the family got out of Brooklyn a long time ago, before he was born. Smartest thing his parents ever did. You've gotta be in Manhattan, downtown; that's where the action is, if you want to get ahead. But his great-aunt is a hoot. He likes the old gal, and she likes him, and she's got a bit of money put away so he visits every month or so.

Andrew Covington is good-looking, tall and slim with dark-blond hair and green eyes. He's a snappy dresser, even when he's going to visit his great-aunt in Brooklyn. Shirt and tie and all that. He works on Wall Street. Sure, business is bad on Wall Street, ever since the Crash. A lot of up-and-coming young guys lost their jobs, but not everyone. Not Andrew Covington. There's money to be made even in a bear market, if you know your stuff and play your cards right. Is she interested in the markets? A little? Well, Andrew Covington is her guy. Has she been up to Manhattan much? No? Sure, you'd like to see more of it. He ends up inviting her to meet him for lunch at the Automat on her next day off.

Rose chooses her dress carefully: her myrtle-green pleated satin, along with shoes, lipstick, hat. Everything has to be right. This is her chance, her big chance. She can't blow it. Andrew Covington, up in Manhattan, has no way of knowing what kind of girl Rose is, what reputation she has – unless his great-aunt has a very unusual circle of acquaintances. She gets off the subway that Wednesday looking like she stepped off a magazine page, advertising the smart young career girl in New York City.

Rose loves the Automat, the neat precision of a restaurant where there's a place for everything and a clearly defined way of getting what you want. She lets Andrew pick out her lunch, though, following his lead, taking his suggestions. She sits across the table and asks him leading questions about his work, his interests, his background. He is happy to talk about himself. But he wants to know about her, too, about Rose. She glances at her watch.

"Oh, goodness, look at the time," she says. "Don't you have to be getting back to work? If you want to know all about little old me, we'll have to do that next time."

"Next time? How about next time is dinner and dancing on Friday night? Dinner at Lindy's, dancing at the Savoy Plaza."

"Oooh, I *love* to dance. Can't wait. Where will we meet? No, you don't want to come all the way down to Brooklyn to get me." Rose is only too happy to meet Andrew on his side of the Brooklyn Bridge, on his ground, which she hopes will soon become her ground.

She spends the rest of her day off in Loehmann's, going through every dress on the rack till she finds one she can wear on Friday night. As she checks it out, she glances up at the top floor. Someday, she'll be there. She's on her way. Andrew Covington isn't a rich guy – she's smart enough to know that – but he's better off than any fellow she's ever gone out with and he's on the way up, too. He's twenty-eight, a year older than her, and he says he's going to be a millionaire by the time he's thirty-five. He would have been a millionaire by thirty if it wasn't for the Crash.

They meet several times over the next six weeks for dinner and dancing, once or twice for lunch. Then, one Friday afternoon, he asks if she can come to a party with him Saturday night.

"It's a dinner party. Friends from work," he adds. "My boss is going to be there."

"Oooh, I'll need a nice dress for that," Rose says.

"Why don't you let me buy you one? May I take you shopping?"

"Weeelllll…I guess I should say yes, if you want me to look nice enough to impress your boss and your friends from work."

"Impress 'em? You'll knock 'em dead, baby. You and me are gonna go far together, Rosie."

Rose floats home that night. She still doesn't let Andrew walk her home, though she's come clean and told him it's because she lives in a poor neighbourhood. Her family back home are good people, but she's on her own in New York, working hard to make her way, and she doesn't want him to see the rundown place she lives now, is that okay? Of course that's okay. And Rose drifts through the sultry streets to Mrs. Borkowski's boarding house, dreaming of the dress she'll let Andrew buy for her. A red dress. Would that be too daring? Black is always classy, of course. Or white. With her colouring, she looks good in white. Only, her period must be due sometime soon; it might not be a good idea to wear white in case…

Her period. When was it? She has to stop and think, though usually she's very regular. She counts back. No, she definitely missed it this month. It should have been weeks ago. She hasn't had one since…before Tony came to her. All those nights with Tony. He never once wore a safe. She was living in a magic spell and he was planning to marry her. Neither of them thought of being safe.

She checks the calendar carefully. Near as she can tell, she has missed one whole period and by now she should have been in the middle of her second one. She's never skipped more than a day or two before.

The next morning, Saturday morning, when she's arranged to meet Andrew to go shopping, she wakes up feeling queasy. Has she felt like this before? Maybe just a touch. She put it down to nerves, excitement over Andrew. Today it could be excitement about the party, worry about Tony. It could be anything. But fifteen minutes later, when she's kneeling over Mrs. Borkowski's third-floor toilet, her cheek pressed against the none-too-clean porcelain, she knows she can't fool herself, or anyone else, any longer.

Rose heads out into the streets, walking blindly, lost in the summer sunshine. Andrew Covington is waiting for her in Manhattan, waiting and waiting. He doesn't have her address or a phone number; he only knows the candy store where she works, but she's not going back there. He'll wait all day but she'll never show up. She'll miss the party; he'll call a secretary in his department to be his date at the last minute and they'll hit it off brilliantly and end up married and she'll be by his side as he rises to be vice-president of the company.

Rose goes to the Loew's Kings and watches two double features, the cartoons, a newsreel or two. She doesn't come out till dusk, hungry and sleepy and bleary-eyed from the moving images that filled the screen. She walks back to the alley where she first went with Danny Ricks after another movie, and looks up at the grey-blue sky between the roofs of the buildings. Her head rests back on the brick wall as her eyes close and her body sags a little. But she's all alone this time. No-one comes to join her.

ETHEL

BROOKLYN, MAY 1932

ETHEL SAT IN JIM'S armchair in the living room, knitting, when she heard the outside door to the apartment open. Jimmy, sprawled on the floor lining up blocks in a patient array, jumped up. "Daddy's home!" he cried. To an almost-three-year-old who adored his father, the fact that Daddy was home at eleven o'clock in the morning could only be good news.

Ethel listened to the sound Jim's feet made coming up the hall toward the living room door. She knew from his feet how his morning had gone, even if she couldn't tell by him coming home so early. First going off, he used to be gone all day looking for work. Then he would come home early in the afternoon. Now he was hardly out before he was back home again. Giving up got easier and easier.

"No luck?" she called out, trying to force something bright and cheerful into her voice.

"Daddy, can you play with me?" Jimmy said. The same words Ralphie always used. Ralphie was in school now, but as eager for his father's company as ever when he got home. Ralphie was old enough, though, to understand that there was something wrong in coming home from school to find his father already home ahead of him. A six-year-old could pick up on things a smaller child would miss. And the new baby, curled tight inside Ethel's womb, knew nothing of job lines and unemployment, nothing of her mother's worries or her father's frustration. This one was going to be a girl, Ethel knew. She was sure enough that she was knitting one little sweater in pink, though all the others were a safe yellow or green or white.

Jim was in the door now, Jimmy up in his arms. "No, nothing on the go," he said. Ethel stood up awkwardly, getting out of his chair. She hated that she was only four months along and already so big. She was carrying this one differently, lower, which was one of the reasons Jean said it must be a girl.

"Come outside and play alleys with me, Daddy?" Jimmy begged. Jim closed his eyes, looking as if he'd just put in a full day's work. Maybe in some ways looking for work and not finding it was more tiring than going to work, Ethel thought. Building was still slow because of the Crash, and what construction work was going on, Jim didn't have a chance at, because of the Ironworkers' Union. Because he'd gone against them, to work on the Empire State Building. He'd taken her and the boys up to Manhattan to see it one day after it was finished. Jim looked proud that day, but now, after weeks and weeks without work or only the odd day's work here and there, he looked beaten.

She thought the baby she was carrying had got started the first night he came home without finding any work at all. After the work on the new skyscraper was finished, they had made do with the money Jim could pick up from odd jobs here and there. They'd gotten used to the awkward coldness that settled between them after Ethel found out about Jim's little fling – that was what she called it, in her mind. But that night in the winter when he came back and told her he'd been out all day looking for jobs and there was nothing out there at all, she knew he was telling the truth. He hadn't been with a woman, not that time anyway. That defeated look could only come on the face of a man who'd been told he couldn't have a day's work to support his wife and kids. He didn't say much, but that night in bed he turned to her and buried his face between her breasts with the sadness of a man who needs a woman's love to make him feel like a man again.

Months had passed since then, and still there was no steady work. Jim sat in his chair and read the newspaper most of the afternoon. After supper, when she'd put the boys to bed, he turned to her and said, "We got to figure something out, Ethel. I don't know what's going to happen to the boys if things don't get better."

Ethel pulled her chair out to the kitchen table and sat down across from Jim. "Rent's due in four days, Ethel, and I haven't got the money to pay it," he said, staring down at his hands, not meeting her eyes.

Ethel felt a little swell of excitement and pride. For nearly seven years Jim had been working to support her and their children. Now it was her time, her moment. She stood up and crossed the room, dragging her chair with her, climbing up to stand tip-toe on it and reach up to the top of the cupboard over the counter, reaching way in back for the biscuit tin.

She had been putting money into the biscuit tin ever since they got married, always keeping it a secret from Jim and even, in a way, from herself, for no matter how badly she wanted to she had never opened it up and counted the money inside. It was mostly coins but quite a few bills too, especially from the first years when Jim's pay was steady. "For a rainy day," her mother had told her. "You puts aside a little, whenever you can." Ethel had gloried in her ability to save a few cents here, a few cents there, out of the housekeeping, to deny herself some tiny luxury and put aside a little more. She pictured the rainy day, raindrops pattering merrily on the tin lid of the biscuit box, the rainy day when she would open it up and reveal her secret.

The effect on Jim was everything she could have hoped. Ethel had been a better saver than even she'd realized. The tin was heavy with coins and stuffed with loose dollar bills.

"Where'd you get this?" Jim said, as if she'd robbed a bank and asked for it all in small change.

"I've been saving it," Ethel said. "Ever since we were married. Saving it for a rainy day."

She had seldom enjoyed a moment in her life when a dream came true, exactly as she'd pictured it, but this was one. Jim's eyes came back to life as he smoothed out the bills, turning them all the right way and counting them, while she piled up the coppers and nickels and dimes and quarters into neat little towers. Ten minutes later, Jim looked up from counting and said, "Ethel, you're a wonder. Do you know there's over a hundred dollars in here? This'll be the savin' of us, girl."

She smiled, letting her smile glow with pride. "Is it really enough to help, Jim?" She knew it was; she just wanted to hear him say it.

"Enough? Sure, even if I never got another day's work this would pay the rent for two or three months. If I can get a bit of work, it'll keep us in rent and food for that long at least, maybe longer."

She let a handful of the shinier pennies trickle through her fingers, thinking of fairy tales about gold pieces, and Jim riffled the pile of dollar bills like a pack of cards. But it wasn't gold, was it? In a moment's silence they both grew sober, and Ethel guessed Jim was thinking the same thing she was: what if he never got another day's work? Everyone said the Depression was going to get worse before it got better. Two months' rent, no money for food, and no more miracles waiting in biscuit tins. And a new baby in five months' time.

"Or," said Ethel, and stopped there.

"Or what?" said Jim.

"Or, there's enough here to buy us all passage home, with some left over." Now it was her turn to look down at the table.

"Home?" echoed Jim, as if the word had lost its meaning. They said it almost every day: "There's a letter from home," "What's the news from home?" They said it, but it was as if they no longer believed it, that a place called home was still there for them.

"Home," she said again. "Back to St. John's. Maybe that's the best place for us, Jim."

Jim shook his head slowly. "You read Annie's letters. Things are as bad there as they are here, maybe worse – men out of jobs, families on the dole. How is that any better than what we got here?"

"Better? Maybe it's no better, but if there's no work and we're going to starve, shouldn't we do it in our own place and with our own people?" As she said the words Ethel knew that once she was home, once she had a child born in Newfoundland, she would never want to leave again. The roots she thought she had put down in seven years in Brooklyn were as shallow as buttercup roots, something you could rip up with one quick tug and never think twice about it. She imagined Ralphie and Jimmy running out Freshwater Road, from her mother's house out to Jim's parents' house in the Valley and into the field behind it.

"It's worth thinking about, Ethel," Jim said. She couldn't recall that he'd ever taken anything she'd said that seriously, really listening to her and saying it was a good idea instead of digging in his heels and complaining. It was like the biscuit tin had given her a kind of power, the power to sit down across the table and make decisions with him.

The idea rolled like a snowball. Jim didn't want to give up their Linden Boulevard apartment, because it was rent-controlled and if they ever did come back to New York they'd never get a place as cheap again. But Harold and Frances lived in a place that wasn't rent-controlled, and the landlord had just raised their rent. Since they wanted to stay in Brooklyn for now, it was decided that they would move into Linden Boulevard when Ethel and Jim moved out.

They would go in June, once Ralphie was out of school. Ethel could see Jim's spirits lift as the day grew closer. She busied herself packing clothes for all four of them, plus the baby things she'd already knitted, in their one big trunk. The rest of their stuff would be there for Harold and Frances to look after, for now anyway.

"It's so wonderful that it's all working out this way," Frances said one day when she came to bring some of her things over to the apartment.

"I know," Ethel said. "It feels right, like this is what's meant to be." She paused a moment, stacking her own dinner plates to put away on the top shelf. "It feels like a new start for us…going back home, having a new baby. Maybe even…a new start for me and Jim, you know? Put the past behind us."

She and Frances had never talked about Jim's little fling. Frances had gotten close to the subject once or twice and Ethel had steered her off it. But she had said enough, now, that Frances was able to say, "It's good to hear you say that, Ethel. I often wonders, you know, how you and Jim are getting on. I mean, it's all water under the bridge and all that, but some things aren't so easy to forget."

"No, they're not." Ethel lifted down her big mixing bowls. "Will you want these left down, or do you want to use your own?"

"Leave them down if you don't mind, I don't have any as big as that."

"All right. No girl, it's not easy to forget something like what happened between me and Jim. I never have forgotten it, I guess, even though I've tried."

"But it's…I mean, there's never been any trouble again, has there?"

"Oh no, no nothing like that." Ethel turned away, back to the cupboards. She wouldn't share her worries, her suspicions, with Frances. Saying them aloud would make them real. Jim said he was out looking for work again today, but was he?

Frances left; Jim didn't come home for supper. Ethel put the boys down to bed and sat looking out the window till nine o'clock. Then she went out into the hall and across the lobby and tapped on Mrs. Liebowitz's door. Mrs. Liebowitz came and stood in the doorway smiling. Ethel had still never been over her threshold. Now she said, "Mrs. Liebowitz, could your Sarah step over to my apartment just for an hour or so? My boys are sleeping, my husband is out and I have to go out. I wondered if Sarah could just sit in our apartment in case one of the boys wakes up?"

"She will be glad to do so," Mrs. Liebowitz said, a little formally. "Sarah!" she called over her shoulder. "Mrs. Evans wants you to step across and mind her boys. They are sleeping. Bring your book with you, you can study your homework over there."

Ethel stepped out onto the street and stopped for a moment just to feel the warm night air. She'd still never gotten quite used to that – how it could be so warm in the evening, even early in the spring. Going back home, they'd have to get accustomed to cooler days, colder evenings, a later spring or no spring at all, really, till summer sprang on them unexpectedly in July. So different from New York.

She walked towards O'Grady's store at the corner of Linden and Flatbush Avenue, just as if she really did have a message to do, then turned south onto Flatbush, past the store, walking almost blindly, looking up as groups of people passed. She glanced into lighted restaurants and soda fountains, moving steadily towards brighter lights. Men weren't very imaginative. Maybe Jim would go to one of the same places he liked to go with Ethel on their rare nights out.

Fifteen minutes later Ethel found herself standing in front of the Loew's Kings, looking at the marquee to see what was playing, and wondering what she thought she was going to do. Go up and down the aisles looking for her husband? She turned back towards home, past the chop suey place, past the dance hall. She turned a corner, onto Church. She should be sensible and go home. She would arrive to find Jim home in his armchair, frowning and wondering what she had been doing out. She needed to think of an excuse, a story. Maybe pick up something in a shop to justify going out.

Then, in the window of a diner, she saw them. Jim and a girl, sitting over half-eaten plates of food, leaning forward, holding hands. She remembered the kicked-in-the-stomach feeling she'd had when she first found out Jim was having…an affair. This was too big for the word "fling" anymore. Jim was unfaithful to her. It wasn't a little thing, something Harold had brushed off with a few words. This was a big thing, a thing that had swollen to the size of her whole world, Jim and this woman he was snatching a few last minutes with even while they were packing up to go back home.

She moved away, breathing heavily, so they wouldn't glance out and see her. She sucked in air like she was drowning. Spots swam before her eyes but she put her head down and pulled herself together. Then she pushed the door open, hesitated on the threshold, and stepped into the harsh light. Nobody noticed her, not even the waitress, so she made herself keep walking, right down to the table.

Jim saw her when she was two paces away. His eyes widened: she saw shock and something like panic. That was to be expected. It was what she'd seen before he noticed her that hurt. She'd seen the laughter in his eyes and around his mouth, the warm, relaxed, light-hearted Jim she glimpsed only rarely now when he played with his boys. His boys. He was cheating on the mother of his sons.

The girl was very young. Ethel herself, though she felt forty-five at times, was in fact twenty-six. This girl looked about nineteen. She wore the kind of bright make-up Ethel hated, and her fair hair was very fluffy and poufy. She put a tiny hand to her rosebud mouth.

"Good evening," Ethel said, laying her handbag in the middle of the table. She put out her hand. "I'm Ethel Evans. Mrs. Jim Evans. We haven't met."

The girl, well trained, took her hand from her mouth and laid it in Ethel's. "Cecilia Fines," she said.

"Ethel, I don't know what you're thinking, but it's not what you're thinking," Jim said. "It's not – we're not – Cecilia is just a good friend…"

Ethel turned to look at him again. "Is that so? And she's been a good friend, has she, all this time? A year and a half – or more – ever since Harold told me you were seeing someone? He told me he'd talked you out of it, too, that you wouldn't make that mistake again. But I guess Harold was wrong, wasn't he?"

"A year and a half!" squealed Cecilia Fines, who seemed completely transfixed by the drama she found herself playing a part in. "Oh no, Mrs. Evans, I've only met Jim here about three weeks ago." She turned to Jim. "A year and a half!" she repeated. "You told me you never...that I was the first girl you ever–"

"Now, now, honey," Jim said in a vague general way, as if that might placate both women at once. Ethel glanced around and realized that everyone in the restaurant, including the waitress, was looking at them. Usually there was nothing Ethel hated more than to be stared at in public. She not only hated scenes, she despised the kind of people who made them. Yet here she was, in a public place, making the very first scene of her life and almost enjoying it.

Jim stood up. "Ethel, I think we should go home." He turned to the girl. "Cecy, I'm sorry about all this." He took two dollars from his pocket and laid them on the table. "Use this to pay for the bill and...ah, buy yourself some little thing with the change, okay?" His voice sounded different talking to Cecilia than it did when he talked to Ethel – less Newfoundland, more New York. She hadn't known he had another voice.

She turned to face him as soon as they were outside. He put both hands on her upper arms, holding her firmly in place. "Now look, I can explain," he began.

"Can you? Can you explain?" Ethel said. She often felt stuck for words but suddenly she had more words than she'd ever known, all waiting to roll out and sweep over Jim. "Can you explain to me who you were with last year, if it wasn't this little...this little tramp? And if you gave that one up when Harold told you off, if you had enough sense to listen when he told you what a fool you were, if you listened to your brother who is ten times the man you'll ever be – then why were you fool enough to go do it again? And again and again. Because this isn't just one girl, or two girls, is it?" She saw it all now. "This is one girl after another, over and over again, a few weeks at a time till the excitement wears off. Just like it used to be before we got married. And just like it has been ever since, I'll bet. What a fool I've been." She stalked away, leaving Jim to run after her.

He caught up with her at the corner. "Ethel, you're being too hard on me, it wasn't like that at all–"

"And what's more," she said, enraged to find herself choking back a sob when all she wanted to feel was anger, the anger that gave her this sudden strength. "What's *more*, while I'm home scrimping and saving and trying to stretch every cent and putting away nickels and dimes in that darned biscuit tin, and cooking horrible cheap cuts of meat and sewing up sheets sides to middle to make them last longer…while I'm home doing all that, you're out here throwing money away on your girlfriends! Laying down two dollars here and five dollars there. All the while I'm saving and mending and working my fingers to the bone – for *you!!*"

She started walking again, fast, but Jim was keeping pace with her now, twisting his face to try to look straight at hers though she wouldn't meet his eyes. "Yes, working your fingers to the bone." He had found his voice at last, and some anger of his own, though heaven alone knew what right he had to it. "You know, when a man comes home from a hard day's work – or a hard day looking for work – did you ever think maybe he doesn't want to find a girl working her fingers to the bone? Always going on about how everlasting hard she's working and how grateful he should be? Ever think a fellow might just like a bit of fun, a bit of a cuddle, a few laughs?"

Ethel turned her face farther away so that though she was still walking beside him she was staring straight across the street, at a row of quiet houses with windows dark. "A few laughs," she said, the words tasting like lemons in her mouth. "You were always a great one for a good laugh, but this is no laughing matter. It's about work, and responsibility, and…and keeping your promises. Making a good home for our children. And I should have known you weren't the man who could do that. Marrying you was a big mistake right from the word go."

Side by side they stalked up Bedford Avenue towards their own neighbourhood, drawing the occasional stare from passersby. Jim was silent for a moment, then he reached out and grabbed her arm.

"Yeah, you made your mistake, didn't you? Too bad you never had another choice. What did you say a minute ago? My brother is ten times the man I am? Ever think about how hard it is to live up to a brother who's perfect, to know my wife would rather be married to another man?"

The world stopped turning for a second and Ethel slowed her pace as his words hit her. *How could he know? Nobody knows what I feel about Harold*, she thought, and then realized that she hadn't ever said it, even to herself, till that moment. She turned to face Jim at last, looking as stunned as he had when she caught him with Cecilia Fines.

Jim went on, "It's no picnic for me, you know, all my life trying to fill a dead man's shoes."

"A dead man's…" The world turned again, though very slowly. *Bert.* "You mean Bert," she whispered. Then, louder. "Bert! Don't you even compare yourself to your brother Bert. Bert was…Bert was a man of honour."

She darted another glance at Jim and saw he was swallowing hard. "Bert was my brother, remember, and you're not the only one misses him. I tried hard enough to make you happy, but I'm not Bert and I never could live up to him."

The picture of Jim in the restaurant, holding hands with that girl, rose in her mind. Bert wouldn't have done it. Harold wouldn't do it. She'd gotten the one bad apple in the Evans barrel.

"No, you're darned right you're not Bert," she said. "I think of him every day of my life, and I miss him, and you can bet your bottom dollar that" – she said the words in a rush now, because it was like walking into the restaurant, if she didn't say it now she never would. And she had to say it because it was the only thing that could hurt him like he'd hurt her, the only weapon she had – "that never in a million years would I have picked you to try and fill Bert's shoes if I hadn't needed a father for his son."

Ethel paused, waiting for her words to hit home. She could tell when they did because Jim stopped walking. She kept on. She was a long ways ahead, maybe half a block, before he called out.

"Ethel! Stop right there and tell me you didn't mean what you just said!"

"What, that I only married you to give Bert's son a home and a name?" She yelled the words out on the empty street, not caring who heard, exulting in the power to hurt.

She expected another angry roar, but she just heard him say, "Ralphie?" in a voice so small and lost she nearly didn't catch it. So, she had hurt him. Good.

"Yeah, Ralphie," she called back, not shouting now but talking loud and clear. He was walking towards her. "What's the matter, Jim, can't you even do your sums? You never counted back when Ralphie was born?" The more clearly she could see his eyes the more she felt the need to drive it home. "Did you really think you were the first man I was ever with? You really…you really thought, all these years, that he was your son?"

When he stood in front of her at last she wondered if she'd gone too far. It scared her, the look on his face. They stood under a streetlight at the corner, looking in each other's eyes, saying nothing. Finally Jim turned onto Linden Boulevard. "Come on," he said. "Let's get home."

There was nothing gentle in his words; he didn't sound as if he was either apologizing or forgiving. But she walked along beside him, as stripped of words as he was, thinking about the balance sheets she kept in her head, her balance sheet with God. Maybe at last everything was paid up.

She didn't guess how wrong she was until they were inside their own apartment, till she'd given Sarah Liebowitz a dime and sent her home. Jim banged around the living room, turning on lights, taking off his coat and shoes, making as much noise as possible. Ethel glanced toward the daybed. "Hush, you'll wake Ralphie," she said.

"Yeah," said Jim. "That's the general idea."

Ralphie moaned and moved in his sleep and Jim sat on the edge of the daybed. Ethel stood still, watching. So many nights she had seen Ralphie stir or wake, and Jim, gentle at his bedside, give him a cup of water or touch his forehead, saying, "Go back to sleep, son. Daddy's here."

Whatever else, he always has been a good father, she thought. *That counts for a lot.*

She didn't realize how much it counted for till Ralphie sat up, looked at Jim, and smiled. "Daddy," he said.

Jim took the boy's face in his hand, tilted it up, searched it till Ralphie squirmed away, closing his eyes. Jim's face was cold and blank, like a fireplace when the fire has not only died but been swept out and cleaned. "Go back to sleep," he said as Ralphie settled back on the pillow. Jim walked past Ethel into their bedroom without saying a word.

She kept telling herself, that night and the next day and all the days after, that it would pass, that when the shock wore off, Jim would be the same as before. In every way but one it was as if that night had never happened: they went on packing and planning for the trip; Jim said nothing to her about Cecilia Fines or anything that had been said that night. He still romped and played with Jimmy, but when Ralphie was home from school and said, "Daddy, can you play with me?" Jim said, "Not now. I'm busy." Ralphie skirted the edge of Jim's and Jimmy's games; he tried to tell Jim what he'd done in school each day, about the year-end concert and the recitation he'd given. Jim never struck him or spoke harshly, but it was as if he was no longer at home to Ralphie. He was cold and distant, as he might be to a stranger's son.

One night as Ralphie sat at the table after supper, watching Ethel do the dishes while Jim and Jimmy played in the living room, he finally asked, "Mommy, is Daddy mad at me? Did I do something wrong?"

Ethel swallowed. "No, Ralphie, Daddy has a lot on his mind right now, with our trip back to Newfoundland and all. You'll see. When we get back home everything will be all right."

"Home," Ralphie said. "I've never been there, have I?"

"No. But it's a beautiful place. You'll meet both your Nannies and your Poppy Evans, and your Aunt Annie, and lots of other relatives and friends, and you'll have a big yard to play in."

"I can't wait to go home," Ralphie said.

There was a knock on the door. "You go get that, Ralphie," Ethel said, glad to have him out of the kitchen, to have a chance to wipe away her own tears. She felt as if, in washing the dishes, she had somehow clumsily dropped a priceless crystal bowl – not that they had any crystal bowls – and now stood looking at the pieces, wondering if it could ever be fixed.

Ralphie came back through the hall. Ethel moved to the kitchen door to see him standing uncertainly, someone else behind him. He looked at Jim, then looked away and turned to Ethel.

"Mommy, there's a lady with a baby here, and she says she's my Aunt Rose. Is that true?"

ANNIE

ST. JOHN'S, JUNE 1932

"DID YOU PUT THE clean sheets on the beds in the children's room, Annie? I think that bit of stew is going to catch, you wants to watch that. What time does the boat come in?"

"Two o'clock. Bill's got a car and he's going down to get them, and there are clean sheets on all the beds," Annie said, coming through the kitchen door and going to the stove to stir the stew. She'd liked to have had something nicer than stew, a nice roast or something, for an occasion like this, her brother and sister-in-law back home with all their family. But she couldn't afford a roast that size. She had already made up her own old bedroom for Ethel and Jim and the spare bedroom for Ralphie and Jimmy; she cleaned the house top to bottom; she baked bread and a cake and made the stew and dumplings for supper, all the while caring for her father who needed something different done for him every half-hour: a drink brought, a pillow turned, sometimes a few pieces from the newspaper read out to him. He could still see fine to read but he liked being read to.

Her mother, meanwhile, directed operations from the armchair in the kitchen. In the two years that her husband had been bedridden, Mrs. Evans had put on a bit of weight and her varicose veins had gotten worse, so that she preferred to spend most of the day in her chair. "I got one bed-rid and one chair-rid," Annie had told Bill the day before. "And now I got Jim and Ethel coming for I don't know how long, and two little boys to look after, and Ethel with a baby on the way, and, Bill, I don't know whether I'm coming or going."

"Ah, it won't be so bad," Bill had assured her. "Sure, Ethel will be able to give you a hand with the housework and with your father, and Jim will probably find a few days' work here and there to help out with expenses."

"I don't know where he's going to find those few days' work. Sure, you're having a hard enough time finding any yourself," Annie said.

Bill touched her shoulder lightly. "Everything will work out," he said.

"I don't know what I'd do without you, Bill."

He smiled and went away to get the car from his brother-in-law. She tried not to say things like that too often. Bill was a great help around the house. He did every kind of little job, he lifted and turned and carried her father when needed, he chopped wood for them and even gave her small gifts of money when he had either bit himself, which she used to think she'd be too proud to accept, but now she thought differently. Pride was something you couldn't afford if you had a bedridden father, a chair-ridden mother, and no man in the house bringing in any pay.

Annie ran upstairs to change into her brown dress with the white polka dots – good as new, she'd made it over completely from an old dress of her mother's – and the hat that matched it, and got into the front seat of the car with Bill. She had only driven in a car a scattered few times in her life and that added to the nervous excitement building in her stomach.

Water Street was busier than usual because of the people gathered to meet the boat. Annie loved being downtown with Bill: with so many people around it was fine to have a man standing by your side. And Bill was tall enough to see over people's heads and tell her that the boat was coming into the harbour. After a bit she could see it herself, a squat black steamer with the Furness-Withy name painted on the side, and soon they were putting down the gangplank and the passengers were walking off.

She scanned all the dark and distant shapes, looking for a man and woman with two small boys. Bill saw them first though, and steered her forward through the crowd till she could pick out that the man was Jim. The woman's face was half-hidden by her hat, but yes, that had to be Ethel. "But what's she carrying?" Annie said. "She got a bundle of something but she's carrying it in her arms like a baby."

"Well, maybe she had the baby already. Maybe it was born on board ship," Bill suggested.

"Don't be so foolish, Bill, that baby's not due till October and 'tis only June. If it were born already it wouldn't be still alive. Besides, you can see from the size of Ethel she's still expecting. Hello! Over here! Jim! Ethel!"

Finally Jim saw them and waved before he led Ethel and the children into the customs shed. Annie and Bill waited in silence until they emerged a little while later, Jim carrying the littlest boy in his arms as the bigger boy struggled to get free from Ethel's hand. And Ethel – who was certainly still in the family way – was indeed carrying a baby.

"Annie! Bill! How wonderful to see you again!" Ethel and Annie sized each other up. Yes, Ethel's dress was more in style for all it was a maternity dress and hidden under her coat. The hat was smart, too. Ethel looked curiously at Bill; Annie realized that in her letters she had not talked about him much and Ethel wouldn't realize what a part of the family he'd become. Of course she'd conclude that–

"And this is Ralphie, and that's Jimmy there with Jim," Ethel said, and looked down at the bundle in her arms, as if she were momentarily at a loss for words. "And this is baby Claire," she said at last.

"Claire? But she's not...I mean, you're not..." Annie stumbled over her words. The baby was big and bright-eyed, obviously not a newborn. Maybe six months old.

"No, she's not our baby. She's..." Ethel glanced from Jim to Annie to Bill and back to Annie. "She's Rose's baby. Rose turned up on the doorstep just a few days before we sailed. We hadn't seen hide nor hair of her in over a year and, well, the long and short of it is, this is her baby and she wanted us to bring it home to you and Mom and Pop."

"Rose's baby." Annie didn't even glance at Bill to see how he took the news. Her arms shifted automatically to take the burden from Ethel, to cradle the baby in her arms. She saw a small round face peeking out from a huddle of blankets: a wisp of Rose's fair hair paired with dark brown eyes unlike anyone in the family. "Claire. Hello, baby Claire," she crooned softly.

Ethel was still gripping Ralphie and now had Jimmy holding her other hand while Jim and Bill went off to get the trunk. Their procession wound up from the wharf to Water Street, where Bill had parked the car in front of the Board of Trade building. The little boys darted away from their mother every chance they got, out into the street, looking into the storefronts. "It's all so different to them," Ethel said. "So quiet, compared to Brooklyn."

It was hard to imagine how anyone could find Water Street on a weekday afternoon quiet. Annie couldn't imagine what Brooklyn must be like.

At the house they all unloaded. Bill helped Jim in with the trunk while Ethel and the children performed the ritual of greetings and kisses and hugs. While they were gone to the boat, Ethel's widowed mother had arrived and was settled in the kitchen too, so that the children could meet all their grandparents at once. Annie stayed out on the back step for a minute, the baby still in her arms, trying to think how to explain the baby to her mother. It shouldn't really be her worry;

she wasn't the one who was entrusted with the baby to deliver, yet she saw already that this baby was her problem, her burden to carry, and she was glad to have it so.

Bill Winsor stepped out of the house, his cap in hand.

"You're going to stay for dinner," Annie said.

"Ah, you've got enough already. And it's all family."

"You're family too. And it's only stew, it can stretch."

Bill moved closer to Annie, moved the blanket that covered most of baby Claire's face. The baby opened her eyes and stared unblinking at him. She frowned and began to whimper. Bill touched her cheek with a fingertip. Annie looked at him; he gazed at the baby so intently that she was free to study his face without his even noticing. This was the man who had loved Rose and wanted to marry her for years, looking down at the baby Rose had had by another man and casually packaged off to whoever might look after it. When she said, "Do you want to hold her?" Bill took Claire, settled her in his arms with an ease that seemed natural, and the baby's whimpering settled down, till she seemed almost content again.

By eleven o'clock that night, when she fell exhausted into her bed, Annie had figured out a number of things. She realized that no amount of explanation would force her mother to acknowledge that Claire was, in fact, Rose's illegitimate child. The baby was there: the baby was a fact, but where she came from was never going to be talked about. Annie saw, too, that Jim and Ethel were shocked by Pop, how wasted and feeble he had become; they were not prepared to find him aged and invalid no matter what she put in her letters. She figured out that Ethel and Jim were not happy; they barely spoke to each other, avoided each other's eyes. Annie saw, too, that Jim, who Ethel had always said was such a good father, was indeed a wonderful father to little Jimmy but barely touched or spoke to Ralphie, who looked ready to turn himself inside out to make his father notice him. And she had figured out that Ethel and Jim were not back here to stay, whatever they might think themselves.

Annie figured out one more thing: that baby Claire was hers, her own baby, the one she had asked God for. Everyone took turns holding her, but they always handed her back to Annie. Ethel, who had cared for the baby all the way from New York, seemed to have no further interest in her once she was safely in Annie's arms. So tonight baby Claire slept in an ancient bassinette that Bill dug out of the attic, hastily lined with a spare soft blanket, pulled up next to the couch where Annie slept in the living room. All night Annie lay listening to the baby's snuffling breath and her father's shallow steady wheeze, and thought of the verse that said *In everything give thanks.*

The summer unravelled day by day, growing warm in late July and cooling down again after Regatta Day in the first week of August. Ethel and Jim had tense, low conversations up in the bedroom at night. Annie heard them as she helped her mother get ready for bed in the next room. She couldn't pick out the words but she knew they were talking about what they were going to do: stay or go back to New York.

"He has to make up his mind sometime soon," Ethel said to Annie as they stood in the pantry washing dishes one night in mid-August. "If we're staying here, Ralphie will have to be put in school. And I'm due to have this baby in October and I'd like at least to know where I'm having it. I can't travel when I'm nine months along. I don't want my baby born on a boat."

This was as forthcoming as she had been all summer about their plans. Annie found it harder to talk to Ethel than it used to be: they had been apart so long, and also Ethel, like all married women, now had secrets to guard. She did not tell Annie why she and Jim were so uneasy with each other, nor why Jim adored his younger son and ignored the older. She only made reference to this once, when the girls were sitting on the step watching Jim chase Jimmy around the yard while Ralphie, solitary, watched from a branch of the dogberry tree. "He wasn't always like this," Ethel said then. "He used to be wonderful with Ralphie. It's only lately…" Her voice trailed off.

What happened? Annie didn't ask. "It must be hard on Ralphie."

"It's tearing him apart," Ethel said. "He adores his father. It's better here than it was back home though. At least here Bill pays some attention to him, and there's you and Mom and Pop too, and my mother. He's got people all around him."

There was so much here that Annie wanted to ask, wanted to pry open Ethel's shell and poke around inside. She had never thought of Ethel, her friend Ethel, as someone who carried a shell, but Ethel had grown a hard outer coating in New York. *She's been hurt bad,* Annie thought, *and I can't get close to her.*

"If you do go back, what will you do about Claire? You don't mean to take her back with you?"

Ethel looked shocked. "No, no, Rose wanted her sent home, she was clear on that. And anyway, I couldn't cope with two babies, and the boys as well." She paused, looking up at Ralphie still perched in the tree. "I don't know but Rose is right. Maybe this is a better place to raise a child. Ralphie couldn't do that, climb a tree, back home in Brooklyn."

Home in Brooklyn. Annie met her sister-in-law's eyes. Ethel looked away and changed the subject.

Jim said something similar a few days later, watching the boys play in the yard. "There's nothing here for me, Annie," he told her after another fruitless day looking for work. "Sure, even Bill is fed up with it, and he belongs here."

"Bill's not thinking of moving away?" Annie said sharply. If Bill went to New York too…

"Not to the States, you'll never get Bill down there. But he's talking about moving out around the bay with his uncle. He says if he can't be in here working he might as well be out there fishing, where at least he can grow and catch and shoot what he needs. I don't know but he's right, but that's no life for me. I'd be better off back in New York, doing what I knows best."

"So, will you go back before school starts?" Annie said. "Ethel's been wondering if she should sign Ralphie up for school here."

"She can do what she likes about Ralphie," snapped Jim. Then, in a lighter tone, he added, "I don't see us leaving here now before the baby is born. And as far as Ralphie goes, he's happy here. I don't know but this is the best place for him."

Slowly, Annie saw what was unfolding around her. "They want to leave Ralphie behind when they go back," she told Bill one Sunday night. He was walking her back from service: she was free to go more often now that Ethel and Jim were at the house.

"Ralphie? Why would they leave their own son behind?"

And Annie, of course, could not explain. "I don't think him and Jim get on very well," she said lamely. "Jim is kind of hard on him, he favours little Jimmy. It's hard to say what's in their minds from one day to the next," she added. "But then it's hard to say that about your mind either. Jim tells me you're thinking of moving out around the bay?" She tried to keep her voice light, but wasn't sure she had succeeded.

Bill looked at her sharply. "I'm sorry, Annie. I meant to say, but it was hard to bring up to you. I don't know what to do. My uncle's getting up there, he could use a hand around the house and in the boat. Fishermen aren't getting much for their catch these days, but at least you got the land under your feet, the fish in the sea, everything you need to survive. People are coming in from the bay to the city and only going on the dole. There's no work for me here and I'd be happy down in Bonavista. I knows I would, but I don't like to leave you."

"I can get by, Bill. I've got a lot of worries I know, but I can always find someone else to help me. People from church will help out now and then, with Pop and all."

"Come with me, Annie," Bill said suddenly. He stopped walking there on the corner of Freshwater Road and Rocky Lane. "Come down to Bonavista with me."

"Bill, that's foolishness. I can't do that. How could I haul Mom and Pop and the baby and Ralphie, if they leave him behind, all down to Bonavista?"

"Not the whole crew! Let someone else in the family take some responsibility, someone else look after them all. I know you couldn't leave the baby, but I'd be glad to have her along with you."

"Along with me?" Annie echoed.

"I'm sorry, I'm doing this all wrong." Bill took off his cap and tried to grin, but it was a little lopsided, like only half of him was smiling. "What I should have said first was, Annie, will you marry me?"

Annie turned, walked a few steps away. "Bill, this is…I didn't expect this. I can't think about all this now, not when I don't know what's going to happen. You have to give me time…time to work it out."

He looked relieved, and put his cap back on. He drew her arm through his and they walked on. "You can have time if you needs it, Annie. I'm not going nowhere before winter, anyway."

No-one, it seemed, was going anywhere before winter. Ralphie started Grade One. Jimmy learned to climb the fence to get out of the yard. Claire learned to crawl. Jim looked for work. Pop developed a flu and they all worried it could turn to pneumonia. And on the first of October, Ethel had a baby girl she named Diane.

After Diane was born Ethel and Annie worked side by side, bathing the babies, changing diapers, preparing bottles. Diane was a plump, contented baby, dark-haired and dark-eyed like Ethel's people, not like the Evanses. One morning shortly before Christmas, as they bathed the babies in the big metal washtub in front of the kitchen stove, Ethel said, "Jim's got his mind made up to go back to New York as soon as spring comes. Harold tells him things are picking up a bit there, he might be able to find work."

"And what do you think about that?"

Ethel was silent, soaping Diane's abundant hair into a curl atop her head. "Annie," she said at last, "there's things I haven't told you. But I can tell you this if you don't ask no more questions: Jim's got his mind made up Ralphie's staying here, not coming back to New York with us. And I can't stand the thought of leaving him, girl, it's tearing me apart. Jim told me last night that he's going back to New York, and he's not taking Ralphie back with us. As for me and the other two, he says, I can decide what I wants: stay here with Ralphie and all of you, or go back to Brooklyn with him, he doesn't care. But his mind's made up to those two things, and I don't know what to do."

Annie nodded slowly, pouring a cup of warm water over Claire's head. She squealed and shut her eyes. "If Ralphie stays behind," Annie said at last, "I'll take the best kind of care of him. I'd treat him like my own, Ethel. And he's good with Claire, he'd be like a big brother for her. If you can't change Jim's mind, Ethel, at least you can rest easy that Ralphie would be well taken care of." She saw Ethel's slow nod, and knew what Ethel would decide. And it was right. A wife's place was with her husband, when all was said and done.

Bill, too, had his plans made. He wanted to live around the bay, try his hand at fishing and maybe a bit of farming. He wanted Annie, he wanted Claire, he wanted them to have a family of their own. Annie sometimes wondered if it was really her he wanted in that life. It had always been Rose he wanted, and now he wanted to look after Rose's baby, Annie was sure. And since he couldn't have Rose, and every man needed a wife, Annie would do. If she said no, he'd find someone else down in Bonavista, that fall or the next fall, Annie thought. But she held her tongue, and only told him she couldn't see her way clear to getting married and moving down there. Maybe next year they'd see.

ROSE

BROOKLYN, AUGUST 1932

DINNER IS A BOILED egg, cooked over the hot plate in her room. Since there's only one burner she uses the egg water to make her cup of tea afterwards, giving the tea a strange aftertaste. It's not the dinner she would have chosen. She wouldn't have chosen to eat at all, in fact: she hasn't eaten all day and feels no hunger, no urge to taste anything. She likes the idea of a restaurant meal: chop suey, or a nice steak. She likes the thought of it appearing all colourful and bright on the tray in front of her, but she cannot imagine lifting the fork to her mouth. The effort seems incredible.

The dingy room has a mirror about one foot square, coated with dust, hanging at chest level behind the door. Rose rarely looks at it. She knows she has gone to pieces. She worried so much about getting fat with the baby, which turned out to be a joke. She was so sick and miserable for most of the pregnancy that she gained barely five pounds. Since the birth those have dropped away and taken several others with them, till her hip bones jut out like spars and her wrists seem as fragile as matchsticks. Every day there is less and less Rose, more and more of the world.

The strange malaise, the world-weariness that muffled her like a heavy blanket in those strange months before she found herself pregnant, only increased once she realized that she had a baby inside her. Tony Martelli's baby, who had stolen her chance at another kind of life with Andrew Covington, who was sucking away her strength, growing bigger and stronger at her expense. A parasite, really. Like fleas on a dog.

The journey toward birth was a long, strange, lonely one. Most of that time Rose saw and spoke to nobody. Every few days the idea of going to see Tony would arise. She was carrying Tony's baby, and the last thing he'd said was that he wanted to marry her. No. The last thing he said was for her to go to hell.

When the money ran out and her time got close she had to look for charity. Her landlady told her about a shelter for girls in trouble. It was run by nuns. Back home, Rose had had Catholic friends who went to school with the nuns and told horror-tales of their strictness, their whippings and beatings and curses of hell that sounded exactly like Tony's mother.

These nuns did not whip or beat or even talk about hell – or if they did, Rose didn't hear it. They were careful and practical and, once in awhile, even gentle, though their disapproval showed clearly in the white-framed circles of their pinched narrow faces. Their hands were kinder than their faces, when the time came to touch her. A midwife guided her through the awful hours of birth, the unimaginable pain, the pushing that felt as if she would be torn apart.

Afterwards, they brought her the baby girl, a scrawny, squalling, appallingly strong red bundle of life and energy. She arched and twisted in Rose's arms without the slightest urge to cuddle or snuggle in. This made Rose like her better.

"Do you want to give her a bottle, or to nurse her yourself?" the nun at her feet said, in a voice that clearly implied that whichever choice she made would be the wrong one.

Rose looked at the baby's hungry little red mouth working. She imagined that little mouth clamping down on her nipple, sucking hard, drawing even more life out of her. As if there was a cord connecting her breast with the heart below it, Rose imagined the baby drawing out not only nourishment but love, sucked from her unwilling heart.

Rose handed her back to the nun. "Get her a bottle," she said.

But she didn't let them put the baby up for adoption. She kept her, and struggled with her tough little body and gave her the bottles herself. She called the baby Claire, a simple and strong-sounding name, and when her recovery was over she left the shelter with Claire in her arms.

As soon as she was out of the hospital, though, out of the care of the nuns, her lethargy and sadness returned full force, and she found herself lying in her bed in the boarding house, listening to the baby scream, knowing she was wet and hungry and yet not being able to get up and pick her up. The cries would go on and on and Rose would think, *In a minute, just one minute I'll get up and get her,* until finally the landlady or the neighbour across the landing pounded on the door and said, "Mrs. Evans! Mrs. Evans! Can you do something with that baby?"

On the days she felt strong enough, Rose walked the wintry streets for hours with the baby, a shapeless bundle of blankets in her arms, while she tried to think what to do. She could only see three possibilities: go back to the nuns and give back the baby, go find Tony and give Claire to him, or see if her own relatives would take in Claire.

Finally she settled on the last choice as the safest. Different as she was from her brothers, they were more like her, because of blood, than anyone else on earth. They were good men and their wives were good, if dull, women. Claire deserved someone sensible and dull to raise her. So one night Rose dressed and combed her hair and took baby Claire to Jim and Ethel's apartment, and when she found that they were going home she asked them, "Please take the baby home to Mom and Pop."

She left Ethel and Jim's place and walked the streets enjoying the freedom: her arms no longer heavy with their burden, her feet lighter. She breathed the air that was free of the hundred and one married tensions she could feel and sense in Ethel and Jim's apartment. She walked back to her boarding house, alone, and felt wonderful.

Now she drifts through the weeks in a daze, eating next to nothing but not feeling hungry, sleeping most of the day and night but always feeling tired. She's heard of women suffering from bad nerves after they have babies. But if the baby is gone, given away, why would her nerves still be bad? And what, if anything, is the cure?

One day she goes downstairs into the hall and sees her landlady's purse lying on the hall table. Rose looks inside and there's a change purse with small change: coppers, nickels, dimes. She takes five dimes and walks out onto the street feeling rich and, briefly, energized. At a diner on the corner she sits down and orders a meal – the first real meal she can remember in a long time, something more than tea and toast and an egg. She orders chicken, always her favourite, with a cup of coffee and a piece of lemon meringue pie for dessert.

The only trouble is, she can't eat more than a mouthful or two, feels as sick when she tries as back when she was pregnant. Back out on the street she tries to think of a way to spend the rest of the money that won't wear her out, won't require a thing out of her. She wanders aimlessly up and down the street, a dingy, dirty grey backstreet where poor people with no colour and no energy, people like herself, are condemned to live. Walks till at last she sees a movie theatre and almost laughs in relief: how could she have forgotten? She hasn't seen a movie since before Claire was born.

The movie is *Laughing Sinners*, with Clark Gable and Joan Crawford. Rose hasn't heard of the movie but she likes Gable and she likes Crawford, so she figures she can't go wrong. She sinks into her seat, glad to have this one escape still left to her.

She's not far in before she learns it was a terrible mistake. Clarke Gable is playing, of all things, a Salvation Army officer, uniform and all. Joan Crawford – blond in this movie – is a wayward girl of the streets who joins the Army. The audience seems to take it all in good fun, but seeing all the uniforms reminds Rose too vividly of Sundays at home, walking into Salvation Meeting next to Annie, Annie dark and sober in her bonnet and uniform, a Salvation Army lassie, and Rose defiant in everyday clothes beside her. Rose remembers it as a sea of black, a swamp of holiness reaching up to suck her under. When Joan Crawford's character slips back into sin and goes to bed with her old, bad boyfriend, Rose wants to stand up and cheer. But Clark Gable ruins it all at the end, showing up all shiny and righteous in the uniform and sweet-talking her into going back with him, back to the black-clad, tambourine-banging, happy-in-the-Lord army of holiness. Rose feels sick once again as she leaves the theatre. But she has a dime left in her pocket, so the day hasn't been a total waste.

Rose walks out of the theatre onto a drab street under a grey sky. She thinks about baby Claire. Rose pictures her, not a baby or a little girl, but grown up, looking like Rose herself but sharper, smarter, able to pull her mother together and get her to shape up. She closes her eyes against the vision, against the troubling sense that she will never see her daughter again.

PART TWO

1944 - 1957

CLAIRE

"I'M GOING TO GET a letter from Diane today," Valerie said, clambering over a snowbank. "I've got a Feeling."

Claire knew about Valerie's Feelings. Feelings, vague but intense and hardly ever reliable, ruled her life. Claire, mercifully free from Feelings, Intuitions, Omens and Presentiments, thought her own life was a lot simpler, though perhaps less exciting.

"Wait for meeeeeee...." came the faint echo of Valerie's brother Kenny, ploughing along through the snow behind them. It was a long walk all the way up from Springdale Street, but this was the worst part in winter, coming through Hennebury's Pinch with the wind blowing snow down from the field on their left and the road a churned mess of icy slush beneath their gaiters.

Actually, Claire corrected herself, *neither* of their lives was interesting at all. They lived in St. John's on the same piece of land in Freshwater Valley in two different houses, Valerie with her father, her mother and her two little brothers, and Claire with her aunt and her grandmother and her cousin Ralph. They were both in Grade Seven at the Salvation Army College. They lived very average, unexciting lives, even though they were living in wartime, which in a book would be exciting but in real life wasn't particularly. But Valerie's life seemed thrilling to her because she had such a great imagination.

They both went in the kitchen door of Aunt Annie's, Kenny trailing behind, stamping snow off their boots, laying down their satchels in the porch, taking off their coats. The heat from the stove hit them both in the face. Aunt Annie had the kitchen done in yellows and reds, bright yellow paint on the walls, red canvas on the floor, yellow and red in the tablecloth. It looked like a room where nothing ever changed, not even the calendar on the wall with the picture of the kittens curled up asleep next to the mother cat. When Claire heard the word "home," a picture of the kitchen came to mind.

Aunt Annie had supper in the oven and tea buns on the table. She stood at the table chopping an onion for gravy, barely even looking up as she said, "Come in, girls, come in. Some cold outside, isn't it? The radio said it was supposed to be mild today but I don't call this mild. Do either of you want a cup of cocoa? Claire, will you get the kettle?" Aunt Annie's words and fingers moved quickly and efficiently. She was a small woman, about the age of Val's mother but with no children of her own. Her light-brown hair was sausage-rolled and neatly pinned; she wore a red-and-white checked dress with a yellow apron and seemed to match her kitchen.

"Come on, let's go up in your room," Valerie said, taking her cocoa and a tea bun. Claire followed her cousin up to her own small room at the end of the upstairs hall, underneath the slope of the roof so it was more like three-quarters of a room than a whole room. She understood Valerie's need to get away from her younger brothers, but Claire was in no hurry to leave the warmth of the kitchen for the chilly upstairs room with the iron bedstead, the heavy dark-brown dresser, the green-fern wallpaper. Nor was she eager to get back to the project she knew Valerie would haul out again as soon as they were settled comfortably upstairs with the quilt tucked over their legs.

"I've got to get at my geography," Claire said. It was only lately she'd had the room to herself, since Valerie's family had built their own house and moved out. For years she had shared with Valerie, and Val sometimes acted as if the room were still half hers. Claire enjoyed the luxury of having a room of her own. Since Pop Evans died, Aunt Annie slept in the back bedroom with Grandmother. The front bedroom had been rented, after Valerie's parents moved out, to a Canadian Air Force officer and his wife, who mostly kept to themselves. Even a tiny room like Claire's, with the ceiling sloping down to make a little cave over the bed, was precious space.

"Let's work on the story first," Valerie suggested, trying to sound as if this had just popped into her head. Valerie possessed all the creative flights of fancy needed to finish the story, but because it was really Claire's story, she couldn't honourably go on ahead with it alone, which left Claire with the upper hand.

Only, Claire reflected as Valerie began digging through the papers in Claire's bedside drawer, having the upper hand with Valerie was really useless. Claire knew herself to be more strong-willed than Valerie, more forceful, and smarter too, in every subject except English literature. But she could not stand up to Valerie and never had been able to. She didn't fully understand why. At school she was clearly the stronger of the two, a leader in their group of girls, but at home she felt younger, weaker, less powerful. It had something to do with Valerie having parents and Claire having none.

"Now, where did we leave off?" Valerie said, thumbing through pages of the exercise book.

"I don't remember," Claire lied.

She remembered every detail of the story, despite trying to act bored every time Valerie mentioned it. At night sometimes she lay awake and scenes from the story played over in her head. Beautiful Rose and the handsome young pilot – Valerie had made him an RAF pilot after first toying with several other branches of the forces – kissing goodbye on the wharf after their secret wedding. In Claire's mind the pilot looked just like Ralph, who in spite of being her cousin was the handsomest boy she knew, with his light wavy hair and clear blue eyes and the little cleft in his chin. The last scene Valerie had written involved Rose leaving the doctor's office, elated at the news that she was having a baby.

"*But little did she know,*" Val said aloud, her pencil scratching steadily at the lined scribbler pages, "*what fate held in store. At home on the floor beneath her front door, next to the mail slot...* No, that's no good, it sounds too fussy. How should I explain about the telegram, Claire? Because the telegram is already there when she gets home from the doctor, see?" She glanced up at Claire, as if remembering that she was supposed to consult her cousin in this fanciful reconstruction of Claire's own personal history.

"I don't know," Claire said. Drawn into it despite herself, she added, "I suppose you could say–"

"Oh, oh, this is good!" Valerie interrupted, and her pencil began to fly across the ruled lines. Claire watched in amazement; she had never understood how Valerie could write so fast when she was spinning pure moonshine, all out of her own head. "*On her way down Merrymeeting Road she passed a telegram delivery boy on his bicycle. As she waved a cheery hello she didn't guess – she little guessed – that just a few moments before he had delivered to her house – her door – a telegram that would change her life forever.*" Valerie read out what she'd written, paused, and started again. "*And shatter forever the beautiful castle of dreams she and Paul had built.*"

"I still don't like the name Paul," Claire said.

"But it suits him! He's a Paul, can't you see it, Claire?"

Claire shrugged. She tugged the quilt up over her knees. It was one of Grandmother's crazy quilts, no pattern or design, just strips and bits and scraps of old clothes that couldn't be mended or let out or handed down any more. She traced a square of the blue dress she wore in Grade Five, and next to it a triangle of Valerie's old purple plaid skirt. An arrow of brilliant green shot down above the two: a dress Aunt Ethel had sent home from New York for Aunt Annie. Aunt Annie hadn't liked it and had worn it only a few times, so the green silk was brighter and less worn than the patches of fabric around it.

"You're always criticizing," said Valerie, mildly. She didn't really mind Claire's criticism: she was so supremely confident in her story that she didn't need anyone else's approval.

"It's just that so much of it is *wrong!*" Claire burst out. She cut off Valerie's usual protest. "No, I know it's just a story and it can't be *wrong*, but it is! Things didn't happen that way. We know they couldn't have! Rose wasn't even living here in St. John's when I was born. She was living in Brooklyn. And my father couldn't have been an RAF pilot because the war hadn't even started then!" It seemed to both of them that the war had been going on forever. Claire couldn't remember what sort of headlines had been on the newspapers before there was war news, or what it had been like when there were no Americans in uniform on the streets of St. John's, but she knew the facts: the war had started in 1939, when she and Valerie were both seven years old.

"But it's a *story*," Valerie began again, and her eyes filled quickly with tears. Watery, light-blue eyes, edged with unromantic short lashes – not the kind of eyes Valerie wanted at all. Val wanted to be pretty and wasn't: the pale eyes and the dull-brown, hard-to-manage hair spoiled it for her. She should have had Claire's shining blond hair, which didn't match at all with Claire's dark brown eyes and strong dark eyebrows.

Downstairs, a door slammed and one of the little boys shouted. Claire jumped off the bed. "Ralph's home," she said. "Let's go down in the kitchen. We could get some more cocoa and find out what he's been up to. Or do you want me to bring some up for you?" she added, seeing that Valerie looked unwilling to move.

"Yes…no, wait, I'll come down," Valerie said, uncurling herself from under the quilt.

They spent the rest of the afternoon down in the kitchen, drafted into helping with supper, listening to Ralph talk about working down on the base. He had left school after Grade Nine and got a job as a janitor working for the Americans at Fort Pepperrell. Ralph would turn eighteen in two months and was counting the minutes till he could join up. Claire saw that Aunt Annie turned her face away whenever she heard Ralph talk about the war or signing up. She was praying, Claire guessed, that the war would be over before Ralph got a chance to go. And Ralph was praying just the opposite – although, could he? Could anyone really pray that the war would go on and on, and thousands of people go on dying? Maybe Ralph wasn't praying exactly that. Claire went back to peeling potatoes, watching with satisfaction the long smooth spirals of peel curling into the sink.

Ralph was putting on an American accent now, imitating one of the fellows down on the base, boys just a few months older than himself but who, with their crisp uniforms and ready cash, seemed to come from another world. Janet Cross, the girl Ralph had liked in school, was going with an American soldier now. But it hadn't made Ralph hate the Americans: if anything he admired them and copied them more than ever.

Claire remembered an evening back in the fall, when it was still mild enough to be outside at night, sitting on the front step and watching a pair of soldiers with their girls going in Freshwater Road.

"We could have been like them," Claire had said to Ralph then.

"Like who?"

"The Americans. We were both born in America, in Brooklyn." Valerie had been born there too, but now that Uncle Harold and Aunt Frances had moved their whole family back to St. John's they seemed to belong here, a complete unit. Claire felt her American roots as a bond shared with Ralph more than with Valerie: she and Ralph both had parents, and a possible unlived life, back in that far-off land. "If our parents had left us there, we would have grown up Americans."

"There's no point thinking about that," was all he'd said. "No point in all that, at all." He talked and looked like a Newfoundlander, just like she did, but as a U.S. citizen he was eligible to join the American army when he reached eighteen. Claire couldn't understand why he wasn't interested in reflecting on what might have been, if their parents had kept them in New York.

Today, of course, as Ralph handed the little boys the sticks of gum he'd gotten from the servicemen, she would not, could not, say anything like that. Nothing about the past could be mentioned in front of Aunt Annie or her grandmother. All Annie had ever told Claire was that her mother's name was Rose, that she had lived in New York when Claire was born, that Rose couldn't handle a baby on her own so she sent Claire home. "And we are your family," Aunt Annie had concluded this brief, awkward talk, "and you're a very lucky little girl."

The door blew open again, whirling in wind and slush and Aunt Frances, Valerie's mother, coming to collect her children. With very little effort Aunt Annie persuaded her to stay for supper. Aunt Frances worked in the office at Ayre and Sons downtown; lots of women had jobs like that now that so many men were overseas. Uncle Harold wasn't overseas; he worked repairing radios, but Aunt

Frances said that with three children every extra penny was a help. She gave Aunt Annie money for looking after Danny all day and Kenny and Valerie after school. Many times, like tonight, the whole family ended up eating supper in Aunt Annie's kitchen.

After supper, when everyone had gone home, Claire laid out her homework on the kitchen table, writing her civics essay in the small circle of yellow light cast by the bare bulb that hung over the red and yellow tablecloth. Grandmother and Aunt Annie knitted in their chairs, one on either side of the stove, and Ralph looked at a comic book. It was quiet and companionable: Aunt Annie turned on the radio at seven-thirty, but that didn't bother Claire because she was used to tuning it out. At nine, Grandmother went upstairs to bed, helped by Aunt Annie, and Ralph took advantage of their absence to say he was going out for a little while and would be back in an hour or so. Claire watched him go, envying his ticket to the world of boys who came and went as they pleased, who stood around on street corners and smoked and looked forward to being old enough to go overseas.

She was back into her essay, just finishing it up, when Aunt Annie came downstairs. Instead of going back to her usual chair Aunt Annie sat at the table across from Claire and said, "Claire, I want to talk to you."

Claire looked up, mildly curious, until she saw Aunt Annie was holding a blue Caribou scribbler. Claire felt sick; her stomach turned and the skin on the upper part of her cheeks got cold and prickly.

"I found this on your bed." Aunt Annie pushed it across the table to her, the scribbler open to the last pages of Val's story.

"That's private! What were you doing in my room?"

"I went in to turn down your bed and put a hot-water bottle in it for you," said Aunt Annie, an answer that completely deflated Claire. "I found this, and I picked it up thinking you might need it for your schoolwork. I opened it to see what it was before I brought it down to you. And then I read…this."

Claire said nothing, looking at the pencilled words blurring on the page.

"This…foolishness." It was Aunt Annie's strongest epithet, the word from which there was no appeal.

"Valerie wrote that, not me."

"I know Valerie wrote it. But it was in your bedroom. You had some say in it. You two girls have been cooking up these stories, these…these foolish tales. And the truth is–"

"Yes?" Claire said, catching an indrawn breath.

"The truth is nothing like this." The word "truth" lay on the table between them like something that almost happened, like the last baby Aunt Frances had: born dead. Aunt Annie snapped the scribbler shut and took it over to the stove, lifting a cover off the stovetop. "I've got a good mind to burn this, Claire, because there's no place in this house, no place in your life, for this kind of foolishness. For making up stories about…about the way you wish things were." She dangled the scribbler over the stove, and Claire saw that Aunt Annie wouldn't really do it: she just wasn't the kind to burn someone else's scribbler, no matter how angry she was.

"Go ahead, burn it. I don't care," Claire said. Aunt Annie's hand hesitated; Claire nodded once. Aunt Annie dropped the scribbler into the fire and Claire heard it crackle and hiss. She felt like an iron band around her chest had snapped. She had known all along that what Valerie was doing was wrong, but she had not known it was possible just to lift the lid of the stove and burn it away, burn away all the past and all what-might-have-been, all romantic fantasies and Feelings.

"Where's Ralph?" Aunt Annie said, looking around sharply. "Gone out, I suppose."

"Yes, he said he'd be back by…well, before ten anyway."

"No more than he should do. I worry about that crowd he hangs around with, there's some hard tickets in that crowd. Those Sullivan boys…" Aunt Annie poked around in the range with her poker, nudging the ashes. With her back to Claire she added, "I don't worry about you, Claire. You're sensible. Sensible people don't get caught up in any old foolishness, any trouble."

"I know," Claire said, folding up her books and scribblers, zipping her pencil and eraser and sharpener away neatly in her case. It was a precise little case with flaps and folds for everything and she loved the orderly ritual of putting each thing back in its appointed spot. Valerie's pencil case was a disgrace, full of inkblots and folded notes and things shoved in any old way at all. Claire's was as tidy as Aunt Annie's pantry shelves. A place for everything, and everything in its place.

ETHEL

⁓

BROOKLYN, JUNE 1944

THE APARTMENT WAS QUIET now, an hour before the children got home from school. Ethel immersed herself in these quiet hours like a bath. Jim worked from eight till six, practicing the trade he'd picked up from Harold – radio repair – at a small shop a few blocks down Flatbush. Diane and Jimmy spent all day at school, came home to change their clothes and then ran out again with their friends. Ethel was alone most of the day. It seemed such a short time since everyone had been underfoot, never giving her a minute's peace. She knew that soon the warm bathwater of peace and privacy would rise like a flood tide and close over her head, and that knowledge worried her. But other times she thought, *Let them go. I'm better on my own anyway.*

Ethel's life was neat and ordered. Her son Jimmy was no trouble, a big hearty fourteen-year-old who liked nothing better than to play stickball all day with his friends in the lot at the end of the street. Diane was another story. She was only twelve but was starting to Develop Early. Also, the mouth on her – Ethel couldn't believe it sometimes, the things she said to her own mother. She would be trouble. Daughters were more trouble than sons.

Ethel creamed a block of butter with a firm hand, wishing daughters were as yielding and predictable. Today was Friday; tonight she and Jim were having three other couples over for cards. They had been doing this for years, though the guest list had changed. Jean and Robert were still the old standbys, like Ethel and Jim themselves. Once upon a time it used to be Harold and Frances, but they moved back to Newfoundland years ago, before the war. Dick and Eileen Mouland were gone too; Eileen had moved back home after Dick was killed overseas last year. So many women, even here in this building, had lost husbands and sons.

Ethel half-listened to a radio serial as she worked, calling it "foolishness" if

⁓

any other woman mentioned it but following the stories all the same. She liked *The Guiding Light* and a few of the others, though she credited herself for not getting all caught up in it like some did. On today's story, Nora was arguing with her daughter Doreen, who she had only discovered was her daughter a few weeks ago, because she had given her up to be adopted at birth. Ethel shook her head. "Where do they come up with the stories at all?" she said to the radio, measuring out two cups of flour from the bin on the counter.

A sharp rap at the door startled her. Ethel wiped her hands on a towel, untied her apron, and went to the door.

The tall young man standing there was nobody she knew. Too old to be one of Jimmy's friends, and dressed in a badly cut, out-of-style wool coat, soaked in the pouring rain, dressed like someone from…could it be someone from home? And then, before he opened his mouth, she saw the ridiculous thin spray of flowers he had clutched in his fist, and knew. Of course she knew.

"Ah…Mother? Mom?" The boy spoke as though it were a new word in an unfamiliar language. Ethel said nothing and his eyes widened; she saw his panic. He stuck out the hand with the flowers, holding the drooping florist's carnations in front of him like a shield.

"Ralph," she said at last, wondering why she couldn't put more feeling into her voice. When Nora on the radio found out Doreen was her daughter they fell into each other's arms sobbing. Here in real life, she stood like a porcelain doll in front of the son she had prayed for and cried over every night since she left him at home in 1933.

She took a step backwards, almost bumped into the doorknob. "Come in, come in." Then, with relief, she recalled a cliché. "This is a surprise! What brings you to New York?"

Ralph was relieved too, she could see. His wide mouth relaxed into a smile. "I just made up my mind to come, you know, come see you and Dad. I told them at home not to write and let you know I was coming, I wanted to surprise you. I came on the boat yesterday, stayed at a boarding house last night; Uncle Harold gave me the name of the place. Walked around the streets for awhile on my way up here, trying to see if I could remember anything."

"Did it…did anything look familiar to you? It's been so long."

"The building kind of felt familiar. But nothing else. I was only…what? Six?"

"Six," said Ethel.

They stood there, three feet apart, in the hallway of what had once been his home. He had been a child here, played here. Ethel found she couldn't think about that. Better to pretend this Ralph was someone new and different, someone who had never been here before. He might as well be, this young man with his strong St. John's accent and out-of-style clothes. Bad teeth, she noticed as he spoke, like everyone at home. His nose was crooked, not the nice straight nose she remembered. Of course – he broke it when he was ten. She remembered his letter, and Annie's. She had saved all the letters.

"Come in, sit down. Will you have a cup of tea?" She led him into the living room, an awkward two-step as she steered him around the furniture. When he was sitting on the sofa he remembered the flowers and passed them to her. He still had not taken off his outside jacket.

"How are they all at home?" she called, going into the kitchen for a vase and the teapot.

"All right. Grandmother's arthritis is bad, of course, like it always is. Aunt Annie is still goin' strong. You knew Bill Winsor was overseas, didn't you? And Uncle Harold is doin' the same kind of work as…as Dad, fixin' radios and stuff. The children are all growing like weeds, of course, Claire and Valerie and the boys."

His voice made a pleasant background hum as the kettle started to hiss. Then the apartment door burst open and Ethel stepped out quickly as she heard Diane and Jimmy arguing in the hall.

"I have a surprise for you," she said, blocking them at the living room door. "We had a visitor, a surprise visitor, someone from home. It's your brother! Ralph!" Her voice sounded as bright and unnatural as the women on the radio. Her smile stretched her lips back into her cheeks.

"Ralph?" Jimmy was the first one into the room. He grinned, opening his arms like Ethel was supposed to have done. All his life he had hero-worshipped Ralph from afar, the wonderful big brother who was never there to smack him or tell him to mind his own business. "Remember me? I know you don't remember Diane; she was only a baby when you left."

They had grown up with stories of Ralph, his letters and a handful of pictures. Ethel had had to invent a story, of course, to explain why Ralph was back in Newfoundland and they were here in Brooklyn. For all Jim had set himself against Ralph – never read his letters or wanted to hear any news about him, never mentioned his name if he could help it – he wouldn't have it said out loud that Ralph was another man's son.

"Those were hard times," she remembered telling the children. "It was the Depression and everyone was very poor. We all went home to St. John's – that was where you were born, Diane – but after awhile your father thought he'd have a better chance here in New York, so we came back. It wasn't an easy place or time to raise children, and in some ways I thought you'd all be better off at home. But you two were just babies, you couldn't do without me. Ralph was older, and his Aunt Annie took a real liking to him. I thought he'd have a better chance, a better childhood, growing up there than here. Of course we'll go back someday, or maybe he'll come to New York, and you'll have a chance to meet him."

Someday was today. Ethel retreated to the kitchen again, pouring the cups of tea, laying out a plate of cookies for the youngsters. Well, for Ralph too; he was still a growing boy, wasn't he?

Her heart had not slowed since she saw him at the door. She wondered if it ever would; or would it just keep racing till she had a heart attack and dropped down dead? She had never stopped praying to see him again. Once she had thought that losing him, Jim turning his back on Ralph and making her leave him behind, was God's punishment and she would finally be even for the sin that had made him, so long ago. But then she began to think of it differently. She saw that this was a new sin, that leaving Ralph was the worst thing she had ever done. Perhaps this unexpected visit was God's way of telling her she had paid her debt. Her boy had come back to her, once and for all.

On that happy thought Ethel put the teacups and cookies on a tray and moved out of the kitchen. Jimmy was saying, "—the boys round here. Don't s'pose you remember any of them, but most of them are gone, joined up. Are you eighteen yet? You ain't joined up?"

The cold finger touched her heart at Jimmy's words, and Ethel looked at her older son, who was just getting to his feet and taking off his coat. She looked at him, knowing that he had kept the coat on to spare her a second shock on top of the first, knowing how Jimmy's and Diane's eyes would widen in admiration and the room would spin when they all saw that under it he was wearing a U.S. Army uniform, brand-spanking new.

"Wow!" Jimmy said.

"Nice," said Diane.

"I signed up and did my basic training with the U.S. Army there at Fort Pepperrell," Ralph was telling his younger brother. He went on, explaining where he was being posted now and how he had a couple of days' leave to come visit his parents in Brooklyn, but Ethel didn't hear his words. She laid the tray down with care but still slopped a little tea out of the cups. To stop her hands shaking she laid them one on each of Ralph's arms, holding him away as if to get a better look, touching him for the first time in eleven years.

She nodded slowly, not trusting herself for words, and Ralph smiled again, seeing the approval and pride he wanted to see. And Ethel saw what God had in store for her and knew she had not yet even begun to pay for her sins and would pay till the day she died.

ETHEL

BROOKLYN, APRIL 1945

"Where do you think you're going, young lady?"

Ethel sighed and laid down her crochet. Behind her, Diane was trying to sneak from her bedroom to the door without being seen by her father. Jim sat in the armchair these evenings, behind his newspaper, and whenever Diane passed, he barked out a line that sounded like some old-fashioned father in a stage play. He had no idea how to handle a daughter who was turning into a young woman too fast, and seemed to have decided that sounding like his own grandfather was the best way to deal with a modern young girl. Ethel knew his crusade was doomed; they were all doomed where Diane was concerned. Ethel turned to see her thirteen-year-old daughter dressed in a bright red sweater stretched tight over her two aggressive little breasts, sharp and unmistakable as ice-cream cones. Her shoulders were padded, though her brassiere didn't need to be. The narrow black skirt was a hand-me-down of Ethel's, and below it Diane had carefully covered her legs with pancake make-up and pencilled pretend seams up the back of both legs.

"Out, I'm just going out. Down to the candy store with Carol and Lorraine," said Diane with the full-lipped pout Ethel thought she must practice in front of the mirror.

"Well, be back in by eight-thirty," Ethel said.

"Carol's allowed to stay out till ten on weekends!"

"Am I Carol's mother?"

"No, but golly, I wish you were!" Diane shot back over her shoulder.

"Don't speak to your mother like that!" barked Jim on cue.

"You and Daddy are so old-fashioned, Mother. You know, I'm a *teenager* now, I'm not living back in ancient times like when you grew up in Newfoundland."

Teenager. Something new, that word, like the bitter sarcasm dripping from the word Newfoundland. Ethel really did feel ancient.

But she tried. She had a quick glimpse of time, life, her daughter, slipping through her fingers like water, and she closed her hand around what couldn't be grasped. She got up and touched Diane's shoulder, felt the warm flesh under the sweater turn hard as bone.

"Daddy and I aren't trying to be harsh with you, Diane. It's just...we just worry about you. You're still just a little girl..."

Wrong thing to say. Of course. Diane turned away and shut the door behind her without a word.

Ethel stood alone in the hall. She thought of Annie's and Frances' letters telling about the girls back home – how Claire and Valerie competed for the best marks in their class, Claire excelling in her math classes, Valerie writing the best English compositions. How Claire still came home muddy and scratched from playing football with the boys in the field; how Valerie curled up in a corner with a book and couldn't be roused from her dream world. How the two girls led Valerie's little brothers, Kenny and Danny, on a raid of the henhouse and then took the eggs and broke them all over the unfinished floor of the new house Bill Winsor's brother was building, and went skating on the slippery mess, and Annie was worried at how little the hens were laying until she discovered the truth. Claire and Valerie were growing up back home as normal, healthy young girls, and here was Diane growing up a New York girl, saucy as a crackie to her mother, with tight sweaters and made-up legs.

Back in the living room Ethel eased down in her chair and picked up her crocheting again. She was surprised when Jim laid down the paper a few minutes later. Often he'd sit behind it all evening until bedtime, only speaking to share aloud a news item that interested him. These days he did that less and less; there was no more war news from Europe since V-E Day and he knew Ethel hated to hear news of the Pacific theatre, though she would take the paper when he was at work and read the stories herself.

Jim folded the paper on his lap and she looked up at him. He was forty-five years old this year. His hair had gone mostly grey, and the lines on either side of his mouth were deeper and more permanent.

"I don't know what to be doing with that one," he said, nodding at the door.

Ethel, who didn't know herself, said, "Don't worry. She's growing up, is all. We can't stop her."

Jim was the one who let out a gusty sigh this time. "They're all growing up too fast," he said. *All*, not both. The word hung between them; the acknowledgment that they had three children hovered in the silence. Fewer and fewer things, as the years went by, were safe to talk about.

"House is quiet with the youngsters out," Jim went on. "I tell you what, Ethel, let's you and me go out. Let's go take in a movie."

This was unexpected. Jim and Ethel went out to dinner and a movie three times a year, on their anniversary and on each of their birthdays. Every Friday night they had their card-party, rotating between their apartment and their friends' apartments in turn. The other three hundred or so nights of the year, Jim sat in one chair and read the paper while Ethel sat in the other and knitted or crocheted, and they turned out the lights and went to bed at ten-thirty.

"What's got into you tonight?" Ethel said.

Jim stood up, paced to the window and back. "Come on, Ethel girl, we don't have to sit here like two old fogies, do we? Our youngsters are out having a bit of fun, why shouldn't we go out too?"

Ethel understood a little of what he felt. As always when she caught a rare glimpse of Jim's inner life, she felt like she was standing at the edge of a foreign country, seeing only the borderlands, curious but not really wanting to cross.

Fifteen minutes later they were walking down Flatbush Avenue towards the Loew's Kings. Flatbush had changed in the twenty years they had lived here: more shops, more lights. And always the boys in uniform these days, young men with girls hanging off their arms, the girls Diane must want to be like, Ethel supposed. She looked at the young men, seeing Ralph in each one, wishing he could turn up safe and surprise her just as he did that day last year.

"They say in the paper it's going well on Okinawa," Jim said. "Our boys expect to have the Jap army cleared out of there in another few weeks. The worst is over, they say."

Ethel nodded. "Please God, he'll be out of there by June. Will it end the war, do you think?"

"How much more can the Japs take?" Jim said. "They can't hold out forever no matter how many of those bloody kamikazes they have. Queer thing, isn't it, a man who'd crash his own plane just to kill someone else?"

No queerer than anything else in wartime, Ethel thought: those boys going overseas, risking their lives and dying to straighten out foreign messes that had nothing to do with them. In spite of the men in uniform, the patriotic advertising slogans and songs and even movies – tonight it was *Blood on the Sun* with James Cagney, all about the Japs and how bad they were – the war still seemed a faraway, pointless adventure.

Since Ralph turned up in uniform Jim's thinking had changed. He had been awkward and restrained with the boy during his visit, but once Ralph was gone Jim put the picture of him in his uniform up on the living room wall and asked, for the first time ever, to read Ralph's letters to his mother. He added one-line messages to Ethel's letters: *Your father sends his love and hopes you are keeping safe and well.* Safe and well. A strange message to send to a boy on a ship in the Pacific, strafed by kamikaze planes. Ethel had his letters, and a blue-star Son in Service flag to hang in the window that faced the courtyard.

The theatre was Saturday-night crowded: young kids Jimmy's age out in crowds, fellows in uniform out with their girls, a few old fogies like themselves. Jim had a bucket of popcorn on his lap and one arm draped over the back of Ethel's seat, just like they were on a date themselves. They laughed along with everyone else at the funny short that began the show, but then the newsreel came up. Ethel saw that it was called *Death on Okinawa*, and the rest of the theatre dropped away.

"I'm sorry," Jim said. "I never knew…well, you know there's going to be something about the war but not…do you want to leave?"

Ethel said nothing, her eyes on the screen, on the black-and-white images of men, boys, running and shooting and falling. It was just what the title promised, Death on Okinawa, and not just dead Japs but American boys and men. She was a taut string ready to be plucked, sitting in the stillness watching the awful mayhem.

Then she saw him. A glimpse, only a few seconds. A bloodied body, one of hundreds, carried past on a stretcher. White face, uniform, gaping chest wound.

"Jim! Jim! I saw him, I saw Ralph."

"What?"

Ethel stared at the screen. Would there be another glimpse? The man on that stretcher could not have been alive. And he could not have been Ralph. Except that he was. The camera closed for a split second on his face, and his mother knew.

"Ethel," Jim said in her ear, "did you say you saw Ralph?"

She whispered back without turning away from the screen. "On a stretcher, he was being carried off. It was him, Jim, I know it was."

"On a stretcher? No, no, couldn't have been. You must have imagined…"

Ethel was silent. The images flickered on but she saw nothing, only Ralph's face, the bleeding body. He was wounded, or worse. She pressed the back of her hand against her mouth, bit hard, felt nothing.

In the pause between the newsreel and the feature Jim leaned over again. "Ethel, don't drive yourself cracked now. You know that couldn't have been Ralph. Sure, these newsreels take awhile to make and send over here. If he was wounded or…if he was hurt we'd have had word by now."

"It was him," she said again.

"No, Ethel, some boy who looked a bit like him, is all. Some other poor sod, not our son." His arm moved from the back of the seat to her shoulders.

The credits rolled, the feature started. As soon as she saw a Japanese face on the screen Ethel stood up, blundered to the end of the row, up the aisle to the bathroom. The bathrooms here were glorious temples of marble and chrome and mirror glass, monuments to cleanliness and comfort. She just made it to a toilet before vomit flooded her mouth.

She stayed there a long time, even after she'd thrown up, kneeling on the floor, shaking. When she came out, Jim was waiting in the lobby.

"I'll take you home," he said. "You shouldn't get all worked up like this. It's nothing."

She fell into step beside him. "I know what I saw."

Out again through the red and gold lobby, under the marquee lights, into the crowded street. "It couldn't happen like that, Ethel. You couldn't see him dead – wounded – on a newsreel before we got a telegram. If we haven't heard from the War Office, then nothing's happened, see?"

It made sense; she knew it was true, but she also knew what she'd seen.

Back at the apartment Jimmy and Diane were home and fighting. "I don't know what you see in that guy Malone anyway, he's a creep," Jimmy said, and Diane yelled, "Yeah, you're jealous because Malone and all his crowd think you and your friends are sooo square."

"Square? Is that a fact? Well, I'll tell you one thing, little sister, I might not know what you see in Malone, but I sure know what he sees in you, and if I catch him laying a hand on you I'll knock him into the middle of next week, I swear."

The fight was so loud they failed to hear their parents coming in through the hall. They fell silent as Jim and Ethel entered. Jimmy said, "Hi Dad, hi Mom, where were you guys?" But Ethel drifted past the whole disturbing scene as if it didn't exist, said nothing to her daughter or younger son, went straight to the bedroom.

Beyond the doors she heard Jim saying, "Your mom's had a bit of a shock. We went to the movies, and the newsreel was about Okinawa. Naturally it's got her thinking about Ralph, so don't be surprised if she's…" Ethel shut her eyes, which was useless since the image she wanted to block out was on the inside of her eyelids.

Jim came in and lay on the bed beside her. They were both fully clothed. "Tell you what I'll do," he said at last. "Tomorrow morning I'll go down to the theatre and ask the guy to run the newsreel again so I can see it. I know it's not Ralph, but you'll feel easier if I've seen it and I can tell you it's not him, right? I'll do it while you're gone to church."

In the morning, for the first time in twenty years, Ethel did not go to church. She got dressed for it, down to her gloves and hat and handbag, then stood on the front step after Jim had gone off to the theatre and Diane and Jimmy had gone out. She couldn't think of a reason to go to church. Her long business arrangement with God was at an end. He was defaulting on payments and she had nothing left to offer Him.

She watched the other women, the other families from the building, leave for church – most, like the Romanos and the Pokornowskis, to the Catholic church, a few to the Episcopalian or her own Methodist church. Only the Jewish women were left, sunning themselves in their chairs on the small square of pavement between the steps and the street, sitting by the sun, as they said.

Mrs. Liebowitz came out, nodded to Ethel, paused. "You're not gone to the church this morning?"

"Not today, no." Ethel looked down at her dress, gloves, handbag, shoes. "I got dressed up to go, but…I had some bad news last night, kind of a shock, I guess, and I don't feel like going."

Mrs. Liebowitz put a hand on Ethel's arm. "Your boy?"

Ethel nodded, then hurried to explain. "We never got a telegram, but I saw this newsreel, the boys on Okinawa. I'm sure I saw his face, him being carried off on a stretcher. Jim says it couldn't be him, but I know it was…"

Mrs. Liebowitz nodded slowly. "A mother knows these things."

"That's it, I know it. I feel it right here." Ethel put her fist just below her breastbone. She first felt the pain there last night when she saw Ralph, like a swift stab from the point of a knife. Since then it had widened to a pain the size of her hand, an irregular burning shape bordering her heart and her stomach. It felt as if a wound there had been bandaged and now the bandage was torn away and she was bleeding. She clutched Mrs. Liebowitz's hand, these two women who had never touched before today.

"You come inside," said Mrs. Liebowitz.

Ethel followed her into the building, through the door across the hall from Ethel's own. There was a smell in the air, cooking odours Ethel couldn't identify. A thin woman stood at the gas stove stirring a pot. With a start, Ethel saw it was Rebecca Liebowitz, the little girl just Ralph's age, in a dark dress that reached her ankles, her hair covered under a headscarf. She wore it in braids down her back till the day she got married, at sixteen. Her young husband had been killed just after D-Day.

"Hello, Rebecca," Ethel said. She had offered the girl her condolences, long ago, and could find nothing else to say now. The older Liebowitz girl, Sarah, came in with her two-year-old on her hip. Mrs. Liebowitz drew Ethel past the girls, out of the kitchen into the room that in Ethel's apartment was the living room. In the Liebowitz apartment this room had a long dining table with straight-backed wooden chairs all around it. Books and papers were piled on one end of the table. Mrs. Liebowitz guided Ethel to a chair and placed a cup in front of her. Ethel took a sip and almost spit: she was expecting tea but this was very strong dark coffee.

"You drink that, it's good for you. What a shock, hey? I never heard of that, seeing someone on the newsreel before you get the telegram. But then, we don't go the movies."

"I hardly ever go," Ethel said, hearing her own voice like an echo. "It was a special treat, last night. Maybe...maybe I was mistaken," she added, trying to convince herself

Mrs. Liebowitz sat down heavily in a chair across the table from Ethel. "I hope it's not true. Your oldest son, that's a terrible thing. And when he just come home again, after so long time away."

Ethel nodded. "It makes me so angry," she said, suddenly finding words. "What's it all for, anyway? All this death, our boys dying in some foreign war. It makes no sense to me. We hear all the time how Hitler was so bad and the Japs are so bad, but why can't we just let them be? Let them live their lives and we live ours? Why do our sons have to die for what's happening thousands of miles away?" Her throat knotted and tears spilled from her eyes; she fumbled in her handbag for a handkerchief and dabbed at them. Looking up, she saw Mrs. Liebowitz's face had changed; the sisterly sympathy, one mother to another, had been replaced by something cold. Foreign, Ethel thought again.

"You think that? It's not America's business?" Mrs. Liebowitz leaned over, pulled a stack of newspapers from the other end of the table, thrust one into Ethel's hands. "You think you got trouble? Look at those people." Her thick finger jabbed at a picture on a page torn from *The New York Times*. Three men so emaciated they looked like skeletons stared at the camera, skimpy clothes hanging from their bodies. Ethel shuddered.

"I saw this before," she said. "Those Nazi camps our boys liberated."

"You think you know suffering, because your son is killed?" Mrs. Liebowitz's face was like stone. "You know nothing. Nothing. This boy...you sent him away to be raised. You were never a mother to him. Why do you cry for him? Ask what happened to my family: my brother, my sister, my nieces and nephews. Then come back and tell me about how Hitler was a bad man!"

She did not slap Ethel but she might as well have. Ethel stood, shaking. She looked at the picture again through blurred eyes and thought that God was not absent from the world, as she'd feared. That would be too easy. What she hadn't realized, in all her long struggle to bargain with God and pay for her sins, was that God was malignant, twisted – that He hated the world. She had thrown her life's energy into trying to appease a monster.

One of the girls – Sarah, it was Sarah, who used to mind Ethel's children when they were little – took her arm as she stumbled towards the door. "Forgive my mama, Mrs. Evans. She is terribly unhappy. She didn't mean to speak to you as she did." Ethel went through the door, turned back only to close it. Sarah tried once more. "I remember Ralphie so well," she said. "Such a bright little boy, such a smile. If I prayed anymore, I would pray for him, Mrs. Evans."

Ethel managed to nod. Then she was alone in the hallway, staring at the door of her own apartment. A man came through the front door of the building, scanning the board for names and numbers. He wore a uniform: he was a telegram delivery man.

An hour later, Jim came home, looking like an old man, walking with a slight stoop. Ethel was sitting in the armchair. Jimmy and Diane were in the kitchen finding something to eat, talking in whispers. Jim walked into the living room.

"I watched it over and over," he said. "Five times I made the guy show it to me." He looked at his feet. "I think you're right, Ethel. I think it looks like him too."

His words fell into a well of silence.

"The guy at the theatre, he said we should contact the War Office if we were sure. He said if we never got a telegram yet, he didn't see how it could be, but my God, Ethel, it looked so much like him. The eyes…"

Ethel still held the telegram crumpled in her hand, the telegram informing Mr. James Evans that Private Ralph Evans had been killed in action on Okinawa on the eighteenth of April. She stood up now and threw it in his face.

"My son is dead, Jim. And for twelve years I never got to touch him, hear his voice, hold his hand. I swear to God I'll never forgive you, not till the day I die. And I hope that's tomorrow."

She turned from him, went into the bedroom and locked the door.

CLAIRE

ST. JOHN'S, APRIL 1945

THE NEWS CAME BY telegram, a cable from Uncle Jim in New York: RALPH
KILLED IN ACTION OKINAWA APRIL 18 STOP.

Stop, stop, stop. The word punctuated the family babble and clatter of the
next few days. Claire wanted to put her hands over her ears, to shut out Aunt
Annie's voice: "I can't believe it, I should have known, I begged him not to go."
Aunt Frances' tears: "Poor Ethel, poor Ethel, this will kill her." Valerie's obsessive
memorializing: "Do you remember how Ralph used to... Do you remember when
he said..." Valerie made a little shrine out of two photos of Ralph, a clothespin doll
he made for her when she was six, and several newspaper headlines about the
fighting in Okinawa. She was working on a poem, a tribute. And Claire wanted
to scream at her, at them all, "STOP."

At night, Claire sat alone in her room while the kitchen below filled up
with relatives and grief. All the Evanses, the cousins, Aunt Ethel's relatives, the
neighbours, the families of boys Ralph used to run around with, some of whom
were overseas themselves now. They sat in the kitchen eating and drinking one cup
of tea after another, hearing over and over the story of how Ethel and Jim saw
him on the newsreel before they ever got the telegram. And Claire hid in her
room, wanting them all to stop, stop, STOP.

She had her geography homework spread over the bed. When Aunt Frances
came upstairs to find out what was wrong with her, she said, "I have homework
to do. I can't do it downstairs, there's too many people."

Aunt Frances frowned, her small face puckered up like a worried bird.
"Sure, you don't need to worry about homework, Claire girl. Your teachers will
understand; there's been a death in the family." Claire noticed that Aunt Frances
wouldn't usually say the word *death* or *died* – people passed away or passed on;
good Salvationists were Promoted to Glory. Soldiers in wartime, like Ralph, were

"lost," a word that suggested carelessness. But the phrase, death-in-the-family, all run together like that, was acceptable as an excuse. It permitted any sort of erratic behaviour.

Please excuse me from the kitchen. I need to stay in my room, as there has been a death-in-the-family, Claire thought. Aloud she said, "I don't want to fall behind. I have exams soon."

"So does Valerie," Aunt Frances said, and shook her head, backing away, pulling the door to behind her. Claire guessed that Aunt Frances was relieved that, for once, Valerie was the one behaving normally: crying, talking about Poor Ralph, sitting around the table drinking tea like a good girl.

Claire wondered how long the parade of people and condolences would last. When Poppy Evans had died – she was only little then – people came by every night before the funeral. But there would be no funeral for Ralph, not here anyway; they would have a memorial service for him at Aunt Ethel's church in Brooklyn, where no-one would remember him. Claire felt cheated. She hated funerals and didn't especially want there to be one, but this way there would be no clear end to the mourning. It could go on forever.

She picked up geography again, a book written before the war, listing the countries of Europe. Ralph had told her once it was a waste of time learning it; all the countries would be different after the war. She had said, "I can't write that on my geography test, Ralph."

"Sure you can. Just put down: *This question left unfinished until the end of the war. Please contact me after peace has been declared for a list of the countries of Europe.*"

Germany. Austria. Czechoslovakia. Poland. She leafed ahead, to the Pacific, a section of the book they had not yet covered. She had already looked there, finding Okinawa on the map. It seemed so small, hardly worth all the trouble.

A light tap at the door. "Come in," sighed Claire.

Valerie drifted in, sat down at the edge of the bed. She shoved school papers aside. "I don't see how you can study."

"Well, I can."

"I finished the poem. Do you want to see it?" Valerie's voice was very tiny, almost breathless. Like it wasn't enough to come in here and make Claire read the fool thing; she had to make Claire beg for it.

"Whatever you want," said Claire, wondering how it would feel to slap Valerie.

"Here." Valerie thrust the paper at her and turned away.

Valerie's handwriting, full of curls and flourishes, filled the torn-out exercise book sheet front and back.

A soldier boy of eighteen years
Full of dreams and hopes and fears
Set foot upon a foreign shore
From which he would return no more....

There was quite a lot of it: fourteen verses. Claire read as attentively as she could: she didn't like poetry. "It's very good," she said.

Valerie snatched it back, eyed her own words greedily. "I don't think it's really *that* good. The last verse...I wonder if it should be *weep his loss* or *mourn his loss*. What do you think?"

Claire shrugged. "I wouldn't have a clue. It means the same thing, doesn't it?" She stared at Valerie, who frowned over the page, hovering with her pen. Claire wondered how at a time like this – well, at any time, really – anyone could waste time or thought on something so insubstantial, so unimportant as choosing one word over another in a stupid poem.

"I'm going to put it up on the wall after I make a copy," Valerie said. "I wish you'd give me the other doll, the one Ralph made for you, if you're not doing anything special with it. I could have both of them up there together, like a set."

"I don't know where it is," said Claire, and looked down at her geography. The silence was sharp, with edges.

"How come you won't come down in the kitchen?" Valerie said, folding the paper. "Mom says it's queer for you to stay locked up in your room doing homework."

"Then I'm queer," said Claire. "An oddball. An odd sock. I just don't want to be down there. Why do all these people have to hang around, anyway?"

Valerie stood. "To show their sympathy," she said. "It makes people feel better, in time of loss." The phrase was practiced, like something from her poem.

When Valerie had gone, Claire opened her bottom drawer. She kept very little of the past, as little as possible. Underneath neatly folded underclothes, slips and stockings, she had her mother's last two letters, and a card Aunt Annie gave her on her thirteenth birthday, with a picture she liked on it. A photograph of herself and Ralph in Uncle Harold's new house before it was all built. Her report card from Grade Six: *Claire is a very bright girl who works hard and shows great promise.* The clothespin doll Ralph made for her when she was six, lying facedown at the bottom of the drawer. Claire did not pick it up, but turned it over with a finger, so it faced up into the whiteness of her cotton underwear.

She went out of the room and down the stairs, pausing at the bottom. Laughter drifted out from the kitchen. Nobody was actually talking about Ralph:

they were talking about some other fellow, some old fellow way back in the first war, the Great War, who went out on purpose trying to "get blighty" so he'd get sent back home. "Of course he came through without a scratch," said old Mr. Winsor. "God looks out for fools."

"Only the good die young," said Mrs. Stokes, and there was a little circle of silence under the hissing of the kettle. In the yellow light of the doorway Claire saw Aunt Annie standing alone at the stove, her hand on the handle of the kettle, frozen for a moment. *He's more my son than Ethel's*, she remembered Aunt Annie saying to Nan, months before, when Ralph went away. She remembered the fierce anger in Aunt Annie's voice. And Claire went down the stairs, into the kitchen, like a good girl.

ANNIE

THE BACK DOOR TO the kitchen opened with a bang. "Hello, Aunt Annie!" Valerie called, as Claire slung her book bag down on the floor.

"I'm only stopping to change out of my uniform and drop off some of my books," Claire announced. "We're going up to Val's house to work on an assignment." She ran up the stairs.

Valerie sat down at the end of the table. "On Shakespeare," Valerie said with a happy smile. "For literature."

Annie shook her head as she kneaded bread dough. "Claire won't be pleased about that," she said. Claire was always complaining about English Literature although her grades in it were just fine.

"No, that's why we're doing it together. She says she needs my help or she'll never get through it," Valerie said, and Annie noted the light in her clear blue eyes, the lift in her voice. There was more rivalry between the girls than there used to be. Time was when they were almost like one person with two heads, always together, but now Claire was coming into her own, a natural leader who was popular with all the girls her age. Valerie, on the other hand, was beginning to seem a bit – well, odd. There was no other word for it. They were both good girls, mind, but different. As they should be. But Annie didn't truly mind that her own girl, her Claire, was turning out the best of the two.

"Come on, let's get going. We've only got a couple of hours for you to explain everything about Shakespeare to me," Claire announced, sweeping back into the kitchen and scooping Valerie out the back door. "I'll be back before supper, Aunt Annie!" she called over her shoulder.

Annie's mother was asleep. She lay down for a nap on the daybed every afternoon now, like a child, and nothing woke her until half an hour before supper when she got up like someone rising from the tomb and demanded a cup of tea. Usually Annie watched Kenny and Danny after school but today Frances had the afternoon off work. Annie was alone in her kitchen.

A tap at the door. "Come in!" Annie called. She heard an odd step – a hesitation, a thump, another step – and Bill Winsor was in the kitchen.

She had heard on Friday that he was back. All through the weekend she'd refused to admit to herself that she was waiting for him to come to the door. Now he was here, not so changed she wouldn't have known him, but changed all the same. He had been thirty-six when he joined up and went overseas; now he was forty-one, but he had aged more than five years. She would have said he was closer to fifty, seeing this man on the street, his heavily lined face, his grey hair.

Her eyes lingered on his face, but when they held too long on his eyes, she shifted hers and could not help looking where she had been trying not to look: to his leg, the one pant leg hanging strangely over the artificial limb. His hand gripped a walking stick and she could see from the cords of muscle in his arm that he was leaning heavily on it.

"Sit down, Bill, do," she said, bustling out from behind the table to pull out a chair for him. He almost tripped over her, trying to get to the chair, and she pulled back, blushing, wondering if she had done the wrong thing. A man pulled a chair out for a woman; you didn't usually do it the other way, unless the man was old or feeble.

But Bill was looking around the kitchen, a smile on his face. "Annie's kitchen," he said. "By the jumpin's, Annie, it's good to be back here. Just like I remembered it too...only you got a different tablecloth on today: I was always thinking about the red and white one."

"That's worn to rags. I threw that out," Annie said. She stood uncertainly in the middle of the room, wondering what to do or say to make this meeting normal, comfortable. Then she remembered. "Cup of tea?" she offered.

"Yes, thanks," Bill said. "A cup of tea in Annie's kitchen." He took it from her and instead of drinking at once, cupped his hands around it as though he were chilled, though it wasn't that cold outside. "I can't tell you, Annie girl, how many times over there – over in England, but all the more once we got overseas – how I'd be lying frozen half to death in some bombed-out house, listening to gunfire off in the distance, trying to get some sleep, and I'd say to myself, 'Now, Bill, just think yourself back in Annie's kitchen, sitting down to that red and white tablecloth, and Annie kneading bread or mixing up a cake at the other end of the table, drinking a cup of tea.' And I'd build it all up like a picture in my mind, not knowing if I'd ever be here again in real life."

There was a small, warm, round silence after he finished speaking. "And here you are," Annie said.

She pulled apart the leftover ends of the dough, making a few toutons to put on for supper. Bill drank his tea and looked around the kitchen as if he couldn't get enough of it. Whenever his eyes lit on Annie she looked back down at the smooth balls of dough she rolled in her hands. She liked pressing them flat between her palms.

"So now I got to think what to do next," Bill said at last, and laid down his cup.

"Oh, no rush for that yet, is there? You wants time to...to get used to everything, you know?" Annie waved a hand vaguely; she had heard enough stories about men coming back, adjusting to life at home after all those years overseas. And Bill had his leg, too. Or rather, didn't have his leg. "Wince and Marge are glad to have you home. I'm sure you can wait till after the winter's done before you have to go making plans."

"Never too soon to start making plans, Annie love, that's what I realized when I was over there," Bill said. "Here I am now, a grown man, past forty, and there were all these younger fellows around me, fellows with wives and children and homes of their own back here. I thought, 'You know, Bill, if one of those fellows were to die tomorrow' – and plenty of them did, girl, plenty of them did – 'at least he's lived, you know? He's had a family, a life, people who love him.' And what did I have? Nothing and no-one, when you come right down to it."

"Don't be so foolish, Bill. You got family, friends, there's plenty would have missed you if you hadn't come back. You know...sure, you got my letters, you know how I prayed for you every night, how I would have felt if you'd...if you hadn't come back."

He nodded. "Oh, I know, Annie. I counted on those prayers. No, it's only–" He broke off, a long sigh interrupting his words. He looked down at his hands. "Hard to put into words," he said, and didn't try anymore. Annie could hear the clock. She threw fatback into the cast-iron frying pan; its sizzle filled the empty air.

"Do you think you'll go back down to Bonavista?" she said at last.

Another deep breath, this one sucked in. "I gave it some thought," he said. "Much like I thought about your kitchen when I was away, I thought about the house down Bonavista – so quiet, so peaceful, like. I'd love to be back there again." Annie dropped touton dough into the spitting fat and waited for him to go on. "But what would I do down there? I can't fish now. Six months it's been since they gave me this leg, and I'm used to getting around. There's a lot I can do, but there's a lot more I can't do."

Annie turned from the stove and at last met his eyes. This time it was Bill who looked away, once again at the yellow walls of her kitchen like it was the walls he was in love with, down at the teacup with a lover's tenderness. Annie moved over and started wiping flour off the table with long smooth strokes.

"You got a lot of responsibilities here, Annie, running this house, looking after your mother and Claire all on your own," he said.

"Claire's a great help. She don't really like housework, but she's a grand hand to do it all the same."

The back door slammed open again and Harold's boys bolted through it. "Aunt Annie, Mom says can we come down here for supper, us and Dad?" Kenny said. "She got to go to a meeting at church, six o'clock. She says she don't have time to give us supper."

"Yes, fine. Mind you, I only got salt fish. You don't like that, Danny."

"I do, I like it now. Can I turn on the radio?"

"Is there drawn butter?" Kenny asked.

"Are those toutons?" said Danny, turning from the radio to the stove.

"Annie! Annie! Come in and give me a hand to get up off this daybed." Her mother's querulous voice drifted in from the living room.

Annie darted a look of apology at Bill, who sat with his teacup, an island in the torrent. He stood up and Kenny stared with open curiosity. "Is it true, Mr. Winsor, you got a wooden leg?"

"Hush, Kenny," said Annie.

"Can we see it?" Danny asked eagerly.

"*Hush!*"

"I'll give you a hand with your mother, Annie," Bill said. She glanced at his leg, at the walking stick, but having just told the boys to hush she could hardly say anything. He limped along behind her, into the front room. Mrs. Evans was sitting up on the side of the daybed. She blinked at Bill.

"Bill Winsor," she said. "Back in one piece, then."

"Nearly, Mrs. Evans," he said. Annie caught his eye over her mother's head and they both smiled.

Bill settled the old woman in her big chair at the head of the table as Annie went back to the stove to turn over the toutons. She heard Bill's uneven step below the clatter of the radio, the boys, her mother's complaint that the tea was too strong.

He came over and put a hand on her waist, bent his head down close to her ear. "Will you marry me, Annie?"

Tears came to her eyes at once and she didn't dare look up, not here, in the kitchen, in the middle of everything. The door banged open again and the boys yelled, "Dad!" Harold was home from work, stamping his boots, hugging his sons.

Annie looked at the toutons and nodded. "Yes. Yes, I'll marry you, Bill, if that's what you want." Fatback spat in the pan as she turned over the last touton.

DIANE

BROOKLYN, SEPTEMBER 1947

SATURDAY MORNING, DIANE AND Carol are having breakfast at the A-1 Diner on the corner down from Diane's building. On Saturday Diane tries to leave home as early as she can, before her mother thinks up a chore for her to do. Today Carol has money because she babysat for the Goldmans last night. Diane thinks how the solid folded pad of money, two one-dollar bills, must feel against Carol's palm. Diane has fifty cents, which will be down to thirty-five when they finish breakfast.

"Wanna go to a show this afternoon?" Carol says. "I heard Davy say yesterday after school him and some guys were gonna go see the Charlie Chan movie today. You wanna catch that later on? My treat," she adds, out of the richness of her bounty.

In the booth behind Diane are two women about her mother's age. Diane has seen them here before. One is dark and one is blond – like herself and Carol. Once she said to Carol, "They could be us, in twenty or thirty years." They had giggled over that, over the idea that in thirty years they might still live on Linden Boulevard, still be best friends, still eat at the A-1 Diner.

The dark-haired woman dominates the conversation in a hard, shiny voice that matches the chrome edging of the tables and counter. "...and I told him, I said, George, it's not natural, is it? *Is* it?" Her voice points the question like a fork at her companion; Diane can almost see the gesture. Carol leans over for the ketchup and slops it all over her eggs. Now her plate matches the seats and the tabletops: red on yellow.

"Whaddya think?" Carol demands.

"A movie? Sure," Diane says. She likes movies, and besides, if Davy Ryan is going, then so are Buster Kemp and Mickey Malone. Last Saturday at the movies, Mickey Malone put his hand on her breast. Just for a minute. She can still feel the handprint there, glowing under her white cardigan.

"No, it is *not* normal. And I mean, for a man, a man who's on the road, what...six days? Six days, and he comes home, and there I am, all ready." The dark-haired woman still holds forth; her blond friend makes small sympathetic sounds. "I have the kids at Ma's place, I bought a new dress, I had my hair done, and George, what does George do? Comes in, kicks off his shoes, lays down on the couch and is asleep in ten minutes. What kind of a man, I ask you."

"We could go down to Macy's on the subway," says Carol. "I want a scarf to go with this blouse and Mom said I could buy what I wanted with my babysitting money."

"If I had money, my mom would make me hand it over," Diane grumbles, poking at her toast with her knife, trying to get the strawberry jam to spread. "She would make me give her every red cent, I swear. She doesn't want me to have anything, any life of my own."

But Diane is only half-listening to her own conversation with Carol: the voices of the women behind them are so much more engrossing. "It wasn't always like this, you know," says the dark-haired one, her words punctuated by the clink of her knife and fork on the plate.

"No, I know it wasn't," says her friend, her loyal supporter. Diane is surprised by how soft the blond woman's voice is. She sounds wistful. "When me and Frank was married first–"

"Same story, I know it, the very same story," says the dark-haired woman. "Back when we were married first, George was on the road then, and when he came home, he couldn't wait to get me into the bedroom. I kid you not, one time – this was before the kids of course – he *couldn't* wait. Right there on the living room carpet. I swear."

Diane feels her toes curl inside her saddle shoes. Quickly she raises her own voice, tries to make it hard and bright like that of her shadow-self in the next booth. "I shoulda gone to Dad for money. Dad's a soft touch, and if he gave me money, it would make Mom crazy."

Carol giggled lightly. "She still doesn't talk to him?" Giggle, giggle. Diane's crazy family.

"I swear, not a word. She won't even give me a message for him. She'll stand in the middle of the kitchen and look up at the ceiling like she's talking to God. 'I don't suppose your father even knows the gas bill is due this week.'" She puts on Ethel's voice, with the faint traces of her Newfoundland accent that Diane can imitate and always crack up her friends, the same way Levi Liebowitz can make people laugh when he pretends to be his mother, crooning, *Ah, mein leetle*

Levi. Mothers with funny accents, funny habits like not talking to your father for at least two years. If you can get a laugh, use it.

Does anyone else notice that Levi makes them laugh with how much his mother loves him, how embarrassing her love is, and Diane gets a laugh with how much her mother hates her, hates Diane's father, hates the whole world? No joke, no fast words for Carol could ever capture the heavy silence of that apartment, where her mother sits at one end of the table and her father at the other behind a newspaper, never saying a word. Diane and Jimmy marooned in the middle, drowning in a sea of silence.

But who cares? School five days a week, choir and Young People's on Sunday no matter how boring it gets, and out all day Saturday with Carol and the gang. Only home long enough to pick up new material for her routines, funny-funny Diane and her funny family.

The girls take the subway downtown, wedged in among crowds of Saturday shoppers. At Macy's, they try on dresses and talk about the junior prom. They are sophomores, but hoping for prom invites from junior boys. Mickey Malone is a junior, if he stays in school for the rest of the year. Diane holds up a pink dress – New Look – and stares at her reflection in the mirror.

Carol holds up something she really can buy: a green scarf that shines like emeralds against her blond hair. Or like Diane imagines emeralds would shine, not having seen any in real life. The scarf looks expensive – it's fifty cents – and Carol is going to buy it.

On the rack next to it is a red one with a gold thread running through it. It slips through Diane's fingers like water. Wraps around her hand while she watches Carol try on the green scarf and take it to the checkout.

Outside, Diane is almost surprised to feel the red scarf still in her pocket. It weighs almost nothing there, does not seem to take up space. Instead, the weight is in her stomach, something cold about the size and shape of a potato. She imagines her mother, Ethel, saying sorrowfully, *I'm so disappointed, Diane. I didn't raise you to be this kind of a girl. Your brother Ralphie died for his country, what would he think of you now?*

Diane stops in front of a store window on Fulton Street and pulls out the red scarf, winds it around her hair, rubies against her dark curls. Carol turns sharply. "Where'd you get that?"

"At Macy's."

"I didn't see you buy it." Carol frowns, suspicious.

"I got it at another checkout. While you were getting yours." She can see Carol doesn't believe her. "I had more money than I thought."

She doesn't, of course. With the subway fare back to Flatbush she has exactly enough left for the movie. But it's worth it, to see the shock in Carol's eyes and know, or imagine, that it's half envy. And the money works out okay after all, because Davy Ryan and Mickey Malone and some other guys are hanging around outside the Loew's Kings, and the girls go up and talk to them.

"So, you going in to see the movie?" Mickey growls, in that voice that makes Diane's toes curl.

"I guess so, unless something better comes along," she says.

Mickey gives a quick jerk of his head. "Come on," he says, putting a hand on Diane's arm, and steers her to the ticket booth, laying down enough money for both of them. Diane knows it's important to have something to say, not too much but a few quick, light, funny words. She looks up at Mickey with his brown hair lit by faint gold streaks and his green eyes with the golden flecks in them. A few childish freckles are still caught on his nose, as if they haven't noticed the rest of his face is a man's face now. Diane feels cold in her stomach, hot in her throat, and in between, on her breast where Mickey is looking, the glowing imprint of his hand.

"Well let's not stand here all day," she says, to Mickey and the others. "I don't wanna miss the feature." And she steps a little ahead, to lead the way into the show.

ANNIE

_⟫_

THE MATTRESS ON BILL and Annie's bed was an old one that sagged in the middle. It was Mom and Pop's mattress and got passed down to Annie. She'd never noticed the sag in it when she slept alone, but now, with Bill in the bed, she found herself rolling into the middle, pressed uncomfortably against his warm back. When she tried to roll back to her own side of the bed it was like crawling uphill.

Maybe, Annie thought, forty was too old to start sleeping with someone else. Not like she'd always had a room to herself. When she was a girl she used to share the bed with Rose, then she had a few years on her own. Then for ages she slept on the front room couch while Pop was on the daybed, in case he'd wake at night and need anything. During the war, when Harold and Frances and all their crowd moved in, and afterwards when they rented out the front room, she shared the bed with her mother. These past couple of years she'd gone back to sleeping alone and loved it. No fighting over the bedclothes. No great lump of body in the bed with you, putting out heat like you were sleeping next to the furnace. No-one always trying to tuck in her feet when she liked them cool, sticking out from under the covers on all but the coldest nights. When they were children, she remembered, her mother would send them to bed in winter with a hot-water bottle and Rose would hug it all night like a lover. Annie only wanted to get as far from the thing as possible. That one thing, at least, Annie and Rose never fought over.

Bill snored, too. Pop used to snore. She'd hear the sound of it coming through the walls and wonder how Mom could sleep through it.

Taken all in all, Annie liked being married. But it took some getting used to, no denying that.

She was forty years old, and a good girl, though not as sheltered as her mother still seemed to think. She knew what men and women did together in

_⟫_

bed, but there was a difference between knowing and – well, knowing. She had washed the bodies of little boys – *Ralphie*, she thought, and tried not to picture him bloody and dying on a battlefield far away – and of old men, Pop and her grandfather before him. She knew what a man's body was like, but not how it felt to have one, alive and vigorous, on top of her. Nothing had prepared her for that.

It struck her as strange, sometimes, that all she would ever know of marital relations would be with a one-legged man, that she'd never know how it might have been with a man who had two good legs. Bill seemed apologetic about that, and she did not remind him that she had nothing to compare it to.

All her life she'd heard women talk about the marriage bed, about having relations, in hushed tones. Their eyes slid away from each other's faces when they discussed it. They curbed themselves if she was there. In the last ten years they'd been less guarded, forgetting perhaps that Annie was still a spinster, or more likely, taking her spinsterhood as so much of a fact it didn't even give them pause. "Well, us married women have our cross to bear too, my dear," Mrs. Captain Avery had told her, patting her on the shoulder.

"Sure, the mister don't want it no more at all now, not since he took that bad fall last year, and that's a blessing, I don't mind saying," Mrs. Stokes had once told Annie's mother.

"You should be on your knees thanking the Lord," her mother had replied.

But in spite of all that, it wasn't so bad. Not painful at all, except for the first time, and she'd been warned about that so she was prepared. After that it was fine. Not as pleasant as sitting with your feet in a basin of hot water after being on them all day, but nice enough. Lately, though, she'd begun to wonder about the point of it. They'd been at it for a year and no sign of a baby at all. And she was forty on her birthday.

Lots of women, of course, had babies after forty; Mom was forty-one when Harold was born. But a first baby? Annie couldn't think of any woman she'd ever heard of who'd had a first baby after she was forty, except for poor Christina Tucker down in Little Catalina, forty-five when she finally got pregnant, and neither her nor the baby lived.

So she hadn't held out too much hope. But oh, she wanted a baby of her own. She remembered bathing Claire when she was tiny, lathering up the soap to make one big curl at the top of her head. Claire would squint her eyes to keep out the soap bubbles. Then Annie would wrap her in a big towel and lift her out of the sink and carry her into the kitchen, to dry her off in front of the stove where it was nice and warm. Ralphie would be there then too, curled up half-asleep on the daybed by the stove, thumb in his mouth.

Last month, Annie had missed her monthlies. She used to be real regular, never skipping it or even being late a day, though in the last year that had changed and she was sometimes late. That was why she didn't think much at first, when it didn't come. But the whole of September went by without getting it, and now they were well into October, up to when she should be having it again. If it didn't come this month…

Well, she wouldn't get her hopes up. Wouldn't tell Bill, not yet anyway. And who else could she tell? She didn't think of telling Frances, who still went to business not because she needed to but because she liked to. Frances seemed to have become somehow – unwomanly. As if house and home were the least of her concerns.

Yet it was Frances, the next evening, who broached a very womanly subject as the two of them sat at Annie's kitchen table. She sipped her tea and said with characteristic briskness, "Annie, has Claire started having her periods yet?"

Annie was startled, though she couldn't think why she should be. Claire was fifteen, nearly sixteen. "No, she hasn't started yet," Annie said.

"Have you talked to her about it?" Frances' nails, shiny with a clear polish, clicked on the tabletop.

"No, I haven't said anything…" Annie's voice trailed off. If she hadn't told Claire, then what did Claire know? What she'd heard from other girls, no doubt. Who else did she have to go to, other than her Aunt Annie?

"Well, Valerie started last year, and I told her all about it, so I imagine she's told Claire the basics. And when she does start, I suppose she'll come to you, so you can give her the sanitary napkins, show her how to use them, that sort of thing." Annie said nothing, feeling the great gulf between herself and Frances. Annie knew what sanitary napkins were, of course, but she used the old-fashioned flannels, washing them out each month. Should she learn the newfangled way, for Claire's sake?

"And one of us will have to have a little talk with her," Frances went on. "I mean, when a girl gets to that age…well, there are things she needs to know. And Claire has no mother to tell her."

Annie nodded. Claire had a mother who wasn't here to tell her, and that was the very reason she needed to know. To be warned. Annie couldn't imagine what she might say to Claire, who at fifteen was already so sensible, so cool, so contained. She'd never said a saucy word that Annie could remember, but she kept her own distance. A private person, something Annie approved of.

"I can speak to her, if you'd rather," Frances said, lifting her eyebrows just a little. Her eyebrows were so shapely, so carefully plucked. Annie just let hers grow in, any which way. It was Frances who taught Claire to pluck her eyebrows. It would be easier to let Frances – a real married woman, a mother, a woman of the world – handle this, too.

But no. Annie laid her teacup down in the saucer and looked at its faded pattern of blue flowers and green leaves. "No, by rights I'm the one should do it, Frances. I'm the one has stood in place of her mother all these years. And anyway, I don't say Claire will need much telling. She's a good girl."

"All the same, there are things she should know. Especially in her case." Frances said no more, but Annie felt the weight of it like a pillowcase full of wet laundry on her back. She carried that burden, of all the things she needed to tell Claire.

She carried it for several more days, while she waited for her own bleeding to start, and weighed what she might say to Claire. She tried to remember what her own mother had said to her and Rose, but could remember nothing. Whatever it was, it must have been very effective in her case, and completely useless in Rose's. So perhaps it didn't matter.

But it seemed the timing was good, or maybe Frances had the second sight, because on Friday evening Claire came to the door of Annie's room while she was turning down the bed. "Um, Aunt Annie, I need…uh, I just need to know…that is, I…" The girl's voice, usually so measured and confident, trailed away.

"What is it, my love?"

"Well, the thing is, I've…ah…I've started having my…you know, my…my periods. Just today. At school. I told Valerie about it, and she gave me a…um, you know. But now I need…"

"I know what you need, my dear. Come with me and I'll show you where I keep the flannels. You can wash them out in a bucket of cold water and then put them in with the rest of the laundry. Are you feeling all right? Do you have any pain or anything?"

"Just a little bit," Claire said. "Valerie told me all about it, so I knew what to expect. Valerie uses Kotex," she added.

"Yes, lots of the younger women do. Maybe you'll want to get some of your own later on. You can ask your Aunt Frances about that. But for now I'll get you the flannels. And just let me get you a hot-water bottle. Sometimes that makes me feel better, to lie down with a hot-water bottle."

Annie went downstairs and filled a hot-water bottle from the kettle, walked slowly back upstairs and into Claire's room. Claire was lying down already, half-curled. Annie handed her the hot-water bottle and paused, looking down at her.

"Thank you," Claire said.

"You know, now, once you starts your monthlies, you can...you can have a baby."

Claire, who had closed her eyes, opened them again, a little startled. "I know about that. Aunt Frances explained it all to Valerie and Val told me."

"Oh. That's good then." So she knew the facts. And what more was there to say? Be a good girl? Don't go into a dark lane with a fellow? Surely Claire had more sense. What Annie really wanted to say was, *Look at you, all grown up.* She recalled again bathing Claire's small body when she was a baby, and felt a physical pain at the knowledge that Claire was nearly a woman and would soon be gone.

"You look so much like your mother," Annie said abruptly, and went out, closing the door.

She went downstairs and made herself a cup of tea. Her mother sat in the rocking chair, endlessly knitting. "Young Claire gone to bed already?"

"Yes, she's not feeling so good. I brought her up the hot-water bottle."

Mom nodded. Her needles clicked.

"Some warm in here," Annie said.

Mom looked up from her knitting and studied Annie's face. "You're right flushed, Annie, and 'tis not warm in here at all, in fact it's a bit cool, if anything. You wants to stir up the stove a little."

Annie waved a hand in front of her face, not wanting to think about stirring up the coals. "Well, it feels warm to me."

"And so it should. I was the same way, my dear, when I was on the change."

Annie looked up sharply. "Oh no, Mom, I'm not..."

Her mother nodded and looked back at her knitting. "Oh yes, just like me. Hot flashes all hours of the day. Of course, I was forty-five, but plenty of women starts it at forty. High time you was finished with all that."

Annie stared at her mother, then at the stove. Two months gone by now. And she had been having hot flashes.

She drew a heavy sigh and went over to open up the stove. *Thank goodness,* she thought, *I never said nothing to Bill.*

CLAIRE

ST. JOHN'S, MAY 1948

VALERIE HAD A TRUNK open on her bed; she was pulling books from her shelves and very slowly placing them in the trunk, a job which took her forever because she would get sidetracked by a book and sit down to read it. "*Little Women*," she sighed as she riffled the pages. A wisp of dust drifted up. "Remember acting this out when we were little?"

"I remember," Claire said. Valerie made her be Beth and she had to cough a lot and die young. Valerie always wanted to be Jo, because Jo was a writer. Claire's own favourite character was Meg, the sensible one who kept them all in line. Valerie used to say Meg and Amy weren't important; if there were only two of them they could do it with just Jo and Beth and pretend Meg and Amy were in another room.

Valerie laid the book down gently on top of her stack of Royal Readers in the trunk. "I'm not going to have any room left for clothes," she said.

"You've got ages, you know," Claire said. "You're not even leaving till school is out. It'd make more sense to be studying for your CHEs. If you want to go to university, you need to spend more time on your exams."

"I suppose so." Valerie sank down on the bed. "I won't ever really get to go to university, will I?" She turned her large pale eyes on Claire as if Claire could somehow look into the future.

Claire shrugged and dropped down on the bed beside her. "I don't know, Val. It's awfully expensive, and I don't think it's easy for girls to get in unless they've got extra-high marks. That's why you need to give it your best shot–"

"I don't know why *you're* not going to university. You've got the great marks and you're awfully smart and ambitious. If you came with me, we could both apply to the University of Toronto." Valerie ran her fingers through her hair and started gathering strands on top of her head, trying, Claire thought, to look like somebody out of one of her boring old Jane Austen novels.

"I don't see the point of it, honestly. I don't want to be a teacher, and what else could you do with a university degree? I want a job, so I took the commercial course. By the end of August I'll be working in an office on Water Street, earning my own money."

"I don't want to be a teacher either," Valerie said, pouting. She stood up and pulled more books off the shelves. "I want to be a writer. But that's not a *job*. Mom says I have to prepare myself for something."

"Valerie? Are you home? Where are your brothers?" Aunt Frances called from downstairs, shutting the door behind her. Click, click, click. Her heels came up the stairs, and she stood in the doorway, smart as paint in her work clothes, her hat perched on her neat curls. She pulled off her gloves a finger at a time, looking around the room with a single frown line between her eyebrows.

"They're over at Aunt Annie's," Valerie said.

"Are you still at those dusty old books? I wish you'd go through your clothes and decide what's worth taking and what to leave behind. Of course most of our things are going to look out of date in Toronto. I'll take you down on Yonge Street, Valerie, and we'll get you some lovely new outfits. Now, Claire, you know it's never too late to change your mind about coming with us," Aunt Frances continued, turning to her. "You're still giving it some thought, aren't you? I've talked to Annie and she agrees it would be a wonderful chance for you. You've got excellent marks in the commercial course, you'll have no trouble finding a good job. You'd really have a chance of getting ahead, meeting someone nice."

"Yes, thank you, Aunt Frances. I'm still thinking it over," Claire replied, and got a beaming smile in return. She had a gift for pleasing other people's mothers: unlike real daughters, she always spoke politely and seemed grateful for advice and attention.

Walking down the lane between the houses half an hour later, Claire wondered what advice her own mother might give her. Rose's letters and cards arrived erratically; one year there might be a card for her birthday, the next year her birthday would pass unmarked and a letter would arrive months later. *I'm sure you are being a good girl for Mother and Annie,* she wrote last Christmas. *Work hard in school and don't go around with boys. Nobody knows the troubles I've seen. Hugs and Kisses, Your Loving Mother.* Claire had been unsure what to make of that letter, and had not been sorry when it was misplaced. One time she used to keep old letters and foolishness like that, but when she turned sixteen she cleared out the drawer where she kept those things and threw most of them away.

Aunt Frances was right, of course. She would have far more opportunities in

Toronto than she'd ever have here. The idea of leaving school, getting a job, making her own way in the world, was exciting. The idea of doing it in a big city, far from St. John's, was even better. Aunt Annie seemed to approve. She said how much she'd miss Claire, of course, but Claire wondered. Ever since Annie and Bill got married they had had family tripping over them. They might like to be able to sit down and eat a meal in peace without the whole family trooping in and out through the back door.

Claire let herself in and sat down at the kitchen table. Aunt Annie was setting the table for supper; she looked up and smiled when Claire came in. Aunt Annie had some grey in her hair now, peeking out among the dusty brown underneath the bandanna she always wore tied over her head in the kitchen, and she had lines around her eyes.

"Where's Bill and the boys?" Claire asked Annie. "I thought I would have passed the boys coming down the lane."

"Oh, they talked Wince Winsor into giving them a ride home in the car," Annie said. Uncle Bill's brother had recently acquired an old Packard and Kenny and Danny thought it was the greatest treat in the world to go for rides in it. "Once they're in Toronto they'll look back and laugh, to think it was such a big deal to ride in a car," Aunt Annie added. "You can hardly walk on the street for all the cars up in Toronto, from what I hear tell. Certainly if it's anything like New York, from what Jim and Ethel says."

"Answer me this," Grandmother said from her chair. "Toronto. With the rest of the family down in Brooklyn. Why couldn't they go to New York along with Ethel and Jim, someplace where they already got people? If they had to go away again, why wouldn't they go back to New York? I never heard tell of anybody going to Toronto."

"Two boys in my class are going to Toronto once school is over," Claire volunteered. "After all, we'll be part of Canada soon enough."

"Well now, that's not a foregone conclusion, is it?" Annie said. She was rather torn on the question of Confederation, as Bill and his family were against it, but Harold and Frances were voting for it.

"Canada!" Grandmother said with some venom. Her only position on the issue – as on any other – was to disagree with the last opinion anyone expressed. "Why not leave well enough alone? There'll always be an England, you know."

"Yes, yes, I suppose there will," Aunt Annie said soothingly. "Of course there will."

"God save the King," Grandmother said. "Canada, my foot. Oh, I dropped a stitch." She handed her knitting needles to Annie.

"Well, of course, there'll always be an England, but England won't always look after us, will they?" Claire countered. "And why would we want them to? The Commission of Government hasn't done a thing for Newfoundland. Mr. Smallwood knows what he's doing if you ask me."

"My goodness, you do know a lot," Aunt Annie said, picking up her mother's dropped stitch and handing the knitting back to her. "I suppose they talk about it at school all the time, do they?"

"Yes, and it's a shame the young people can't vote, because it's our future that's being decided." Claire was all for Confederation; she'd competed in a debating contest at school and her team – pro-Confederate – had won easily. She was one of only two girls on the debating team and Mr. Hobbs had told her she ought to go to Memorial College – which just seemed to bring everything back from the broad question of Newfoundland's future to the narrower one of Claire Evans' future.

"Aunt Frances was talking to me again about coming with them," she said, taking chicken from the frying pan to a plate and laying it on the table. She looked quickly at Aunt Annie, thinking that maybe if she could catch her aunt off-guard, she might see what Aunt Annie really felt about the idea of Claire going to Toronto. But Aunt Annie's face looked as composed and sensible as ever.

"It's something to consider, indeed," Annie said, putting out the creamed potatoes. "It's a great opportunity. Seems there's more people every day going away, off to the States or to Canada. Makes you wonder if there'll be anyone left here in twenty-five years." She stirred the gravy and sprinkled another pinch of salt into it. "One thing I keep thinking of, is how much you'd miss Valerie when she goes. Sure, you and her have been like two twins almost since you were born."

Claire busied herself with the carrots, straining them into the sink and turning them out into a dish. The same thought, albeit from a different angle, was on her mind. If she went to Toronto with Valerie's family, she'd never get shut of Valerie. They'd be doomed to go through their whole lives lashed together like some poor pair of losers in a three-legged race.

Bill came back in and sat down at the table. Grandmother shuffled over and Claire took her own seat as Aunt Annie brought the gravy boat over and set it down. "I hope that gravy's not too salty, Annie," Grandmother said. "You got too heavy a hand with the salt, I can't stand salty gravy."

"Last time you said it was too fresh," Aunt Annie said, but she didn't sound as if she minded at all. Claire knew that she herself would go crazy in a second if she had to keep house under Grandmother's nose and keep up with all her whims.

After supper Claire sat at the table with her books spread out, studying for her geometry exam. Aunt Annie was washing dishes, Grandmother was still knitting, and Uncle Bill listened to the radio with the sound down low, which was supposed to keep from disturbing her while she studied but was in fact more annoying than if he'd had it going full-blast. Mr. Smallwood was on talking about Confederation again, and the words drifted in and out of Claire's mind, twining together with the proof of the Pythagorean theorem until neither one made any sense.

The back door opened and Valerie came in, her own geometry book under her arm. "Can I study with you?" she asked Claire, slipping into the seat beside her.

"What, you mean, can I explain it all to you while you draw pictures in the margin of your exercise book?" Claire said sharply.

"Don't be mean. You understand it and I don't, and we've got an exam in three days. I keep forgetting what the hypotenuse is."

"It's the long side on a right-angled triangle," Claire said for what must have been the hundredth time, and she quickly sketched the diagram on the edge of her paper. "There. That's one picture you *can* draw in your exercise book, perhaps it'll help."

"You're the one who should be a teacher: you're mean enough," Valerie said, copying the triangle on her own paper.

It proved almost impossible to concentrate on geometry with the radio going, all the adults in the room putting in comments in reply to Mr. Smallwood. When Uncle Harold and Aunt Frances came in, Claire began to gather her papers. She loved studying in the brightness and warmth of the kitchen, but she'd have to retreat to her bedroom, cold and dim as it was, if she wanted to really get anything done tonight.

"Well, Fred says he'll put me in touch with a fellow named Harris who runs a shop in Scarborough, that's just on the outside of Toronto. He thinks he might be able to give me a job or help me find someone who can," Uncle Harold said to Uncle Bill. "Of course there's no problem finding jobs in Toronto, not for a man with a skilled trade like electronics. It's an up-and-coming city, Toronto."

Uncle Bill nodded and grunted; he was still listening to the radio, his face screwed up in a frown.

"Yes, you want to listen to that, that's a smart man there: Joe Smallwood," Uncle Harold said. "He's tomorrow's man, and fellows like Major Cashin are yesterday's men, yesterday's men." Aunt Frances laid her hand lightly over Uncle Harold's and patted it.

"Oh, so you think bowing and scraping and going cap in hand to a bunch of mainlanders is the way of the future, is it?" Uncle Bill growled. "And looking after ourselves, managing our own country, that's a thing of the past?"

"He didn't mean it that way, Bill," Annie said, coming in from the kitchen with her dishcloth in hand.

"Come on, let's go upstairs," Valerie whispered to Claire, sweeping her own books and papers into a pile. Arguments made her fidgety.

But Claire shook her head slightly. "In a few minutes," she said, watching Uncle Harold's face. He lifted his voice to cut across the sparrow-like fluttering of the women.

"I do mean it that way. I'm sorry, Annie, but Bill is right. That's exactly what I mean. Yes, I mean yes, if there was some way Newfoundland really could go it alone, be a nation, sure, that would be fine. But that's a pipe dream and you know it, Bill. That crowd at Government House wants to string us along with promises of independence, and we're at the mercy of a bunch of fat-arsed merchants and English lackeys. If you think they've got the good of Newfoundland at heart—"

"Oh, and I suppose you think Joe Smallwood has the good of Newfoundland at heart, does he?" Uncle Bill spoke Smallwood's name like his mouth was filled with vinegar. "Talk about a lackey...going to Ottawa for handouts."

"Those handouts, as you call them, might be the difference between life and death for some poor family in an outport with thirteen children. Imagine what a difference the baby bonus will make to a family like that! Or to veterans. You'll be much better off under a Canadian government. Sure, even Mother here will get the old age pension."

"That's what you think, is it, that Newfoundlanders can be bought with Canadian dollars? Is that all our country means to us...something to barter and trade?"

Uncle Harold made a fist and didn't exactly bang it on the table, but thumped it lightly a few times. Neither of them was the kind of man to get worked up, and they liked each other, but when it came to Confederation, Claire thought, Uncle Bill just couldn't see sense.

"Send him victorious, happy and glorious, long to reign over us," said Grandmother unexpectedly from her chair, her small dark eyes opening like buttons popping through buttonholes. "God save the King."

"God save the King, and God help Newfoundland," Uncle Harold said, standing up. "Come on, Frances girl, we got to call those boys in and get them to bed. Valerie, don't be down here too late with Claire now." He turned to Bill and stuck out his hand. "No hard feelings now, Bill. I s'pose we'll never see eye to eye on this, but we'll all see what's what next month when we has the referendum."

Up in her room later, after Val and the others had gone home, Claire rolled and put away her socks and decided her sock drawer was untidy. Time to straighten it out. If she really did have to pack it all up soon, it would be best to have it well organized. She pulled the drawer out: socks, underwear, slips. She began to sort and fold.

As she laid the drawer back in, something at the back of the dresser, down inside, caught her eye. Claire pulled it out. It was a cheap birthday card, with a picture of a little blond-haired, blue-eyed girl with a simpery smile. She couldn't remember what birthday it had been sent for – certainly not for this one, her sixteenth. Maybe last year or the year before.

Inside, her mother's spidery handwriting: *Happy Birthday to my darling daughter Claire. I thank God every day my dear that you have such a good Home.*

Claire laid the card on top of the pile of underwear and old socks she was throwing out, but couldn't quite do it. She always managed to lose her mother's cards and letters; she had never actually put one in the waste basket. Instead she tucked it in her Bible, at Habakkuk, a book rarely read and poorly understood. She slid her tidy underwear drawer back in the dresser, cleared off the old clothes to put in the trash, and went to bed.

ETHEL

BROOKLYN, SEPTEMBER 1949

ETHEL SAT IN HER living room, listening to *The Guiding Light* and crocheting. She had taken up crocheting doilies because she was no longer at the age when her friends were having babies and not yet at the age when they were having grandchildren. Without babies to knit or crochet for, she was reduced to doilies.

Jim and Jimmy would be home from work soon; their dinners were in the oven. Diane had been home, had her dinner, and gone out again. Diane had just started her last year of high school, counting the days till she would graduate and go from working afternoons and Saturdays at Macy's to working there full time. After that, she and her friend Carol Dobrowski were getting their own apartment. Ethel looked around her living room, where for almost seventeen years Diane had slept on the fold-out daybed and Jimmy had slept on the couch. When Diane went, they could fold up the daybed and put it away. Right now, this was all Ethel could bring herself to feel about her only daughter leaving home.

This doily she was working on was white with pink and green trim, part of a set she was making as a gift for her friend Irene at church, who was having a dinner and dance for her twenty-fifth wedding anniversary. Next year would be Ethel and Jim's silver anniversary.

When she heard Jim and Jimmy at the door, she got up and tucked her crocheting into her work basket. From the hall she heard Jim's easy laughter as Jimmy finished the punch line of a story: "...and so I told her, lady, save yourself a coupla bucks next time; don't call me till you check first and see if it's plugged in!"

The men's voices mingled in laughter, and inside the laughter she caught Jim's question, "You charged her anyway, for makin' the trip?"

There was a pause and she could hear Jimmy kicking his boots off. "Naw, I was gonna charge her fifty cents but I didn't have the heart." Jim laughed again. Ethel looked at the table, where two hours ago she and Diane had sat at either end, eating in silence. Why did fathers and sons get on so much better, easier, than mothers and daughters?

Then father and son were in the kitchen, and the laughter was stilled. Jim pulled out his chair and sat down. Jimmy came over to the sink where Ethel stood and gave her a quick sideways hug before he sat down. "Hey, Ma," he said. "How's your day?"

"Fine, my day was fine," she said, wondering what he would think if she recited a litany: *I got up. I made your breakfast. I cleaned the toilet. I crocheted a set of doilies to give to a woman I don't like much. I listened on the radio to stories about women who have real lives, lives where something happens.*

"I don't know what we're gonna do about these televisions," Jim said, directing the comment across the table at Jimmy.

"I tell you, Dad, I can fix televisions. They won't need another guy. Trust me. I been studying it." He glanced up at his mother with a quick smile. She smiled back. He was a good boy, her Jimmy. Not brilliant. Not like Ralphie. Ralphie could have gone on to university, Ethel thought, forgetting that Ralph had never gotten his Grade Eleven. Look at all those boys who went to college on the GI Bill, and here they were now, college graduates. That's what Ralphie could have done.

She looked at Jim, saw he was giving Jimmy the same proud look she had given him herself a moment ago. Jimmy didn't notice either parent; he was buttering his bread. Over his bent head his parents' eyes met for a minute, and Ethel turned away – not just her eyes but her whole body, back to the sink, where she began scrubbing at a stain that wasn't there.

"So young Taylor called me into the office today," Jim said.

Ethel assumed he was speaking to Jimmy, but Jimmy's chair scraped back along the floor and he stood up. "I gotta run," he said. "Gotta meet some of the guys." Then she understood that Jim was talking to her, directly to her, and that Jimmy did not want to be there, to stand between them and be the channel for this conversation.

She turned slowly and stood with her back to the sink, watching her husband chewing another mouthful of roast before he spoke again. The dishrag was knotted between her fingers; she was playing with it like Mrs. Romano did with her rosary beads. She stared at Jim's face, watching his eyes meet hers and then shift away again.

"So he calls me into his office," Jim repeated, "and he tells me that since the old man died, he needs someone to live over the store. A manager, like. Till he decides whether to sell it or not. He's waiting to see about this television thing…whether it catches on or whether it's just a flash in the pan." Jim's hands moved on the tablecloth, lifting his fork, playing with it, putting it down.

Ethel said nothing, and Jim went on. "Poor old Taylor…he put his whole life into that store. And for what? To hand it down to his son. And all young Taylor cares about is real estate. Not radio." In a small silence, Ethel heard the clock. Tick, tick, tick. She looked down at the pointed toe of her shoe. A scuff-mark showed white against the beige. When she glanced at Jim again, he was still at the fork, poking the end of a tine through a small hole in the tablecloth.

This was the most words she'd heard Jim say to her, all at one time, in four years. Five full minutes of words, and she still didn't have a clue what he was driving at. Finally, like it was dragged out of him, he turned to her with the first direct question he'd put to her in all that time.

"Well, girl, what do you think?"

Ethel's mouth was dry. She wasn't sure what the question was. Old Taylor, Young Taylor: what did it matter what she thought? She shrugged. "I don't know. What am I supposed to say?"

"It's a good opportunity, Ethel. More money. But if I don't take it, he'll bring in some other guy and I might be out on the street without a job." Tick, tick, tick. This time when he looked at her he held her gaze and spoke very slowly. "He wants me to take over as manager. He wants us to move down there and live over the shop."

She pulled out Jimmy's chair and sat down in front of the half-eaten dinner. "What does Jimmy think?" she said, as if, even though Jimmy wasn't here, they could still speak around and through him.

Now it was Jim who shrugged. The tine of the fork slid in and out of the hole in the tablecloth. She wanted to tell him to stop, he was ruining the tablecloth, but after four years of silence it seemed she should weigh her words more carefully.

"Jimmy thinks it's a good idea," Jim said. "He thinks it'll be a long-term thing. Jimmy says there's gonna be a big boom in the business with this television thing, and we should take advantage. Stay with it. And if I don't take it, what else will I do?"

She nodded. Jim had made one big change, when he was thirty and couldn't work as an ironworker anymore. He learned something new: radios. Now he was over forty. It wasn't the time for learning another new trade.

"It's not as nice of an apartment," he offered, apologetically.

Ethel unclenched her hands, moved Jimmy's plate aside, made herself lay the twisted dishtowel out on the table. She smoothed it and folded it, in half and then in thirds. "It's not easy, to start over in a new place," she said. "But what choice have we got?"

She heard the rustle as Jim picked up the newspaper he had laid beside his plate. "That's it, then," he said. "I'll tell young Taylor tomorrow."

DIANE

~

BROOKLYN, DECEMBER 1949

DIANE SITS BESIDE MICKEY at the soda fountain, her ankles twisted around the stool. She watches as his long slim hands stir his coffee, cradle the cup, lift it to his mouth. His mouth is full-lipped and kissable in his thin, strong-lined face. She lets her eyes slide down to his body, long and lean with a hard layer of muscle over his chest and upper arms, sharp as a knife under his white T-shirt. She reaches out to lay a hand on his arm, not for any reason but to touch him.

Mickey smiles, not at her but into his coffee. "Take it easy, Di," he says. Then he looks at her sideways out of those green eyes she loves so much, and the long crease in his cheek, like an elongated dimple, folds into a deeper smile. "Everybody's gonna know you can't keep your hands offa me."

He reaches up and puts his hand at the nape of her neck, under her hair, a gesture that makes her shiver. "It'll be nice when you get your own place," he says, very quietly.

This is the plan. High school graduation is six months away. Diane now works part-time at Macy's in Brooklyn, but her plan is to get a job at Macy's in Manhattan after graduation. Carol is going to do the same thing and they're going to get their own apartment. And then Mickey can come over any time he wants, any night at all, and there won't need to be any more sneaking around and doing it in cars and stuff.

Diane and Mickey have been having sex for over a year now, since they started going steady at Christmas of her junior year. It should have been Mickey's senior year but he'd dropped out by then, to nobody's surprise, and was working at his uncle's garage. That made him seem older, more serious, than guys who were still in high school.

After the first time, Mickey always used a safe. He knew how to get them and he told her not to worry. Diane knows from Carol, who has done it with two different guys, that not all guys are willing to take the responsibility, to make it their business. It's one more reason to love Mickey, as if she didn't have enough, like his beautiful body or his incredible eyes or the way he kisses or the dark, lonely anger that sometimes drops down on him out of nowhere like a blanket.

"Anyway, first I gotta get out of my folks' place," she says. "It's even worse now we're in the new place. We're tripping over each other all the time, and I never thought Ma could be in a worse mood than she usually is, but it turns out, yeah, she can."

Mickey shrugs. "It's not such a bad place. Close to me."

It's true, the apartment over the radio repair shop is only two blocks from the garage where Mickey works and, sometimes, sleeps. Diane senses that he likes her living there better than living in the apartment building where she grew up, perhaps for some of the same reasons her mother hated the move. It seems to have moved them down a notch in society; living in four rooms over a store someone else owns is a step down from living in four rooms in a rent-controlled building. *Down* is not a direction Diane's mother Ethel has ever planned to move in life. Neither has Diane herself, for that matter. She sees herself moving up, up, into Manhattan, into the stars, but she doesn't consider that the move over the radio shop really counts. It's her family that's moving, not really Diane herself. She does not feel her fate is tied to theirs.

But talk of families and living arrangements has turned Mickey's thoughts in another direction. "Ma's gotta get out of that place," he says, as if picking up the thread of a conversation recently dropped. "Dad came home again the other night and beat the shit outta her. Someday I'm gonna get him by himself and he's not gonna know what hit him."

"Were you there?" Diane says. She puts her hand on his arm again, but it's a different gesture this time, a desire to heal rather than just a desire, and what she feels from him is not heat but a cold deeper than she can imagine, an absolute zero colder even than the chill between her mother and her father.

"'Course I wasn't there! He never woulda done it if I'd been there. He's scared of me, and so he should be. No, I came in Sunday morning and saw her with the black eye and the fat lip. Like most every Sunday morning of my life. The only difference now is I'm not there on Saturday night when he comes home."

"Good thing you're not," she says, remembering Mickey's other stories, never told but only hinted at, Saturday nights when Gerry Malone would finish with his wife and start in on the kids. Mickey has scars: she's seen them, traced them with a fingertip across his back, the backs of his legs. The old man used a belt sometimes.

But Mickey shoots her a look of contempt. "What do you think, I'm still a kid? He couldn't beat me now. I should be there, to stand up for Ma. But I'm no better than Johnny or Frank. Stupid jerks, off with their cars and their girlfriends, never lifting a finger to help Ma. And now I'm just like 'em." He stares into his coffee cup, won't meet her eyes.

"That's not true, Mickey. You do lots for your mother. She counts on you, you know it." Diane's hand makes little soothing circles on his arm, but he shakes her off.

"Yeah, do everything but what I should do: hang around and wait for Dad some night when he's coming home from O'Donnell's and strangle him with my bare hands."

Diane searches for words. She knows words are no good, that anything she says will make Mickey angry. She's glad when Mickey says, "Come on, let's get outta here."

In the alleyway next to the candy store he takes her hand like he's leading her into some fancy Manhattan hotel room. Draws her in behind him, slips his arms around her waist. She links her own arms around his neck and pulls him as close to her as she can get, opening her mouth to his, warm and generous. Their bodies are so close she can feel the tensed-up muscles in his chest and stomach, feel him slowly relax in the heat of their kiss. She feels his hands on her back and gives herself up to her own inner rush of pleasure, and also to that other pleasure, of knowing that she can heal him, can make him forget, can, for a moment, kiss and make it better.

ROSE

BROOKLYN, JANUARY 1950

ROSE KNOWS THAT HER brother Jim works at Taylor's Radio Repair at Flatbush and Beverley. She passes the store now and then and stands in front of the window, looking at the crowded display of radios and phonographs, the signs advertising the brand-new 45 RPM records, the huge console television with its $400 price tag. She wonders if anyone will ever buy it. One day she goes past and it's gone. *So, there are still rich people in the world,* Rose says to herself.

She never goes inside. Watches her favourite brother, the handsome one, the carefree laughing one, grow old and grey and grim. *That hard little bitch Ethel,* Rose thinks, *she ain't givin' him much of a life.*

She is sure Jim would not know her: she doesn't know herself, most days. She, too, is greying, her hair spidery and frizzled under an old cloth hat. There was a time, Rose dimly recalls, when she cared about having the newest, the most fashionable of everything.

She leaves her boarding house early this chilly morning; it's a crowded tenement in Fort Greene where Rose sleeps on a mattress on the floor in a room no bigger than a closet, with a blanket across the door. The landlady, who is used to seeing the least of these washing up on her doorstep like driftwood, is getting nasty about the rent. Rose walks down Flatbush Avenue towards O'Donnell's Saloon where today, and for the past several days in fact, she has a job. Sometimes she doesn't. She has gone to charities and street missions for something to eat, a place to sleep. She doesn't remember pride. Like the polished cabinet of the TV set, pride has an impossible price tag.

There are many things Rose doesn't remember, and a few she recalls with startling clarity. She remembers Claire, the small solid weight in her arms. The brown eyes. Sometimes, for hours at a time, she doesn't remember what happened

174

to Claire, and goes about with a vague sense that she's misplaced something. Then she recalls: Home. Claire is safe at home.

Paddy O'Donnell is already at work, washing up glasses, wiping down the bar. "Good day, Rosie," he calls. Rose has worked for him before: he has a soft spot and they have a flexible arrangement which suits them both. He pours a drink for her and she picks it up when she comes back from the cupboard with her mop and bucket. She drinks it leaning against the counter like a customer, like a man, and feels that sense of pieces fitting together, of all-wellness that only the first drink of the day can produce. When she's done, she goes out back to fill the bucket.

She mops the dust and boot-marks and beer-spills on the floor, while O'Donnell washes glasses and brings up the beer from the cellar, and sings things like "My Wild Irish Rose" and "The Rose of Tralee" to see if he can get a rise out of her.

"Can ya stick a wild Irish sock in yer wild Irish gob?" she calls out after the third rendition of his favourite tune.

"Not in a fine mood this fine morning, are we, Rosie? Do you know what your problem is?"

This is such a huge question Rose is glad he allows a moment's silence for her to consider. She wrings out the mop, then gets down on her knees to scrub at a stubborn spot.

"My problem," she says when she gets to her feet. "Yeah, I know what my problem is. My problem is, I was born ten years too early. I was too old for the war."

"I thought it was only fellows who said they were too old to go overseas."

"Not to go overseas, you old fool. To stay right here. I had a great time during the war. Rosie the Riveter. Remember her? Well, that was me. Rosie the Riveter."

"Yeah? You worked at the Navy Yard?" O'Donnell sounds mildly interested. Surely he's heard this before.

"You betcher life I did. Great work, great pay, great bunch of gals. Those were my best years, Paddy, the best years of my life." Rose goes to the back door to throw out the dirty water and refills her bucket. "Sure, I had some rough times before the war." The Depression – well, both depressions really, her own and the country's, having and losing Claire. Her time in the hospital, that strange shadow-world of doctors and pills and the shock treatments that made her feel crazier than she did before. "But when 1941 rolled around and I got a job in the Navy Yards, that was a great time."

O'Donnell is silent, and she wonders if maybe he lost a son or something. The war, she reminds herself, wasn't so hot for everyone. But Rose Evans had a good war. Working in the factory, feeling like part of a team, the friendship of the other women – it gave her back something she had lost.

But she was over thirty then, ten years older than the girls she worked with. She was too old for the main point of the war: falling in love with a man in uniform. There were thousands of them on the streets of Brooklyn, but they were just boys. Sure, once or twice she had a date, even had the pleasure of showing a young fellow how it was done a few times, young farm boys just up from wherever, never been with a woman before.

During the war, sleeping with a fellow didn't make you a bad girl. It was just doing your patriotic duty for a boy who might not come home. Lots of those patriotic girls did their duty with one sailor after another, and still wound up with husbands after the war. If all those men in uniform, desperate in the face of death and hungry for love, had come rolling Rose's way when she was nineteen or twenty-two, her life might have been entirely different.

"I was too old, by the time the war came along," she repeats.

O'Donnell doesn't seem to need any more explanation, or perhaps he's lost interest. He's getting his bar ready for the day's customers, washed-up old Irishmen who will come in as soon as the doors open to drink steadily all day, working men who'll come in for a few on the way home when their workday is over. All welcome at O'Donnell's, including the cleaner, Rose Evans.

But then, as she's getting ready to go a couple of hours later, taking one for the road, she says, "I need some cash, Paddy."

He raises his eyebrows. "I thought we had a deal, Rosie."

"You know I'm working more than I'm drinking."

"That's how you see it." He flicks a suddenly cold eye around the barroom. "I might say the opposite. Get on home now, before opening time."

"What home, Paddy? I don't have anything you could call a home, and I won't have even that if you don't give me a few dollars to give to the old bat. She's threatening me, Paddy."

He shrugs. "We got a deal, Rosie. I can't be giving you handouts whenever you run short."

"How is it a handout if I clean the place for you?"

"Drinks are not on the house, Rosie."

She sags against the bar, draws idle designs on the countertop with her finger, then meets his eye. He has to know what she's thinking, to spare her the shame of having to say it. Rosie's arrangement with O'Donnell, over the years she's worked sporadically for him, has been flexible. There have been times when he's been willing to provide extra cash in return for additional services. O'Donnell is a widower, and lonely.

But he shakes his head before she can say anything. "No, Rosie, there's nothing you can do for me and I got no extra money. Don't go making a charity case of yourself, I'm not the Salvation Army." She has a sudden mental picture of the paunchy old Irishman fitted out in an Army uniform, humping and pumping away in his narrow upstairs room to the accompaniment of the band and tambourines. She almost laughs, but then sees what he is saying. *Don't go making a charity case of yourself.*

Rose pushes her empty glass across the bar at him and goes out into the sunshine.

She walks for a long time through the streets of Flatbush. She's cold. She's hungry. She has no desire to go back to her boarding house.

There's a Salvation Army mission downtown, near the Citadel. Rose tries not to go to the Army. When she's cold or hungry or in need of a handout she prefers the Catholics, St. Vincent de Paul or some other crowd with no ties, no memories. She wonders if everyone feels this way when they're down and out. Is the Salvation Army mission crowded with old Catholic bums who don't want to see accusing pictures of the Blessed Virgin and the Sacred Heart staring down at them every time they get a bowl of soup? Mary and Jesus don't bother Rose one bit, but the uniforms, the music, the haunting memories of testimony meetings and services back home – it's like a net, reaching out across the miles and years, something she's afraid will get tangled around her ankles. Yet her long walk today brings her to the door of the Salvation Army mission – because she's tired, and it's the nearest place, and she doesn't have the strength to run away.

Inside, she sits at a long table sparsely populated with a few other abandoned women. The men, far more numerous, eat at another table. The soup is good, and hot. It would be nice if she could have a drink. Now that would be a real mission of mercy. Why doesn't someone start one of those? Missions where they hand out gin and rum for free to washed-up old rummies and whores. Why don't the people who want to save humanity ever give humanity what it actually wants?

Despite her doubts, Rose stays not just for the meal but for the service afterwards. It's so cold outside, and so warm inside. As warm and familiar as being tucked into an old patchwork quilt, the kind your grandmother made out of your own discarded dresses, down by the woodstove in the kitchen on a winter night when you were cold and sick and tired. The meeting hall, shabby with its wooden chairs and peeling paint, is hot with the press of bodies: the bodies of the faithful and the bodies of the lost, distinguished by cleanliness and uniforms.

From the voices around her Rose picks out several Newfoundland accents, some quite strong, as if the speakers or singers have lately arrived on the boat. Of course, the Salvation Army in Brooklyn is full of Newfoundlanders, especially the Citadel. She's heard that before, though she hasn't had opportunity to discover it herself. The lively bespectacled man leading the singing is a Newfoundlander: Sergeant-Major Noah Collins, he's called. He dances up and down across the platform. "The Lord saved every part of me when I got saved," he says, "except my feet! The Lord never saved my feet!" Rose joins in the answering chorus of laughter: those lively step-dancing feet certainly don't look saved. It's been many years since Rose has been in a room where someone can make a joke like that – in a voice that clearly labels him as someone from Bonavista Bay – and others can understand and laugh. Rose stops fighting the familiarity, relaxes into it.

Feet stamp and hands clap in vigorous rhythm, raising the roof, raising the temperature even more. An old fellow with three days' growth of stubble leans over to her. "I don't know about this crowd," he says, a hint of Irish mingled with the whisky on his breath. "They keep talkin' about goin' up to glory, but with all this stompin' I think they've got the floor drove down and they're six inches farther from heaven than when they started."

Rose laughs, under cover of music. It feels good to laugh, good to have this whole old world to wrap herself in and even to laugh at. She is relaxed, she's happy, her stomach is full. When singing turns to preaching, she drifts off to sleep.

She startles awake as the Captain's voice peaks to emphasize a point. He's preaching on the Prodigal Son, and as she dozes again she finds scenes from his sermon mingling with her dreams. She always pictures the far country that the boy went to as being like Brooklyn: busy, crowded, full of strange people. It seems to her now that she herself was a good girl back home and didn't become a bad girl until she came to Brooklyn. Like the prodigal, she met her downfall in the far country.

Captain White describes the father of the prodigal, walking day by day on the road in front of his house, waiting and watching. Rose sees the road looking like Freshwater Road at home, rutted and unpaved, grooved with cart tracks, dusty in summer. The house of the prodigal's father is her parents' yellow clapboard house. At the front gate she sees not a father or a mother but her sister Annie, who must be just home from Holiness Meeting, because she's wearing the uniform, bonnet and all.

"And the father of the prodigal runs toward him," Captain White says. "Forgetting his age, his dignity, he picks up the skirts of his robe and runs! Runs with open arms toward the boy who has so disappointed him, has hurt him, has squandered his inheritance. Can you see it, brothers and sisters? Can you see the Father running towards you? Nothing can hold him back. If he sees you taking that first step on the road home, he'll be there. Because he's been waiting, waiting all this time. And now he's running to welcome you home."

Rose is fully awake now. The piano comes in under the Captain's words, and he shifts from speaking to singing as the melody builds.

Softly and tenderly Jesus is calling
Calling, O sinner, come home…

One by one, people around her go up to the mercy seat. If she were really on Freshwater Road, if home, Annie, Claire, peace, forgiveness were just a few steps up the road, what would hold her back? Why wouldn't she step forward, as she does now, and take those few simple steps up the road, and fall on her knees?

One of the women officers kneels beside Rose, offering her a hanky and an arm to tuck around her. "God bless you, sister, God bless you," she says. Rose feels something physical, something definite, happening to her heart. It feels as if it has been tied up with twine, the kind you use on brown-paper parcels, and now someone is cutting the strands, one by one. She feels them snap free.

The next day, Rose returns to the mission as soon as it opens. Over the days and weeks that follow, the place becomes her new home. She eats there, helps out in the kitchen, worships at the meetings. The officers and the volunteers give her hugs and gentle smiles. She is a success story, one of the saved. The unsaved eye her suspiciously, as if she has let down their side.

One night during a testimony meeting, Sergeant-Major Noah Collins, the lively old fellow with the unsaved feet, tells how, as a young man, he went to the ice on a sealing ship and was stranded out there for three days. Men froze to death on their knees in prayer; the survivors walked around constantly, singing hymns like "Does Jesus Care?" Rose, hearing this testimony a few weeks ago, would have thought it was pretty friggin clear Jesus didn't care, seeing as how over eighty of the men died. She hears it differently now. She imagines Jesus, wrapped in a wool coat stiff with ice, stumbling around the ice beside those men, peeling off his own frozen mitts to put on someone's bare hands. He feels that close, right this minute. Buoyed up by the new joy inside her, Rose gets to her feet.

"Yes, Sister Rose," says the Captain. "What would you like to share with us, Sister Rose?"

There is something of a formula to testimonies and Rose knows it well. She does not search or scramble for words, but lets familiar phrases carry her into this unknown territory. "My friends, my brother and sisters, I want to thank Jesus for taking away my sins, for rolling all my burdens away." She feels a wave of energy, something that might come from God, but might also just come from the fact that people are listening, paying attention.

"I led a life of sin before I came to this place," she continues, mingling the known words with words of her own so that she does not know where memory leaves off and invention begins. "I was a slave to the bottle and a slave to the lusts of men. Yes, I sold both my body and my soul, time again, and what did I get in return for it?" She pauses, feels the power of that moment of silence. Around her she sees people shake their heads, mouthing the word: *Nothing.* "That's right, brothers and sisters, I got nothing in return. Nothing! Nothing but a few hours' pleasure and a bottle of cheap wine! Nothing to fill my soul, nothing to ease my burden, nothing to take my pain away." As she says the word over, "Nothing…nothing," and feels its driving force, she hears other words below the surface of her mind, Bible verses and hymns, the sediment of memory laid down when she was too young even to rebel against it. "And when I was weak and heavy laden, when I had need of rest, I came to this place, and do you know what I found here?" The pause again. This time they do not anticipate her answer: some of them shape the word *Jesus,* but she surprises them when she repeats, "Nothing! Yes, my friends, I found nothing…nothing…nothing but the blood of Jesus!"

"Amen! Hallelujah!! Praise the LORD!!" The voices rise around her, hands reach out to clasp hers, she sits down. The pianist, who is quick, strikes up the tune and Rose catches her breath and joins the others, perhaps even leads them.

> *No other fount I know*
> *Nothing but the blood of Jesus.*

DIANE

BROOKLYN, OCTOBER 1950

"MOM, YOU GOTTA DO something. We're not going to just ignore it, pretend it's nothing."

"I can ignore it if I want to," Ethel says, pushing her mop over the linoleum with dogged determination. "I hate the way the dust gets in here," she adds. It's one of her ongoing complaints about the new apartment. Right on the street, it seems to eat up dust and grime from Flatbush Avenue. Ethel wages a constant war against dirt.

Diane watches her mother, dressed in a cotton print housedress, her hair tied up under a scarf, her feet laced into sensible shoes. Diane sits on the couch in her bathrobe, her hair in rollers, eating a slice of toast and drinking coffee. It's her half-day off work. She knows idleness drives Ethel insane.

"Everybody makes a big deal out of their silver anniversary."

"Silver anniversary!" Ethel spits the words out like a curse. "Twenty-five years of married life and what have I got to show for it? Living in four rooms on top of a radio shop, working my fingers to the bone day and night, four grown adults tripping over each other in a space not big enough to swing a cat in? What have we got to celebrate?"

"Love. Romance. Staying together," Diane says, and is rewarded, as she expects, with a look of mingled fury and despair.

"Don't you have to get ready for work?" Ethel says. "I don't need you under-foot when I'm trying to clean this dump."

"Gosh, give me a break, I'm on my way. So glad I could stay home and spend the morning with you, loving mother." Diane gets up slowly, stretches, lays down her plate of toast crumbs and her coffee cup on the end table. She hears Ethel's sigh and a grumble about people who can't even be bothered to pick up after themselves, and the clink, tinkle as her dishes are brought in the kitchen and set in the sink. By that time Diane has squeezed into the tiny bathroom, where she unrolls and brushes out her hair. Today could be a big day. Diane has the chance to help arrange a new window display. She isn't crazy about being a salesgirl, not like Carol who is a born salesperson, could sell refrigerator-freezers to the Eskimos. Diane loves arranging displays in the store, figuring how to lay things out in a way so attractive, no-one could resist, even if they've only come in to look and not to buy.

Once she is out of range of her mother's voice, Diane forgets all about her parents' twenty-fifth wedding anniversary. She loves the subway ride uptown, the walk along Sixth Avenue, loves moving as part of a crowd, the huge rushing torrent of people going places, more people on a single afternoon on Sixth Avenue than walk on Flatbush Avenue or Fulton Street in a whole week. Different people, too. Men in sharply pressed suits, women in dresses at the height of fashion. *This is my world*, thinks Diane, *this is where I belong*.

As she goes through the glass front doors of Macy's, into her world of light and colour and retail sales, she thinks briefly of Mickey Malone, who never leaves Brooklyn at all. Her insides turn to water at the thought of Mickey, at his voice or his touch, but she cannot imagine a place for him in the clean, bright Manhattan life she imagines for herself. So it's good that it's time for her to start work and stop thinking.

She gets home that night to find that the idea of a silver anniversary dinner has been taken up with great enthusiasm by her brother Jimmy. All four of them are at home for dinner, squished around the kitchen table, eating fried chicken. Diane, Jimmy, Mom, and the sports page of the *Brooklyn Eagle*, behind which Dad is buried, following the Dodgers' uncertain fortunes.

"Well it was just an idea," Ethel says, buttering bread. "Just something Diane said."

"I think it's a great idea!" Jimmy says heartily. Jimmy is always hearty. Diane rolls her eyes. "Me and Diane are both working now. We'll treat you to a real nice dinner. Hey, why don't we go to Gage and Tollner's?"

"No," Ethel says. "I wouldn't know what to do with myself. No place fancy."

"How about Junior's?" Jimmy says. "The new place where Enduro's used to be, you know? You been there, Diane? Me and Joyce ate there last week. It's nice. A real family place."

Ethel frowns, pushes her mashed potato around on her plate. "Maybe Junior's," she says.

Jimmy turns to the *Brooklyn Eagle*. "Whaddya think, Dad? An anniversary dinner at Junior's for you and Mom?"

A faint rattle. "Whatever your mother says. I don't want no big fuss." Jim's voice comes from behind the paper.

"No fuss," Ethel echoes. For two people who virtually never exchange a word, and haven't as long as Diane can remember, it's amazing how much alike they are. Probably that's what marriage is all about.

With that ringing endorsement, plans for the anniversary dinner are laid. Of course, everything starts to fall apart within days. Exactly at the point when Jimmy explains that he's borrowing his friend Jake's car to drive them to dinner. "It's a brand-new Packard," he says. "Lots of room for the five of us to go in style."

"The five of us?" Diane repeats. They are again in their parents' kitchen, late at night. Mom is in bed and Dad is down in the shop.

"Yeah: Mom and Dad, you, me and Joyce," Jimmy says, as though she has difficulty counting.

"You're bringing Joyce?"

"Of course I'm bringing Joyce. She's my girlfriend."

"Then I'm bringing Mickey."

Jimmy freezes in the act of buttering a piece of toast. "Diane. You are not bringing Mickey Malone to our parents' anniversary dinner."

"Why not?" Diane turns a chair around and sits down on it backward, like a guy. "You're bringing Joyce, she's your girlfriend. I'm bringing Mickey, he's my boyfriend."

"It's not the same thing at all. Me and Joyce are serious."

"Me and Mickey are serious." *You want to know how serious?* she almost adds, really wanting to push him over the edge. She's pretty sure Jimmy and Joyce have never actually done it. But he is still her big brother, after all, so instead she says, "We've been going together for two years. That's longer than you and Joyce."

She breaks the news to Mickey that night. "You're kidding me," he says. "Go to dinner with your mom and dad and Jimmy and his girlfriend? Couldn't you just shoot me now and have it over with?"

"You're so funny," she says.

"I'm not goin'," he says.

Diane nestles into his arms. She can time this right. There will be a moment when he can't say no to her, when he'll go along with whatever she asks. For now, she drops the subject.

Sure enough, the following evening at five-thirty they are all on the sidewalk in front of Taylor's Radio Repair: Ethel, in a blue dress; Jim wearing pressed pants, a shirt and tie, and a suit jacket Diane hasn't seen on him in at least five years; Jimmy and Joyce; Diane and Mickey. Everyone is dressed up except Mickey, who wears jeans and a T-shirt. Jimmy shoots Diane a look that says he could kill her, and Mickey a look that says he actually will kill him, later on. After the parents' anniversary dinner, which nobody wants to spoil.

The Evans family can seldom think of much to say when four of them are sitting around their own cozy kitchen table. Here, amid the aggressive orange splendour of Junior's, they are as subdued as people at a funeral. The waiter shows them to their table. "And are we celebrating a special occasion this evening?" he asks. Apparently he recognizes that this odd assortment of people would not go out to dinner with each other for anything but a very special occasion.

"It's my parents' silver wedding anniversary," says Jimmy, rising to the moment. "James and Ethel Evans, twenty-five years married." The happy couple, sitting at opposite ends of the table, look away from each other but cannot find any eyes they are willing to meet.

"Well, well, well. Congratulations. Twenty-five years," says the waiter, handing them all menus. "Can I get anyone a drink while you're waiting? Champagne, perhaps?"

"Oh no, no, not *champagne*," Ethel says, as if he had suggested drinking the blood of a goat. "I'll have…let me see…may I have a cup of tea? Very, very weak tea," she adds. And of course, after that it's impossible for anyone else to order champagne or indeed anything particularly festive, except for Mickey, who goes last and doesn't seem to have any difficulty asking for a beer.

When the waiter is gone they are alone in the echoing silence that follows Mickey's order. The restaurant is in fact quite noisy, couples and families and friends all chattering happily away, apparently having many subjects they can safely discuss. But a glass bell seems to have dropped over the Evans table. Jimmy peruses his menu. "I think I might have a steak. Whaddya think, Dad?"

"Steak is good," says Jim.

Joyce plunges in. She is not a girl who has difficulty finding words, Diane has noticed, nor is she particularly good at picking up little subtleties. "I always order chicken when I go out," she begins chattily. "Or fish. I love going out to dinner, don't you? Junior's is really nice. Don't you think so, Mrs. Evans?"

Ethel shakes her head. "We don't eat out very much, these days."

"But I'm sure you did when you were dating, didn't you?" Joyce burbles happily. "Now you know, a silver anniversary is time to look back on your courting years. At my parents' silver wedding they had all their old friends get up, and everyone had to tell a story about when Mom and Dad were dating each other. Oh, it was so funny." Another little well of silence. "So, Mr. and Mrs. Evans, don't you have any romantic stories? How did you meet?"

Ethel looks at Diane in mute appeal, but it's Jimmy who steps in. "Well, that's kind of a funny story, Joyce. Funny I never told you before. My mom and dad, you see, they grew up together, back in Newfoundland. And when they first came to New York, it was actually my dad's brother, his brother Bert, that Mom was engaged to."

Joyce's very blue eyes open wide, then she smiles her dimpled smile and shakes a finger at Jim. "Oh, Mr. Evans, did you steal your brother's girlfriend right out from under his nose? How naughty!"

Again, silence. Jimmy opens his mouth but nothing comes out. Ethel finally speaks, her voice as dry as layers of tissue paper rustling. "Well, it wasn't quite like that, you see, Joyce. My – Mr. Evans' brother, Bert – you see, he had an accident. He fell from a building and was killed."

Mickey, who has also never heard this story, looks interested now. Diane and Jimmy have only heard the story of Bert as a distant legend. No-one has ever elaborated on how Ethel went from being Bert's fiancée to being Jim's wife. Romantic courtship stories have never made up part of their family lore.

"So she married me instead," Jim finishes, in a tone usually reserved for judges pronouncing sentence of death.

At this moment the waiter arrives with their drinks. Very, very weak tea for Ethel. Coffee for Jim and Jimmy. Ginger ale for the ladies. A nice big frothy mug of beer for Mickey. Jim and Jimmy eye it enviously. The waiter takes their orders and abandons them to their fate. Everyone takes a sip of their drink at the exact same moment. Diane meets Mickey's eyes over the rim of her glass and sees that he wants to laugh, and knows that if they look at each other a moment longer, she will laugh too. She kicks him under the table, but her mother glances up with a sharp look of surprise and Diane realizes she has connected with the wrong ankle.

"So," says Joyce, as if gathering her strength, "so, Mr. Evans, you were there for Mrs. Evans in her time of grief. I'm sure you were a great comfort to her. How very sweet."

Jim nods slowly, and all four Evanses look at Joyce with new respect, not to mention relief. She obviously has a talent for finding the right thing to say in difficult moments. A gift that will come in handy in this family.

Jimmy suddenly picks up a knife and taps it against his glass, as though they are all talking with such animation that he needs to do this to get their attention. As they are, in fact, all sitting in silence, the effect is startling.

"Well, uh…ladies and gentlemen," he says, looking around at their table in a self-conscious speechmaking voice. "It's, ah, it's an honour to be here tonight to celebrate my father and mother's twenty-fifth anniversary and the, ah, accomplishment they've made in raising such a wonderful family." Mickey rolls his eyes. "It's only, ah, it's only too bad, too sad, that my brother Ralph can't, uh, is no longer with us to, ah…I'm sure we would all be very happy if Ralph could be here with us too tonight." Ethel looks as if someone has punched her in the gut, and raises her napkin to her eyes. Jim looks away, over at the people at the next table, as if wondering whether he can detach himself from his family altogether. Joyce's eyes widen a little more. Diane wonders if she's even heard about Ralph. Has Jimmy told her *anything* about his family?

Jimmy, for his part, ploughs on. "In spite of, uh, all that, it's wonderful to be here this evening and I want to congratulate my parents and wish you, ah, a very happy anniversary, Mom and Dad." He hesitates, then raises his cup of coffee. "To Mom and Dad."

Everyone raises their glasses or cups. Diane echoes, "Mom and Dad," and Joyce quickly mumbles, "Mr. and Mrs. Evans." Mickey says nothing but takes a long pull at his beer in obvious relief.

This would be the time for Ethel and Jim to look at each other tenderly, raise their tea and coffee cups, and say "To us." Ethel blushes, looks embarrassed, and sips her very, very weak tea. Jim, however, actually does say, "To us, Ethel girl!" rather loudly, and she looks up as if someone has kicked her again.

Diane looks around for the waiter, but of course he's not back yet. At least, she figures, her brother has had his little speech now and no longer needs to pretend he's speaking in front of sixty people at a rented hall. But Jimmy has a surprise for them. He goes on.

"Since we're celebrating the, uh, joys of marriage tonight, it seems…ah, it seems appropriate that, I mean, I think this is a good time to announce, that, ah, Joyce and I…"

Diane sees her mother freeze, and for a moment feels almost sorry for Ethel. Not that Ethel disapproves of Joyce, or wouldn't want her to marry Jimmy. But Diane can almost hear her mother's thoughts: *Not tonight. Not one more thing, after all this!* She places her hand on top of her mother's for a moment.

"…we've set a date, and decided, and, uh, Joyce has agreed to do me the honour of becoming Mrs. James Evans. The Second. In June."

In the stunned silence, Mrs. James Evans the First pulls her hand out from under her daughter's and begins to clap very quietly, and the others follow her lead. Ethel leans forward, past Diane, to Joyce. "Joyce, dear, my very best wishes. I hope you and Jimmy will be very happy."

At that moment the waiter arrives with their meals. Once food is in front of them they can talk about the food, and about Jimmy and Joyce's wedding plans, about Jimmy's wonderful opportunity to manage Taylor's new store out on Long Island, about where they will live. To other tables around, they no doubt give a good imitation of a happy family celebrating not one but two special occasions. A keen observer might pick up tiny strains: the handsome young man dressed entirely inappropriately to whom no-one ever speaks, or the fact that the older couple, presumably the guests of honour, never actually look at each other all evening. But they finish the evening with ice cream sundaes and everyone goes back out to the car feeling that, on at least some levels, the evening has been a success.

Diane has waited through the whole endless dinner to get Mickey alone, to laugh with him about her ridiculous family. After Jimmy drives them all home she stands in the street with Mickey, looking oddly mismatched with her new pink dress and pearls next to his jeans and T-shirt. Without saying anything, they begin walking down Flatbush. Diane puts out her hand and brushes Mickey's hand, and he holds hers, but without any real warmth or pressure. Just as if it's something he's carrying for a few minutes. Mickey stops suddenly next to a lighted sign that reads "CANDY...CIGARS."

"That's what you want, isn't it?" he says.

"Candy cigars?" Diane says, feeling the need for a joke. The night is chilly, and so is Mickey's glare.

"Candy cigars, Jimmy and Joyce. You know. Nice little place on Long Island. He's gonna be manager of the store, good prospects. Babies comin' along in a coupla years...a nice little life. That's what you want too, isn't it?"

"No! No, that's not what I want at all!" Diane says. She thinks of walking down Sixth Avenue, carried on the current of rich, successful people all striving for something more. "I don't know exactly what I want, but it isn't that."

Mickey starts walking again, fast. She has to almost run to keep up. "You know where Joyce and Jimmy are gonna be in twenty-five years, huh?" he says. "Right back at Junior's, same table, their kids in between them, making a toast. Can't even look at each other, they're so sick of the sight of each other after all these years. Just like good old Mom and Dad."

"Hey, that's not fair," Diane protests, though she's said a thousand times worse herself about her parents. "Anyway, I told you, that's not what I want. Maybe that'll be Joyce and Jimmy someday, but it's not going to be...us."

"Us." Mickey stops again, turns to look at her. A streetlight illuminates his thin handsome face, the sharp jawline, the nose just a little too long. "What other choices do we got, Diane? Wanna be like my mom and dad instead? Want me to come home drunk every night and beat the crap out of you and our kids? Would you like that?"

"Mickey! No! Of course not." She reaches out to touch him: his arm is cold and hard as metal. "You're not going to be like your dad."

He laughs. "Think again, sweetheart. Everyone turns into their parents. Can't you see that?" He looks away again, swallows hard, twice. "I'm joining the army."

"You're what?"

"Joining the army. I already been to see about it. It's the best thing for me."

"Mickey, don't be stupid! You join the army now, you'll get sent to Korea. You might..." She remembers her mother crying the day they got the telegram about Ralph. But Mickey just laughs again.

"Yeah, go to Korea and get my ass blown off. From where I'm sitting right now, it don't look like a bad deal." He grips her upper arms and she looks into his eyes and sees all the pain there, all the darkness, everything she's tried to patch up and make better. Sees that she's been like a child putting Band-Aids on someone whose throat is cut.

"I love you," she tries. "I thought...you loved me."

He shoves her away, so hard it almost hurts and she reels for a moment. "I don't know about love, Diane. But if I did – if I loved anybody – here's what I'd do." He turns and walks away from her, down a side street. When he's about fifteen feet away he turns back. "Don't come after me, Diane. This is for your own good. I'm leaving now, because I love you, okay? Go home now. Go home to Mommy and Daddy."

She watches, wanting to follow but nailed to the spot, till he turns another corner and is gone. And then she goes home to Mommy and Daddy.

ANNIE

ST. JOHN'S, JUNE 1953

"TELL ME THE TRUTH, Aunt Annie. What's wrong with me? I'm a fine figure of a fellow, wouldn't you say?"

Doug Parsons sat at Annie's kitchen table, drinking a cup of tea. He was indeed a fine figure of a fellow, twenty-three years old with a good job with the *Daily News*. Annie wasn't sure exactly what he did, but Doug's mother assured her it was a good job. His family went to Number Two Corps with Annie and Bill; she had known Sarah and Abe Parsons all her life, seen their children grow up. Doug had had his eye on Claire since she was fourteen. But Claire never paid him no particular mind, no more so than just one of a crowd of friends, which Annie thought was right and proper when she was a young girl in school.

But now Claire was twenty-one and here was Doug Parsons, still hanging around. Not making a fool of himself waiting, now mind, not like her Bill did over Rose for all those years. Doug took out other girls: last year he went around with a girl called Theresa Walsh for five or six months. Anybody who heard the name Theresa Walsh could have told you what was wrong with *that* match, and his poor mother was practically in tears at the thought that her boy might end up marrying Catholic. Annie watched closely during those months to see if Claire showed any signs of jealousy. But Claire, as always, was busy with work, going out with a crowd of girlfriends and sometimes with one fellow or another, doing things with the Young People's Fellowship at the corps. When the Theresa Walsh fiasco ended, Claire had barely even seemed to notice.

Now here was Doug again, in Annie's kitchen, dropping by on a pretext of returning some dress patterns Annie had loaned to his mother. "Aunt Annie," he said – the young ones who grew up with her nieces and nephews all called her Aunt Annie – "I'm not such a bad catch, am I? Why do Claire think I'm not good enough for her?"

"Now Doug, 'tis not a matter of you not being good enough for her. I'm sure Claire don't think that way. She's just very...choosy, I guess," Annie said gently. Doug posed his questions like jokes but you never knew with young people. She guessed he really had feelings for Claire, underneath all his carrying on. He was a good boy, even if he didn't go to meeting. She didn't want to see him hurt, though of course, if he ever hurt Claire, Annie would tear the eyes out of him.

A clatter of feet and high girlish voices on the back step made Doug glance to the door and sit a little straighter in his chair. "Look at that, my white shoes are filthy now, where they oiled the road again today." A girl's voice, not Claire's but one of her friends.

"That's her, home from work now," Annie said.

Sure enough, Claire came through the door, trailed by her girlfriend Phyllis from work. It wasn't so very different from the days when she used to come home from school with Valerie, all chatter and giggles. Claire was taller and more elegant, even more confident now that she was earning money, buying her own clothes, having her hair permanent-waved.

She was a good girl, but she seemed so cool sometimes, so distant. What was the word? Aloof, that was it. Annie rolled the word in her mind, liking the sound of it, the way it captured Claire. Aloof. From where Annie sat, aloof wasn't such a bad thing. She could see, though, how Doug Parsons might not like *aloof* so much.

"Doug! How're you doing? What brings you here? Just stopped in for a chin-wag with Aunt Annie, did you?" Claire's eyes sparkled: she enjoyed teasing him.

"What're you at, Doug?" Phyllis asked, sliding into the chair next to his. Annie got up and went into the pantry where she began slicing onions, blinking back the tears. She listened to the conversation in the other room, not wanting to miss it.

"Not much, girl, not much," said Doug. "Just stopped in to drop something off for Mother on my way home from work."

"This isn't on your way home," Claire pointed out.

"Well, in a manner of speaking, you know. After all, it is Friday night, so I was thinking I might find a pretty girl – or two – who wanted to come out to Barney's for supper with me tonight."

"You might find two," Claire said. "Pretty girls only come in pairs around here."

"Well, if I looked hard enough, I might find another fellow on the way," said

Doug. "I could swing by and pick up Gary Follett. What do you say to that, Phyllis?"

"Why not ask me what I say to it?" Claire countered. "You might end up with Phyllis and then I'd be the one stuck with poor old Gary Follett."

"There'll be no reason to pity Gary if he winds up with you," Doug said. "As for me, how can I lose? It's a win-win situation."

They were so easy with each other, boys and girls these days. Annie was glad she heard a lot of it or she might have thought badly of Claire. In her day she could only ever remember Rose talking so freely to fellows, and if she didn't know better she might have thought Claire was a copy of her mother. But the world had changed, Annie knew. Girls like she had been herself – modest, shy and quiet – were out of style. Claire was quiet enough, compared to some of the young ones she ran around with, but she could hold her own in any conversation with a fellow.

Annie wondered how much she really knew about Claire, what the girl could be getting up to behind her back. Young people weren't always straightforward, she knew. But all signs pointed to Claire being exactly what she appeared: a nice girl. Smart, and strong-willed in her way, but always respectful and polite. Always ready to lend a hand around the house, even though she never had learned to enjoy cooking and cleaning. She brought money home to contribute to the household, every payday, before she ever touched a cent herself. She was in meeting twice every Sunday and down to Young People's every Tuesday night, a senior soldier, though she didn't wear the uniform and wasn't the sort you'd ever expect to find going off to officers' training. But that was all right with Annie.

She didn't really want to see Claire married off to some young officer, in charge of a corps down in a tiny little outport, slaving day and night to keep the church on its feet. Claire would do the job well, of course – Annie couldn't think of a job Claire wouldn't do well – but she wasn't cut out for that kind of life. She suspected if Claire were away from home she might not go to church all the time, or at least not to the Army. She'd seen Claire's distant look sometimes when the testimonies got heartfelt and people began to weep. Claire might even go to a movie or a dance if she were living away, but here at home she did what was expected, followed the rules, and never suggested by a word or a glance that those rules held her back.

They were back again by nine o'clock, the four of them crowding into the kitchen as Claire and her friends often did after an evening out. Claire made cocoa for everyone, and Annie, who had just gotten her mother settled in bed, brought out a plate of cookies she made that morning and set them on the table. Bill was sitting by the stove with his feet up, reading the paper, the cat curled on his lap. The scene was warm and familiar. It took Annie a moment to notice the one unfamiliar thing: the young man accompanying Claire, Phyllis and Doug was not Doug's friend Gary Follett but a stranger, a tall, strikingly handsome boy with glossy black hair. When he spoke, she knew he wasn't a Newfoundlander.

"Aunt Annie, this is Eddie Tanner," Claire said, and the young man stepped forward with a hearty handshake. "He's down here visiting his mother, Mrs. Curtis."

The pieces fell into place. Herb Curtis was a Salvation Army man who had come home from Toronto a few years ago married to a widow whose own children were all grown up. This must be one of those children, Eddie Tanner from Toronto.

He was as handsome as a movie star, good teeth, healthy glowing skin. His suit seemed a little flashy; it was powder-blue and he was wearing a foolish little string tie. But he positively glowed with warmth and energy as he pumped Annie's hand and said, "Pleased to meet you, Mrs. Winsor. My mom's told me so much about you and your family."

"Has she now?" Annie said, trying to make her voice as warm as his, but failing. She was sure none of the young people noticed but Bill cocked an eyebrow at her over the edge of the paper. Then he laid down the paper and stood up to be introduced to Eddie Tanner.

"Oh yes, she's told me all about how nice you folks in NewFOUNDland have been to her, how friendly everyone is, the hospitality. And now I can see she wasn't exaggerating. Why, in Toronto, if you drop a young lady off after a date, that's it, goodnight at the doorstep. Here you get invited in, get cocoa and cookies. My word! It's a whole different world, I can see that now."

"Eddie's in university, he's applying to medical school next year," Claire said, taking Eddie's coat to hang up on the hook by the door. "Sit down now, Eddie. Don't just talk about the cookies, have one." Claire's voice was as pleasant and calm as usual, but Annie, who knew her so well, saw something in her eye, heard something in her tone, that Doug Parsons had never put there. And she saw by the way they were all sitting that Doug and Phyllis were paired off after all, two castaways in the storm, while Claire was circling Eddie Tanner like a miller around a lamp.

Sunday morning at Holiness Meeting, Eddie Tanner sat not with his mother and her husband, but on the bench with Annie and Bill, sharing a songbook with Claire. His voice rang out strong on the choruses. In the evening, he came by to walk Claire up to church for Salvation Meeting.

His mother was vague about how long Eddie planned to stay in St. John's, but he had the whole summer free from university. And clearly there was plenty of attraction. He and Claire were a number. Not only did he come by to take her out on the weekends, he also picked her up and dropped her off after work in a car he had mysteriously gotten the use of – certainly not his stepfather's, since old Herb Curtis never drove in his life. Apparently it belonged to one of Herb's sons and Eddie was borrowing it for as long as he stayed.

Annie had never seen Claire like this. Or rather, she had often seen Claire like this, but never about a fellow. When Claire talked about her work, she had a focused, purposeful kind of excitement that made her light up from the inside. She was the same way when she was social convenor of the Young People's group, or last summer when she organized the Songsters to go on a tour, travelling about and singing at the Salvation Army corps around the bay.

Now Annie saw her focus all that glowing attention on Eddie Tanner. Claire, always so careful about her hair, her clothes, her grooming, now went the extra mile. She came home one Saturday from a trip downtown carrying a new dress, a pink so soft it was nearly white. Annie touched the fabric almost reverently, it was so delicate. "That'll be hard to wash," she said.

"I know," said Claire with a sigh. "But it's worth it. Eddie's taking me to Frost's Restaurant tonight, then to a symphony concert at Pitts Memorial Hall." Frost's was a cut above Barney's and the Chuck Wagon, places Claire and her crowd usually went to eat. That evening when she stepped out the door on Eddie Tanner's arm, wearing the pink dress, Annie couldn't begin to explain to herself, much less to Bill, why she didn't trust the boy.

"You're just afraid he'll marry Claire and take her away from here," Bill suggested, up in their bedroom one night in early July. The fog and cold of June's caplin weather had slipped back out to sea and even the nights were warm now. The flowers had taken heart and started to bloom in earnest.

"No, it's not that." Annie shook her head. "She's fond of her home, I know that, but I've always expected her to go away sooner or later. I wouldn't be surprised if she took up with a fellow from away."

"But not this fellow," Bill said.

"No, not this one."

Claire changed that summer, but only in the sense that her happiness had a sharper, brighter edge, and was clearly focused on Eddie Tanner. Otherwise she was the same, still Annie's good girl. Despite her whirlwind romance she did not stay out late or give her aunt a moment's worry. She and Eddie Tanner went out to supper, they went for walks and drives, they went to meeting. They joined friends from the Young People's Fellowship for get-togethers at someone's home or afternoons trouting and picnicking in the woods. Annie didn't worry about her virtue. Perhaps, she thought, it was Claire's heart she worried about.

In the middle of August, Eddie Tanner disappeared. The first Annie knew of it was when Mrs. Captain Avery sat at Annie's table having a cup of tea and she said, "Ada Curtis misses her son some lot. My, that house just came alive when he was in it. It must seem some quiet now."

"Gone back, is he?"

Mrs. Avery raised her eyebrows. "Oh, I thought you'd know all about it, him and your Claire being so close and all. He didn't come in here to say goodbye to you crowd?"

Annie looked down; she had miscalculated. Now half St. John's would know that Eddie Tanner left town without saying goodbye to Claire Evans' family. What did this mean? Clearly Mrs. Avery had come here to tease out this very information. "Oh, you know the young folks are always coming and going," Annie said, thinking quickly to make up for her blunder. "Claire had a grand time with young Eddie, but I don't think she was any more fond of him than any of the others, not that I know of. I don't know that he'd feel the need to come in here and say goodbye before he went back to university."

"Oh, but he's not gone back to university," Mrs. Avery said, leaning in a little. "Ada says his classes don't start till second week in September. She expected to have him here till Labour Day at least. But he took off right sudden, only gave her a day's notice. Bought the ticket one day and was gone on the train the next."

"You don't say," Annie said mildly. "Well, no doubt he got a little tired of it down here. Must be very quiet, compared to what he's used to."

Claire came home from work that afternoon and Annie searched her face for signs of a change. She was quiet, but then Claire was often quiet. Annie couldn't think of a good way to bring up Eddie Tanner, so she waited. And waited. A week slipped by and no mention of Eddie's name. On Saturday afternoon, Claire and Annie sat on the back step fanning themselves with the *War Cry*. It was muggy and overcast. The yard was heavy with the scent of the wild roses, deep pink and smelling like heaven. Laundry hung limp on the line. Every Saturday this summer, Claire had gone somewhere with Eddie Tanner. It was only natural to ask.

"So Eddie's gone back, is he?" Annie said finally.

Claire leaned back in her chair, closed her eyes, fanned herself a little more vigorously. "Yes, he's gone back to Toronto."

"I'm surprised he never came over to say goodbye, he was over here so much,"

Annie said, keeping her voice level. "We'd all got so..." she was going to say, "fond of him," but honesty compelled her to say, "used to him."

"He made up his mind very quickly," Claire said. "He hardly said goodbye to anyone."

And that was all. There was so much more Annie would have liked to ask, but Claire remained aloof.

In the second week of September, the temperature dropped sharply. Annie looked out one morning and saw a tracing of frost on the grass. Her wild roses, still open yesterday and spilling their scent into the air, had shrivelled and closed like brown-edged fists. Annie pulled on her jacket and went out to inspect them. She found a single rose, sheltered under some leaves, still open and untouched by the frost. Taking scissors from her apron pocket, she snipped the rose and carried it in to place in a glass on the table.

Claire came down in her dressing gown – it was a Saturday morning. "Grandmother's still asleep," she said, and saw the rose. "Oh, did all the other roses die?"

"Yes. The frost, you know."

Claire filled her bowl with Cream of Wheat from the pot on the stove, poured herself a cup of tea, and sat down. "You want toast?" Annie said, cutting the bread.

"Yes, please." From where Annie stood in the pantry she could see the pink rose against Claire's white cheek, both of them beautiful, perfect and untouched.

ETHEL

~♦~

BROOKLYN, MAY 1955

CLAIRE ARRIVED IN NEW York on a spring evening when the air was warm and the sky was blue and gold. Ethel heard the downstairs door open at six o'clock and she could hear girls' voices, light feet on the stairs. Diane came in first, carrying a powder-blue train case, and behind her, lugging a large suitcase, was a fair-haired girl in a green-and-white striped suit. Jim folded the paper and got up at once to take the suitcase from her. "So, Claire," he began. Then, as she straightened up, his voice dropped for a moment. "Glory be, you look just like your mother."

Ethel stepped forward, holding out her hands. Jim was right. Replace the haircut and dress with the styles of 1925 and Rose might have been standing before them: tall, fair-haired, pretty, except the girl's eyes were brown instead of the Evans blue. But this girl did not have Rose's brashness; she looked polite and eager to please. To cover Jim's gaffe, Ethel said, "We're so glad to have you, Claire. I'm your Aunt Ethel, of course. And how was your journey?"

Claire looked around her at the tiny neat kitchen, the faded wallpaper, the well-scrubbed linoleum. "It was fine, thank you," she said. Her voice had the slightest trace of a St. John's accent, nothing heavy, but it warmed Ethel's heart. All her friends had lost their accents; Brooklyn sounds overlaid the old rhythms of their speech. Claire sounded fresh, like something just unfolded and taken out of a drawer, clean and pressed.

Through supper, the girls did most of the talking. They seemed to hit it off right away. Diane had suggested weeks ago that Claire should stay with her and Carol in their apartment in Manhattan, rather than with Jim and Ethel in Brooklyn, but Ethel had vetoed that. "I owe it to Annie to look after her properly," she had told Diane.

Diane's lip curled. "So, if she was with me, she wouldn't be looked after properly?"

"She should live with a family," Ethel said. "That's all I'm saying. Your place is too small, anyway."

Ethel knew Diane and Carol lived a fast, immoral New York life, and she had accepted that there was nothing she could do about it. But Annie's girl, little Claire, deserved something better. She was nearly a year older than Diane but would seem younger, Ethel was sure, having been raised at home. She would enjoy their sheltered, quiet family life. She would be company for Ethel.

Now, listening to the girls talk, Ethel wondered if Claire wouldn't prefer to live in Manhattan with Diane and Carol after all. Diane chattered about her new job at an advertising agency, which she loved. Claire talked about the course she was going to take so she could be a legal secretary, and whether it would be easy to get work in a law office once she was finished. They sounded so smart, the two of them. She couldn't ever remember hearing girls talk that way when she was young. The only jobs she ever knew of for girls were working as a maid or working in a shop. She passed the salt and the butter and poured iced tea from a glass pitcher, thinking how this was as it should be: children were meant to rise above their parents, to go farther and higher.

Ethel had laid aside any hopes of herself and Jim ever doing any better for themselves. *This is my life now*, she reminded herself, looking around the four tiny rooms above the shop. *This is what I have.* She had a daughter in Manhattan, a smart-mouthed career girl who knew everything and couldn't stop criticizing her mother. She had a good son with a nice wife out on Long Island, where she was lucky to see them once a month, and no grandchildren yet. She had a husband who worked downstairs all day and climbed the steps at suppertime and hid behind his newspaper, who cared more about whether the Dodgers won or lost than about whether his wife was dead or alive. She had her church, which had continued to be a habit even after she and God had gone their separate ways. She had a few old friends from home; she had a photograph, a telegram, and a Gold Star to mark the place of her eldest son, dead on Okinawa. She had a pain she carried between her stomach and chest, dull but large and hard as a fist. After thirty years in New York, she didn't ask much, Ethel told herself, but was it really fair she'd landed in an apartment as small and shabby as this one?

After supper, Claire helped Ethel clear the dishes, bringing her up to date on news of Harold and Frances and their family, with whom she had stayed for a few days in Toronto on the way down. Diane sat at the table with her father and lit up a cigarette. Ethel hated it when Diane smoked in the apartment, which was probably why Diane always made a point of doing it.

Ethel enjoyed having Claire to work with, liked the soothing rhythm of two women working together, something she had never enjoyed with Diane. It reminded her of years ago, clearing a table with Frances or with Jean, or with Annie, during that year they'd spent back home. Back when Claire and Diane were both babies, which meant it must have been more than twenty years ago.

Over the next weeks, Ethel thought back to that summer often, remembered herself and Annie side by side at the washtub, soaping the hair of the two baby girls, rocking them together on the back step. She wondered if, somehow, amid water and soap bubbles, or in the crib where they slept head-to-toe at nights, baby Claire and baby Diane got switched, so that without knowing it, Ethel had left her own daughter for Annie to raise up at home, and accidentally brought Rose's daughter back to Brooklyn with her. Despite physical likenesses – Claire was the spit of Rose, while Diane was small and dark-haired like Ethel herself – the girls' personalities made her think this was possible. She had too often thought of brazen, brash Diane as another Rose, had said, "You watch out, you're going to turn out exactly like your Aunt Rose."

Now she discovered the delightful other side to that coin: the girl birthed by Rose, raised by Annie, was in every way the daughter Ethel would have wanted for herself. Claire rode the subway into Manhattan every day to go to her course and came home to sit in the kitchen with Ethel and tell stories about her classmates and what she'd learned that day, the things she saw on the subway. She helped in the kitchen and pitched in with the housework. She was cheery and pleasant and soft-spoken, and did not try to shock Ethel.

One Saturday afternoon in the fall, when Claire had been with them half a year, Ethel came out of her bedroom to see Claire standing in the living room with her cheek laid against the window glass, looking down onto Flatbush Avenue. Ethel said nothing, thinking how alone, how separate the girl looked, and she felt a pang of protective love she had not felt towards her own daughter since Diane was twelve.

Claire looked up, her dark eyes clouded and distant. "Aunt Ethel?"

"Yes, my love?"

"Do you ever hear anything from my mother?"

Ethel sat down, crossed her legs, pulled her skirt down over her knee. It was a measure of Claire's reserve, her polite reticence, that this question had taken six months to emerge. Ethel thought back carefully, wanting to get this right.

"Well now, Claire, the last time I can recall seeing your mother would be…I'm not sure now, it must be ten years ago now. During the war, or just after.

You know, she had a job at the Navy Yards. She was quite the working girl, just like you are, I suppose." She remembered Rose, her chin jutting, her eyes hard, perched on the edge of a chair in the Linden Boulevard apartment, looking pleased with herself. "Since then, we haven't seen her. But she's written you, hasn't she?"

Claire moved slowly to the sofa and sat there, her hands folded in her lap, still looking at the window. "Yes. She used to write me about every year or so. Sometimes it would be around my birthday, but other years it might be…oh, just anytime. I suppose the last time was about two years ago. She never said much about herself, but her letters always had a New York postmark, and in the last one she said she was happy and doing fine, that the Lord was taking care of her. Aunt Annie said that was a surprise; she said my mother wasn't ever the religious type. But I guess people can change, with time, can't they?"

Her brown eyes fixed on Ethel, who was also surprised that Rose would give the Lord credit for anything. She did not tell Claire that Jim had made several efforts to locate Rose, even putting a small ad in the Personals section of the *Brooklyn Eagle*. All she said to Claire was, "Yes, honey. A person can change."

Claire picked up a magazine from the coffee table and was silent so long Ethel thought the conversation was over, but then she said, without looking up, "Do you know anything about…about my father?"

This question, too, Ethel had known must be in the girl's head, but she hadn't been sure either how it would come out, or how to answer it. There was no delicate way to tell a young girl you loved that her mother had been such a tramp her father could have been anybody, any man at all. Carefully, she said, "Even back in those days, before you were born, we didn't see a lot of your mother. I don't know who she went around with." She cast back through memory for any information, something to give the girl a sense of roots. "Once we met an Italian boyfriend of hers, a fellow named…let me see, what was it? Martelli, I think? Something Martelli. I believe she said he was in the fruit and vegetable business. Before that, she was seeing a Navy man, but I don't recall his name. Or was it a police officer?"

Ethel made herself stop there, before the litany of vaguely remembered boyfriends made Rose sound like the loose woman she in fact was. She added, "All of those were a few years before you were born, honey. I really don't know who she was keeping company with at the time." She liked the sound of that phrase, *keeping company*. It covered a multitude of Rose's sins.

Claire stared out at the street, but said nothing.

Next time, Ethel thought, *I'll be more careful what I say to her.* Better for the girl to have a story, some story in her mind than to know nothing at all.

She thought of a story: yes, there was a fellow Rose was really serious about. They were engaged, in fact. But he was – it would be best if he could have been killed. More respectable than leaving her, and it would forestall any chance the girl might want to find her father. Ethel decided she needed to polish the story up a little before presenting it to Claire. Also, she would have to take back some of what she had said about not knowing who Rose was seeing. *I didn't know if it was my place to tell you*, she practiced. *But I think you deserve to know.*

But all Ethel's efforts at story-weaving and dissembling were wasted. Sometimes, on Saturday or Sunday afternoons, Claire went by herself for long walks, and Ethel wondered if she was looking then for either of her parents, trying to find clues to her past. She might be, or she might just enjoy the exercise. Ethel didn't know. Claire never raised the subject of her mother – or her father – again.

ROSE

~

BROOKLYN, MARCH 1956

ARE YOU WASHED (are you washed)
In the blood (in the blood)
In the soul-cleansing blood of the Lamb?

Rose beats the tambourine vigorously. Her feet – which, like Noah Collins', are not altogether saved – tap a steady rhythm on the floor beneath her. She stands in front of the altar, wearing the uniform, leading the other worshippers in song.

"For yes, brothers and sisters, I am washed! Are you washed?" she shouts at the congregation as the hymn ends.

"Praise the Lord!" the people chorus back at her, their voices like a mighty current carrying her above them.

"Praise Jesus, you are washed! Redeemed, how we love to proclaim it! Redeemed by the blood of the Lamb!" The band strikes up the tune and Rose's fine strong voice chimes out in the first notes. She loves hymns about the Blood. Redeemed by the Blood of the Lamb, washed in the Blood, power in the Blood. The soul-cleansing Blood. She pictures a great red tide of it, rising to swallow her up, ebbing away to reveal a new, cleaner Rose.

Rose is a fixture at the Brooklyn Citadel now. She is a senior soldier: Welcome Sergeant Rose Evans, her voice frequently raised in testimony and song. She also serves soup and prays with people at the mission. Some of the other saved sinners there look at people just in off the street and shake their heads. "There but for the grace of God go I," they say. "It seems so hard to believe just six months ago – a year, two years ago – I was just like them."

Not hard at all for Rose to believe, for though it's been six years and she now wears a uniform and is washed in the Blood, she still feels like one of them. One of the sinners from the street. Most people come in, get saved, and then become

~

respectable. The men shave, cut their hair, and get steady jobs; the women get married to good men. They live in better apartments than they did before they were saved, and sometimes they leave Brooklyn altogether and go live on Long Island. And this is a sign of success, Rose understands: failure and poverty are supposed to be washed away just like sin and guilt. One young fellow, only about twenty-one, came in off the street in terrible shape, not only a drunk but doing the heroin too, looking like he was at death's door. And in a matter of months wasn't he all shipshape, not only cleaned up and sober but headed off to officer's training college. He came back once to visit, in uniform, with a pretty little wife and a baby. How pleased they all were to see him, to see what a nice job God had made of him.

Rose's life has not changed much. She lives in a rundown boarding house in Crown Heights. She cleans shops and offices, sporadically, for her rent and food money, though much of the time she eats at the mission. The hymns and prayers and testimonies are her lifeline. Throw out the lifeline, throw out the lifeline. Someone is sinking today. Rose was sinking, deep in sin, far from the peaceful shore, and now she has been saved. She's not on the peaceful shore; she's in deep water, miles of black ocean below her, but she's clinging to a life preserver. She likes it this way. If she were on shore, she thinks, would the life preserver seem so dear, so necessary? Wouldn't it be harder to see the other folks out in the water? Pull for the shore, sailor, pull for the shore, Rose advises others in song, but she herself is content where she is.

"You'm finished them pots, Rose?" Marjorie says. They are in the kitchen, doing the washing up now that the evening service has finished.

Rose is humming, *Pull for the shore, sailor, pull for the shore.* "Got a few more to do, Marjorie," she says.

"Well put them over on the counter when you'm done. I got h'eleven big knives 'ere where there should be twelve. Is there one over there?" Marjorie's accent is pure Bonavista; she and her husband came to Brooklyn just after the war and she couldn't be taken for anything but a Newfoundlander.

Until Marjorie came, Rose steered clear of discussing her family back home with Newfoundlanders at the Citadel. "Now which Evans would you be?" they'd say, but she used to sidestep the question. It was Marjorie who finally pinned her down, because she saw the ad in the *Eagle* looking for Rose Evans. Jim must have put that in, Rose thinks. When Marjorie showed it to her they had a long chat which ended up with Rose finally telling which Evans she was and Marjorie saying that her husband knew Mom and Pop and Annie and all their crowd from his time in St. John's.

Rose asked Marjorie not to tell anyone; she says she's not in touch with her family anymore and there's bad feeling there. All the same she's grateful for the bits of news Marjorie gives her; she likes being distantly attached to the Newfoundland grapevine, whose branches filter news of home through the streets and churches of Brooklyn. Still, Marjorie's words this particular night catch her by surprise.

"One of your nieces is moved down 'ere, is she? Will we 'ear tell of her coming to the Citadel, I wonder, or is she not in the Army?"

"What niece would that be?" She hasn't spoken to any of the family in…what is it? Ten years? More? It was like she had disappeared, and she liked it that way. The old Rose is gone, and the Evans family never really had any place for her anyway. What would they make of a whole new Rose? She lifts a heavy pot out of the water, wondering what niece – Harold's girl, perhaps? – might be in Brooklyn now.

"I don't know her name, but my cousin Barbara said she was talking to Annie Winsor – that's your sister, isn't it? – and she said Annie was right lost, didn't know what to make of herself, because her daughter was gone to New York. Now I don't know Annie. How old would her daughter be? I thought Annie only married Bill Winsor after the war?"

"Claire, that would be Claire," Rose says, speaking the name aloud like a word in a hymn. *Blessed. Holy. Claire.* "She's not…not Annie's daughter by rights. Annie reared her up."

"Oh, make no wonder then. Well there's no doubt, you can get just as fond of them you rears up as of your own. My own mother now, she died when I was only five, and me and my sister both was reared up by H'Aunt H'Agnes Mitchell, no relation now, but we called her H'Aunt H'Agnes, of course, and she was as good to me as any mother could have been," Marjorie says, wiping her eyes with the edge of a dishtowel.

Rose takes up another towel and begins drying the pots that lie on the drain board, slowly and methodically, her mind racing. Claire is in Brooklyn. Staying with Ethel and Jim no doubt. How old would she be now? 1931: Rose is not good with dates, but that one sticks. Claire would be twenty-five this winter coming. And Rose has never seen her, not so much as a picture even since Claire was about ten years old.

That night she leaves the mission kitchen late and pulls on her worn grey raglan over her uniform, leaving on the bonnet. She takes a bus down Flatbush Avenue and stands, as she has not done for years, in front of the night-darkened radio shop above which her brother's family lives and works. Up there, behind one of those windows, her daughter is sleeping. Or not yet sleeping, perhaps. A bluish glow flickers: the television light, which shines from more and more windows these evenings. The streets of Brooklyn always used to be crowded in the evenings, kids playing in the street, older people sitting and visiting on the stoops. Now she notices the streets seem quieter at night, more people inside behind closed doors, watching that blue light.

In the squatty, shared bathroom in her boarding house that night, Rose strips off her uniform blouse and brassiere to wash herself. She remembers standing in front of mirrors as a girl, admiring herself. Vanity, vanity, as the preacher says. Her breasts lie almost flat now, hanging down on her chest like flags at half-mast. Her skin is wrinkled and spotted. She thinks of Claire again, wondering what the girl would think if she could see her mother. The threadbare pink washcloth, rubbed with an unyielding bar of old Lifebuoy and soaked with chilly water, traces the outlines of her thin body, lingers a moment at the base of one slack breast.

Rose feels it then, but convinces herself she has not; it is her imagination. She's overwrought by the late hour and the news of Claire. But later, lying in her bed listening to the sounds of traffic and the obscene yells of coloured boys outside, she lets her hand creep up under her nightdress, to that spot again. Now, when she presses it, it feels tender. And there is definitely a lump. Not as big as a marble but bigger than a pea.

She lives in an uneasy balance until Sunday, thoughts of Claire and of the lump jostling in her mind, pushing out everything else, even Jesus. She must do, should do, something about one or both of them, but taking any definite action seems impossible.

On Sunday morning she comes down to the penitent form for prayer. Just as she is, without one plea. With two pleas, it turns out. She kneels amid the crowd of her brothers and sisters, her true family, most of them Sunday-washed and polished, but a few still with the telltale smell of their own bodies, of the street, clinging to them. Words and music wash over her. *All to Thee, my blessed Saviour, I surrender all.* But she is not ready to surrender, not her life, it turns out. A new fire fills Rose, starting in the warm spot under her breast and spreading through her whole body. For the first time she wonders if contentment might not be the only sign of God's presence. Perhaps that old, driving need for something else, something more – perhaps God was in that, too.

Rose prays, *Dear Jesus, heal me. I'll go to the doctor or the hospital or whatever You want. Or You could heal me with just a touch, just the hem of Your garment, like the woman in the story. But I want to live. And if You give me back my life, I'll do something great for You, Lord, I promise. Give me a little more time.*

CLAIRE

MANHATTAN, MAY 1956

YOU SHOULD MOVE IN with me. You'd love it," Diane told Claire over lunch at Chock Full O'Nuts. It was a Saturday and Claire had come in to Manhattan, as she often did, to do some shopping and meet her cousin for lunch. Diane's roommate Carol was getting married and she was looking for someone to share the Greenwich Village apartment.

"I don't know," Claire said. She was cautious of Diane, though she liked her. "It's working out okay for me with your folks. And it's cheap. I don't know if I want to move."

"You're crazy. I don't know how you can put up with my mother." Diane wrapped her perfectly moulded, lipsticked mouth around a sandwich.

"Because she's not my mother, I guess," Claire said.

"She loves you. She thinks you're the cat's pyjamas."

Claire sipped her coffee. "Anyway, I know what would happen. I'd move in with you, and next thing you'd get married to Handsome Henry and I'd be the one stuck with an apartment I couldn't afford. Don't say it's not going to happen, because it is."

Diane shook her head but her smile was pleased: she liked Claire's assurance that this would someday happen. "Henry's worried about getting married too quickly. He thinks he'll get a promotion this summer, though, and if he does, I'd say that's when he'll propose. If he ever does."

"He'll propose. You wait and see. And where would I be then?" Claire made a face and Diane laughed. Diane wiped her mouth with a napkin, then took out her lipstick and compact mirror to touch up.

Claire thought Diane really was movie-star gorgeous, with her dark glossy curls, her long black eyelashes, her wide painted mouth framing white teeth. She was five foot three, which seemed perfect to Claire, who was five foot eight. And she was curvy, with a generous bosom and full hips. Diane worried about her skin, which was not quite perfect, and her weight, which she constantly feared would get out of control. She told blond, slender Claire that she looked like a china doll, or an angel. But Claire knew china doll angels were not in vogue. Diane looked like Jane Russell, or like a dark-haired Marilyn Monroe.

"You lead such a boring life," Diane said now. "I feel it's my mission to bring some excitement into your life."

"My life's not so boring," Claire said, although she secretly agreed. She got up every morning, caught the subway at Church Avenue, rode into Manhattan, got off at Times Square, went to work, and did the same thing in reverse every evening. "I suppose I don't see much, outside of home and work," she conceded. "I haven't even really seen that much of Brooklyn, and I've been living there for half a year now." The only thing she did in Brooklyn was go to church with Aunt Ethel, and go for walks.

Diane made a gesture like brushing away a fly. "You're fine there. There's nothing to see in Brooklyn. But you need to see more of Manhattan than just the subway and your office."

"I went to Macy's this morning. I'm eating at Chock Full O'Nuts," Claire said.

Diane gathered up her purse, her own shopping. "Come with me," she said. "I'll be your tour guide. What's the most tourist-y thing you could ever do in New York City? Something you'd never do on your own. Something I'd never do if I didn't have an out-of-town cousin to drag along."

That was an easy one. "Go up the Empire State Building," Claire said. "I've always wanted to."

Diane rolled her eyes. "Well, now I really do feel like the country cousins are up from Hicksville for the weekend. But sure, we'll go. I've never been up either, you know, and I oughta, because my dad helped build it, as he tells me at least once a year."

"Really? I didn't know that," Claire said, following Diane out of the restaurant.

Up on the 86th floor, the winds blew briskly and the walls were lined with people staring down at the buildings and streets below. Diane leaned against a wall and pointed things out to Claire: the Chrysler Building, the Queensboro Bridge, the Brooklyn Bridge. Brooklyn was distant and hazy, unreal and insubstantial. "Maybe I should move to Manhattan," Claire said aloud.

"Sure you should. This is where everything happens," Diane said.

"I'm glad this fence is here," Claire said, putting her hand against the ropes of steel that caged her in. "I think I'd be scared if I were just leaning over the edge."

"Well, you would have been, if you'd come a few years ago," Diane said. "Henry told me it used to be all open here, but so many people jumped off and killed themselves, they had to build the fence."

"I wonder what makes a person do that," Claire said so quietly that Diane asked, "Beg pardon?"

"Oh, just what would make a person do that...jump, I mean."

"It'd take a lot of guts," Diane said, almost with admiration.

"If you felt that bad, it might take more guts to stay alive," Claire said. She imagined it again: the free-fall, the floating. She felt that way herself sometimes, like she was attached to nothing, suspended between the past and future: no father, a disappearing mother, no sure sense of who she was or would become. But jumping off a building? No, it wasn't something she could imagine. Stupid, really.

"They say a lot of rich people did it in the Depression, after they lost all their money in the stock market," Diane said, leaning back against the wall so the city was behind her. "But I bet a lot of people did it for love, too. Broken hearts."

"I don't believe that," Claire said. "That's only in movies. In real life, nobody would be that foolish, to kill themselves over a fellow." She remembered the summer Eddie Tanner came to St. John's, the giddy feeling she thought might be love, the sharp pain when he told her he was going back home, for no reason at all that she could see. Never, in a million years, would she have jumped off a building for that.

Diane half-closed her eyes and looked at Claire sideways. "You think you know so much about real life? I think you're wrong. There was a time I woulda done it."

Claire looked at Diane sharply. Such things ought not to be put into words. It was like a bad-luck charm. *Don't say that*, she wanted to say, but bit it back, knowing she'd sound like Ethel and that would irritate Diane. Instead she said, "Serious? Who was it?"

"Oh, a guy I used to know in high school. Just nobody," Diane said, cranking up the tough-girl voice a couple of notches. "He dumped me, and I thought I was gonna die. I wanted to, actually, for a long time. I really had it bad."

"But you didn't," Claire said.

"No, I did. I really had it bad, head over heels, you name it. Couldn't eat, couldn't sleep. I wouldn't chase after him 'cause I was too proud for that, but I used to lie awake on the daybed in Mom's living room and cry my eyes out."

"No," Claire amended. "I mean, you didn't kill yourself. You went on living."

Diane pulled a cigarette from her purse and lit up. "Yeah, I guess so. I did, didn't I?" She sounded pleased, as though it had not occurred to her before what an accomplishment this was. "And I'm gonna go on living. I'm gonna make a great life for myself, and forget all about him. He was no good for me anyway. That was why he left – 'cause he said he was no good for me – and now I know it's true. If a fella tells you he's bad news, believe him." She took a long drag on the cigarette.

Claire wondered if she would be able to make a great life for herself. At work she felt a combination of fascination and envy for the junior partners; she sometimes wished she had been a boy, and rich, so she could have gone to law school and been like them. Not just for the money – though that would have been great – but for the work itself.

"So what about you?" Diane asked, and as Claire, still thinking about work, was about to explain, she added, "You haven't gone out with anybody since you landed here. Aren't you ever going to find Mr. Right?"

"Oh…that," Claire said, looking across the river where the ships drifted lazily up and down on its green surface. "There's someone back home. Sort of."

"Sort of? Gosh, you're such a romantic."

Claire pulled her light raglan around her, tied the belt. The wind up here really was cool, even though the sun shafted through the clouds and lit the skyscrapers, turning all their windows to silver, making it look like the Promised Land.

ROSE

⤳

BROOKLYN, JULY 1956

ROSE STEPS THROUGH THE doors of the hospital, clutching her bag. Outside, cars shoot past, blurring against the brightness of the summer day. She feels unsteady, as if the world is spinning. She walks half a block or so to a bench by a bus stop where she has to sit down.

When the bus comes, Rose gets on, even though it's not her bus. She can always get a transfer. A bus feels like a safe place, surrounded by other people, a driver in charge. For awhile, she doesn't have to think or make any decisions.

Marjorie and Frank would have picked her up from the hospital. In fact, Marjorie probably would have brought her in this morning and waited for her while she had the treatment. They've been so good. Everyone has been so good. Ever since the doctor told her it was cancer and her breast would have to come off, her family at the Citadel has encircled her like a warm pair of arms, not only praying for her loudly and regularly, but raising money for her surgery and treatment, bringing food and flowers, visiting faithfully while she was in the hospital.

Marjorie and Frank made the greatest offer of all: they asked Rose to come stay with them, in their small but tidy spare bedroom, in their neat little apartment on President Street. They are twenty years younger than she is, hardworking people with two small children. And they are willing to take an old woman of fifty into their house for no better reason than that she's a child of God and she comes from home.

She said no. Told Marjorie she was better off on her own, though she can't articulate in what way her cramped dark room with its single bare light bulb, its peeling wallpaper and worn linoleum, makes her "better off." Perhaps it's just the fact that there's no-one here but her and God. Back in that room after an hour and a half of bus rides and transfers, she makes herself kneel on the hard floor beside the bed, feels the floorboards bite into her knees. The surgery was, in its way, successful, and the radiation, though horrible, is supposed to "make sure" they had got it all. But she can still feel cancer like a dark suspicious man following her home through the night: you don't want to turn and look it in the eye but you always know it's there.

She pictures Jesus, tall as the Williamsburg Savings and Loan building, walking down the streets of Brooklyn in his long white robe, looking into the upstairs windows of houses, passing a hand through the walls to touch this one and that one. The way things are these days, he might skip Crown Heights altogether, she thinks, what with all the fighting and the Negro gangs and all. Or maybe he wouldn't. It's hard to tell, with him. But she sees him very clearly, coming down her street, this wretched little line of sagging boarding houses. His sandaled feet carry him past; perhaps there's a coloured child with a praying mother sick in the house at the end of the street. Or some old saint on her deathbed. It would be so easy for him to miss Rose Evans, with her room on the back of the house and all. *While on others Thou art calling, do not pass me by!*

Before she can finish her prayer she feels the familiar tingling in her neck and below her chin, the faint sour taste in her mouth, and knows she's going to vomit. She presses a hand against her mouth and looks around for the tin basin. She grabs it from the nightstand and holds it on her lap with one hand, using the other to hold back her hair as she heaves and retches into the basin. There's little to bring up because she hasn't eaten all day, and she can feel her stomach clenching with the dry heaves as she chokes up a few pitiful mouthfuls of bile. She lays the basin on the floor. It reeks, but she can't find the strength to get up and take it to the bathroom. Instead, she takes a sip of the glass of water that's been on her table since morning; it's warm now but it tastes as sweet as wine in her mouth. She lies down on the bed, drawing the threadbare chenille bedspread up over her, feeling not just exhausted and empty but clean, drained of doubts and fears.

On Flatbush Avenue, two weeks later, Rose sees her. Rose hasn't come here to lurk or snoop around on purpose: she's trying to give that up. No, she came down here because a woman from church invited her for a visit, a good meal, and it's been awhile since Rose has had a good meal. Then, walking back up towards her bus stop, she sees Ethel Evans and a young woman. The girl is fair-haired, tall, wearing a pink suit with a matching hat. Ethel and the girl look into store windows and talk together, their heads close. Ethel puts a hand on the girl's arm.

Rose passes so close behind them she could touch them. She is sure she will stop, will say something. But she has no idea what to say. She pauses just past them, pretends to bend down to pick up something she has dropped. Long enough to hear Ethel say, "Now that would look lovely on you, Claire."

"Oh, do you think so? I think that would be more Diane's style. I could see her in that."

Hearing Claire's voice, Rose is riveted to the sidewalk. She turns back and eyes the girl again, hungrier than she was this evening when they put a good hot meal in front of her. She can't get enough of looking at the girl, listening to her. Rose feels like the world has stopped turning, like when Joshua made the Lord stop the sun in the sky. She can stand here forever, watching the daughter she has never known while a pain that has nothing to do with radiation treatments twists inside her stomach.

Rose continues walking, because she has no excuse to stand there any longer, and they're walking away in the opposite direction. She looks back, just once. The tall fair girl, the small dark woman. Well matched, all the same. Claire's aunts have done well by her, anyway, even if her mother hasn't.

Rose wanders blindly, past groups of people on the sidewalk, till she hears singing that, although it's no hymn she knows, she recognizes at once as a holy sound.

Inside a storefront, a crowd of people is gathered, singing, hands raised over their heads. Nobody passing by seems to give them a second glance. Their song flows out into the street and swirls around Rose.

Glory glory, hallelujah,
Since I laid my burden down...

Rose pushes the door open and slips in under cover of the music. Once inside, she sees that nearly all the people there are coloured, with only a few white faces among the crowd. It doesn't surprise her: the music has a dark and vibrant sound that she doesn't associate with people of her own kind, lively though the crowd at the Citadel is. This is like a whole other kind of music, stripped of the blare of trumpets and the pounding of the piano and the clanging tambourine – an earthy, strong sound carried only by human voices rising up and plunging down the scale.

An old coloured man stands up at the front, wearing a red and white robe. His hands are raised; his hair is white. The music does not exactly stop; it lowers to a hum, a murmur, that continues to twist and writhe beneath his words.

"Oh, my brothers and sisters, is there anyone today who has come here for healing? Is there anyone here bound by Satan, caught in chains of alcohol or drugs? Snared in the trap of cancer or tuberculosis? Ravaged by disease, wrecked by despair? Come down, come on down, my brother, come down, my sister, kneel and receive healing, healing, through the precious blood of Jesus. Come now! Come now!"

It is as dizzying as the first altar call Rose knelt for at the Citadel, when she was saved. Now she is answering another call – not to be saved, but healed. They have prayed for her healing again and again at the Citadel, of course. But it was a polite request, something they'd like the Almighty to do if He could fit it into His plans. And if not, Thy will be done. After all, they bury their saints every year, as every church does; they have to hedge their bets. She has never heard them pray for healing as this Negro preacher prays, like it's not a request but a demand, like he has the authority to call down God's power from on high.

She is kneeling at the front, but strong hands pull her to her feet and she stands before the minister. His black face seems huge and staring; she has never been this close to a Negro man. "And what is your burden, my sister? What do you need deliverance from?"

"I…I have cancer," she says. "I've had treatment but…I don't think it's really gone. I want to be healed." He takes a breath as if gathering his energies, and she adds, "And I lost my daughter."

"Are you saved by the blood of Jesus?"

"Yes. Yes, I am saved."

"Then be *healed* by the power of the Holy Spirit!" He leans back and brings his hand forward onto Rose's head with enough force to knock her to the ground, but she feels no pain as she hits the floor. Instead, she is flooded with energy, with joy. Around her, she hears voices rising in words that are not words, a melodious babble of sound, and opens her mouth to find she is making the same sounds. Tears pour down her face. Black hands reach out and hold her, and she holds these unfamiliar bodies close.

"Do you believe in healing?" Rose asks the Captain at the Citadel after Sunday evening service.

"Yes, of course, we believe God can heal the sick. We believe He's healing you, Rose."

"I don't mean a bit at a time, with the surgery and the radiation. I mean all at once, like Jesus did. A miracle. When somebody lays their hands on you."

He nods, obviously trying to encourage her, but worried, she can see. He'd be even more worried if he knew she'd been to a place called The Miracle Healing Temple of the Precious Blood, but he probably guesses it's something like that. After all, she's not likely to have had hands laid on her by the Methodists or the Episcopalians, is she?

But Rose's inner certainty is unshakeable. She does not go back to the doctor or the hospital. No more radiation; she is free from the stink of vomit and fear. She does return to the Citadel, for awhile, to those kind friends who helped her and prayed for her. But her real life now is at The Miracle Healing Temple of the Precious Blood. Despite the garish name and the ugly storefront, despite the black faces and the unfamiliar hymns, Rose belongs there. She stands to testify there and the voices rise around her like waves. *Amen, sister! Glory hallelujah! Preach it, preach!!*

And she does preach it. She lays aside the neat black Army uniform for a dazzling red and white robe. She stands at the front of the small shabby room beside the Reverend Vernon Peters, the kindly old man with the authority of an apostle who healed her. Here, Rose shines; she is incandescent. She can lay hands on someone and pray for their healing, and see in their eyes that God has touched them.

Other things slip away. Not just the Citadel, not just cancer. She no longer feels like she wants a drink at the end of the day, a feeling she has battled for years. She no longer has to restrain herself from walking past Jim and Ethel's place, looking for Claire. Her one glimpse of Claire was a gift from God, a message that her girl will be all right. All Rose has to do is keep serving Him. And she has found the place to do it.

CLAIRE

BROOKLYN, JULY 1956

CLAIRE LIKED TO TAKE long walks on warm weekend afternoons. She looked in store windows, at the fronts of houses, trying to imagine her mother walking here thirty years earlier. She had asked Aunt Ethel about her parents only once. In her aunt's vagueness and discomfort, Claire had all the answer she needed. Aunt Ethel obviously had no idea who Claire's father was, and just as obviously she hadn't thought much of Claire's mother. She had hinted at numerous, nameless "men friends," but come up with only one name: an Italian fruit-seller named Tony Martelli.

It was foolishness, really – one name in a borough of two million people, one man among probably dozens her mother went out with. Claire knew it was foolish to pause at every fruit store she passed, to check the proprietors' names on the signs. Foolishness was something for which she had little tolerance, in others or, especially, in herself.

So when, after a year of long walks, she passed a fruit store in Williamsburg with the name "T. Martelli" over the door, she made herself walk past, not looking back. Claire told herself she had seen nothing important, nothing that mattered.

The next day, Sunday, she went with Aunt Ethel to the Methodist church. Claire enjoyed the services there. There was none of the fervent emotional baggage that was attached to Army services at home. No testimonies, no shouts of "Hallelujah!" or "Praise the Lord!" It was quiet, dignified, decorous. A person could go to church there and not even have to think about whether she believed in God.

After Sunday dinner she went back to the fruit store, which was closed. She told herself there was no need to come back here, yet the next Saturday she found herself walking down the same street. This time she saw a middle-aged man behind the counter. She went inside and bought a bag of peaches.

The man behind the counter was burly, red-faced, with black hair turning to grey. He was loud and friendly with three neighbourhood children who each went away with an apple. Then he turned to her.

"This is a good choice," he told her as he rang up her purchase. "Redhaven peaches. You like Redhaven peaches?"

"I suppose so," said Claire. "Back home, the only peaches I ever saw came out of a tin. I thought they grew on the tree that way, tinned."

T. Martelli laughed, a big warm laugh. "Yeah, I can just see that. The canned-peach tree." He looked up from the cash register, lowered his furry eyebrows. "Back home, eh? Where's that, where's back home, young lady?"

"Um, in Canada, a place called Newfoundland," Claire said.

He laughed again and pointed at her. "You see, I was right! I knew you was from Newfoundland. I knew some Newfies, years ago. Well, I still know some, we got a few right in this neighbourhood." Now she got the bushy-eyed stare again. "You never knew a lady name of Rose Evans, did you? Years ago, years ago. You ain't related to any Evanses, are you?"

It was that easy. Two million people, one year of long walks, one fruit store, one middle-aged Italian man, and Claire had found, at the very least, someone who once knew her mother. Maybe she had found more than that.

"Rose Evans is my mother's name," she said. "I'm Claire...Claire Evans."

She tried to read his face, but all she saw was a broad grin. "Well, Claire, welcome to Brooklyn. You been here a long time? How's your mama? How's she doin' these days?"

"I'm sorry, I really don't know." Claire laid the bag of peaches on the counter. "She's...I haven't had much contact with her, these last few years. My Aunt Annie, back home, raised me, and now I'm living with my Aunt Ethel and Uncle Jim here in Brooklyn."

He frowned, searching his memory. "Ethel and Jim. Yeah, I remember them. He worked up on the high steel, didn't he?"

"A long time ago. Not anymore."

The man laughed again. "Well, it was all a long time ago, wasn't it?"

She wanted to say, *I'm almost twenty-five years old. I was born in 1931. Does that mean anything to you?* That would be impolite, of course. Not sensible. But she nudged as close as she could. "When did you...I mean, how long ago did you know my mother?"

"Oh, ages ago. When I was young and foolish, right? Back in...oh, back in the twenties, I guess. Prettiest girl I ever went out with. What a dancer."

"You…you went out with her?"

"Oh yeah, she was my girlfriend. My first big love. We all gotta have one of those, don't we?" Mr. Martelli lowered his eyebrows and looked at her. It was impossible for him not to be thinking what she was thinking, wasn't it? Had he even known Rose Evans had a baby in Brooklyn and sent her home to Newfoundland to be raised? If he knew, surely he must have wondered what became of her.

"You look like her, like Rose, you know. Just like her," he said. "That's why I asked if you were related."

"People tell me that a lot," said Claire.

A plump, dark-haired woman came into the shop from the back door, the door connecting it to the apartment above. There was a door just like it in Uncle Jim's shop. "Angelo!" she called back over her shoulder. "Get out here and give your father a hand unloading these boxes!"

Mr. Martelli pulled the woman next to him, squeezing her against his side. "This is my Gina, my wife," he said. "Gina, this girl is from Newfoundland. She's Rose Evans' daughter. You remember Rose, dontcha?"

Claire wondered what memories Tony Martelli's wife could have of the woman who was supposed to have been his first great love. Gina looked her up and down, then looked back at Tony. "I don't remember no Rose," she said.

Through the open storefront three old women entered amid a swarm of small children. Gina's smile grew wide and she moved to serve them. She shooed the children, not out of the shop but upstairs.

"Some of them are mine," Tony Martelli said. "The rest, who knows? The whole neighbourhood comes in and out. I don't even keep track." He leaned his elbows on the counter, smiling at Claire, in no hurry to ring in her peaches.

Gina took over the cash, ringing in purchases for the old ladies. She invited them, too, up the stairs. The store was growing loud, noise cascading down the stairs from the kitchen above. Claire could smell something cooking.

It wasn't hard to imagine the scene upstairs. The Martellis' kitchen, though foreign, would also be familiar. If she stood in the middle of that crowded room, it would remind her of Aunt Annie's kitchen and dozens of other kitchens back home, where food was always cooking and being eaten, children played around the stove, old men and women sat to the table, telling stories about the places they came from and how they got here. Noisy, crowded kitchens full of life. Claire supposed that these Italian kitchens and Newfoundland kitchens were only part of a web that stretched world-wide, Brooklyn-wide too: Spanish kitchens and Jewish kitchens and Black kitchens, all full of voices and smells and faces. It was all very picturesque, but what Claire loved was Aunt Ethel's kitchen, small and clean and sparkling with Formica and linoleum and chrome, where no-one ever went except to cook, eat, or clean up after a meal.

Claire felt she had stayed too long, peering into Tony Martelli's shop and apartment and life. She picked up the peaches. "I have to go now," she said.

"But you'll come again, right? Come again, drop by any time," he said, waving his hand like a king offering her half his kingdom.

"Maybe. I...I don't live around here. But it was nice meeting...someone who knew my mother."

Tony Martelli's face looked sad for a moment. "I miss her, sweetheart. She was a great gal. The love of my life."

Without meaning to, Claire let her eyes flicker to the stairs, half-expecting Gina to come into the room again. Tony followed her glance. "Don't get me wrong," he said quickly. "My Gina, she's a princess, she's a queen. But your mother, Rose...well, that was love. Me and Gina...this is a marriage. It's two different things. You don't wanna get them mixed up." He smiled at Claire again. "You take care of yourself, now, you hear? You tell your aunt and uncle Tony Martelli says hi."

Claire went home that night to the clean quiet of Aunt Ethel's house, where she did not tell her aunt and uncle that Tony Martelli said hi. Instead, she went to the bathroom and looked at her own face in the bathroom mirror. Tony was right; everyone was right: she looked like Rose. Like pictures of Rose, like the Evans family. Fair hair, fair skin. Her brown eyes were the only thing that might seem remotely Italian, hardly enough to link her to Tony Martelli and his dark, lively tribe of children. She was left with that thought, and with the only piece of fatherly advice Tony would ever give her. "That was love. This is a marriage. It's two different things. You don't wanna get them mixed up."

ANNIE

ST. JOHN'S, FEBRUARY 1957

"ABIDE WITH ME, FAST falls the eventide, the darkness deepens, Lord with me abide," Annie sang under her breath as Bill unlocked the door. "Funny thing, isn't it, how Mom always hated that hymn, yet she said she wanted it at her funeral?"

"She hated it because she said it was dreary and put her in mind of funerals," Bill pointed out. "I s'pose she figured there was a time and place for it."

"She never liked dreary hymns, though," Annie said. "She was always more for the lively ones, the ones you could clap your hands to." Funny, she thought, since she didn't think of her mother as a happy person. But she was a grand one to belt out a hymn.

Harold had flown home for his mother's funeral. He couldn't have made it to be at her deathbed: there was no deathbed. She lay down one night as alive and cranky as ever, woke up calling for Annie at two in the morning, and was dead before Annie got into the bedroom. Her heart, of course. Eighty-five years old. A good long life, though very narrow these last years. And not a bad way to go, everyone said.

Annie had phoned Jim with the news; he said he was sorry he couldn't come. Only Harold and Annie, of her five children, to stand by her graveside. None of her grandchildren. All scattered, all so far away, one dead before her. But the house was full of friends and relatives, church people and neighbours, all reminiscing and catching up.

Harold moved up beside Annie. "Jim would have liked to have been here," he said.

"It's a shame he couldn't come then."

"Don't blame him, Annie. Things are harder for him and Ethel than they are for me and Frances. I'm my own boss, you know."

"You always said any man who had his own business had a slave driver for a boss," Annie remembered suddenly.

Harold laughed. "That's what I said, and it's true, too. But at least I can give myself a few days' leave to go to my mother's funeral, and scrape up the money to go. Like I said, 'tis not as easy for Jim and them."

"And all your crowd, how are they doing?" She hadn't had a chance to talk with Harold yet: he arrived this morning, barely in time to get ready and go to the funeral. Bill had picked him up at Torbay airport.

"Oh, not bad, not so bad, you know. The boys are doing well. You know Ken's graduating from university in the spring. Says he's going to be a teacher. Danny, now, he's finishing up high school, but he's not the university type."

"Will he come work for you?"

"He might, he might for awhile. His real interest is in cars. And poor Valerie, well, she never changes."

"No signs of her getting married?"

"No, and she don't seem to have any interest even. But she's not career-minded either, except for this writing she keeps on about. She's not like Claire, now, or Jim's Diane. Those are two smart young girls."

"How is Claire doing in New York?" asked Ethel's sister Ruby, drifting over.

"Oh, she's doing marvellous by all accounts," said Annie, warming with pride.

"Not married, is she?"

"Not yet, but she's working hard. She's secretary in a lawyer's office."

"She's smart, that one," Bill said, moving up to join their small circle. "Could have been a lawyer herself, if she'd been a man."

"Does she mean to stay there, or come home?" Harold asked.

"Oh, I don't know," said Annie. "She doesn't say, in her letters. I s'pose sometime she'll meet someone down there and get married, settle down in the States." Across the room she saw Doug Parsons, his head a little above the sea of women around him. "But she does say she'll come home if I ever needs her, you know."

Annie looked around at the kitchen and imagined what it would look like when everyone was gone. It had been quiet these last two years, with Claire away. Now, without Mother in her chair knitting away and throwing in the odd comment, it would be quieter still. "I'll hardly know what to do with myself when I'm not looking after someone."

Ruby laughed. "Well, you still got Bill to look after."

"Yes, but Bill looks after me too," Annie said. "I know some husbands are not like that. Need to be waited on hand and foot." Ruby, a spinster, nodded sagely. "But Bill does for me, and I do for him. Not like looking after children, or old people, where it's all give and no take."

"So you'll be looking forward to this, then, to having some peace and quiet and the place to yourselves."

"I've been looking forward to it a long time," Annie said. It seemed for years now, she had been waiting for the day when she wouldn't have to jump up to make anyone a cup of tea, when she'd have no-one but herself and Bill to think of. It was a sin to think of her mother's death as a relief, but it was, in its way. And yet. She held herself tensed up inside, unable to relax, because of a secret she had been guarding these weeks now – something held inside her that would not allow her to enjoy the long-deserved rest.

Finally they were all gone, except Harold of course. He was flying out tomorrow. He sat at the table with Bill, exchanging family news. They would like to come home for a holiday sometime, him and Frances. Maybe next summer.

Maybe, maybe. Annie sat with her feet up and sipped her tea. Her free hand strayed to her side, just above the line of her bra, her fingers searching. But Bill glanced her way and she let her hand drop. She had said nothing to him, because she could not frame it into words. *I found a lump. There's a lump in my breast.* She needed another woman to tell it to, but there was no other woman: no sister, no daughter, now, no mother. If it really was – anything bad – she couldn't do it alone. Bill was the kindest man in the world, but he was still a man. She hated to put the thought even into words – hated the words even more than *I have a lump* – but the words she was thinking, and could not keep back, were: *I need you, Claire. Please come home.*

PART THREE

1974 - 1989

ANNE

ST. JOHN'S, APRIL 1974

ANNE'S PARENTS ARE FIGHTING. Anne lies on her stomach in bed and pulls the covers over her head but she can still hear them. There's no yelling, just loud talking. When Tammy Simms' parents fight, they yell at each other and her mother breaks glasses. Anne's parents don't ever fight. But for the last few days something has been different. On Friday her mom got a letter in the mail that made her really happy and they all went out to the Kenmount for Chinese food to celebrate, Mom and Dad and Stephen and Anne. They got Chinese take-out food too and dropped it off to Aunt Annie and Uncle Bill.

Then on Saturday and Sunday, Mom and Dad had Long Talks. Every time Anne or Stephen went in a room, Mom and Dad would stop talking or change the subject. "What are they talking about?" Anne whispered to Stephen in the back seat of the car on the way home from church on Sunday.

"Moving away," Stephen said.

"We're moving away? Who is? All of us?" Anne's panic made her voice rise and carry to the front seat. Mom turned around.

"We're not moving anywhere, Anne. Stephen, don't get her worked up over nothing."

Then Dad. "Claire, don't go telling her that when you haven't even—"

"*Doug.*"

Anne pulls back the covers and can hear words again. Only none of the words make sense.

"...your decision, Claire, not mine. I think it's a mistake but it's your mistake. You take responsibility for it."

Her mother's words are so fast and run-together Anne can't pick them out. Then her dad again.

"...fine, but don't try to cast me in some male-chauvinist-pig role because you're too scared to take the bull by the horns and..."

Bulls. Pigs. What the heck are they talking about? Anne wishes she could slip across the hall to Stephen's room and see if he is making any sense out of it. He's eleven, two years older than she is. He understands a lot more things, though usually he doesn't explain them to her. Or she could just sit there on the foot of his bed. Maybe they could turn on the light and play Battleship. It would make her feel better, just to be with someone. The words her parents are saying are not making sense. Not just bulls and pigs, but Dad said Mom was scared. That can't be right. Mom is never scared. She is the bravest person Anne knows.

People say, "Your mother is amazing, Anne." Last spring, when Mom had her graduation and wore the long black dress with the flat hat, people said, "You should be very proud of your mother." Anne's mother has been in school for as long as Anne can remember. In the day she goes to work and at night she goes to school. In between she picks up Anne and Stephen from Aunt Annie's and takes them home for supper, except for the nights they stay and have supper at Aunt Annie's. Those are the best suppers.

The voices get quieter. A door closes, probably the door to Mom and Dad's bedroom. Anne lies awake and wonders what her parents are fighting over. Something to do with moving away. Why would they move? They have a house. Sometimes people move when they don't have a job. But Mom and Dad both have jobs. Anne would hate to move. She loves her school, which is St. Andrews, and her church, which is St. James. Right next to each other, two saints. In St. John's, which makes three. School is just ten minutes' walk from Aunt Annie's house and Anne can walk home to Aunt Annie's after school as long as Stephen is with her. Then she can watch TV and do her homework and usually have a snack. Uncle Bill shows Stephen how to tie different kinds of knots and takes him out in the shed to make things with wood. Anne learns from Aunt Annie how to make chocolate chip cookies. If they moved away, they would have a different church and school and not live in St. John's and be far from Aunt Annie and Uncle Bill. All bad things.

Later, when she goes to the bathroom, Anne stops by the door of her parents' room. It is open a little bit, but she stands where no-one can see her. She stands there for a minute, to see if they say anything about moving away.

Mom is talking. Anne hears "...responsibilities..." and then "...Annie and Bill." She edges closer to the door.

"Lots of people their age manage, Claire. They're both in good health."

"You only see what you want to see. Bill is going downhill every year. And

Annie, it's a game of Russian roulette. She has another check-up tomorrow. Seventeen years of good reports. That could all be undone in one minute."

"You can worry about things till you drive yourself crazy, honey. But you have a responsibility to yourself too. You worked your tail off; you sent out applications. Even your cousin Valerie went off and—"

"Don't talk to me about Valerie, there's no comparison. A Master's in Creative Writing? You know what that was, Doug? An excuse to go to Arizona and sit in a circle with a bunch of hippies getting in touch with her feelings. And Valerie can bloody well do that if she pleases. Harold and Frances don't need her. She's got no responsibilities."

It's quiet for a long time. Anne goes back to her room and pulls the covers up over her head again.

She wants to talk to Stephen about it, but when they get to school the next morning he takes off for the Grade Six room right away and she doesn't see him anymore. After school he walks home with Andrew Clark and Jamie Cross, while Anne trails behind.

When they get to Aunt Annie's house, only Uncle Bill is home. "Your mom's taken your Aunt Annie to the doctor," he explains. "Just a check-up. I guess you two are stuck with me for the rest of the afternoon."

"Can we go out in the shed?" Stephen suggests.

Uncle Bill looks at Anne.

"Could I come out in the shed too?" She likes the shed, with the wood-shaving smell and the radio that plays old-time favourites on VOWR. "I could just, you know, sit and watch or something."

When Claire and Annie come back from the doctor's office that's where they all are, out in the shed. Stephen is trying to build a birdhouse and Uncle Bill is sanding the edges for him. Anne sits on the floor with several small odd ends of wood, trying to build something.

"Get up, Anne, you're sitting in the sawdust. Have you still got your school tunic on? That's going to be filthy, you should have more sense." Mom says these things before hello, before she even really looks at Anne. She seems more impatient than usual, jingling her car keys, looking around the shed without meeting anyone's eyes. "Anne, Stephen, get up to the house and get your book bags and put your jackets on. I need to talk to Uncle Bill for a minute. I'll be right up."

As the shed door shuts behind Anne, she hears Uncle Bill say, "What is it, Claire?" in a voice that doesn't sound like him at all.

They run up through the garden, getting their feet wet in the grass. Up the back steps and into the kitchen. Aunt Annie sits at the kitchen table, looking out the window. She looks up when they come in, and smiles. "Did your Uncle Bill take good care of you? You got sawdust all over your tunic, Anne. Is he making a little carpenter out of you too?"

"No, I was just fooling around with wood," Anne says. She's about to follow Stephen to the front porch where her jacket is hanging, but something pulls her back. She says, "How was your check-up, Aunt Annie?"

Aunt Annie looks startled. "Imagine you asking me that, Anne. You're growing up so fast. Well, my check-up was fine, just fine. I've got to go back next week to have something looked at, just a little thing. The doctor says it's probably nothing."

"Good." Anne goes over and gives Aunt Annie a quick, fierce hug. She's not used to seeing Aunt Annie dressed up for the doctor, with a good skirt and blouse on and her hair brushed out. The only time she looks like that is sometimes on Sunday nights when Anne comes over to go to Salvation Meeting with Aunt Annie and Uncle Bill, which she likes because it's so different from her own church on Sunday morning. On Sundays, Aunt Annie wears the uniform. Here in the house she usually has an apron on and a bandanna tied around her hair with a few grey curls coming down on her forehead.

Probably nothing. Anne hears those words again before supper, as her dad stands at the counter making hamburgers and her mom leans against the counter talking. Anne sits in the dining room doing homework. She hears unfamiliar words: *mammogram, suspicious, biopsy.* Out of them she picks the familiar phrase: *probably nothing.*

"Well there you go," her dad says. "The doctor thinks it's probably nothing. There's no reason to get all worked up about it."

"If he thinks it's worth a biopsy then it's not nothing. She's been down that road already, lost a breast, and survived. Every time she goes to the doctor I'm terrified. How could you expect Bill to cope with all that himself? At his age, in his state of health? It makes no sense, Doug."

Anne's pencil stops moving. Her mom's voice sounds like it did when they were fighting last night. She sounds angry, but at who? Not at Anne for something as simple as sawdust on her tunic. She's angry in a bigger way.

"So you're back to square one? As far as law school is concerned?"

"Yes. Back to square one," her mother says.

There's a lot Anne still doesn't understand. Aunt Annie losing a breast doesn't make any sense. How could you lose something that's attached to you? It's like her mother says, *Anne, you'd forget your head if it wasn't screwed on.* And she doesn't know what law school is, or where Square One is. But the days unravel one after another and there are no more fights. Life is normal. Aunt Annie has another doctor's appointment, but it's in the morning so she's there when Anne and Stephen get home from school. After that nobody says anything more about breasts or doctors, so it was Probably Nothing. Nobody says anything more about moving away either, not ever again.

ETHEL

~~

BROOKLYN, MAY 1974

SHE HEARD JIM COMING up the back steps from the shop at four-fifteen, a quarter of an hour earlier than usual. Ethel stood at the sink peeling carrots, feeling the spidery fingers of pain shoot up the backs of her legs. Jim must feel the same way, standing behind the counter all day long. No wonder he wanted to come up early, to put his feet up and rest.

The steady rhythm of his steps was broken as he paused, turned back. Going back down for something he'd forgotten, she thought. He was getting like that, forgetful. She wondered why young Taylor still kept him on. It must have been a kindness, maybe a favour for Jimmy, who was one of his most successful managers.

From below, a voice rose to a shout. No-one ever shouted in the store. She heard the words: "Mr. Evans! Mr. Evans!" It sounded like Martin, the boy in the shop. What was so wrong that Martin couldn't handle it himself? Then another voice, not Jim's – loud and sharp and rough. *Trouble*, Ethel thought.

"Freeze! Don't get in my way, I got a gun!"

Just like those cop shows on TV, Ethel thought. Just like the nightly news reports about crime, more of it every day, right here in Flatbush. All those foreigners, all those coloured. It wasn't safe here anymore.

She stood crouched on the stairs, out of sight from the store, terrified. She could hear the men's rough voices, hear them making threats and lifting things – TVs, she supposed – out of the store. If she went upstairs, she could call the police. But they might hear her on the stairs. She heard no sound from Jim, or from Martin. Of course, Martin could have been in on it all. He was coloured, after all. Maybe these were Martin's friends, his gang members. She had never really trusted him.

Then she heard the smash and tinkle of broken glass. After that, the door slammed, with the little ping that used to welcome customers. Silence. Ethel crept a few steps farther down, almost to the door. Then she heard Martin.

"Mr. Evans, Mr. Evans, you all right? Mr Evans!"

Ethel was through the door and in the shop, not seeing the disarray, the broken glass near the door, the missing TVs and radios. She saw Martin, a short round boy whose eyes were wide with terror, shaking Jim's shoulder. Jim was at the counter, slumped forward, his head on his arm.

He's been shot, she thought, looking for blood, a wound, then remembered she had heard no gunshot.

Martin looked up at her, the whites of his eyes staring in his dark-brown face. He was obviously scared and truly concerned for Jim, but all Ethel could see was his black skin – the same as the men who broke in here and hurt her husband, the same as all the people who had moved in and changed the neighbourhood, made it so a decent woman couldn't walk the streets and a decent man couldn't make a living in the shop where he'd worked for over twenty-five years.

"Get away from him," she ordered coldly, and went over to Jim.

He struggled to open his eyes, to lift his head. His mouth groped for words but could not form them. "Hush, hush," she said, in a voice she had not used since the children were small. "You're going to be all right." She looked across at Martin, moving dazedly around the broken glass, the places where the missing items were. "What happened?" she said, freezing him with her glare.

"I don't know, Mrs. Evans. It happened so fast. Some guys came in, they had a gun, they started taking stuff. Me and Mr. Evans, we just shut up and stood here." His toe nudged the broken glass. "They didn't need to break anything. One guy just kicked the glass out of the door as they were going out."

"Just for badness," Ethel said. "What happened to Jim?"

"He was fine, ma'am, just fine up till they went out the door, just standing there like I was, trying not to do anything that'd get them mad at us, and then…then he just went like that. I mean, he just kinda fell forward with his head on the counter like that. I was scared. I thought maybe he had a heart attack…"

Ethel's hands were still moving gently over Jim's head, his neck and back. "Get on the phone," she ordered Martin. "Call the police and then an ambulance. You'll have to stay here and talk to the police, tell them what happened. I have to get my husband to the hospital." As Martin moved to the phone on the counter nearby she wondered what they would do about locking up. Martin hadn't been trusted with the keys. That reminded her of something, and she said sharply, "Martin."

"Ma'am?" He looked up, receiver in his hand, finger on the dial.

"These men…the men who broke in here. Did you know them?" He shook his head, but she pushed. "They weren't…friends of yours? Fellows you go around with?"

He frowned; his face closed. "Mrs. Evans, I never saw those men before in my life," he said, and turned back to the phone. She could see the difference now in his face, in his attitude. Before, he'd thought he was on her side and Jim's, all of them victims of crime together. But she had pushed him back over a boundary, placed him on the same side as men who broke into stores and smashed windows and threatened old men with guns. Now, she knew, she could never give Martin the key.

What came to her, in the ambulance riding to the hospital, was how she had no-one nearby to call on. For years, it seemed, she had been part of a community. She had friends from home, family nearby. Church friends. Neighbours in the apartment building when they lived on Linden. Someone who could come with you to the hospital, or watch your shop for you, or just be there to help in time of need. Somehow, without her really noticing, all those people had disappeared: moved back home, moved out to New Jersey or even down to Florida. Her church had closed down, actually closed because there weren't enough white people to keep it going, and the nearby churches were full of coloured people, so of course she didn't go anymore.

It was a stroke, she learned at the hospital. A massive stroke, but he was going to live.

"You'll come stay with us, with Jimmy and me and the kids," Joyce said, patting her hand as she sat with her beside Jim's hospital bed. Joyce was a gem, an angel, a pearl. She was here doing what Diane should be doing, while Diane was off living her fancy, high-priced California life.

Diane phoned long distance and asked if there was anything she could do. *Yes*, Ethel thought, *you can be here for me and your father, beside us, where your place is.* "No, dear," she said into the phone.

"No, dear," she said to Joyce. "Not right now, at least. You don't have room anyway, and it would be so difficult, so confusing for the children."

Jimmy carried his father up over the stairs the day they brought him home. And that was all they would need to worry about the stairs, Ethel figured, because Jim would never go down them again. He sat in the armchair in the living room, half his body slumped and immobile, his still-handsome face twisted, his eyes staring into a vague distance. She switched on the TV, and he focused on that.

Later, when Jimmy and Joyce had gone, Ethel brought him supper on a tray and sat beside him as she had done in the hospital, helping the fork find its way to his mouth. He tried to help capture the food, to chew and swallow as best he could, but did not acknowledge her, or her help, in any way. The doctors said they couldn't tell how damaged his brain was, how much he understood, whether he would get back some of his abilities, or none. Several times in the hospital he seemed to be fighting for words, trying to speak to the doctors or the nurses, or to Jimmy and Joyce. Once he was home alone with Ethel, he stopped trying to talk. They sat by the blue light of the television, in their accustomed silence.

One night as Ethel picked her way across the living room, around Jim's inert figure, she realized how many years she had spent secretly wishing Jim were gone, were not part of her life. She would never have wished him ill, never have wanted him dead – just wished for him not to be there. And now here he was – not dead, and yet not here. It was one more of God's little jokes. A reminder to be careful what you wished for.

In August, three months after Jim's stroke, she got a phone call from Harold. Harold and Frances were good about keeping in touch, as were Annie and Bill, Claire and Doug. But they were all so far away. "How are you managing, Ethel?" Harold asked, taking the phone after she'd had a long chat with Frances. The gentleness of his voice was like a warm arm around her shoulders.

She opened her mouth to say, "I'm doing fine," like she said to everyone, but what came out was, "I don't know how I'm going to go on, Harold."

There was a pause on the other end of the line. "How about if I come down for a visit, Ethel?"

Harold and Frances came down almost every summer to spend a week. Usually the four of them went and rented rooms in Ocean City or Asbury Park; those were the only vacations Ethel and Jim had ever taken together. Harold had never come for a visit by himself, and Ethel wanted him to come so badly it felt like a sin.

Jimmy met Harold at Grand Central and brought him out to Brooklyn. "What you should be doing is helping her pack up," he told Harold as they came into Ethel's kitchen. "She and Dad need to move out with Joyce and me. Out near us, anyway. I've been telling them for years. Even before this happened."

Harold nodded and smiled at Jimmy but didn't say anything about Ethel moving out. He laid down his small bag – Jimmy had his big suitcase – and went straight over to the chair where Jim was slumped in front of the television. At first, Jim didn't look up, didn't seem aware that anyone was there. Harold stood in front of him, then slowly, painfully, squatted down so he was at eye level with Jim, and took one of Jim's hands between his own.

"Jim. James b'y, I'm here. Harold. I'm here now."

Ethel saw Jim's vacant eyes focus on Harold's face, then Jim's other hand darted forward and gripped Harold's wrist so hard it had to hurt. His mouth worked frantically, but all that came out was a garbled, grating sound, and his eyes flashed with the terrible anger of the caged animal.

"You see what he's like," Ethel said.

Harold showed no sign of shock. He patted Jim's hand steadily, saying in his low voice, "Frances sends her love, and Val and the boys...I've got a couple of grand boys, Jim, and you've got a grand young fellow there too, your Jimmy. He picked me up at the station. Had a good ride down on the train, not like it used to be though. Trains are more crowded, not the same comfort at all." As his voice murmured on, Jim calmed a little; his lips still twitched and his hands jerked slightly, but he no longer looked angry or panicked.

Having Harold around made all the difference. The long silence of the apartment – deeper and darker since Jim's stroke, but stretching back long before that, back to when Jimmy and Diane moved out – was banished under a spell of laughter, of gentle words, of long conversations about old times. Harold liked to sit in the living room with them, the sound on the TV turned down low so only the flickering picture lit the room. Jim didn't seem to care that the sound was gone. He still looked at the screen, but his eyes sometimes darted back and forth from Harold to Ethel as they unravelled the skein of years, remembering the time they all went to Coney Island, the time Jimmy got lost when he was only a little fellow, the Friday night card games they used to enjoy.

They talked, too, about their children. It had been so many years since Ethel had had anyone to talk to, anyone to whom she could say, "Jimmy's the best kind, he really is. He's making a grand job of his shops, going right ahead. And Joyce is good. She's steady. And she's always been good to Jim and me. More like our own daughter than Diane is, really." The only lamp on in the room was the knobby brass table lamp on the end table by Harold's chair, its yellow light highlighting the crinkly cellophane covering the lampshade. The TV flickered. The blinds were drawn against night-time on Flatbush Avenue, but sounds drifted up: shouting voices, curse words, a basketball bouncing on the pavement. A car horn blared, then a second on a different note.

"Diane's had a hard time, though," Harold said, his voice as soothing as when he talked to Jim.

"Hard time? She left her husband, Harold. He wasn't a bad man, he wasn't cruel to her. She was just tired of him. Tired of him! Imagine, now, what kind of world it would be if everyone up and left when they got tired."

"It's a different world now, though," Harold said. "Dan and Joanne, now, they had a rough time there last year. Dan moved out for awhile. But he saw sense, in the end. Left off with the other one and went back to Joanne."

Ethel nodded. "Well, I can't talk no sense into Diane. She never listened to me, more's the pity. Now what about Valerie, what is she doing these days?" It wasn't that she wanted to hurt Harold, but he sounded so satisfied about Dan's good sense, and she'd talked about her problem child, so it was only fair they both air out the closets, skeletons and all.

Harold sighed, took a long sip of tea, looked down into his cup. "Well, girl, 'tis hard to know what to make of Valerie. Frances is like you are with Diane. She's like to tear her hair out about Valerie, worrying about her, you know. There she is, forty-two years old, no hopes of getting married and nothing to do with herself. Valerie got the top floor of our house turned into her own apartment. She comes and goes as she pleases, but she don't seem to have no..." He groped for a word. "She went away down to the States somewhere for awhile there, a year or so back, some kind of course she was on, but nothing more came of it. She just came back home and went on writing. She's working on a book, it seems. Has been this ten year. The Great Canadian Novel, I s'pose." Harold laughed, a short laugh without humour, and stared into his tea again. "Did I tell you Ken got moved up to principal? Principal of the biggest high school in the district," he said, looking up.

One day, Joyce arranged to come and stay with Jim for the day. "You never get out, Mother," Joyce said. "Now that Harold's here, he can take you out somewhere. You can have a nice little day to yourself."

"Don't be so foolish, Joyce. Where would we go? Coney Island?"

Harold loved the idea of a day on the town. "We'll go to Prospect Park," he announced. "The Botanical Gardens."

Ethel looked at him as if he had grown another head. "Prospect Park," she repeated. "Do you know what Prospect Park is like? It's full of rubbish and gangs and winos sleeping on the benches. Nobody goes to Prospect Park anymore."

Harold crumpled; the lines in his face seemed heavier, and his eyes dull. "Hard to believe, Ethel girl." He looked out the window. "What happened to Brooklyn? Toronto, you know...Toronto's a big city, but you can still walk the streets, go into the parks. It's a beautiful city."

"Well, Brooklyn's not," Ethel said. "There's nothing beautiful about Brooklyn, I assure you."

"That's a sad thing," he said, shaking his head. "What about the Botanical Gardens? Are they as bad as the park? Does anyone go there now?"

"I don't know. I don't think…I mean, it's behind a gate, not all open like the park. I still hear people talking about it on the television like it's a nice place to go. I couldn't tell you for certain. I haven't been there in twenty years."

"Well, let's go there tomorrow," Harold said. How quickly he perked up again, like the hard realities of life could never get him down for long. Ethel looked at Jim, hauled off in his chair, knowing no more than a two-year-old child, she thought. Let Harold have to look after Frances like this for a few years and see how cheerful he was. See if he was so anxious to head off to Prospect Park then.

They went on the bus, a thing Ethel hadn't done in years. The bus was terrifying. They were the only white people aboard, two old white people wearing sweaters in the August heat, targets for gang violence if anyone on earth was, Ethel thought. But the coloured people on the bus didn't seem particularly interested in them. They were busy talking to each other, in those heavy accents that didn't even sound like English. There were mothers with babies, men and women as old as herself and Harold, stout women in cotton dresses and hats who looked like they might be steady, sensible churchgoers, in their own kind of churches, of course. Then three teenage boys got on at the front of the bus. The boys were loud, shoving and pushing each other, sprawling over three double seats, not getting up when an older man with a stick got on and couldn't find a seat. The old man was white, but he was one of those Jews with the hat and the long sideburns, as foreign in his way as the coloured.

Stepping inside the gates of the Botanical Gardens was like taking a step outside of the real world of Brooklyn into a saner, simpler time – the time when they were all young, and it was safe to ride a bus or take a subway. Pale green trees formed an archway over the path, blocking out the worst of the sun's heat. Couples and families – white people, ordinary people – strolled past, some pushing babies in strollers. Ethel felt safe. Harold shuffled along, pausing every few feet to squint at the little markers stuck up in front of the flowers.

She stopped to lean against a wall, looking down at the Cherry Esplanade below. Some young people had spread out a picnic on the grass; their laughter drifted up to her. Harold leaned beside her.

"Can't quite make it as far as I used to," he said. "I remember when I lived here, I used to walk all over New York, blocks and blocks every day."

Ethel nodded. "I remember pushing the little ones in the stroller, down Flatbush Avenue, for hours. Nowadays I can barely get across the kitchen without having to sit down."

"You're pushing yourself too hard, Ethel. Day in, day out, in that apartment with Jim. Doing everything for him. It don't make sense."

By the time they reached the Japanese garden, they were both ready to rest again, and the bench was empty, so they sat and looked out at the murky green water. The flowers all around the bench would have been lovely if the water didn't look so dirty, but even so it was a peaceful place to stop, and there was a bit of much-needed shade. Ethel wiped beads of sweat from her brow. A swan glided past, white and erect. Harold said, without looking at her, "Ethel girl, you got to give it up."

"Give it up? What am I going to do, Harold, put him in a home?"

"No, no, no," Harold said, as though the very thought made him nervous. He reached down and took her hand in his. "But it's terrible for the both of you, going on the way you are. I know you wrote us about it, but until I saw it myself – there in the apartment with the two of you – I never really magined, I suppose, how bad it was."

Ethel had nothing to say to this. She was glad, actually. Happy that Harold, that somebody, had noticed how hard her life was. She wondered how much else Harold understood. Did he know that it wasn't only since the stroke that things had been hard? He'd always understood her so well. Surely he'd guessed how bleak her life with Jim had been for…oh, so many years now. She used to date it from the time Ralphie died, but that wasn't it, not really. Years and years before that. It had been wrong so long she wondered if it had ever been right. Jim's stroke was really just the straw on the camel's back, you might say.

"It's kind of you to come down here," she said.

"Oh, I couldn't stay away," Harold said. His hand, with its staring veins and brown age spots, tightened on hers, and Ethel felt its surprising warmth. "I mean, how could I? When you love someone so much, to see what they're going through. You have to be there, to do whatever you can to help."

Something happened in Ethel's chest like a balloon bursting. At first she wondered if she was having a heart attack. But it wasn't pain, only a sudden openness, pinpricked by Harold's words, the words she had wanted, needed, for so long. *When you love someone so much.* A lifetime of propriety, of caution, of measured words suddenly slipped from her as she turned her face up to him.

"Harold, do you mean it? I'm so glad. I always thought, you and I, we would have been–"

"I mean, he was my hero when we were growing up, and to think of him there, struck down like that…" Harold went on, speaking at the same moment Ethel did, so their words twisted and tangled. Beneath the breathless rush of her own words she heard his, and understood. Prayed her first prayer in nearly thirty years: *Oh God, let him not have heard me, not have understood what I said.*

But God said No, as He always did. Harold's words stumbled to a halt; she saw the confusion in his eyes. In that moment Ethel understood that this love that had been plaguing her since, oh, 1928 or so, had never once, not once, crossed his mind. It had been all in her mind, her own mind. There was a moment of silence so long Ethel felt it contained years. Harold's hand still covered hers.

"That's right, girl, you know what I mean," he said gently after a moment. "You and me, we always understood each other, didn't we? You were as much like a sister to me as Annie was, tell the truth…or more. I couldn't stand the thought of you here all alone, taking care of poor Jim, nor of him suffering like that, and I thought, b'y, if there's anything at all you can do for Ethel, for her that's always been so good to you, well you get yourself on that train and get down to New York, now. And Frances agreed with me, one hundred per cent."

Ethel could hear her own heart beating, the shouting voices of two children on the path behind them, a faint breeze that moved the leaves above her head. She looked away from Harold, down at the pond where a girl of about thirteen knelt at the water's edge, holding out a piece of bread to a swan.

Harold still held Ethel's hand, patting it now. "Come on now, let's get up. If we sets here too long my knees are likely to lock and I'll never get up again," Harold said, chuckling. He got slowly to his feet and offered her his arm as they walked on.

Ethel shuffled as she walked; her knees still ached and her right ankle felt like it might turn over at any moment. Yet she felt lighter, somehow. Maybe all that unspoken love she'd been carrying around was heavier than she realized.

"You're a kind man, Harold," she said. "Always were. And you may be right." She let a little pause grow and then said, "About Long Island. Maybe it is time for me to talk to Jimmy and Joyce about moving out there. I never wanted to be a burden on anybody, you know."

"I know," Harold said. "I think the same thing about my boys. I don't want to be a burden. But my time will come. Just like it has for poor Jim."

"Like it will for all of us, I s'pose," said Ethel.

DIANE

MANHATTAN, JUNE 1975

DIANE STANDS IN FRONT of the mirror in her hotel room, turning, touching up her lipstick, viewing herself from different angles. This morning she packed her daughters off to Henry's place before catching her plane from LAX to LaGuardia. Tomorrow she will get a train to Long Island, to her brother's tacky little suburban home, and see what kind of shape her parents are in. Tonight is an island in between, a space of time that's just Diane's. Tonight she's going to a dinner and dance in honour of her high school class's twenty-fifth reunion.

Diane turns once more in front of the mirror, admiring her tanned legs under the pink mini, her neat figure, slimmer than when she was in high school, her shoulder-length glossy dark hair. She wants people to say, "Diane *Evans*? Is that *you*? You're a knockout. I never would have recognized you!" And then she will talk about her work in public relations for a major Hollywood studio, and her home in L.A., and her beautiful teenage daughters. Her high school is famous for high achievers and success stories; Diane knows she will have to work hard to shine.

But she's used to that – working hard, and shining. She picks up her purse, goes downstairs and catches a cab to the hotel where the reunion is being held. Men and women who look only vaguely familiar arrive in couples and groups. For a moment Diane wishes she had kept in touch with someone from high school, someone she could have arranged to meet beforehand. Then she decides it's okay, maybe even better, to sweep in alone, head held high.

"My *gosh*! Diane *Evans*? Is that *you*? I'd have known you *anywhere*!!" The high-pitched blond woman with the accent that sounds cartoonishly New York to Diane now, after her years in California, bears down with her arms outstretched. Diane catches her name tag: Carol (Dobrowski) McLean.

"Carol! How fabulous! You look great!" Diane holds her former best friend at arm's length, and yes, she can see Carol at fifteen, at seventeen, at twenty-one, tucked inside this forty-two year old woman with the bouffant blond hair and the lime green pantsuit. "What are you doing now?"

"Well, I'm living in Jersey. We moved to Jersey, me and Clint, you know," Carol says, putting her arm around Diane's waist and drawing her over to a table full of people, also all vaguely familiar.

"Clint, hi! Tina…oh gosh, yes, Frank Murphy, I would have known you anywhere. Anywhere." Diane makes the rounds of the table, the rounds of her old friends. She has many opportunities to repeat the carefully rehearsed one-minute version of her life that she has prepared for the occasion.

"Well, I live in California, in L.A. actually. I'm in P.R. Kids? Yes, I have two daughters, two beautiful girls, Christine and Laurie. I did the housewife thing for a while there, you know, out in California, had my babies, raised them, and then one day just kind of thought, Is this *it*? Is this my *life*? The girls were in school by then, so I got a job. Kind of had to start from the bottom up, you know, since I'd been out of the work force for nearly ten years, but I love it now, it's such an interesting field. Henry and I split up, oh, about five years ago. No, nothing nasty, no hard feelings, just, you know, we'd outgrown each other. And hey, it's great to be back in New York!"

Everybody smiles and nods at her story, takes it at face value, which they should, because it's the truth, the varnished truth. And there are much weirder stories out there, both from people who made the reunion and about people who didn't. The graduates of 1950 were a little too old to be hippies and dropouts, but the sixties sidelined some of them anyway: Shirley was living in a commune in Vermont; Darrell was a folksinger. Many of the men, and more than a few of the women, had successful careers and a lot of money. And then there were women like Carol, who appeared to have missed the whole women's movement somehow. Carol was happy as a clam out in Jersey, ironing Clint's shirts – Clint was in real estate – and raising their four kids.

"Wow," Carol says, wide-eyed, when Diane talks about her job. "You always were so smart, so ambitious."

Dinner comes; Diane is wedged at the table with Carol and Clint and a small group of others she remembers vowing eternal friendship with twenty-five years ago. Nobody lives in Brooklyn anymore; it seems nobody's parents even live there anymore. They have moved to the suburbs or retired to Florida.

"You wouldn't know Brooklyn now, if you went out there," Frank says.

"Oh, I know!" Carol adds, rolling her eyes. "You know, I went to see my mother, before she moved out with us, and driving down Flatbush Avenue, it was like being in another world. Not like you're in America at all."

"It's totally changed," Carol's husband Clint puts in. "The crime rate there is incredible."

"Brooklyn's never been the same since the Dodgers left," says Frank.

Tina gives him a look of something near disgust. "Brooklyn's never been the same since all the niggers and the spics moved in," she says, not even bothering to lower her voice. Diane is a little shocked, not by the sentiment, which she has heard often, but by the words. Out in California, all her friends are liberals like herself, in favour of integration and equality. She doesn't hear words like "niggers" and "spics." But she also lives in an all-white suburb, where her daughters have friends as fair-skinned and golden-haired as themselves. She looks away from Tina.

After dinner, there's dancing, with a live band playing hits from their high-school years. Diane dances with Clint, with Frank, with guys she liked in high school who have turned out balding and paunchy and boring. At one point, she sits alone at a table on the edge of the dance floor, cradling her drink, wondering when it will be okay to go home.

Hands rest on her shoulders; someone has come up from behind. "Well, well, Diane Evans," says a voice that has not changed much at all in twenty-five years.

Diane twists to see him and is annoyed to notice that the bottom seems to be falling out of her stomach. Mickey Malone stands behind her, and she quickly gets to her feet to be on a level with him, while at the same time he pulls out a chair and sits down. They laugh, and Diane sits back down.

She hasn't seen him since the night in 1950 when he told her he was joining the army and she'd be better off without him. She heard news of him for awhile, of course, when she still lived in the area: she knew he went to Korea, and that he came back alive. But they've never talked, never had one of those casual adult conversations that is supposed to draw the sting from a high-school love. Now, she supposes, it's time to do that.

"Mickey Malone," she says, smiling.

"Mostly I just go by Mike these days," he says, also smiling. His face is a little heavier and more lined, but it creases the exact same way when he smiles. "I outgrew Mickey, I guess."

"Yeah, you don't look much like a Mickey anymore."

He is still handsome, his hair cut unfashionably short with a little grey at the temples, his body more solid, no longer as slim but still looking muscular and trim. When she imagined him – and of course she imagined bumping into him back here: how could she not imagine that? – she had seen him either as a carbon copy of his teenage self or, more realistically, old and fat and gone to seed, a paunchy old

Irishman with a whiskey nose and bloodshot eyes. If she'd imagined him looking like this, she would have told herself she was dreaming, being unrealistic.

"How's the world treatin' you?" he asks. The woild. His accent is still pure Brooklyn.

"Not so bad, not so bad. You?"

"Oh, fair to middlin'."

Diane crosses her legs and smiles again, feeling like her face might crack. This is what a twenty-fifth reunion is all about: running into the guy who broke your heart, the one you thought you'd love forever, and finding you have nothing to say except the most appalling clichés.

She thinks of a real question to ask. "How'd you get in here? You're not class of '50."

"Nope...shoulda been class of '49, if I'd graduated. My cousin Charlie—" he gestures at a short, bald man a few table away "—he was in your class. Remember?"

"Yeah, I remember Charlie." Only as Mickey's cousin, of course, not as a human being in his own right.

"So, Charlie's wife didn't want to come, seein' as how she's busy having an affair and getting ready to dump Charlie, so I told him I'd be his date." There's a pause, and Mickey says, "I was hoping you'd be here."

Diane stares down into her drink. Here she was feeling smug about how trite their conversation was, and Mickey has just upped the ante. She won't pass back the compliment, though. "I had no idea you'd be here," she says instead. "I didn't even know if you were still in the area."

"Yeah, more or less. I'm in Brooklyn Heights now," he says.

"Still in Brooklyn?" She's surprised. "I think you're the first person I've met tonight who's still living there."

"Pretty much, I'd say." He takes a look around at the crowd. "Jersey, Jersey, Jersey, Long Island, a few here in Manhattan – doin' pretty well for themselves – and some from places unknown, like you."

"California," Diane says. She's finished her drink and could use another one. Mickey's drinking what appears to be rum and Coke and it's still half full.

"California, hey? Nice place."

"It's different from Brooklyn, that's for sure," she says lamely.

Mickey shrugs. "Well, Brooklyn's different from Brooklyn, these days. Here we are, a bunch of kids from Brooklyn, havin' our twenty-fifth reunion – well, your twenty-fifth reunion, anyway – in a hotel in Manhattan."

"They say the crime rate there is awful."

This time Mickey looks down and smiles. "Well, we're doin' what we can about that," he says, and pulls out his wallet to show her his badge: NYPD. She looks up, surprised.

"You're a cop?"

"Wouldna thought it, would you?" Mickey says, and pockets the badge again. "Yeah, after the army it seemed like the thing to do. I've seen some tough things on the streets. But it's tough for those kids too," he adds, staring down into his glass. "Not much to look forward to. You can see why they get into drugs and crime, I guess. And the parents come here, you know, from Haiti or Puerto Rico or wherever, looking for something better. Kinda like our parents and grandparents came. To us it seems like Brooklyn's changed, but to them... I don't know, I think it's pretty much the same."

The band starts playing "Tennessee Waltz" and suddenly Mickey stands up. "Well, listen to that, Diane. They're playing our song. Wanna dance?"

Now she's really surprised, though she stands up and lets him lead her out on the dance floor. "You? Dancing?"

"Tennessee Waltz" is "their song," kind of, in that they both used to like it and listen to it a lot when they were going out. But Diane has no romantic memories of floating around the dance floor in Mickey's arms to this tune, because Mickey never danced. He was one of the guys at school dances who would hang around on the edges, keep going out to the parking lot for a drink and coming back in, eventually to start a fight and get kicked out by the chaperones.

"Just an excuse," he says. "You're lookin' great by the way. You look ten years younger than half these gals."

She laughs, a slightly brittle laugh. "Well, you know how it is out in California. It's all about looking good. The fountain of youth."

"Are you married?" he asks, apparently giving up on any idea of working the question into the conversation subtly.

"I was." She gives him the same pared-down version of her life story she gave everyone else. "And you?"

"Yeah, I was, too." He looks over Diane's shoulder as if concentrating hard: frown lines cut down between his green eyes. "I married a girl from Queens a few years after I got out of the army. Her name was Julie. She was nice; we had three kids. I'm the one who screwed that up. Divorced eight years now."

"Sorry to hear that," says Diane, thinking how inane and, in many ways, untrue this is.

"Are you?" Mickey says. "That's funny, 'cause I was so happy to hear you were divorced." There's a pause, and he laughs. She thinks it's funny, how direct he's gotten, how good he is at being honest, which is not a talent she would have predicted Mickey Malone would develop.

After that dance, Mickey says he needs to go say hi to some guys, and drops her back at the table where Carol and her friends are sitting. "Do you have plans, afterwards?" he asks.

"My gosh, Mickey Malone," Carol says, when she and Tina have Diane to themselves. "Who'd have thought. I figured for sure he'd end up in jail or something."

"He's still very good-looking," Tina says, lighting a smoke.

"You and him were hot and heavy, one time," Carol says, nodding slowly at Diane.

"He told me he was nothing but trouble and I'd be better off without him," Diane says. "He said he was going to go get his ass blown off in Korea."

"Obviously he didn't," Carol says, watching Mickey walk across the floor to talk to someone.

"Good thing too," Tina says. "Damn fine ass."

Diane looks too, and has to agree. "*Damn* fine," she says, and all three women giggle, feeling for one more minute like high-school friends.

The evening winds down; the band plays "Goodnight Irene." Diane says goodnight to Carol and Clint, Tina and Frank. Declines offers to share a cab. She hasn't seen Mickey for an hour and wonders if she's going to be fool enough to hang around waiting for him. But then, there he is.

"Want to go somewhere else?" he says. "We could go for...for a drink, I guess. I'd like to talk some more."

She puts her arm through his and they leave the hotel and go out into the street. He picks a small, not very trendy-looking bar where Diane orders a gin and tonic and Mickey, to her surprise, orders just a Coke.

"I'm glad I took the chance on coming tonight," he says. "It was good, seeing you again."

"Yeah, considering the last time I saw you, you said you were on your way to get your ass blown off in Korea." She smiles, remembering Tina, but decides not to share the joke.

Mickey looks down into his glass again. "I gave it my best shot, but it wasn't in the cards."

There's a silence between them, though not around them, as music pulses through the dark air. "See?" Diane says finally. "You were wrong. You told me we didn't have that many choices, that you could go get killed in the army, or else we'd wind up just like my parents, or just like your parents. But we didn't. We made different lives for ourselves."

Mickey looks up, meets her eyes. "You still remember that night."

"I think I remember every word you said."

"I remember it too. And every word was true. I was headed for trouble, and it wouldn't have worked out. You made a good, clean getaway."

"But you were wrong," she repeats. "We didn't turn out like our parents, either of us."

"Well, maybe not," Mickey says. "I think just because the world changed, though. Like divorce. Hardly anybody got divorced in our parents' day. Now everybody's doing it. Isn't that the only thing that saved us from being stuck in dead-end marriages like our parents were?"

Diane is quiet, considering this. She felt a kind of desperation the last years she and Henry were together, as if she were being smothered in layers of pastel chiffon. It wasn't really fair to Henry, because she married him hoping that he could take care of her, look after her, and he did exactly that.

She isn't about to reveal all that to her high-school sweetheart. They have one evening together – maybe one night? It's a possibility – and Diane has already polished and prepared the self she's going to show on this trip. Just as Mickey has, no doubt, prepared his own persona: the Good Cop. "Look at you, though," she says, keeping it light. "A fine upstanding member of society. People in the neighbourhood thought you'd come to a bad end. And you said yourself you were going to end up a drunken bum like your father."

This time, he doesn't smile, or look away. He looks as serious as he did twenty-five years ago when he told her she should stay away from him. He holds up his keychain and she recognizes one of those little AA chips. "A cop can be a drunken bum just like the rest of them. Just like my old man. Don't let the uniform fool you." He's not in uniform tonight, of course, but she knows what he means.

Diane takes the keychain and fingers the red plastic disc. She has friends who are in AA, who call themselves recovering alcoholics, but she has always thought of this as a California thing. The chip says "Ninety days." She looks back at Mickey, cradling his glass of Coke.

"Three months, this time. I was sober for six years after Julie left me. Started again two years ago. I've been lucky to hold onto my job – it's about all I've held onto."

Diane stares at him in the dim and flickering light, seeing the curious double image: the boy who said he would come to no good, and was right; the man who has done well for himself. And this third man, the honest one, who feels he has to tell her all this. She puts out her hand and covers his lightly. "Mickey," she says. It's the first time she's said his name since he came up to her at the party. "Sorry…Mike," she corrects. "But I don't think I can call you anything but Mickey."

"That's okay," he says. "Do you want to get out of here?"

She does. He pays the bill and they go out onto the sidewalks of New York, through the night that is never really dark or quiet, past the flashing signs and the bars pouring noise into the streets. For a while they walk without saying anything.

"I used to work here, when I first came to Manhattan," Diane says as they pass Macy's. "I thought it was the doorway to heaven, that I could be or do anything if I could get a job here."

Mickey takes her hand in his and squeezes it. "And see? You did. You got what you wanted."

Now Diane is the one to shake her head, as if she owes him something for his honesty back in the bar. "Don't be fooled by the uniform," she says.

She doesn't mean to tell him everything, but her story comes tumbling out – not the polished one she had prepared for meeting old friends, but the truth, or as close to truth as she can get. At some point – maybe when she's talking about the postpartum depression, or maybe it's the part about the suicide attempt – she realizes tears are pouring down her cheeks, making a mess of her makeup. Mickey hands her a three-ply Kleenex, large and manly, which unfolds like a bedsheet in front of her.

They are still staring at the window display, a vivid splash of rainbow colours. Mickey puts his arm around her waist. "And now… how are you doing?"

"Not bad." That's the official line, the happy ending she'd decided on after he told his story and she knew she'd have to tell part of hers. "Yeah, things are pretty good now. I like my job, and the girls are pretty good, even though they're getting to that difficult age. And I don't come home much, because I still have… issues, I guess, with my parents, but I'm hoping we can get over that. My dad's sick; maybe Mom will need me. And I've dated a few people, but I haven't really met anyone, and sometimes I feel kind of lonely and…there's a lot of pressure, you know?" Her words are blurring, running together, like the lights in front of her eyes, and she's shaking, though it's a warm night. "I shouldn't…I mean, I still see a doctor. I take these pills…mostly I keep things together. The last time I… well, it comes back, you know? And–" she blew her nose hard "–I was so *mad* at myself, because I was supposed to be all better, there was no *reason* to be depressed. That's supposed to be all behind me, and it scares me to find out that it's not."

"Yeah," says Mickey. "Yeah, I know what you mean."

She stops walking and swipes at her eyes and nose with the giant Kleenex. They are standing under a brilliant neon sign advertising XXX Live Nude Girls, All Night Long. Mickey puts both arms around her, makes a little circle for the two of them to stand in. "I know what you mean," he repeats.

Diane starts sobbing for real, like something has been untied, or unlocked, inside. She cries, and leans against Mickey's shoulder, and he holds her while she cries in a messy, unpretty way, blowing her nose into the Kleenex. An unshaven, bleary-eyed drunk careens past them towards the blacked-over door of Live Nude Girls.

"This is so funny," Diane says. "All those years ago, when we were together, I always thought I had to look out for you, take care of you, be the strong one. And here we are, twenty-five years later, and turns out you're being the strong one."

"No." Mickey's voice is surprisingly hard, like it used to be when he got angry years ago, like she imagines it might be when he's interrogating a suspect. The Bad Cop. "No, Diane." He doesn't push her away, but he lifts her face away from his chest, up towards his, so their eyes meet. "Don't make me the strong one. You know who I am, what I am."

"But you quit drinking…again," Diane says. "*You're* strong. *You're* a good person."

"You're strong. You're a good person." He smiles, and it transforms and gentles his whole face. "See, this time it can't be about anyone saving anyone. We can be here for each other. That's all."

Diane reaches her mouth up to his, and only as they're kissing does she realize he's not talking as if this is a one-night reunion fling. He's talking as if they have time, a future together. When they stop kissing, she's going to have to tell him how impossible that is. And it's too bad, because she sees now that he's absolutely right, that she wasn't meant to be either the girl locked in the tower or the knight on the white horse, that nobody can be anyone else's saviour, or else that everyone is.

She puts her arms around Mickey, lets her hands slide up his back, remembering the scars he used to have there, as if her fingers can still feel them. And he moves his hands on her back, as if searching for hers.

ROSE

BROOKLYN, JUNE 1977

THE PRAISE TABERNACLE CATHEDRAL of Miracles, Reverend Rosamond Maranatha, Pastor, Come Expecting a Miracle, sits between the Lamb of God Hairstyling and a boarded-up convenience store. Above the Tabernacle Cathedral is Madame Yvette Tarot and Palm Readings. Clients who take the stairwell to the second floor will find Madame Yvette's rooms on the right. On the left, a similar set of narrow rooms is home for the Reverend Rosamond Maranatha, who climbs these stairs four nights a week after prayer, praise and healing services in the Cathedral below.

The Cathedral used to be a 99-cent store, but after her original church home, the Miracle Temple, closed down, Reverend Rosamond and some followers from the Miracle Temple congregation worked together to gut out the store and cover its cinderblock walls with a coat of vivid pink paint. One of the members built a small platform at the front of the room, and they took up a collection to buy seventy-five folding chairs. With that, the Praise Tabernacle Cathedral of Miracles was in business.

There are services on Monday, Wednesday and Friday nights, and pretty much all day on Sunday. Reverend Rosa, as the people call her, preaches at every service and heals the sick. Reverend Rosa is distinctively different from most of her congregation, all of whom are black. She is an elderly white woman who wears robes of vivid green and gold, or pink and purple, or red and white: she owns several sets of vestments. They're about all she does own, though. Reverend Rosa is not getting wealthy off the people of Crown Heights.

She has a one-room bedsitter with a hot plate. A picture of the Sacred Heart of Jesus hangs above the iron bedstead. The Tabernacle Cathedral is a very Protestant church, but there's something about the vividly coloured, exposed, bleeding heart of Christ that appeals to Reverend Rosa, born Rose Evans long ago in another world. She has only one other picture on her wall, a faded snapshot of a blond girl about ten years old.

Most evenings, Rose does not cook on the hot plate in her room but goes down to the end of the street, to the Western Cafeteria, which is as much a cafeteria as Rose's church is a cathedral. She sits at a corner table and orders a bowl of soup, Today's Special, and watches her neighbours come and go. She reminds herself to feel love and compassion for the boys who come in cursing and swearing, obviously hopped up on drugs. The Tabernacle Cathedral has had several break-ins, but the collection is rarely more than twenty dollars on any given Sunday and Rose gives the money to Gavin Bennett to take home right away, so nothing is kept in the church. Nothing of value except a stack of Bibles and the folding chairs.

Loving people is the hard part of being a minister, that and thinking holy thoughts all the time. The easy parts are wearing the robes, singing, preaching, healing and casting out demons, all of which Rose enjoys. She also likes performing both weddings and funerals, though, as she frequently tells people, funerals are best because those poor souls have no more troubles ahead of them.

Ten years ago, Rose wrote away to a place that advertises in the back of magazines, and they sent her a ministerial license. She chose a new name to go on the license, to signify a new start. Rosamond reminds her of a flower opening, something new budding out of the simple and overused name *Rose*. And Maranatha means The Lord is Coming. Rose devoutly hopes He is. She preaches this hope weekly, telling people that the earth is the Lord's harvest field and it is ripe for the picking, that if they want to be plucked from the fire they must come, kneel, lay down the burden of sin and take up the cross.

All the childhood years of Army sermons have soaked into Rose deeply, the Bible words she hated learning, the unlikely hymns her mother chose as lullabies. *There is a fountain filled with blood, drawn from Immanuel's veins.* The words and rhythms are forever part of Rose now, rooted so deep that years of unbelief and drink and even shock treatments didn't budge them. She can't recall her mother's face but when she stands in the pulpit and raises her hands to heaven, the words of Revelation come rolling out of her: *And I John saw the Holy City, coming down out of heaven as a bride adorned for her husband. Amen, amen, Jesus. Come on down. Come on down and take us out of this hellhole.*

Rose walks down her street. Winos and drug addicts lie in doorways; gangs of teenage boys hang out on the corners. Spray-paint graffiti messages scar the buildings. On the corrugated steel door drawn down over the front of the

Tabernacle Cathedral, one message reads, "Jesus Saves!" which is encouraging. Another reads, "Fuck the Rich."

She goes upstairs to change into her robe and fix her hair, mostly grey now and worn in a tight curly perm. Hairdressers, like Lamb of God next door, specialize mainly in straightening the hair of black women who want to look more white, but the girl there is an old friend and is always happy to do Rose's perm and rinse. She's chosen the pink and purple robe tonight, and feels stronger, more Spirit-filled, just standing there in it.

Downstairs, Gavin Bennett is rolling up the big metal door and unlocking the church entrance. He is a handsome, broad-shouldered young man in his early thirties, and Rose is ashamed to admit to herself that she has felt stirrings of carnal desire for him. At seventy-plus, she expected to be over all that kind of thing. And for a black man, too. Gavin Bennett is a Spirit-filled young man, a powerful preacher, with a nice little wife and two fine babies. The congregation sees him as Rose's successor, the same way some of them once saw Rose as Vernon Peters' successor. Reverend Peters turned against Rose in the end, not ready to hand over the reins. Rose can understand that with her mind, but her weary body feels all too ready to give over, to let Gavin take over the preaching and the healing.

Tonight, the worshippers trickle in. The regulars: Sister Andrews with her knitted pink and blue hat, clutching her battered Bible; Sister Phelps, vast as a mountain, enfolding people in her gigantic embrace; Brother Ashe, his long thin face sour as if he's sucking a lemon. Children swirl around Rose's feet like a shallow river.

Rose, Reverend Rosa now, holds hands, puts her arms around people. As she moves into the room she starts to sing. Quickly, Gavin Bennett joins her with a deep chocolate baritone that takes the music and lifts it up to someplace above where ordinary music can go.

> Oh-o you can't stand up, all by yourself
> You can't stand up alo-o-one

Rose is on the platform. She can't stand up alone, but she can stand here, supported by something that might be the Spirit or might just be the spirit of all these hungry, needy, faithful people believing her, listening to her, loving her. Their voices, their hopes, carry her like a tide. Gavin Bennett climbs the platform to stand beside her as she moves the congregation into another song.

The service is long, exhausting. Rose preaches for forty minutes about Jesus who will heal them, Jesus who will mend their broken hearts. They sing some more, and then there are the prayers. A knot of women comes to the front to be healed. Young Missy Elliott comes to pray that the Lord will touch her womb and take away her barrenness. Like Sarah, like Hannah, like Elizabeth of old, she wants a baby. Rose prays over her, thinking that maybe she should tell Sister Elliott that having no baby can be God's blessing. How can you raise a child in this city, on these streets? How can you walk past the gangs, the graffiti, every single day and know what that baby will grow up to become – and still rejoice? Of all the choices Reverend Rosamond has ever made, the one she's certain was good and true – apart from kneeling at the altar the night she was saved – was sending her baby Claire home to Annie.

Rose lays on the hands and prays for the healings. Some nights she feels energy tingle in her palms, as though she is drawing from a great reservoir of power and channelling it through to those who need it. Other times, she feels only like a woman praying, begging God for mercy and not sure if he hears. Tonight is one of those times. When Sister Andrews looks in Rose's face and says, "Reverend Rosa, I been to see the doctor and he says it's cancer," Rose's heart falls. She has told these people a hundred times that God can cure cancer because God cured her. But she has buried them, too, saying the funeral rite over the same people for whom she's prayed. God loses more than He wins when the doctor says it's cancer.

Rose wants to be upstairs, in her own rooms. This might be one of the nights she goes into Huldah's room for a cup of tea. Huldah – known to the world as Madame Yvette – likes to sit back and put her feet up after a hard day reading the cards for people. Sometimes she and Rose compare notes, talking about their day's work, which is not altogether different. Once Rose finished a cup of tea and passed it back to Huldah. "Can you read tea leaves?" she asked.

Huldah looked down in the cup and frowned. "No, don't do the tea leaves," she said, shaking her head.

This surprised Rose. Surely if you had the second sight, it would work no matter what tools you used? But Huldah said no, it wasn't like that. Rose still wonders if that's true or if Huldah made an excuse, not wanting to say what she saw in Rose's cup.

When the service is over and everyone has left, she gets ready to go. "You watch out there, Reverend," Gavin says. "Those boys are soundin' nasty out there. You better wait for me and Sheilah."

"I've only got to go out this door and in my own door," Rose says. "It's not two seconds. I'll be fine."

And she would have been fine, really, if she'd been content not to interfere. The circle of boys is not directly in front of the door; they are standing in front of the Lamb of God. One looks up as Rose exits and says, "Hey, you better watch yourself, bitch!" but his tone is perfunctory, as if he can't be bothered to make a real threat. Rose ignores the language: she has been called worse, in fact said worse, in her own day. When she gets to her room she will say a prayer for these boys, so lost and lonely.

Then she hears the cries. "Help me! Help!" A girl's voice. From the middle of the circle.

"Get her out of here. Get the fuck out of here," one of the boys says to the others, glancing back at Rose.

"What's she gonna do, man? You scared of that old bag?"

"Shut up, man. She could call the cops. Shut up!"

"Help me!" Then a cry, as if someone has been kicked.

Rose doesn't want to be involved. There are fights on these streets all the time. The struggling knot of boys and whatever, whoever, is in the centre now move away, down past the Lamb of God. And Rose, who should be glad to get quietly up to her bedsit, who dragged herself through a service of preaching and healing this evening because the Spirit left her to stand up all by herself, now feels the Spirit enter into her. She pulls herself up to her full height, five foot six, and hears her own voice crying out, "You! Stop! Stop what you're doing, this minute."

"Stay out of it, bitch!" one of the boys calls back, almost kindly. He could be the son of one of her parishioners – though surely he would have called her Reverend, wouldn't he? Most of the boys do, even the ones she knows are smoking the dope and holding up stores for money.

Instead of taking his advice, Rose runs down the sidewalk after them. "Leave that girl alone! Let her go!!"

"Yeah? You gonna stop us, preacher lady?" So someone does recognize her. Rose has caught up to them now; the boys tower over her. She catches a glimpse of the girl pinned struggling in one boy's arms: a black teenager with her shirt torn away, terror on her face.

Rose's next impulse races ahead of her thoughts: the words are out almost before she knows what she will say, but they feel right, for if the Devil is any-where he is here. "In the name of Jesus Christ, I command you to leave this girl alone!"

Rose has cast out demons. She has seen tormented people writhe on the ground before her, heard strange ugly words leave their twisted lips, then watched them lie still, sobbing gratefully, restored in mind and spirit. She almost expects something like that to happen now. But there are more demons here than Rose's faith can handle. From behind she hears a voice that must be Gavin's, shouting. The struggling girl locks eyes with Rose, and Rose sees a fist coming towards her face. Then nothing.

She opens her eyes again in a grey room full of people and noise. She can't focus clearly on anything. Gavin's face is near hers. "Reverend, Reverend, can you hear me? Can you see me?" Rose wants to nod but the pain in her head is intense. She tries to form words, to ask where she is. But everything swims in front of her. She closes her eyes and drifts down to the dark again.

The next time she wakes everything is clearer. She is on a bed, with flimsy greenish curtains drawn around it. On the other side of the curtain a man is moaning, "Don't leave me alone here. Oh God, don't leave me alone. Somebody come. Please, don't leave me." She is in an emergency room. She hasn't been in a hospital for – what is it? Years, years. Since her operation.

Later, a young Spanish woman with a clipboard comes in and asks Rose questions. "The young man who brought you in, he tells us your name is..." she squints at the paper "...Rosamoond Mara-nata? This is right?"

"Yes. No. My name – my legal name – is Rose Evans." That was her name the last time she was in hospital. It's on her birth certificate, wherever that may be.

"Your age, Mrs. Evans? Date of birth?"

"Miss. I'm seventy, seventy...two? three? I'm over seventy. My birthday? November. November the fourteenth." She's pleased at having pulled out that memory. "Where am I? What happened to me?"

"You are in the hospital, Miss Evans. Of what year?"

"What..." Rose draws a blank. Is this a test, to see if she still has her wits about her? What year is it, anyway? What day is it? The last thing she remembers is leaving the Tabernacle Cathedral, Friday night after service. Something happened on the street.

"November the fourteenth of what year, Miss Evans? Your birth date."

"Oh. I...I'm sorry. I don't remember." The girl – a nurse? – looks unconvinced. "It was a long time ago," Rose explains.

The girl asks more questions: her address, her next of kin. For next of kin Rose says Gavin and Sheilah Bennett, which should give the hospital staff a turn when the Bennetts show up. No, she has no medical insurance. She doesn't have a family doctor. She still wants to know what happened.

"I don't know what happened, Miss Evans. The doctor will see you when she's available. We're keeping you in overnight for observation."

The doctor comes next morning. It's a woman doctor, which seems strange;

although being a woman minister, Rose figures she can hardly complain. The woman doctor seems very young. But she speaks with calm confidence and tries to answer Rose's questions.

"We don't know what happened to you, Miss Evans. You were brought in suffering from a concussion; apparently you received a blow to the head. We need to keep you here for observation and for some tests. In a woman of your age an assault like this is not to be taken lightly."

When she goes, Rose turns her face to the wall, like old King Hezekiah. He asked the Lord for fifteen more years and the Lord turned back the sundial to show him his prayer was granted. Rose has had her fifteen years and more. She does not feel like asking God for miracles. Her faith is not what it was twenty years ago. She no longer feels the Spirit pulsing through her veins like fire in the blood. Blood and Fire: that's the Army motto, isn't it? If they ask, does she want a clergyman, she'll call for an Army officer. She's been her own minister for too long. She knows Jesus cares, but she also knows he's not always in the miracle business. Right now he's sitting in the visitor's chair, looking at her. Not saying or doing anything: just being there.

After supper, which Rose doesn't eat, Sheilah Bennett comes and sits in that chair. "Gavin's home with the boys," she says. "He's been on pins and needles to know how you are, ever since he brought you in the other night," Sheilah says.

"You tell him thanks for me," Rose says. "I don't know what I'd've done without him."

"You're the one we should thank," Sheilah says. "That girl – the one those boys were after? That was Sister Penney's daughter, poor little thing. They all ran after you got hit, let her go. The Lord used you, Reverend, to save that poor girl. I brought you a nightgown," she adds. "I didn't know if you had one. Is there anything else you need? When are they letting you go home?"

"They won't tell me," Rose says. "If you could…I hate to ask another favour, but I have a little suitcase in my room up over the church. I've got a few clothes, a dressing gown, slippers, in my dresser drawer. Put that in, but leave the few things that are already in the suitcase. Some…a few personal items. I'd like to have them, to go through them. I don't like the thought of leaving my things there. Oh, and the few pictures on my wall, put them in the case too. Could you pack up that suitcase and bring it to me? It's no rush."

Gavin comes with the suitcase the following evening. "You don't need to worry about a thing, Reverend Rosa," he says. "I'm running all the services. We haven't closed the church doors once. I did the healing service last night, and we had a special season of prayer just for you. The Spirit was movin' in that room, Reverend, movin' in a mighty way."

"Praise the Lord," says Rose wearily. He goes on with news of the congregation, his energy and enthusiasm reminding her of herself ten years ago. Whatever happens here, she thinks, her time is over. It's Gavin's turn now. *My day is done*, she thinks, and then remembers how often she's believed that before, and how the Lord keeps coming up with surprises.

But one day, even he'll run out of tricks up his sleeve. "Brother Gavin, I need to ask you. If the time comes…if I should pass on, I want to leave something in your care. A little box, a few belongings. Can you send them on to…well, I'll leave you the address. My daughter. She lives far away from here, and I don't want to trouble her now, but I want to leave her a few small things. Will you take care of that for me? If need be."

Some time later – after complications, after surgery, after prayer and anointing, after the lights in the room grow dim and flicker out for the last time – certain items do pass into the hands of Reverend Gavin Bennett of the Praise Tabernacle Cathedral of Miracles. The untidy note accompanying the small suitcase instructs him to send it to Miss Claire Evans, St. John's, Newfoundland. Gavin has lived all his life in Brooklyn and cannot conceive of a place so small that this address will find the person intended. He will have to do some digging, he tells his wife, to try to find out if there's a proper address for this person Claire Evans, if such a person even still lives in St. John's, Newfoundland, wherever that might be.

But the Reverend Gavin Bennett, who works eight hours a day cleaning a department store and ascends the platform at night to preach the word of the Lord, is a busy man. This complicated task gets pushed to the back of his mind as the suitcase with the note gets pushed to the back of one closet after another. His business is with the living, not with the dead, and no-one can really blame him.

ANNE

ST. JOHN'S, MARCH 1983

"SHE THINKS...WELL THEY both think...this is just going to be the ideal set-up, but you mark my words. This is going to end in absolute disaster."

Anne tries to nod noncommittally. Claire turns on her with an impatient sigh. "You think it's going to work out just fine, don't you?"

"Mom, I don't think anything, I just *hope* everything works out." Anne and her mother are having coffee at Intermission in the Avalon Mall after a shopping trip to find some new sheets and blankets for the fold-out bed in Aunt Annie's back bedroom.

"It's going to take more than hope, it's going to take a miracle," Claire says. She checks her watch. "I've got to get in to work for a couple of hours. Can I drop you at Aunt Annie's with this stuff?"

"Sure. I need to go into the university library and work on a paper, but I'll walk in from there."

"The thing is," Claire says, gathering up shopping bags, "just because two people were best friends fifty years ago does not mean they're going to be able to live together when they're nearly eighty years old. Ethel thinks she wants to come back to Newfoundland, but it's going to be a different story once she gets here, let me tell you. And your Aunt Annie's got very set in her ways since Bill died. She thinks it's going to be wonderful having someone in the house again, but it's not as simple as she'd like to believe."

"I guess not," Anne says. She realizes she has been caught up in Aunt Annie's version of how nice it will be to have Ethel home again.

"Are you *coming*?" Claire says in the voice she used to use when Anne was five years old, standing in a puddle outside the front door.

Aunt Ethel arrives a week later, with the whole family out to Torbay airport to meet her. They strain to see over the heads of the disembarking passengers. Happy reunions bubble all around them. Anne, on tiptoes, is the tallest of her family, now that Stephen's gone, and she's the first to see a little old lady – she really looks exactly like a Little Old Lady – coming off the plane clinging to the arm of a flight attendant.

Her hair is very white, almost blue-white, and her face, though wrinkled, is carefully made up. She wears a light blue raglan over a darker dress, and leans on a walking stick. The flight attendant holds Aunt Ethel's carry-on bag, part of a matched set with three much larger pieces, which, in their own good time, tumble down the carousel.

"My, my," Aunt Ethel keeps saying, looking around at the crowds. "So this is St. John's. My, I wouldn't know but I was still in New York. Nothing like this here in my day, nothing at all."

"Well, it's not exactly LaGuardia, now, Aunt Ethel," Doug says, straining as he lifts one of the gigantic suitcases off the carousel and onto the cart. "But at least we've got the walkway now. You don't have to walk down the steps straight onto the tarmac anymore."

"No, it was a lovely flight, lovely," Aunt Ethel says vaguely. Anne can't tell yet if she's just disoriented from travel or actually a bit senile. "My word, Annie, hard to believe, isn't it, how the world has changed. Flying around on airplanes… I never thought I'd see the day, did you?"

"No, never," says Aunt Annie, who has never been on a plane and never intends to be.

In the car Ethel still seems disoriented. "Now, where are we now, Claire?" she keeps asking, twisting around in her seat to pose questions to Claire, although she is riding in the front seat next to Doug. "Are we out in Torbay? You said this was Torbay airport. Now I remember Torbay was only a little fishing village."

Claire leans forward from the back seat where she's squashed with Anne and Annie and Aunt Ethel's carry-on. "No, the airport is on the road out to Torbay, but we're headed back into town now. See here, at the lights, now this is Allandale Road. That's the university, where Anne goes."

"Oh, very good, very good," Aunt Ethel says, according the sprawl of university buildings a cursory glance. "Diane's youngest, Laurie, is studying marine biology. Did I tell you that? In graduate school. She's already got the one degree and she's gone back for another. She won some kind of award, there last year, for research. Such a smart girl."

"This is Empire Avenue," Doug offers as they turn onto it. "I guess it's changed quite a bit since you were here last, hasn't it?"

"Oh my, yes, look at how it's all built up. I think this was what we used to call the old railroad track if I'm not mistaken. This was all open fields when I was a girl. And even when we came back in '32, it was nothing like this. My, if poor Jim could see this now. He used to say, 'Ethel girl, I'd rather be back in Newfoundland on one meal a day than living here, even with all we got.' My, how he would have liked to come back home."

"Well, we're glad *you* were able to get home anyway," Claire says firmly into the little silence that follows. Doug turns the car onto Freshwater Road. "And when is Diane coming to visit?"

"She says she's going to try to get down for two weeks in June. Come in June, I told her, the lilacs in Annie's garden will be blooming. You still have the lilac tree, Annie?"

"Better tell her to wait till July, or pack some heavy sweaters," Claire says. "June's not the best month for the weather."

"Oh, I always remember it being lovely in June," Aunt Ethel says, staring out at the brick sprawl of the taxation building. "Diane's going to try to get the girls to come up with her. None of them have ever been back here, and she wants to give them a sense of their heritage. Chrissie – that's her oldest – she's very interested in history, you know. Old buildings, architecture. She and her husband Barry designed their own house. Amazing, it's like a mansion."

The drive home sets the tone for Aunt Ethel's visit. She has three topics of conversation, Anne discovers: How Things Have Changed; Poor Jim; and My Wonderful Grandchildren. After about three weeks have passed and Aunt Ethel has exhausted much of the subject matter in the Big Three topics – not that she ever lets them go entirely – she finds a fourth area of conversation: Complaints.

How Everything Has Changed slips easily into Complaint: it was never this cold, people used to be more friendly, you can't find your way around St. John's anymore. As well as deviating from its former self, St. John's also errs by not being New York: not enough buses and taxis (although Ethel approves of the fact that all the taxi drivers are white and speak English); the stores aren't the ones she's used to; it rains so much.

Anne hears these complaints when she sits down at Aunt Annie's kitchen table for a couple of hours after her classes finish at university. She's in the habit of waiting there for one of her parents to pick her up after work. ("Your mother is still a secretary, is she?" Aunt Ethel says. "Jimmy's wife, Joyce, she's never gone out to work. Wonderful housekeeper. You could eat off her floor. Diane, now, she's with a big firm in Manhattan. Very big office. She'll retire in a few years with a grand pension plan.") Aunt Ethel always smiles pleasantly at Anne when she comes in, but once, when Anne was curled up on the chesterfield reading a book, she heard Ethel in the kitchen saying to Annie, "Is that all she does? Hang around here and read? Fine big girl like that, you'd think she'd be more help to you." Which makes Anne feel guilty, but also makes her think that Aunt Ethel is a venomous old woman.

She learns, after awhile, to tune out Ethel's personal attacks, the ways in which Anne does not measure up to Ethel's own grandchildren. She can also ignore the general complaints about Newfoundland. What she can't ignore are the digs at Aunt Annie's home and hospitality. Fiercely loyal to Aunt Annie, Anne bites her tongue – hard – when Aunt Ethel gets up slowly from her chair. "I find I'm awful stiff these mornings, in my back and down into my hips. That mattress is not very firm. Of course it's only a sofa-bed."

So it begins. Within a month the hints have gotten broader. Well, they really can't be called hints anymore. "Oh, I don't know what I'm going to do, my back is so bad," Ethel says. "Annie, when Harold and Frances were home a few years ago, they said they had a lovely room, nice comfortable bed. What bed was that? Where did you put them to?"

Aunt Annie looks up from the cake batter she's stirring. "That was my bed. When Harold and Frances came down I moved out of my room. For two weeks."

Aunt Ethel looks away, out the window. "Oh. That was nice." She draws a long, deep sigh. "I can't get used to looking out the window and seeing all these other houses around. Seems so crowded here. Remember how open it used to be, Annie?"

Anne corners Aunt Annie the next day, when Aunt Ethel's own sister Ruby has taken her out to supper. "How can you put up with it, Aunt Annie? Making little digs like that? It's like she's suggesting you should have moved out and given *her* your room!"

"Well, and I would have, Anne, if it was only for a couple of weeks like when Harold and Frances came. But she's talking like she's moving back here forever, or at least for as long as she pleases, and I'm not…I'm just not willing to be put out like that, not knowing how long it'll be."

Spring arrives. Anne's first year of university ends and she has a job with Parks Canada for the summer. To get the job working at Signal Hill she had to go through an interview where they asked her all about the history of St. John's and Signal Hill, and she performed admirably, but the job actually involves painting the steps and railings on the scenic walking trails, which doesn't seem to require much knowledge of history.

In the last week of June, Aunt Diane arrives for a visit, accompanied by her daughter Laurie and Uncle Jimmy's daughter Katie. Anne finds, as she stands in the Arrivals area of the airport, that she's actually scared of meeting Laurie and Katie. Both are older than she is, but more importantly both are more beautiful, brilliant and sophisticated than she is – at least, if Aunt Ethel is to be believed. When she sees the three women coming out of the gate Anne is inclined to believe Aunt Ethel, for once.

Aunt Diane – not really an aunt, of course, a first cousin once removed – has dark hair and very bold, striking make-up. She's wearing a long leather coat and high leather boots. Behind her are the two girls, one a couple of years older than Anne, wearing a college sweatshirt, tight jeans and a denim jacket. Her ash-blond hair hangs straight to just below her shoulders, with bangs feathered back around her face. The other girl is older – that must be Laurie, the marine biologist – also a blond, who looks so much like Princess Diana, ruffled blouse and all, that Anne feels her heart drop.

A flurry of hugs and kisses is followed by an interminable wait for luggage. They get most of it in the end: a large suitcase of Diane's and a bag belonging to Katie are missing, which involves trips to the office to report the bags missing. "Oh my gawd, I don't have, like, my toothbrush or *anything*," Katie says. Her accent is like a TV-sitcom-New Yorker: Anne didn't think anyone in real life actually talked like that. "Underwear, everything. Can you even buy underwear here?"

"No, we mostly go without it. It's sexy and it feels so...so *natural*," Anne says, wide-eyed and hating her new cousin already. "But for times when we absolutely *have* to have it, we mail-order it in from the States. I can loan you my back-up pair if you want."

For a horrified moment Katie stares at Anne, then Laurie bursts out laughing. "Way to go, Anne. That's telling her. Don't be an idiot, Katie. Give me a hand with this freakin' bag, wouldya?"

Anne likes Laurie.

Anne and her parents drive the three guests to Aunt Annie's house, where the two aunts have cooked a turkey, but decided, since it's so warm, to serve it cold, with salads, instead of doing dressing and mashed potatoes and gravy. While Aunt Annie explains this decision, Diane peels off her leather jacket and shivers. "Oooh, you think this is *warm*? I'm really finding it chilly."

Doug laughs as he hangs up her coat. "No, this is what we call a heat wave, Diane."

"Oh gawd," Katie says again, refusing to relinquish her denim jacket. "I could never, never live here."

Several responses spring to mind, but Anne bites her tongue.

Katie's attitude does not improve, but the visit in general gets better after its awkward start. Claire takes Diane, Laurie and Katie up to Signal Hill one day when Anne is working. Anne gets off early and they all stay up on the hill to watch the Tattoo, which is pretty impressive – although Laurie points out that she's been to a Civil War re-enactment with her sister and brother-in-law "because they're into that kind of thing," and that the Tattoo is pretty small by comparison. "But it's really nice, for what it is," she adds kindly.

"Mike would love this. He was really sorry he couldn't come," Diane says. "I gotta bring him back here sometime." Aunt Diane's second husband is a New York City police officer named Mike Malone, and he's the reason she moved back to New York. Laurie, who grew up in California, describes herself as "bicoastal": she attends grad school in California near her father, but spends vacations with Diane in New York.

Katie has lived all her life on Long Island. Except for a trip to Florida with some girlfriends last spring, this is the farthest she's ever been from home. "Edge of the freakin' world," she says. "My dad is *always* going on about wanting to come up here again. I'm going to tell him: Newfoundland? Been there, done that."

"Oh shut up, Katie," says Laurie. "You've done nothing but bitch since you came here."

"Give it a rest, you two," Aunt Diane says from the bleacher seats behind them.

"I'm going inside to find a bathroom," Katie says, wandering off towards the interpretation centre.

Anne doesn't look at her, but she can tell from the sound of Diane's voice that she's rolling her eyes. "Honest to God, she's a little pain in the ass, isn't she? I mean, I had the best of intentions, bringing her along. Jimmy and Joyce thought it wouldn't hurt her to see a little bit of the world, discover her roots. But she just doesn't travel well."

"She's immature," Laurie says. Anne, two years younger than Katie, although better travelled, stays quiet.

"Yeah, well if she doesn't grow up a bit soon, Jimmy and Joyce are going to have their hands full. They've already got enough trouble with Dennis."

Laurie laughs. "We shoulda brought *Dennis*," she says. "Dennis with his green hair. Rebel without a clue."

Aunt Diane changes topics in midstream without warning. "I phoned Air Canada this morning, Claire, and I got reservations for Mom to come home the first week of September. I told Joyce to start looking for another place for her. She can't go back in her apartment – she's not able to manage on her own – but she doesn't want a nursing home either. A place with some care, but a little independence too."

"Oh. She's not...I mean, she's not still thinking of staying longer?" Claire's voice is light, but Anne, who knows its every nuance, can hear several things in her mother's tone.

"No, well, you can't go home again, can you? I think Mom finally has that figured out. She called me the end of her second week here and told me, 'Diane, I can't stay here with Annie.' It only makes sense, two women their age. They're set in their ways, aren't they? And nothing home is the way she remembers it. Except for Aunt Annie and Aunt Ruby, she's got no-one here. All her old friends are dead. She's been thinking for fifty years she wants to get back to Newfoundland, but the fact is, her home is in New York, you know?"

"Oh, I agree completely," Claire says.

"I told her as soon as I called, I said, 'Mom, come back with me and the girls when we come up to visit.' And she thought she might, but now she says she'd like to see out the summer. It's like part of her wants to go and part wants to stay, you know?"

"But you made the reservations?" Claire says. There's a hint of concern in her voice now, no doubt wondering which of Aunt Ethel's divided halves is going to carry the day.

"Oh yes, reservations made and paid for. Tuesday after Labour Day. I told her this morning, and I think she was satisfied."

"Well," says Claire in a voice that betrays nothing, "that's all you can do, isn't it?"

CLAIRE

TORONTO, MAY 1984

THE DAY THOU GAVEST , Lord, is ended
The darkness falls at Thy behest

Claire stood with head bowed in the spare funeral chapel where artificial light glowed through artificial stained-glass windows. Uncle Harold, at the front of the room, looked artificial too, with his hands folded over his chest. "My but he looks lovely, doesn't he," the women around the casket at the wake had crooned. Lovely, except of course, dead.

All the women in the family were weeping: the daughters-in-law discreetly, dabbing Kleenex around their eyes. Aunt Frances fought it, screwing up her face. Only Valerie gave way to grief, tears pouring down her face, her great shoulders heaving. Valerie had become a big woman who looked ten years older than Claire. Valerie had let her hair go grey but didn't have a short sensible cut or a perm. Long grey hair draggled down her back, or was pinned in haphazard loops and coils atop her head. She wore a flowing black dress like a tent, accented by silver bangle bracelets and a jangly silver necklace. Claire shook her head. Valerie wasn't stupid. She knew she was outlandish and didn't even care; she did it by choice.

"I wasn't prepared for it, not a bit," Aunt Frances said as the coffin was lowered. "I always thought Harold would live to be ninety, he was so healthy, so spry for his age. Seventy-five years old...sure, he had years and years ahead of him. I was never prepared for him to go so sudden."

A massive heart attack had killed Uncle Harold instantly. "Better to go sudden than like poor Uncle Jim," Claire reminded Frances, who was immediately cheered by the comparison. Uncle Jim had lasted seven years after his stroke.

Claire patted Aunt Frances' hand and said, "There was a nice turnout at the funeral."

Aunt Frances reached in her purse for a Kleenex. "Yes, wasn't there? Of course Harold was very well liked."

There weren't really many people at the funeral. Thirty or forty at the most. Claire knew that people used funerals as a way to measure how successful a life had been. She was sure Uncle Harold was well-liked and well-respected, but he and Frances lived in a small world – a tiny circle of expatriate Newfoundlanders, old people like themselves. A handful of these had shown up, and the family, and some men who had worked for Harold in the shop. One of Ken's fellow teachers had come, and a row of women in gauzy dresses and improbable hats who turned out to be Valerie's writers' group. Claire had not envisioned writers as creatures who roamed in packs, but references to "the group" peppered Valerie's conversation.

Aunt Frances' little house was cozy and shabby; the furniture and decor hadn't been updated since she and Harold bought the place in the mid-50s. There was the old chrome kitchen set, the chintz chesterfield and matching wing chair covered with hand-knitted afghans, the set of framed Scenes of Newfoundland put out by one of the oil companies a few years ago. Photos of the grandchildren dominated the living room wall, and the gigantic TV set loomed in the room. Frances stood in the middle of her own living room as though she were in a foreign country, shaking her head. "Poor Harold, poor Harold," she said. "I can see him sitting there in his chair, as plain as if he was there."

Once Aunt Frances was asleep, Valerie said to Claire, "Come upstairs to my place. Mom and Dad's living room gives me the creeps."

Claire was not particularly fond of the living room decor and she understood Valerie's need to decorate her own space in her own taste. But to tell the truth, it was Valerie's bedsitting room upstairs that gave Claire the creeps, with dark foreboding pictures and African ceremonial masks hung on the walls. One whole wall was floor-to-ceiling bookshelves, crammed full, and even then there were piles and boxes of books all over the place. Claire would have loved to get hold of this place and organize it. But, she thought, even if you sorted the books properly, by author or subject, and had them all on shelves, the room would still be weird. Valerie had beads instead of curtains hanging over her windows. She was like some kind of fifty-year-old hippie.

Valerie poured herself a glass of wine and offered one to Claire. "No thanks. I'll have ginger ale or something if you've got it," Claire said.

"Oh, that's right, you don't drink. Good Salvation Army girl," Valerie said with a chuckle.

Claire sighed. "I haven't gone to the Army in years, Val. I go to the United Church, where you can have all the wine you want. But I never got in the habit. Not raised up to it, I guess."

"Yes, it's hard to shake off the shackles of how we were reared," Val said, curling up on a cushion on the floor. Claire, perched on a spectacularly uncomfortable wicker chair, thought that even if Valerie looked sixty with that dishevelled grey hair, she must have the joints of a much younger woman, to be able to sit on the floor so easily. "I wouldn't call myself a Christian anymore," Valerie went on, "but I do feel there's *something* – a deep spiritual something at the core of our being, at the core of all life, wouldn't you say?"

As was often the case with Valerie, Claire felt completely at a loss, as though she and her cousin were the print and the negative, opposite in every way. Claire went to church and considered herself a Christian but had no opinion on the deep spiritual something at the core of everything.

"I've been reading a great deal, visiting with some friends who worship in…well, different ways," Valerie went on. "More in touch with nature, with the Spirit in us all. I'm interested in finding more woman-centred expressions of spirituality, unleashing my inner goddess, if you will."

Unleashing my inner goddess, if you will. Claire was storing moments from this conversation, little gems to bring back to Doug.

"…and what I really feel, after all these years, is that I'm finally beginning to find my voice, my feminine voice," said Valerie, ironically, because her voice was actually quite low, even gruff. "I look back now at my work over the past several years, and you know, I struggled so with that, struggled to get it published, and now I just feel such *relief.* The universe was so kind to me, not allowing any of that to be published, because none of that was truly me. Here, this is my latest story."

Valerie thrust into Claire's hands what appeared to be a paperback book but was actually some kind of book-like magazine called *A Room of One's Own.* "Women's writing," Valerie said. The title rang a bell with Claire, though she couldn't recall from where. Anyway, she figured, a room of one's own was what Val had here, in every possible sense.

The story was called "A Peace of My Mind" and at first Claire thought it was a misprint, then realized it must be a clever pun, the point of which she would get if she read the story. It started with a woman sitting in an empty house on a cliff while the wind howled around her and the grey sea was churned into white-topped waves below. Claire read two paragraphs in which nothing happened except the woman sat there. She knew with absolute certainty that she would rather take a good solid kick in the teeth than finish reading this story. She looked up. "This is set in Newfoundland."

"Yes, it's about a woman who returns to her roots and lives in an isolated house in Conception Bay. Just as I've done...returned to my roots, spiritually, that is. I feel Newfoundland in my blood so strongly these days, drawing me home."

Claire looked up sharply. Valerie had made three visits home in her life and each one had been an ordeal for Claire, with whom she always stayed. "You're thinking of coming home again?"

"Well, perhaps. You know, life may imitate art. I may just find myself a little property somewhere in the outports—"

Claire actually snorted. "Why on earth would you do that? Look at everything you have access to here in Toronto: your writing group, your book club, art, theatre, museums, fine restaurants, all the things you enjoy. Living in some remote rural cabin through a nine-month winter sounds romantic enough, but you'd go crazy within a week."

The idea of Valerie reclaiming these supposed Newfoundland roots, after all this time, was actually an affront to Claire. It was offensive, and in poor taste, and totally unrealistic, since even when she was a child Valerie didn't exactly live in a fishing village and spend her days gutting and splitting fish on the flakes. "I can see travelling, but you'd be nuts to move away from here permanently. Honestly, Val, I don't know what more you could want."

"No," Valerie said, staring out the window. "No, you never did see what more I could want, did you?" Rain splattered against the window. "And what about you? Are you content with the way you've lived your life?"

"What a way to put it, Valerie. I'm hardly dead yet." At fifty-three, Claire felt it was as good a time as any for taking stock, but only Valerie would be willing to put such a bizarre question so bluntly.

Content? Claire did not think of her life in those terms. She thought of her marriage, good and stable, if lacking in excitement – which suited her fine; excitement was overrated. She thought of Annie, still hanging in there twenty-seven years after her cancer, stubbornly independent but needing someone to look out for her. She thought of Stephen, her firstborn, immersed in studying obscure computer languages. And Anne – her bright, wonderful, frustrating daughter – studying English in university, sounding dangerously like Valerie sometimes. She thought of her own job, which, with all the raises and new responsibilities, still added up to managing the office for the men who did the real work, making their days smoother and their jobs easier.

Claire looked around again at Valerie's room, which in one way was cluttered but was, in another sense, painfully simple. Nothing in this room – no picture, no book, no stick of furniture – reflected anyone else's needs or priorities other than Valerie's own. *It's my life that's cluttered*, Claire thought. *My life is all about other people. Valerie's life is only about Valerie.* And this revelation irritated her even more, made her want to say, *What the hell kind of a question is that?* although she never swore, considering it a sign of poor taste and limited education. She took a deep breath instead.

"So tell me all about your nieces and nephews, Valerie…Ken's and Dan's young ones. What are they like?"

Valerie smiled, poured herself another glass of wine, leaned back against the wall. She raised a glass to Claire, as if they'd just finished playing a game together and she was toasting Claire's success. "Yes," she said in that husky voice, still smiling as if she had a secret joke. "Yes, let's catch up on all the family news."

ANNE

∿

NEW YORK, OCTOBER 1986

ANNE GRADUATES WITH A degree in English from Memorial University. She wants to be a writer, but her mother, who finds this ambition alarming, leans heavily on Doug's newspaper career to suggest that Anne study journalism. Anne goes to Columbia University to do this, as well as to immerse herself in New York, and, of course, to fall in love. She knows the kind of person she is going to fall in love with: he will be tall, with dark unruly hair and long, thin hands that are in constant motion. He will be an artist trying to make a name for himself in New York, tortured by his inner demons and teetering on the brink of madness, from which she will pull him back.

She meets Brian in the sculpture garden outside the Cathedral of St. John the Divine. Brian sits at the edge of the fountain, staring at the bronze giraffes. He is tall, with unruly dark hair and long, thin hands; his thumbs twiddle as they rest in his lap. He wears acid-wash jeans, a white shirt with a collar, and a brown leather jacket that looks like it cost a mint. Anne sits down next to him, looks at the giraffes and says, "Do you think they're screwing?"

He looks at her, then back at the giraffes. "I think it's more metaphysical than that." Anne remembers she intended to fall in love with someone who used the word *metaphysical* in sentences.

"Maybe they're composing metaphysical poetry," she suggests. "Like John Donne."

"*License my roving—hooves—and let them go, before, between, beneath, behind, below,*" he says, still staring at the giraffes, and Anne feels as if her whole body has been dipped in hot water.

"That's my favourite poem," she says. "It has the name of the place I come from in it. 'Oh my America, my New Found Land.'" When he doesn't respond, she adds, "I'm from Newfoundland. It's…you know, east of Nova Scotia."

He nods. "I know where it is. My parents took me there once on vacation. But I can't remember much about it. I was really young."

"Oh." After a minute's silence she says, "So, are you studying English?" Then she remembers that she doesn't even know for sure if he's a student.

"I was. I had a double major in English and biochemistry. Now I'm in med school. I'm thinking of cardiology."

"*Really?* And you read John Donne?"

"Well, I *have* read John Donne. I wouldn't say I have him on my bookstand and read him every night before I go to bed." For the first time he looks at her full on, with the light switches on behind his eyes.

"What is on your bookstand?"

"Right now? An anatomy textbook, a *Penthouse* magazine, and *The Catcher in the Rye.*"

"That's quite an eclectic assortment," Anne says, thinking she ought to be able to draw some conclusion, to pull something together out of these pieces of information.

"So, what's on yours?"

"On my..."

"*Your* bookstand. I told you what's on mine; now what's on yours?"

"Oh...mine?" Her experience of college dating has prepared Anne for asking men interesting, leading questions about themselves. It has not prepared her as well for answering questions about herself.

"A biography of George Eliot, my journal, the *New Yorker*, and *The Fellowship of the Ring*," she says after a quick visual recall.

"Aha! Reading or re-reading?"

"Tolkein? Re-reading, of course."

"In undergrad, I used to re-read the entire *Lord of the Rings* every exam week."

Anne tells nobody in her family about Brian for a month. The first person she tells is not her mother or even Aunt Annie, in her frequent calls home. Instead, she sits in Aunt Diane's kitchen in Brooklyn Heights, at the small Formica table, drinking coffee on a Sunday afternoon while Diane clears away the debris from Sunday dinner, and describes Brian Hayworth. Aunt Diane chatters as she clatters. In the adjacent living room, Mike watches the football game.

"So why didn't you go to his place for Sunday dinner, if he asked you?" says Aunt Diane, swishing water over the dinner plates.

"It's a big thing with them. They're rich...sort of, I guess. They have this apartment a few blocks from Central Park."

"Oh yeah, they're rich."

"Right. And the whole family comes for Sunday dinner."

"And you're scared to go?" Diane asks.

Anne turns her coffee cup round and round on the tabletop. "No, it's not really…I mean, I wouldn't say I'm scared, exactly."

"Not scared? Geez, I'd be *shitbaked*," Aunt Diane says. Anne laughs so hard it's a minute before she can stand up. She picks up the dishtowel, which is a souvenir of the Cayman Islands.

"So, you coming out with us to see Mom, or do you want us to drop you back to your place?" Aunt Diane wants to know as they finish the dishes.

"I'll come with you. I guess."

Three quiet steps, and Mike's in the kitchen. "We better get going if we're driving out to Jimmy's," he says. He comes up behind Aunt Diane, puts his arms around her from behind, and kisses the back of her neck.

For a moment the kitchen is so still Anne almost forgets to breathe. Then Diane says, "I'll finish up here, you go get the car."

A Sunday afternoon trip to see Aunt Ethel involves first driving to Jimmy and Joyce's, then all setting off together on pilgrimage. Jimmy and Joyce's older two, Junior and the infamous Katie, don't live at home, but Jimmy's youngest boy, Dennis, is still there. He's Anne's age and this Sunday afternoon he decides to come along to visit his grandmother. "Do something with your hair, Dennis," Joyce says in despair as she scurries about the house collecting magazines and fruit to bring to her mother-in-law. Dennis makes a face at Anne.

"I could shave you bald," Anne whispers as he pulls on his jacket. Dennis' hair is a dead-white mohawk, leaving the tattoos on either side of his skull visible. For a punk, he's mild-mannered and funny. He hangs drywall for a living.

"So, d'you go home for Christmas?" he asks Anne as they squeeze together in the back of the station wagon.

"Yeah," Anne says.

"I'd like to go home sometime. For a visit, you know. Guess I'd scare them all up there, though."

"No, we've got punks in St. John's too. They wouldn't look twice at you," Anne assures him. It's important to her to keep updating Dennis' ideas about "home" – the place his grandparents came from, a place he's never been.

Aunt Ethel lives at a place called Shady Acres, a long one-storey complex of seniors' apartments and nursing-home rooms. The trees are narrow and spindly, recently planted, so Anne assumes the name is more an act of faith than description. Aunt Ethel has a roommate, Mrs. Clarke, who glares suspiciously at Ethel's family as they gather around her armchair. When Anne walks past,

Mrs. Clarke beckons her over. Anne goes to the woman's bedside and stoops to listen.

"That woman...she's watching me," Mrs. Clarke says, pointing at Aunt Ethel. "Last night...I saw her. I was lying in my bed, and she had...a *flashlight*. Pointed right at me. She watches me while I sleep."

Anne joins the family group to find that Aunt Ethel is complaining, fairly loudly, about Mrs. Clarke. "That one there, I don't know why they got me in here with her. Can't you speak to them, Joyce? Don't you think they'd put people in with others of...of like interests? I don't think she should be on this wing at all. There's a wing, you know, for people who are bed-rid and mental."

"Look, Mom, Anne came with us again today. You remember...Claire's girl, Anne?" Diane's voice is a little hesitant at the end, prompting.

Aunt Ethel leans forward, peers at Anne through old-fashioned cat's-eyes glasses. "I know who Anne is, Diane, I'm not senile yet. How are your mother and father, dear?"

"They're fine. I saw them when I was home Christmas."

"Oh, I'd like to get home again," Aunt Ethel says. "I often have a mind to write to Annie, say to her, Annie girl, can you fix up a little room for me? Off in a corner anywhere, it doesn't have to be anything special, but I'd like to die in my own place among my own people. Is that too much to ask?" Anne wonders if Aunt Ethel remembers the four months she spent in Newfoundland, four years ago. Aunt Annie certainly remembers.

Joyce pats Ethel's hand. "You are among your own people, Mother. Look, we're all here."

Ethel shakes her head; Anne has noticed that no matter what Joyce says Ethel is never sharp with her, whereas Diane can't make even the most innocent comment without earning a reprimand. Ethel's voice now is sad rather than angry: "You'll never understand, Joyce girl. Newfoundlanders, you know what they say, you can take the girl out of Newfoundland but you can't take Newfoundland out of the girl. Poor Jim understood that. To his dying day he wanted to go back home. He would have been so happy, just to sit on the back step of Annie's house again, just to see all his old friends. No, Joyce, you don't know what it is to be uprooted from the place you were born, and live out your life among strangers."

A small silence follows this melancholy speech. Dennis breaks it, saying, "I'm buying a motorcycle, Nan." This change of subject does nothing to lighten the mood.

"He was a wonderful man, was Jim," Aunt Ethel says, fumbling for the box of Kleenex on the nightstand. Joyce hands them to her. "A perfect gentleman, right to the end, that's what I always said."

"Do you want to go for a little walk, Ma?" Jimmy says. "Down the hall, as far as the lounge?"

Ethel looks up through misty eyes. "My, yes, Jimmy, I think that'd be nice. Get me up out of this chair. Take my mind off things. Just bring me over my walker now, that's a good boy, Dennis. What a shame about your hair, can you have anything done for it? I don't suppose it'll be long growing out, will it?"

"Everyone in my family is obsessed with *home*," Anne tells Brian a few weeks later, walking in Central Park in a drizzling rain. "My Aunt Ethel wants to die at home. I have this cousin, Dennis, who's never been in Newfoundland in his life, and he says he'd like to go *home* sometime. Home is a place he's never been. Isn't that weird?"

"It is weird," Brian says. "I can't imagine that. It's like they're immigrants or something."

"Well, they were, I guess. Maybe I'm an immigrant too."

"And are you obsessed with going home?"

"Um...I don't know. Not right now. But on the other hand, I knew all these people in high school, and in university at home, who were like, *I can't wait till I can get off this godforsaken Rock.* I never felt that way. But here I am."

"Do you think you'll go back there sometime?"

"I...yeah, maybe. I want to travel, do the whole see-the-world thing, work overseas. But yeah, I guess I do have that sense of roots. Like I know where I belong."

Brian frowns, but says, "That's nice. In a way."

"What about you? Do you have any feeling of roots? I mean, is New York home for you, in that way?"

He shrugs. "Not really. I was born here, but my dad is from Chicago, and my mom comes from Virginia. Neither of them has that kind of feeling about *home* like your people do. I think the only Americans I've ever met that feel that way were some Southerners...not my mom's family but, you know, people who can't wait to get back to the grits and gravy. I grew up thinking *grits* was plural. When I finally went to visit my grandma in Virginia and she asked if I wanted grits, I said maybe just the one grit."

Brian laughs, then looks quickly at Anne who is smiling, but uncertainly. "You thought it was plural too, didn't you?" he says.

"Grits." She pictures three long fried things on a plate. "Well, you could see how I might. If I offered you fish and brewis, how many would you have?"

He takes her hand. "Just one. A fish and brew. You take me home sometime and I'll try that."

ETHEL

~3~

LONG ISLAND, JULY 1989

ONE NIGHT, IN HER bed in Shady Acres, Ethel has a dream.

She dreams about heaven – not surprising, perhaps, given that it's Sunday night and the church crowd have been holding services in the chapel. Ethel always goes, even when she's not feeling well. She likes when they sing the old hymns, not the young crowd with the guitars and jangly new music, but the crowd that sings "When All My Labours and Trials Are O'er" and "We Are Nearing Home" and all the old favourites. Ethel likes to think about heaven. She imagines it in the usual way: mansions, streets of gold, angel choirs. Promoted to Glory.

In her dream, when she finds herself in heaven, it's nothing like that. Heaven, it turns out, is Annie's backyard in Freshwater Valley in St. John's. Except a little bigger than Ethel remembers it. But she knows right away it's heaven. She's sitting on the back step, wearing a blue dress with white sprigs that comes just below the knee, a dress she owned in 1928 and particularly liked. She has a white cardigan over it, because there's just a bit of a breeze, but not too much. Heaven is a July day in St. John's, warm but not sultry. Annie has a line of wash out: the wind fills the white shirts and they dance on the line like angels.

Bert sits on the step beside her, looking just like he did the last time she saw him, twenty-two years old, one arm laid on her shoulder. On her other side, sitting just as close, is Harold, about the same age, smiling like he's just told a joke. Annie is somewhere inside the house making supper. In the yard below, Ethel can hear the children playing: Jimmy and Diane, five or six years old, their voices ringing with laughter.

She looks at Bert, and then back at Harold, thinking she should feel uneasy though she doesn't. "It's all right, girl," Harold says.

"Is it?" Ethel asks.

"Yes, it's really all right."

"Everything," Bert echoes. "Everything's all right." And hearing them both say it, she knows it's true.

Some people are not in the yard but she knows they are somewhere around; their absence does not feel like a loss. Frances must be in the house with Annie, and Ethel's own family, her parents and her sister, are probably in there too. The younger ones, the grandchildren – she can hear them laughing from somewhere in the distance, even though their parents are only children themselves. All children, playing together, and everything is all right.

And Jesus. She almost asks Harold where he is, because Harold would know if anyone would. As it's heaven, she expects to see him. But then she doesn't need to ask, because she's sure he's around. She can feel him. Probably sitting down in the kitchen with Annie, having a cup of tea. Ethel thinks she should go in and find him. She owes him an apology for something, some misunderstanding years ago. But he'll probably come out and sit in the yard in a few minutes, it's so nice out, and whatever misunderstandings there were between them she's sure he won't hold it against her. He's bound to be in a good mood. Sitting at Annie's table having a cup of tea and a slice of homemade bread with molasses is enough to put anyone in a good mood.

Then she remembers she hasn't seen Jim. A flutter catches her heart, her first moment of discomfort since waking here; she feels as if she's misplaced something important. Harold lays a hand on her arm. "Everything's all right," he reminds her.

That's when she sees them, over by the lilac tree. Jim is standing there, young and strong, spinning around in the grass. In his arms, high above his head, he holds Ralphie, who is about eight years old. Ralphie is silhouetted against the blue sky high above Jim's head, arms outstretched, spinning in the air making airplane noises. Both their faces are alive with laughter, echoing each other's smiles, no eyes for anyone but each other. Ethel watches them till the picture is seared into her eyelids, then closes her eyes.

The morning nurse finds Ethel when she makes her rounds. As she says later to Joyce, in thirty years of nursing she has cause to know that not many deathbeds are like in the movies or in books. People don't usually die with a smile on their face; it tends to be messier than that. "But your mother-in-law, Mrs. Evans, was one of the few. One of the few I can honestly say died with a smile on her face."

EPILOGUE: ANNE

BROOKLYN, MAY 2004

THE BARNES AND NOBLE bookstore in Park Slope is like every Barnes and Noble everywhere: tastefully cream and dark green, two levels of books with comfy chairs which Anne has never seen unoccupied, a cafe serving Starbucks coffee, scones and cheesecake.

It's just a few blocks from the house Anne and Brian bought three years ago when their daughter Hannah was born. Before that, their home base was an apartment in Manhattan, where Brian worked and Anne came home between overseas assignments. Anne used to joke to friends that her parents were shocked that her brother Stephen and his girlfriend were living together and not married, and equally shocked that Anne and Brian were married and not living together.

The year she turned thirty-five, the turn of the millennium, the year Aunt Annie died, Anne decided it was time to stay in one place, live with her husband, make a baby. She's always wanted to live in Brooklyn, and Park Slope is now a very trendy neighbourhood. Pricey, too, but they rent out the downstairs apartments of their solid old brownstone on Carroll Street. Anne took a year off after Hannah was born and now has a job with the network in New York. No more travelling for a while.

They do travel to Newfoundland almost every summer; last year she and Brian bought a house in Elliston, as a summer place. Since the collapse of the cod fishery the little Newfoundland outports are gutted, and well-to-do Americans can buy beautiful old saltbox houses for twenty thousand cheap Canadian dollars. Anne's still not used to thinking of herself as a well-to-do American.

This is Claire's first visit to the brownstone in Brooklyn; she and Doug have been to visit Anne and Brian in Manhattan, but for this trip Claire has come by herself. Claire still finds it hard to believe her daughter has chosen to live in Brooklyn. Yesterday Anne and Claire drove through boarded-up, burned-out streets in Bedford-Stuyvesant, walls painted with lurid gangland graffiti, garbage on the streets. Claire said nothing at the time, staring out the window like she was touring the streets of Baghdad. She kept quiet last night and this morning, in front of Brian, but now, sitting in the Barnes and Noble cafe waiting for Diane and Valerie to arrive, she says, "I don't see how you can raise a child in this city, Anne."

Anne sighs, looks at her mother over her mocha frappucino. "I don't live in Bed-Stuy or Crown Heights, Mom. I live in Park Slope." She waves a hand at the street outside the bookstore's window: the stone Baptist church, the small trendy shops. The beautiful, well-dressed, multicoloured people all talking on cellphones. The line of SUVs, minivans, BMWs parked at the curb. The mothers walking past with children in strollers, Snuglis, slings. Then she sees a woman entering the store. "Oh good," she says. "Here comes Aunt Valerie."

Valerie drifts into the store like a feather blown on the breeze. Bangles at her wrist jingle as she holds out both arms towards Claire and Anne in a theatrical gesture. "Darlings!" she says.

She is barely settled, catching them up on the story of her reading today in Manhattan, when Aunt Diane finds them. "Well hel-LO!" she bellows, and there are hugs all around. Diane gets coffee for herself and Valerie.

Sitting around the table as they talk, Anne studies the three older women. Her mother, slim and elegant with the high proud tilt of her head on her long neck. Valerie, more comfortable in her own skin than anyone Anne has ever seen, long white hair flowing down her back. She looks like a Victorian virgin gone to seed. And Diane, the only one who still dyes her hair, looking glossy and lacquered, her bright red lipstick standing out oddly on her creased face, her laugh as loud and unrestrained as ever.

Seventy, Anne thinks, sounded so old until just a few years ago, when her parents reached that milestone. She herself is dealing with Nearly Forty, and is happy with her choices: a child, a home, a career change. But she still feels half-hatched, feeling fourteen some days, twenty-two others. Once in awhile, after a hard day at work and a sleepless night with Hannah, she feels fifty-six. She still doesn't feel she's arrived. What can happen in the next thirty years to give her the confidence she sees in her mother and her mother's cousins, these women barrelling so brazenly into old age?

"It must be a long time since the three of you have all been together like this, is it?" Anne says.

The other three women look at each other, then at her, then back at each other and burst out laughing.

"You know what, honey?" Diane says. "We have *never* all been together. Not once in our lives, till tonight."

"You're kidding me. How is that possible?"

"Well," Diane says, "we never all lived in the same place at the same time. We've kept in touch, visited each other on trips, but honestly, this is the first time all three of us have been together." She sips her coffee and smiles. "The Evans girls, together at last."

"I did not think about that at all," Valerie said. "It really is an historic moment."

Valerie's reading is downstairs in a corner of the bookstore cleared for the occasion, tucked between self-help and sexuality. As they follow her downstairs, Valerie gushes to the nervous young store employee about how wonderful it all is, how special it is to come to Brooklyn, where she was born but has never lived as an adult. Anne suggested the reading here and made the arrangements. Valerie's publisher, in planning to promote the book in New York, had only thought of her reading in Manhattan, despite the fact that a significant chunk of the book takes place on Flatbush Avenue.

"Yes, it's quite lovely here," Valerie tells the bookstore girl in her mid-Atlantic voice. "I feel quite at home, even if it has been nearly seventy years since I left here." A polite murmur from Bookstore Girl. "Oh, don't be surprised, my dear. I have no problem admitting I'm over seventy. I don't know why women feel so embarrassed about their ages. I *revel* in old lady-hood. Now that I'm in my seventies, I've told myself, Valerie dear, it's time to cease being conventional, kick over the traces, let yourself be flamboyant." She gestures broadly, her fingertips knocking over a copy of *The Bad Girl's Guide to Good Sex*. "I'm planning to be a truly *eccentric* old lady."

Claire leans close to Anne's ear. "The mind boggles," she whispers. Anne chokes back her giggle.

After being a late bloomer, publishing her first book at fifty-five and then being published for fifteen years by small presses with minuscule print runs, Valerie surprised everyone three years ago with a book that made the Canadian bestseller list and was nominated for the Giller Prize. Her latest book, just released, was another surprise in that it was just as good. The new buzz on Valerie is that she's going to be the oldest woman ever to win the Governor General's award.

Only fifteen people show up for Valerie's reading: a big success in Canada does not necessarily mean you've been heard of in Brooklyn. But the small group settles under the spell of her voice, her words, as she opens the book and begins to read.

Despite all the mockery of Aunt Val that she and her mother have shared over the years, Anne has always been drawn by Valerie's writing. Now she sits in the straight-back chair and the green and cream room full of books falls away as Valerie reads, leaving Anne alone on a Brooklyn street eighty years ago.

"*They came like other immigrants,*" Valerie finishes, "*but they were not like other immigrants: they spoke English; they were not believed to carry disease. They crossed not the entire ocean but one corner of it, and because of that, they believed they were going to a place much like home. And they were just like other immigrants, because they barred their doors and shut out the world that was so different, and made for themselves a world like home. They ate with and slept with and married one another, and in the evening they took the subway to the Loew's Kings to laugh and cry at the lives of people they believed were quite unlike themselves. But before they went in they paused outside to hang their harps on the willows, for they were immigrants, could not sing their own songs in this strange land.*"

Valerie's voice ends; the strangeness drops away; the room comes into focus again. The small audience applauds as she finishes. Valerie doesn't care about the size of the crowd. "It's just such a pleasure to be here," she gushes during the signing afterwards. She sells three books and signs four: one hard-core Valerie Evans fan shows up with a well-thumbed copy of her last book and gets it autographed.

A young African-American man, well-dressed, wearing small wire-rimmed glasses, waits among the small group of fans. When he reaches Valerie he says, "I enjoyed your reading." He has a new copy of the book for her to sign. "I hadn't read your work before today, but I'm looking forward to getting home and reading this."

"Thank you, thank you so much," Valerie says. "And your name is?" Her pen hand hovers over the title page.

"Bennett. Gareth Bennett," the young man says. As Valerie signs, he says, "Actually, it's an interesting story, how I came to be here tonight. I teach English at Brooklyn College. A lot of ads for readings come across my desk. I was about to pin yours on the bulletin board and forget about it when I noticed you were originally from Newfoundland and the book is partly set there."

"Oh, have you been to Newfoundland?"

Gareth Bennett shakes his head. "No, never been farther north than Boston," he confesses. "But it was the Newfoundland connection, combined with the fact that your name is Evans. You see, I came across that name recently. Do you know, would you by any chance be related to, a Claire Evans from St. John's, Newfoundland?"

Claire's head lifts like she's scented something on the breeze, and she moves forward with her hand outstretched. "How interesting...I'm Claire Evans. Well, Claire Parsons now. Evans was my maiden name. I'm from St. John's."

Gareth shakes her hand. "Nice to meet you, Mrs. Parsons. Can you think of any reason why a suitcase with your name on it would be in the back of my mother's bedroom closet?"

"Nothing comes to mind," Claire says carefully, "but who is your mother?"

"Her name is Sheilah Bennett. But she thinks the suitcase belonged to my father. We can't be sure, because my father passed away two years ago. I was helping my mother clean out her house, to move into an apartment, you know? And among all these odds and ends we found this." He paused. "I have it with me. I brought it, just on the off chance Newfoundland might really be that small a place."

He goes back to where he was sitting and pulls from beneath his chair a very small, battered cardboard suitcase, perhaps twice the size of a shoebox. On the outside is written: *Claire Evans, St. John's, Newfoundland.* Claire stares at her name but makes no move to take the suitcase.

"I...I suppose it might be mine," she says. "My family...some of my family lived in Brooklyn. A long time ago. I don't recognize the handwriting," she adds, looking up again at Gareth Bennett.

"It's my father's handwriting. My father was a minister, Mrs. Parsons. He was a very generous man, always doing favours for people. My mother and I wondered if this was something given to him to hold onto, perhaps for someone who was going to pick it up and bring it to you, but never came. It's hard to tell now, so many years later. There were a number of things in the closet just as mysterious as this. It just so happens that the names Evans and Newfoundland crossed my desk only a few weeks after finding this, so they caught my attention."

"Well, this is really one of those stories, isn't it?" Diane says, having muscled her way to where the action is. "You know, like you hear about love letters that go astray in the mail and finally get delivered fifty years later?"

"Serendipity," says Valerie, listening with rapt attention. "There are forces at work, forces at work."

When the four women leave the bookstore to walk to Anne's place, Claire carries the unopened suitcase. It's a warm May night, one of those lush spring evenings that still seem like a gift to Anne. A Newfoundland upbringing is hard to erase even after twenty years, and she's still amazed by spring as a distinct season. The streetlamps of Park Slope cast a gentle glow on the tree-lined streets. People are out walking their dogs and children, or sitting on their stoops. At Anne's house, the babysitter is watching TV; Hannah is asleep and Brian is on call at the hospital tonight. Anne pays the babysitter and puts the kettle on. Her mother and the two cousins settle themselves in the living room.

"It must be from your mother. It must," Diane insists. Claire sits on the couch, looking down at the suitcase on her lap.

"How did a black preacher get hold of a box belonging to my mother?" Claire wonders.

On Claire's previous visits to New York she and Anne have done some family-history research, but have found nothing conclusive. They found numerous death certificates for women named Rose Evans, most of whom had to be disqualified because the birthdate or birthplace was wrong. Only one was vague enough to possibly qualify: this Rose died in 1977, but neither birthplace nor birthdate was listed. Her occupation was "Minister," which seemed unlikely, to say the least.

They found another death certificate on one of their searches, a couple of years ago, for an Antony Martelli. The address was the same one Claire remembers from her visit to the fruit store. He died in 1981. But again, there's nothing to prove Tony Martelli was even her father. Still, Claire has kept copies of both death certificates, carrying them around in her purse for the last few years: they seem as close as she's likely to get to having parents.

"No-one will ever know," Valerie says mysteriously.

"Unless there's a note inside the box explaining," Diane suggests.

As Claire runs her fingers over the suitcase, Anne remembers herself as a child, poking around in corners of Aunt Annie's house, looking for a trunk filled with old clothes and diaries, a box that would give her the key to her past. It's smaller than she had imagined it would be.

"Okay," says Claire. "This is it. I'm taking the plunge."

She flips up the rusty clasps of the suitcase. Inside, nestled in a water-stained red lining, are two smaller boxes. One is a shoebox, very battered, with a loop of string loosely tying it shut. The other is about the same size, but looks sturdier and more official.

Claire pulls the string off the shoebox and lays it on the coffee table. They all cluster around to see. On top is a card that says, "Get Well Soon." Inside, the signature (*We're all praying for you, The Carter Family*) is crossed out in pencil. On the empty page opposite, another note is pencilled in a different hand. "That's my mother's handwriting," Claire says. "I remember it. She used to send me cards and letters when I was little." She reads aloud: "My dear daughter, just a few things for you to remember me by. God bless you, your Loving Mother." Claire looks up. "Well, that was informative," she says.

The few things are few indeed. There's a snapshot of a little girl. "That's me," says Claire. A lurid calendar poster of the Sacred Heart of Jesus. A folded paper that turns out to be a ministerial license, granted to someone by the name of Rosamond Maranatha. A small pocket New Testament, well-worn with pages falling out and verses underlined in red pen. A cheap-looking pair of dangly earrings. Brown things that might be pressed flower petals, rose petals perhaps. A single yellowed baby sock. Claire holds the sock in her palm, staring at it. It's the last thing in the box.

All four women gaze at the tiny pile of memorabilia. Valerie reaches forward and picks up the Bible; Diane turns over one of the crisp flower petals and sniffs it.

"What's not there is a lot more striking than what is there," says Valerie. And this is so true that for a moment no-one can think of anything else to say. A few things to remember me by. Remember who? Rose Evans? Rosamond Maranatha? Your Loving Mother?

"I don't know what to make of it," Claire says. "Imagine this stuff, stuck away on a shelf all these years, and him finding us tonight. What a coincidence."

"What's in the other box?" Diane says.

They have all been so taken with the contents of the shoebox that no-one has spared a thought for the second box, which is much heavier. When opened, it is found to contain a wooden vase or jar with a sealed lid, about ten inches high and quite heavy. Everyone stares at it.

"It's an urn," Valerie says finally. "It must be your mother's–"

"Ashes," Anne says.

"Remains," says Diane at the same moment.

"Actually, the word they use now is *cremains*," Valerie says.

Claire is still staring at the urn. Finally she says, "My mother left instructions to have her...her ashes...packed up and sent to me, and then left them with someone who forgot all about them. She's been sitting on a shelf for heaven knows how long."

"Maybe since 1977," Anne suggests. "That death certificate...Rose Evans, the minister? It could have been her."

"Sweet land of Goshen," Claire says. "What am I supposed to do with these?" She makes a move as if to unscrew the lid, then stops and lays the urn down on the coffee table. "Take them home and bury them, I guess. I suppose that's what she wanted, to be buried back home. Otherwise, why send it to me?"

"You could scatter them," Valerie suggests.

"Where?" Claire says. "It makes more sense to bury them."

"I wonder if she really belongs back home," Diane muses, picking up the urn and turning it in her hands. "Cheap finish. I guess this was all she could afford. I mean, she lived most of her life here, in Brooklyn, or so it would seem. Wouldn't she want to be scattered, or buried or whatever, right here?"

"Well, she's *been* right here for nearly thirty years," Anne points out, and tries to suppress a giggle. But it's contagious. Diane laughs her loud, unfettered laugh, and Valerie joins in. Then Claire is laughing too, all four women laughing so hard that tears stream down their faces.

"Just think, Anne," Claire says. "All these years I've been coming to New York trying to find my mother. And all the while she was in the back of someone's closet in Crown Heights!"

The laughter passes after awhile, leaving them all weak. "I think you should scatter them off the Brooklyn Bridge, or the Staten Island ferry," Valerie says.

"What a tacky idea, Val," Claire says. "It's the kind of thing people do in books, not in real life. And I think it might be illegal. You need a permit or something, don't you? The sensible thing to do is to take her home and put her in the family plot, with Nan and Pop and Annie and Bill. I wouldn't even know how to go about scattering someone."

"Me either. All our people were always buried," Diane says.

"Oh, I've done it," Valerie assures them. "A dear, dear friend of mine, three or four years ago, passed away. Tom Sutton, a lovely gay man, died of AIDS, sadly. A group of us went to his garden and scattered his ashes at night, by candlelight. A beautiful ceremony. We had a piper, too. I like the idea of doing it over water."

"Someone does that in a book. Off the Staten Island ferry, or maybe between Brooklyn and Manhattan," Anne recalls suddenly, and looks to Valerie for confirmation. "Remember? Is it in *A Tree Grows in Brooklyn*?"

"No, but you're right, I remember the scene," Valerie says. "Not *A Tree Grows in Brooklyn*, but something like that. It's not the way you'd think it is," she adds. "Not like fireplace ashes or cigarette ash. They're very gritty, and they cling to your fingers. As if the dead don't want to let go."

Claire looks up from the urn to Valerie. "I don't think letting go was anything my mother ever had a problem with," she says.

Valerie is in town for one more day, so they agree to get together the next afternoon and do some sightseeing. "No ashes, no cremains," Claire warns. "But maybe we could take a bus tour, or walk across the Brooklyn Bridge. I've never done that."

"Neither have I," says Valerie.

So the next day they take the subway to Battery Park, where you can get on the trolley tour of Brooklyn. Anne brings Hannah and an umbrella stroller; Diane brings her husband Mike, who Anne always thinks is strikingly handsome for a man in his seventies, with snow-white hair over a strong-boned face with vivid green eyes. He takes Hannah on his lap as soon as they're settled on the trolley. "How's my little angel?" he asks Hannah.

"I'm not an angel, I'm a princess. A *ballerina* princess," Hannah informs him solemnly.

"God, she's a doll," says Diane.

Valerie, who has never seen Hannah before, says, "What a shame Annie never lived to see her."

"Yes, she would have loved to," Anne says, swallowing down the lump that quickly rises in her throat. Aunt Annie outlived all her siblings, dying at ninety-two in her own house on Freshwater Road. She was proud of Anne and got cable TV just so she could see her girl on the American news, even though she always worried when Anne was reporting from those dangerous places where the bombs were. She would have loved to see Anne settled down with a little girl, but nobody lives long enough to see everything, Anne thinks.

The trolley tour guide makes a number of jokes, none of which are funny, and tells them the wrong date for the construction of the Brooklyn Bridge as they drive over it. When the trolley stops at the Marriott hotel he tells them they can get off to walk across the bridge if they want, and catch another trolley later to continue the tour. They climb off, a large and awkward crew. The trolley ride has made Hannah drowsy and she is draped over Anne's shoulders like a very heavy scarf while Mike opens the umbrella stroller. The three older women all have extra-large purses and Valerie has shopping bags as well. When Hannah is buckled into the stroller with the sunshade pulled down, they begin their slow trek across the bridge. The day is warm and golden, sunshine spilling down on them. Claire, Valerie and Diane all wear hats.

Many people are walking on the bridge today. Traffic roars beneath them, so noisy they can't even talk to each other. Mike stops to read each of the informative historical plaques, but the women wander ahead, finally finding a place to lean on the railings and look out at the river. It's sluggish and slow-moving, with a few boats lazily ploughing their way through. "They say once upon a time it used to be filled with boats from one bank to the other," Valerie shouts.

"They say that about St. John's harbour too," Claire yells back.

Different times, Anne thinks. The river seems almost irrelevant now, just a backdrop for the real current of humanity that rages back and forth over the bridge.

Claire reaches into her carry-all. "Guess what I brought?" she shouts, pulling the urn out of the bag.

Valerie looks so excited she actually claps her hands. Anne is shocked. Once Claire has said a course of action is foolish, tacky, and possibly illegal, that's generally the final word on the subject.

"You're going to scatter them from here?" Val shouts.

"I thought maybe just a few! Bring the rest home to bury! But I still think it might be illegal!" Claire yells, turning from one to the other. She looks uncertain, and seeks out Anne's face first. "What do you think I should do? Is this the right thing?"

In thirty-eight years, Anne cannot recall her mother ever asking this question – of her, or of anyone else. She feels a huge wave of love for Claire, so certain, so brittle. She moves to put an arm around her mother's thin shoulders and speaks right in her ear. "I think if you want to do it, then it's the right thing," she says.

Diane and Valerie nod vigorous agreement. Mike is some distance away, immersed in reading a plaque. The four Evans women – five if you count the one asleep in her stroller, six if you count the one in the urn – are alone together on the Brooklyn Bridge. Claire takes the top off the jar and looks around quickly, perhaps for the Cremain Police.

"Go ahead!" shouts Diane.

Claire tips the jar. Nothing comes out, and she tips it a little more, then reaches up with her fingers to hook the ashes loose. A light drift of grey, gritty stuff falls out and is caught by the breeze, swirling down to the water.

"Not like they're going to notice a few more bits of dirt in the East River," Diane says in Anne's ear.

"Here." Claire hands Anne the urn. "You do some. But save some for home!"

Anne takes the urn, hoping it doesn't slip from her hands and fall into the water below. Her hand shakes a little as she jiggles the urn, dislodging a few more particles of her unknown grandmother who crossed this river so long ago, leaving behind one life to find another. The grey swirl drifts down and they all watch eagerly till it is invisible. Anne tilts the jar back upright, making sure to save some to go home.

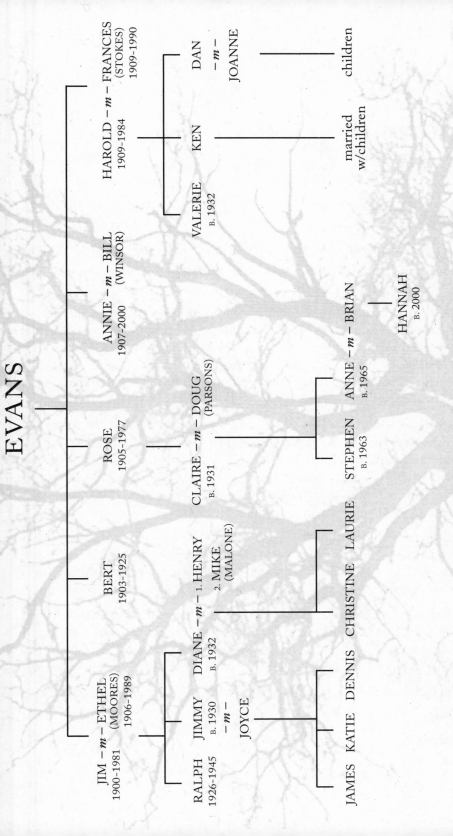

EVANS

ALBERT – *m* – LOUISE

JIM – *m* – ETHEL (MOORES)
1900-1981   1906-1989

BERT
1903-1925

ROSE
1905-1977

ANNIE – *m* – BILL (WINSOR)
1907-2000

HAROLD – *m* – FRANCES (STOKES)
1909-1984   1909-1990

RALPH
1926-1945

JIMMY
B. 1930
– *m* –
JOYCE

DIANE – *m* – 1. HENRY
B. 1932   2. MIKE (MALONE)

CLAIRE – *m* – DOUG (PARSONS)
B. 1931

VALERIE
B. 1932

KEN

DAN
– *m* –
JOANNE

JAMES   KATIE   DENNIS   CHRISTINE   LAURIE

STEPHEN
B. 1963

ANNE – *m* – BRIAN
B. 1965

HANNAH
B. 2000

married w/children

children

EVANS FAMILY TREE

ACKNOWLEDGEMENTS

I AM VERY GRATEFUL for financial assistance from the Newfoundland and Labrador Arts Council and from the City of St. John's for grants which allowed me to research and write this book.

Support and critique are essential to the writing process. I have been very fortunate to be a member of the Newfoundland Writers' Guild, whose members have listened to and critiqued portions of this novel at workshops over a period of several years. Likewise, I owe an eternal debt of gratitude to the Strident Women for loving and reliable cheerleading, hand-holding, butt-kicking and coffee-drinking as required.

I am particularly grateful to several readers who took the time to read and comment on the entire manuscript in an earlier form: Helen Porter and Joan Clark in St. John's, and Yona Zeldis McDonough in Brooklyn. Two other early readers without whom this book would have been impossible were Donald and Joan Morgan, not only wonderful parents but the best research assistants one could hope for, especially in matters concerning St. John's history.

To all these people, and to the many others who helped me find obscure bits of information or talked to me about their experiences, or those of their family members, in Brooklyn, I am deeply grateful. Any errors which remain after all these thoughtful readings and conversations are, of course, entirely my own.

Many thanks to everyone at Breakwater Books, especially Annamarie Beckel, a wonderful editor who convinced me I could substantially shorten the original manuscript of this book without it bleeding to death from the cuts. I also thank Rhonda Molloy for her lovely creative work on the cover design and interior.

Most of all, I am forever grateful to Jason, Chris and Emma for constant love and support.

TRUDY J. MORGAN-COLE is a writer and teacher. Her previous works of historical fiction include *The Violent Friendship of Esther Johnson*, *Deborah and Barak*, and *Esther: A Story of Courage*. She lives in St. John's with her husband and two children, and teaches English, writing, and social studies to adult learners at The Murphy Centre. Awards won include one fiction win and one non-fiction win for the Newfoundland Arts and Letters Competition and the H.R. (Bill) Percy Unpublished Novel Award.